...ity of Good...

CITY OF GOOD DEATH

CHRIS LLOYD

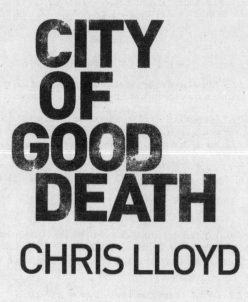

CANELO

First published in Great Britain in 2015 by Canelo

This edition published in the United Kingdom in 2019 by

Canelo Digital Publishing Limited
57 Shepherds Lane
Beaconsfield, Bucks HP9 2DU
United Kingdom

A CIP catalogue record for this book is available from the British Library.

Print ISBN 978 1 78863 556 1
Ebook ISBN 978 1 910859 93 3

Look for more great books at www.canelo.co

Printed and bound in Great Britain by Clays Ltd, Elcograf S.p.A.

For Liz. For everything.

Chapter One

It began with the tiny effigy hanging from the Verge de la Bona Mort.

No one knew its meaning.

Not that first morning, anyway.

And that was what proved to be the problem.

The Verge de la Bona Mort. The Virgin of Good Death. Such an overwhelming name for such a small statue. Standing in her narrow niche between the ancient stone towers of the Portal de Sobreportes, high above the slender cobbled street below, she had in medieval times been the last sight that condemned prisoners had of the city. A final blessing before they were led beyond the city walls to die.

That late summer morning no one knew what it meant. Least of all Andrés Soriano. An immigrant from Andalusia some thirty years earlier, he had cleaned the streets of the city for the last ten. That was after the factory where he'd first found work all those years ago had finally folded. No crisis, no great drama, just a victim of changing times. He didn't know the city's history. He barely spoke the language. Thirty years and proud not only to keep his strong Andalusian accent in Spanish, but prouder still he'd failed to master Catalan. They all speak Spanish, he'd argue to anyone who cared to hear, why should I learn Catalan? His children spoke it, though. Not at home. Never at home. But first at school and then at work. A boy and a girl, both doing well. Both more Catalan than Andalusian. Sourly, he spat a thick gobbet of phlegm at the ground and immediately hosed it away, the heavy pipe snaking from the little municipal cart with its pregnant metal tank of water.

He only saw the figure suspended from the ancient statue because a pigeon resting in the niche shit over his uniform.

'*Hijo de puta*,' he growled at the bird, instinctively pointing his jet of water upwards to give it a good drenching.

And there above him was the little effigy, hanging down four metres or so above his head.

'*Hijo de puta*,' he cursed again. This time in surprise. It was a saying he used often.

Looking around him to make sure no one saw him disrespecting one of their wretched icons, he sent his powerful spray up again to dislodge the figure, letting it fall to the ground by his feet.

'Ugly little bastard, aren't you,' he said, stooping down with difficulty to pick it up. Just a little wooden stick doll it was, with an oversized head carved out of soft wood fastened with twine to the top. Huge circles for the eyes on a moon face and big pointy ears going straight up. 'So what are you supposed to be?' he demanded, shaking his head. Looking around one more time, he tossed it into the thick plastic basket for rubbish hanging off the side of his vehicle and turned the water off.

Spitting once more on to the grey cobbles, he coiled up the hosepipe and hurled it along with the coarse broom into the back of the little motorised cart. Cursing at the pigeon shit on his uniform, he trundled off under the Verge de la Bona Mort and out through the old city gate for the long hike back to the depot south of the city.

He was the only one to see the effigy.

Chapter Two

Carrer Pla i Cargol was a narrow street in a city of narrow streets.

Elisenda Domènech looked at it now.

It had little to mark it out from many of the tiny alleyways around it, she thought. Worn cobbles stretched from the smartly renovated building on the left to the series of smaller, rougher houses on the right, still to be regentrified. On the left, a smart coat of paint on narrow blue balconies and old stone buffed and polished to a new glory. To the right, rusted iron balconies in crumbling stone. One house already under the care of a sympathetic builder, others to follow. Just like so many of the streets in the old city.

Except for the body of the man swinging below one of the ancient windows. That was different, Elisenda decided. She looked back along the street to the crowd gathering on Carrer Ciutadans and back up to the figure above. His feet two metres above her upturned face, his arms tied above his head to a rope leading out of the glassless window, his nose gone. Cut off. Blood dried around his mouth like a once-fashionable goatee beard and down the front of his shirt and trousers, no longer dripping into the congealed and rusted pool on the stones below.

Six members of the Policia Científica were still looking for his nose.

'Sotsinspectora?'

Elisenda turned on hearing the voice from behind her. A young mosso in the Seguretat Ciutadana, flecks of vòmit

3

streaking the front of his dark blue uniform and a dusty, light patch on his sleeve where he'd hastily tried to brush the stains away.

'You were the one who found him?' Elisenda guessed.

'Yes, Sotsinspectora,' he replied. 'On patrol.'

Elisenda nodded. 'What is it?'

'The judge is here, Sotsinspectora.'

Elisenda looked over the mosso's shoulder to the end of the street and sighed. 'Jutgessa Roca. My day is complete. I take it the pathologist isn't here yet.'

'He's already inside the building, Sotsinspectora,' the mosso informed her. He looked paler by the minute. 'Supervising.'

'I'm sure he is,' Elisenda commented. The mosso stifled a smirk. 'What's your name, Mosso?' she added.

The young man in front of her stiffened. 'Mosso Paredes, Sotsinspectora.'

'Your first name.'

'Francesc, Sotsinspectora.'

'Well, Francesc, just for now, my name's Elisenda.' The mosso nodded, relaxing. 'And just round the corner from here there's a bar called El Cercle. Go in there and tell them Elisenda sent you, and get them to give you a brandy. You look like you need one.'

'Yes, Sotsinspectora. Thank you.'

They both turned as the judge and the far too expensively-dressed court secretary announced their regal passage along the narrow street, nosing haughtily through the lines of white-suited Policia Científica inching painfully along the cobbles on their knees.

Elisenda sighed. 'And get one for me while you're at it.'

–

'Useless bloody judges,' Elisenda swore, kicking the door open and crashing through, a bundle of files in her left hand, a mobile phone in her right. She walked on through the outer

4

office she shared with the Local Investigation Unit to her own department, the newly-formed experimental unit that worked exclusively on serious crimes throughout the whole of the Girona police region, and kicked a second door open. The room was empty, everyone either still at the Carrer Pla i Cargol scene, out at court or not on shift yet. Checking her watch, she went into her office, flopping all the files on to her desk and sitting down.

'Bloody judges,' she muttered again, sifting through the paperwork that had already been generated by this morning's suspicious death. Suspicious death, she murmured, echoing the words of the judge.

'I can confirm it as a suspicious death,' Jutgessa Roca had announced finally, the court secretary busily filling out forms, using the back of her briefcase as a rest.

Elisenda had simply nodded her head. Man hanging by a rope tied to his wrists from the window of a derelict building, pool of blood on the ground below, man's nose a distant memory, and the judge had taken an hour to come to the conclusion that it was suspicious. 'I'll just write that down, shall I?' Elisenda had asked her. In the meantime, crowds of the curious had piled up at the end of the street, leaving a traffic tailback along Carrer Ciutadans that had ended up affecting half the city centre, and schoolchildren and office workers had started out from their homes, catching glimpses of the hanging man through the makeshift barrier put up by the Seguretat Ciutadana unit.

The judge had turned on her. 'I don't like your tone.'

'Don't worry,' Elisenda had reassured her, 'I'm sure I'll get over it.'

Leafing through a copy of the court secretary's report in her office, Elisenda leant forward over her desk and took in the page after page of fluff and waffle needed before the judge finally declared that the body could be moved and the Mossos could get on with their job. In theory, whenever there was a suspicious death, a judge, the court secretary and the forensic doctor were all supposed to be present to authorise the removal of the body. In practice, many judges delegated this to the forensic doctor. Unfortunately, Jutgessa Roca wasn't one of them.

'New police, same old legal system,' Elisenda complained out loud to the empty office when she'd finished reading. What she found most galling was that the judge wasn't some ancient throwback to the bad old days before policing had been devolved from the old Spanish national police to the Mossos d'Esquadra, the Catalan regional police force, but was only two years older than she was. Two years ahead of her all through school and then university, and they'd exchanged more words in the last year than they had throughout their entire education. Elisenda could see why.

The phone on her desk rang.

'*Elisenda?*' the voice on the other end said. '*Pep Boadas.*' A sergent in the Policia Científica, two years below her at school. Small world, Girona, Elisenda thought. Very different from the days of her childhood, when all policemen were either Policia Nacional or Guardia Civil and were drafted in from other regions of Spain, arguably more willing to put down popular revolt than fellow Catalans would be in the days when that was deemed an infinitely more important aspect of policing than crime detection or prevention.

'*Got an ident for you,*' he told her. '*You're going to love it. Daniel Masó.*'

Elisenda whistled. 'Daniel Masó? Are you sure?'

'*Positive.*'

'Well, well. I didn't recognise him without his nose on.'

'*You're heartbroken, aren't you?*'

'Devastated. Truly devastated.'

'*Me too.*'

'Not in the least bit surprised, mind.'

'*Is anyone? I'll get a preliminary report to you this morning. I imagine it'll be our number one priority.*'

He rang off as the outer door to the unit banged open and shut. Two caporals walked in, deep in discussion, and went to facing desks. Elisenda considered them. The woman, Montse, a Gironina like her, brought up knowing everyone and everything in the small city, their extensive network of acquaintances spreading vertically through family and laterally through peers. The man, Josep, posted to Girona from Hospitalet, the sprawling city sprouting from Barcelona's southern border, after passing his caporal's exams. Only been here a few months. Few friends outside the force, no local girlfriend, sharing a flat with a caporal in another unit, also from outside the city.

Elisenda went to the door into the outer office. 'Montse, Josep,' she said, 'could you come through a moment?'

'Sotsinspectora?' Josep questioned, closing the door behind them. Very tall, he had a habit of stooping to try to appear the same height as everyone else, which made him look rather gloomy. Elisenda always had to fight the urge to tell him to stand up straight.

She motioned them to sit down. 'How would you like to solve the murder of a local entrepreneur?'

Chapter Three

'No, Sotsinspectora. I don't recognise the name.'

'Good,' Elisenda replied. 'Now write his full name down, Daniel Masó Comas, and go and spend the morning looking him up on NIP.'

'He's on NIP?' Josep asked her. 'What sort of things was he into, Sotsinspectora?'

Elisenda considered that for a moment. 'He had a pretty varied portfolio, but where he made his millions was in loans to the poor and needy. The very poor and the desperately needy. With a pretty robust after-sales service if you didn't make the repayments. He will not be missed.'

'Right, Sotsinspectora,' he said, closing his notebook.

'And don't go listening to anyone else telling you stories about Daniel Masó. You don't have any prejudices against the victim. I need that. I want you to find out everything you can on NIP. Associates, rivals, most recent victims, any complaints in the system, anything. You have any questions, you ask me.'

'Right, Sotsinspectora.'

'And when you've done that, come back and I'll give you a copy of the judge's report and the Seguretat Ciutadana report and any other bit of unnecessary paper I can find, so you can enter it all into the records.'

Elisenda turned to Montse, who shrugged in admission. Born and raised in Santa Eugènia, the suburb between Masó's home ground of Salt and the centre of Girona, Montse would already know more than enough about the loan shark as his claws had stretched well into the immediately neighbouring areas.

'I do know Masó.'

Elisenda nodded. 'I know. And I know you'll be just as prejudiced against the little bastard as I am. I want you to check out victims and victim's families. Anyone who seems to know more about things than they should. Anyone making noises, anyone with a particular grievance. Daniel Masó might have been a scumbag. But he's a murdered scumbag and he's a murdered scumbag on our watch. And I don't want anyone accusing us of not pulling our fingers out on this one.'

The two caporals stood up. A twice winner of the annual run to the top of the Els Àngels mountain, Montse looked slight next to the towering Josep.

Elisenda watched them leave and picked up the judge's report. 'Suspicious death,' she muttered to herself, thrusting it in a buff folder.

Checking her watch, she called Àlex, the only sergent at present in the nascent Serious Crime Unit, but his mobile was switched off. He'd arrived at the Carrer Pla i Cargol scene after her and had accompanied the body to the Institut de Medicina Legal once the judge had allowed it to be removed. She texted him to tell him to call her when he came out and picked up her things to leave.

Across town, at the Fiscalia, the public prosecutor's office, on Avinguda Ramon Folch, she was told by Laura Puigmal that the Fiscalia wouldn't be directing the case as Elisenda had expected.

'Jutgessa Roca will be in charge.'

Elisenda just dropped her head. 'Give me strength.'

In the same building, nearly an hour later and still waiting to see the judge, Elisenda thought that Roca must have seen some political weight to be gained by directing the investigation. She couldn't see what it might be, unless she had designs on bringing down the Masó clan.

'How much longer will the judge be?' Elisenda asked the harridan in a dated plaid skirt sternly guarding the judge's door.

9

'I have told Jutgessa Roca you're here, Sotsinspectora Domènech,' the woman told her, unhurriedly moving flimsy bits of paper from one side of her desk to the other. The woman took a phone call and went through a door behind her, to emerge ten minutes later. She sat down again and spoke to Elisenda. 'Jutgessa Roca has requested that you return on Friday. She has been called away.'

'You must enjoy your job,' Elisenda told her, getting up to leave. She knew the pointlessness of arguing with this sort of good old-fashioned officialdom.

Taking her jacket off in the heat outside, she saw that it was lunchtime. She called Josep. She knew where she would find someone nearby with much more of an idea of what was going on than the judge and with only marginally less of a moral compass.

–

The toasted slice of country bread was a bit overdone, Elisenda thought, but the *escalivada* was good, the red pepper, onion and aubergine baked, then allowed to cool slowly and smothered in olive oil. Even the wine was reputable, a red from a co-operative up in the mountains of the Alt Empordà, an hour or so north of Girona. Not bad at all, she decided.

Unlike her fellow patrons.

And the owner.

She watched him now. Rings of sweat darkening the front and sides of his pale brown polyester shirt, one leg hitched high up on the rear of the counter, the wattles on his face red and shining in the heat from the kitchen behind him where three young Asian guys were hard at work.

The man Elisenda had come to see was standing opposite him. A razor-thin profile of sunken cheeks and narrow jaw atop a body so slight his shirt kept popping out of his saggy trouser belt no matter how often he tucked it back in. His prominent Adam's apple bobbed nervously behind turkey skin every time he gulped. It bobbed now as his eyes flickered warily in Elisenda's direction, so she raised her glass at him. Slung across his shoulder was an enormous light-brown leather satchel, the kind Elisenda remembering postmen carrying in her childhood. Reluctantly, he dipped into it and pulled out a small pile of garishly-coloured DVDs. The owner took them and put them in a drawer behind the counter and turned back to the thin man. 'My commission for letting you sell in my bar.'

His business over, the thin man had no other option but to walk over to Elisenda's table.

'Siset,' she greeted him affably, 'sit down.'

'Can't, Elisenda. Got to go home, look after my mother.'

'She ill?'

'Yes.'

'Sorry to hear that. Sit down.'

Grumbling, he scraped the chair opposite Elisenda across the tiled floor and sat down.

'You might want to pull your chair a bit nearer,' Elisenda told him.

'I'm fine.'

'Suit yourself.' She slowly cut up some aubergine and placed it carefully on a piece of toast. 'So, got any more information for me today?' she added in a louder voice.

'Shush,' he hissed at her, pulling his chair right up to the table, his Adam's apple almost bobbing over Elisenda's lunch.

'Now isn't that more comfortable?' she asked him.

'I don't know anything.'

'About what?'

'I don't know.'

Elisenda looked at him, chewing slowly. 'This really is very good, you know,' she said, her voice loud. She saw the owner looking over to them. Her voice dropped again. 'Daniel Masó.'

He recoiled, as though she'd stabbed him with her fork.

'I don't know anything.'

'You keep saying that.'

'But I don't,' he hissed back. 'Really I don't.'

Elisenda called the owner over. 'Can I have a glass of wine for my friend?'

'Stop it, Elisenda, you'll get me hurt,' Siset pleaded when the owner brought the drink, looking from one to the other of them. He picked up the glass in both hands and swallowed the wine in one gulp, a tiny belch emerging from his pursed lips. Elisenda could see his hands shaking as he put the glass down. The ends of his fingers were scabbed and raw where he bit them. He was wearing the same black T-shirt announcing a faded concert that he always wore, the armpits stiffly white and concertinaed with years of sweat and cheap anti-perspirant.

Elisenda shrugged. 'Sooner you tell me, sooner I go. Less damage I do. Now tell me what you know.'

'But that's the thing,' Siset whispered urgently at her. 'I don't know. No one does.'

'You see that's impossible, Siset?' Elisenda put the last of her lunch into her mouth. 'Someone must know. One person at least. Fancy a coffee?'

'It's no one in the world, Elisenda.'

'No one bragging?'

'Would you?'

Elisenda called over to the owner. 'Could I have a *tallat*, please? And whatever my friend wants.'

'Please, Elisenda,' Siset pleaded, his head in his cupped hands, oily brown hair spilling limply through his fingers.

Elisenda kept quiet while the owner brought her small white coffee over. 'So what are people saying?' she asked Siset after he'd gone.

'Everyone reckons it's vigilantes,' Siset replied hopefully.

Elisenda nodded. 'Because if it's vigilantes, you think I won't come back asking more questions. But I will. What else are they saying?'

'Foreigners. Lots of foreigners in Salt now. You can't move for them all eating their food and praying funny.'

'Try again.'

'I tell you, Elisenda. Everyone's as puzzled as you are.' He looked thoughtful for once. 'No one can think of anyone who'd have the balls to do it.'

'One of his victims?'

He shrugged, his head almost enveloped up to the ears by bony shoulders. 'Could be.'

'I take it Masó's bunch have thought of the same thing.'

'They've asked a few questions.'

'I'm sure they have.' Elisenda made a mental note to have Josep look into anyone with a new and unusual injury in Salt. 'What about other gangs? Incomers?'

Siset shook his head. 'Masó's family are too powerful. There's no way anyone would try and muscle in on Salt, least of all by killing Daniel.'

Elisenda nodded her head slowly. 'Was Masó looking to go into other neighbourhoods?'

'No need. The family's got Salt tied up so much, there's no need to take any of the new gangs on. They live well where they are,' he added without any irony.

'Don't they just.' She stirred her coffee, spooning through the light milk froth. 'So what about Masó's family? What are they doing about it?'

'They've put themselves about a bit. Got heavy with a couple of the Latins. No one important. They're more worried about keeping their business going than they are about revenge.'

'Sure they didn't do it?'

Siset paused a moment too long. 'You know Masó's lot wouldn't do that. They're all family. They wouldn't dare.'

Elisenda considered the Masó clan. The father and the uncles presiding over the old town in Salt. The grandfather presiding over prison on his latest conviction. A warren of cousins, brothers and nephews held in place by fear and loyalty, their sway extending into Santa Eugènia and Sant Narcís. She found it hard to imagine any of them going against the family.

'What aren't you telling me, Siset?'

Siset sighed, almost crumpling. He pushed an unruly strand of hair behind his right ear and absently wiped his hand on his shoulder. 'Please, Elisenda,' he finally said in a low voice. 'You didn't hear it from me. There's talk of one of the uncles, Joaquim. He wants in.'

'Enough to take on his own family?' Elisenda thought out loud.

'It might not be true, though. I tell you, everyone's in the dark.'

'OK,' Elisenda said, gathering her bag and getting up to pay at the bar. 'The moment you come into the light, you call me.'

'I will,' he promised.

'Because otherwise I'll call on you.'

At the bar, the owner told Elisenda lunch was on the house.

'No, it's not,' she said, reaching into her purse.

Outside, Elisenda waited around the corner for Josep to catch up with her.

'You get that?' she asked him. He'd been sitting at a table on the square, listening over his bluetooth. He nodded. 'Did you see anyone paying undue attention? Anyone leave in a hurry?'

'Only the owner of the place. He wasn't happy.'

'Bad for trade,' Elisenda agreed.

'Apart from him, no one. Some of them in there recognised you, but they didn't seem over-worried. Apart from that, lot of tourists.'

'Strange place, isn't it? Nice terrace, good food, plenty of passing trade and it's stuffed to the gills with the arse-end of the fauna of the city.'

'There are a couple of things he said that I can try following up,' Josep offered.

'Good. And check on anyone known or thought to be one of Masó's clients with dubious injuries in the last couple of days.'

Josep noted it down in his notebook. 'You were pretty tough on him,' he commented when he'd finished writing. 'The little guy.'

'Look him up on NIP,' she told him. 'Then tell me I was tough on him.'

Chapter Four

'Joaquim Masó?' Àlex asked.

'Uncle of our very own Daniel Masó. Runs a parcel delivery firm. Small-scale. Very much on the fringes of the family.'

'Legit?'

Elisenda shook her head. 'He's a Masó.'

Àlex smiled, a wicked, dark grin. The edgy, knowing smile that excited half the women at the station and angered the other half. Too many bad boys outside the station, the second group said. Exactly, the first group argued.

He edged forward in the stop-start traffic snarl heading for Salt, Daniel Masó's stamping ground. Once a town, then a suburb, now a town again, Salt sprawled in a humble, troubled ribbon from the western fringes of Girona to the motorway connecting France with Barcelona.

'I still find it hard to imagine a Masó taking on the family,' Elisenda added.

After seeing Siset, she'd told Josep to go back to the station and had called Àlex, who'd just left the Institut de Medicina Legal, not far from the law courts, to get him to pick her up to drive out to Salt. He'd told her of the preliminary opinion that Albert Riera, the pathologist, had given. The post mortem proper was scheduled for two days' time.

'He had two stab wounds to the chest,' Àlex told her. 'Probably either could have been the fatal blow, Riera reckons. Quite a fight, evidently. He had defence wounds to both his hands and his forearms.'

Elisenda tried to imagine the scene in the derelict building. And the killer then hanging Masó out of the window. She wondered where his nose being cut off fitted in. What at first sight seemed a straightforward killing of a vicious criminal who operated in a world where that was always a possibility took on puzzling dimensions. And now they were going to see the Masó family to question them about his death. She sighed heavily.

'We're here,' Àlex told her.

The clans had gathered.

Four generations of delinquency at the red-check plastic tablecloth restaurant owned by one of the uncles as a front. Even the children in sombre mood, not running about or hiding under the chairs, all infected by the dark anger of the three tiers of adults above them. With the grandfather in prison, it was Jaume Masó, Daniel's father, who was the head of the family.

But before him were the cousins on the door, barring Elisenda and Àlex's entry into the restaurant.

'Family only,' one of them told Àlex, placing a hand weighed down by a thick gold chain on the Mosso's chest. Àlex smiled at the man and gently removed his hand, continuing to stare at him. The man put his hand back and pushed slightly.

'We're just here to pay our respects,' Elisenda told him.

The man at the door didn't take his eyes off Àlex. 'Family only.'

A second man moved closer, flexing his chest and thrusting his shoulders forward.

The restaurant door opened and Jaume Masó came out. 'It's OK,' he told the men on the door. 'You go in. I'll deal with this.'

'Jaume,' Elisenda spoke. 'I've come to offer my condolences.'

He looked surprised at first as he stared into Elisenda's eyes, but then softened. Nodding his head slowly, he thanked her. 'You understand.'

He invited them in, but only as far as the bar. The restaurant was closed to the public but was filled with family members, who stared coldly at the two Mossos. Elisenda spotted Joaquim seated at a table away from the senior family members, near the window, where the sun was shining in, bringing him out in an uncomfortable sweat. He spoke little to the people around him.

Jaume offered them a glass of market-stall cava and a tray of cured ham, sliced from a whole ham wedged in a stand behind the bar.

'This is my sergent, Àlex Albiol,' Elisenda said, thanking him.

Jaume nodded. 'I thank you for your condolences, Elisenda, but the family would prefer you not to be here.'

'I understand that, Jaume, but a murder has been committed. We will need to interview some members of your family. To help us in our enquiries and to eliminate them from them.'

Jaume's voice dropped in temperature a few degrees. 'Eliminate them?'

'It's standard procedure, Jaume.'

Another of Jaume's brothers and his two sons, the ones on the door, came to stand nearby.

'This is my family, Elisenda,' Jaume told her. 'We look after our own.'

'And we don't need the Mossos to do it for us,' one of the cousins interrupted. Jaume gave him a stern look and he shut up.

'You know that's not possible, Jaume,' Elisenda said. 'We will need your co-operation to find whoever did this to Daniel.'

Jaume just looked at her and around the room at his family. 'But we won't need you, Elisenda. We can find whoever did this and we will deal with it. You have my word on that.'

'I'm sorry about that, Jaume. Because you have my word that if you do take the law into your own hands, I will deal with that.'

Two more members of the family came over, one of them standing very close to Àlex. Every other head in the room was facing their way, every other pair of eyes focused on the two Mossos.

'I think you should go now, Elisenda,' Jaume told her. 'Leave my family to grieve.'

Elisenda turned to go. 'I will have to come back, Jaume.'

The men around them jostled Àlex's shoulders as they walked out of the restaurant but moved aside to let Elisenda pass, their antiquated attention automatically focusing on the man, not the woman.

'So what did you make of that?' Elisenda asked Àlex when they were back in the unmarked pool car.

Àlex eased out onto the main road back to Girona. 'Uncle Joaquim seems to be a long way down the pecking order. Maybe he didn't like that.'

'Did you see the way he was dressed compared with the others? And their jewellery? You can see why he would want a piece of the family silver.'

Àlex nodded. 'Which is as good a reason as any for someone in that family to kill.'

Back at the Mossos' Vista Alegre station, the most recent addition to the team, Pau, another caporal, told them that Montse and Josep were in Salt, checking up on Masó's victims.

'Good,' Elisenda told him. 'There's something I want you to take a look at. Joaquim Masó. We need to know the state of his business. I'll be applying to Jutgessa Roca for a warrant to get his bank account details, if he uses one, but I want you to find out if his business is healthy or if he looks like someone who needs to take over the family empire. While you're at it, anyone else in the Masó family who looks a likely contender to kill Daniel.'

'Yes, Sotsinspectora,' Pau replied. 'I've got this for you.' He showed Elisenda a spreadsheet on the computer in front of him. Arranged in rows were the names of the Masó clan members, with a series of columns detailing criminal records, business interests and even their probability of being involved in Daniel's murder. 'I hope you don't mind.'

Elisenda looked astonished. 'Mind? Anything but. This is excellent.'

Looking slightly embarrassed, Pau told her that Joaquim was the unfavoured arm of the family. 'But he does look like someone who should interest us. His business is healthy enough, mainly thanks to being a Masó, and he's been suspected of fencing in the past, but he earns nowhere near the amount we calculate Daniel or some of the other members would be making. I think he's worth looking at.'

'I think you're right.'

Pau turned back to his computer and Elisenda watched him work for a moment, his slender honey-coloured fingers spidering gently across the keyboard, his long black eyelashes barely flickering. Private in nature, he'd been born in Girona to Andalusian immigrants, originally christened the Spanish Pablo, but he'd had it legally changed to the Catalan Pau when he turned eighteen.

'Meeting tomorrow morning at eight,' she told him and Àlex. 'Let the other two know.'

Elisenda spent the next two hours in her office going over the notes they had so far, reminding herself of the Masó family crimes. She was surprised no one had taken Daniel out before, surprised anyone had had the nerve to do it now.

'You leaving, Elisenda?' Àlex asked her as he was getting ready to go. Pau had left a few minutes earlier.

'I'll stay here a bit longer.'

She watched Àlex leave and thought of her empty flat.

'Just a bit longer,' she murmured to herself.

Chapter Five

This was the bit that hurt.

Elisenda pushed a strand of wet hair out of her face and wiped her forehead. She had made good time along the paths skirting the east of the city outside the medieval walls, jogging on the spot to watch the sun climb above the distant hills, but the sound of a small aircraft from somewhere behind her had made her stop and turn to look for it. A single-engine plane. Low in the sky but climbing, heading towards the coast and, beyond it, the sea. Watching in silence, she'd waited until it was no longer a dot in the distance and turned away to carry on running. Numb now, she'd sprinted back into the old town past the quiet houses of the Fora Muralla before gingerly crossing the cobbles of Plaça Sant Domènec.

But this was the bit that hurt.

Running up the stone flight rising to the cathedral in little dolly steps as the slabs were too shallow to take comfortably, she could feel the bite down from the gluteus maximus, through her thighs and calves, to the Achilles. She pulled air into her lungs, grimacing with the toll the steps were taking on her legs, and waited for the perfect moment when she got to the top of the steps and curved back down along the narrow road to return to the bottom, freewheeling like a child on a bike. It was all downhill from here, back to her flat on Carrer Ballesteries.

'Hey, Elisenda.'

She stopped at her name being called and leaned forward, her hands on her knees, before standing up straight. She was almost at the bottom of Pujada de Sant Feliu, where it ran into her street.

'Xiscu,' she said, no sign of breathlessness in her voice.

'You're running,' he told her.

'I know.'

'Quiet, Pujol.' The last comment was aimed at a jerky white Scottie dog, tugging at the red and black cotton scarf rolled tightly and slipped around its neck as a lead.

'Hi, Pujol,' Elisenda greeted the dog, which wagged its tail once. It was named for its squat little legs after a diminutive former president of the Catalan government. 'You're up early, Xiscu.'

The slight young man in front of her looked surprised at that. He didn't have a watch on his wrist. Elisenda knew he never wore one.

'No,' he said doubtfully. 'Late. I don't think I've been home.'

Elisenda smiled at him. 'You're probably right. How's Joan?'

Joan, Xiscu's older brother and Elisenda's contemporary at school, lived on the coast, where he owned a successful restaurant, a small yacht and a share in a vineyard. Xiscu sculpted clown figures out of coat hangers for tourists and spent most of what he earned on Pujol and coke.

'Doing all right.' He wobbled as he spoke, his eyes looking tired. 'You were always the coolest friend Joan had.'

'Things change, Xiscu.'

'You don't, Elisenda. Not at heart.' He suddenly brightened. 'See you finally got that Masó.'

'We didn't get him, Xiscu. Someone killed him.'

'Bet you're pleased, though. The Mossos. Someone doing it for you. Makes your job easier.'

'Not really,' she told him wearily, turning away. 'Take care of yourself.'

She left him looking uncertainly at the road and ran home for a shower and a quick breakfast before the walk to Vista Alegre.

She just had time for a second cup of coffee before the meeting started. Standing in front of them, she considered the members of her team. They were all relatively new to each other and she was just beginning to know their strengths.

'Daniel Masó,' she announced. 'Surprisingly, no one has come forward to confess to the crime and claim their star prize. Josep and Montse, you were out and about in Salt yesterday. How many people have rushed forward to help you find who killed him?'

'None,' Montse told her.

'Anyone abusive?'

'A few.'

'Anyone physically attack you for trying to find his killer?'

'No. No one.'

'I'd say you've come out on top so far then.'

'No one yet,' Montse clarified.

'Strong community spirit,' she told her. 'Give them time. They will.'

'Have you seen the morning's paper, Sotsinspectora?' Josep asked her.

'Yes. I don't think our friends in the press are too worried about our finding whoever did it, are they? Until we don't find them, that is, then they'll be on our backs. Anyway, what's your gut feeling about it?'

Josep thought for a moment. 'I'm not sure we're looking in the right place. All his victims are obviously happy he's gone, and no one wants to talk about it to us, but I don't get the feeling that there is anything they actually know that they're hiding. I think there's something else going on here.'

Elisenda looked at the other three people in the room. 'Are we all agreed on that?'

'I don't think we should rule out the idea of one of his victims killing him in a fight,' Àlex pointed out. 'I think it's still there in the mix, even if no one's talking about it.'

'True. No one in their right mind would talk about it if they were involved, so I think we need to follow that up. Montse, you've been looking into victims, can you take care of that?'

'Yes, Sotsinspectora. Following on from victims, it stands to reason that we should also consider some sort of vigilante action.'

'I was hoping you wouldn't say that,' Elisenda commented. 'You're perfectly right. And it's the one explanation we really don't want. Everyone will be on our backs then.'

'Logically, any vigilantes who start by targeting Daniel Masó would be most likely to be victims of his,' Àlex said.

'True. Keep an open mind on that when you check them out, Montse. Other possibilities?'

'Gang war,' Josep offered.

'That's the other one we really don't want,' Elisenda muttered. 'Can you look into that, Josep? The usual suspects. Anyone moving into Masó's old business. I suspect if there is anyone trying to muscle in, they'll be doing it through Santa Eugènia and Sant Narcís first, before attempting anything in Salt itself. I hate to say it, but you will have to check out the foreign gangs.'

Pau spoke up. 'And there's the Masó family, of course.'

'Indeed there is.' Elisenda explained to the rest of the team what she'd learned from Siset and about her visit with Àlex to Salt. 'Àlex, I want you to check out Joaquim Masó. He's the individual most clearly in the frame right now. Pau, you help Àlex with the background searches. Also, I want you to collate all the information from the rest of the team. Besides that, all co-ordination goes through me. Montse, I'll be coming with you to Salt this morning. I want to see what people are saying. Any questions?'

No one had anything to ask, each one silently taking it in.

'Good, so go and investigate.'

Chapter Six

Elisenda had never seen so many hangovers.

Everywhere she and Montse looked.

From the greengrocer to the DVD club owner. The guy in the *estanc* to the woman in the internet café. Old ladies in the queue for bread and young men in overalls in greasy garage workshops. Young, old. Men, women. Poor, poorer. Everywhere.

She'd never seen so many.

And she'd certainly never seen any with broad, helpless grins shining through them.

Parking the car on Carrer Major in Salt, their last stop was an *estanc*, one of the state-run tobacconist's shops that sold cigarettes, stamps, official papers and lottery tickets. All the country's guilty pleasures under one roof, Elisenda reflected: smoking, bureaucracy and gambling.

Inside, they waited for the shopkeeper, a tall, gloomy man with thick-rimmed glasses and a permanent five o'clock shadow, to finish serving a young woman with a child in a pushchair and then showed him their badges. An elderly woman was standing to one side of the shop, clutching half a dozen lottery forms and sorting through her purse.

'Nice you finally came around now,' the man greeted them testily. 'Nothing from the Mossos for years, and now you suddenly all show up.'

'I think there's some misunderstanding here, sir,' Montse replied. 'We're inquiring into the death of a local man.'

'I know you are. Daniel Masó. That's who you're asking about.' At the sound of his name, the elderly lady stopped searching for coins. 'Where were you when he was alive? That's what I want to know. We got precious few visits from your lot then.'

'I'm afraid I know nothing about that. I'm looking into his death.'

'Well, you're wasting your time coming here, then. I wouldn't tell you anything even if I knew.'

'I heard they sliced his face off,' the elderly woman butted in.

'Good,' the shopkeeper commented. 'I hope they made the bastard suffer the way he made us suffer for years.'

The young woman with the child nodded in agreement.

'He was an evil little shit,' the elderly woman added. Elisenda looked away, coughing to hide a laugh. 'I only wish my mother, God rest her soul, were here to see this day.'

'And the only time your lot comes round this neighbourhood,' the shopkeeper grumbled on, 'was when we all celebrated last night, and you sent two cars to tell us to keep quiet. I tell you, Caporal whatever your name is, whoever did for him is a hero round here. You won't find anyone wanting to help you find them.'

The young mother finally spoke. 'I can buy all the food I want today, without having to worry about whether I have enough money to pay Masó what I owe him.' A broad grin illuminated her face. For the first time, Elisenda saw the red eyes and open pores of her hangover shining through. 'And it was a hell of a party,' she added.

The shopkeeper nodded in agreement, a smile finally breaking through his features.

'Look at this,' the elderly woman insisted to the two Mossos, waving the sheaf of lottery forms in Montse's face. 'We're all playing the lottery today. If some good soul has got rid of Daniel Masó for us, then this has got to be our lucky day.'

Outside the *estanc*, Montse stared glumly at the town carrying on its business in a happy alcohol haze. Immigrants and locals rarely united in celebration.

'That's what I'm finding across the board, Sotsinspectora,' she told Elisenda.

Elisenda, too, looked at the renewed spirit of the humble town. 'I don't think we're going to get much help from anyone in this investigation.'

Chapter Seven

On the drive back to Girona, Elisenda's mobile chimed with a text message. It was from Àlex, to remind her that he'd be meeting her in court at four o'clock.

'Damn,' she muttered to herself. She'd forgotten.

She opened the inbox on her phone and reread the mail sent to her the previous evening by Laura Puigmal from the Fiscalia.

'And damn again,' she said when she'd finished.

The hearing at four wasn't her unit's case, but both she and Àlex wanted to be there. It was an appeal. Unfortunately, it was an appeal that was likely to prosper, according to Laura Puigmal's e-mail.

A discrepancy, Laura had written. Between police reports. The Policia Municipal gave one time for the facts and the Mossos gave another. And no one had noticed until yesterday. That was until the defendants' lawyer, Gerard Bellsolà, had spotted it. Laura's take was that there was a strong possibility that Bellsolà would be able to get them off because of the discrepancy.

Elisenda scanned the attached medical report and swore at the thought of the four thugs who'd brutally beaten an elderly man for a handful of euros getting off. And not for the first time. One of Àlex's first – and few – failures on arriving in his new post in Girona from Barcelona had been not to put them away for an attack that had ended in a vagrant being beaten to death. Everyone knew they'd done it but there wasn't enough evidence to bring it to court. It still ate at Àlex, Elisenda knew. And it was going to happen again. All because of an inconsistency between the reporting of the two police forces who patrolled the city: the local Policia Municipal, run by the city council, and the regional Mossos d'Esquadra, under the auspices of the Department of the Interior of the Catalan government. Nothing ever changed, Elisenda thought. Despite the politicians' best efforts. Or because of them.

–

Elisenda found Àlex already outside the court when Montse dropped her off on the small cobbled square in the shadow of the cathedral steps. She didn't even have to ask him how it had gone. For the outwardly most laid-back guy she'd ever met, his face was capable of showing quite shocking rage.

'Bastards,' he spat when she walked up to him, 'bastards, bastards, bastards.'

'I'm sensing a definite theme here,' she told him.

'Technicality,' he replied. 'What about the technicality of an elderly man too frail to have reconstructive surgery to his face?'

'So tell me what happened.'

He explained to Elisenda about the different times recorded by the two police forces. 'And that creep Bellsolà completely resisted any attempts to allow the medical report to be considered. Reckoned the extent of an elderly man's injuries had no bearing on guilt or procedure. And I am quoting here.'

'Hasn't the judge called for more evidence?'

'No. Thrown out. No further avenues.'

'Bastards,' Elisenda finally agreed with her sergent.

They were dislodged from their place in the doorway by a commotion from inside. Bellsolà, the defence lawyer, was first out, scuttling past them, heading for the haven of his office, an ancient leather pouch clutched to his chest.

'Pleased with the result, Senyor Bellsolà?' Àlex asked him. Elisenda signalled him to keep calm.

The lawyer turned to face him. 'Yes,' he said, pulling himself up to his fullest height. 'Yes. As a matter of fact I am, Sergent. Or would you prefer a return to the days when people like you were judge, jury and executioner? You want justice in Catalonia, then you work within that justice.'

'Justice?' Àlex spat, but Elisenda silenced him.

'I think you'd better go, lawyer,' she told Bellsolà.

'Threatening me, Sotsinspectora?'

Elisenda cocked her head. 'No, not at all. But if you listen, you might just hear the victim's family coming out and they might have a slightly altered view of justice thanks to you.'

'Then it would be your job to protect me.'

'Wouldn't it just? But I imagine I'd be far too busy making sure I was recording the time of the incident exactly right to ensure that justice was done.'

The hubbub from inside the building rose and the lawyer thought better of replying, hurrying away instead to the top of Carrer de la Força, where he stopped to look back for a moment before carrying on slowly down the steep road to his office.

'Lawyers,' Elisenda told Àlex. 'Always stay on their good side.'

The elderly victim shuffled out, visibly aged since the last time Elisenda had seen him, supported on one side by his wife and on the other by his son, both also worn down by the morning's trial. They were followed by a small group of shaken and red-eyed family members. Too defeated and too appalled ever to have launched any attack on Bellsolà. Elisenda could sense Àlex stiffen next to her. The small group walked wordlessly past the two police officers, equally silent, equally impotent.

Finally, the erstwhile defendants made their exit. All four of them looked and acted like the latest freaks from all these reality shows clogging up the national television networks these days, Elisenda thought, with that overwhelming and unwarranted arrogance in their cruelty and ignorance. They liked to call themselves by their first name and the two initials of their surnames. It was their trademark. A conceit brought about by the press not being allowed to print anything but that information about detainees before they were tried, and since the four of them were constantly in the papers for some offence or other, that was more often than not how they saw their own names.

One of the four, the leader, peeled off and swaggered up to Àlex, his face barely centimetres from the sergent's. Àlex pushed him back, his forefinger pressing lightly against the man's chest. A crowd had gathered around the doorway and at the foot of the cathedral steps. Past Àlex and the thug, Elisenda could see Laura Puigmal looking on intently.

'Chema Guijarro Martín,' she heard Àlex say to the figure leaning towards him, his eyes expressionless.

'Chema GM to you,' the young man growled back, pushing Àlex's hand away. 'You're a useless son of a whore.'

'Is that right?' Àlex replied. Elisenda was always amazed at how Àlex could soak this up without letting loose. He'd calmed down instantly from his anger of a few moments ago, but she knew that it was all being filed away for another day.

'Fuck you.' Chema GM let out a loud belch and sloped off to rejoin his friends. Another of the gang, Juan Serrano Prieto, Juan SP in his world, flicked the finger at Àlex, and the four of them walked away through the Portal de Sobreportes, staring down anyone not getting out of their way.

'No,' Elisenda heard Àlex reply under his breath, as he watched the four young men go. 'I will fuck you.'

—

Elisenda put down her heavy, white coffee cup. Her second large milky *café amb llet* in five minutes. She couldn't decide if it was to calm her nerves or to keep the rush going. Oddly, it seemed to be doing both. Her head and shoulders rocked gently back and forth. Hidden under the table, one leg was crossed over the other, the foot briskly shaking. She knew Àlex could sense the movement. His own pose was in counterpoint to hers, leaning lightly back against the uncomfortable upright of the wood and raffia chair, both feet resting on the crossbar under the table. Laid back, Elisenda reminded herself. But the constant tapping on the table leg told her that one of his knees was jiggling in nervous tension the way she'd seen so many times, sending shock waves through his feet on the crossbar and making the table vibrate slightly. She stared at the blurred circles lapping back and forth in her glass of water. Outwardly laid back, she corrected herself.

They were in L'Arc, at the top of Carrer de la Força, taking a coffee to quell the anger each knew the other was feeling. One of the city's earliest bars, L'Arc was still held in veneration by a dynasty of fading bohemians who once eagerly and inactively plotted Franco's downfall over hot brandy and chocolate milk. Àlex grunted and finished his tiny cup of treacly black coffee. Ready to go. He always said he could never see the point of the large white coffees that Elisenda always drank, more often than not needing two to get the right adrenaline intake. He preferred his in one short, single caffeine rush. Over and gone in a moment. Elisenda finished her second coffee and took a sip from her glass of mineral water. Another of her routines. Àlex's knee jiggled even more impatiently.

'I will have them,' he suddenly said out loud. Not so much a comment to Elisenda as a voiced thought. She simply stared back at him.

They were disturbed by a figure approaching their table. 'Elisenda,' the man greeted her. He glanced in Àlex's direction. 'Sergent Albiol.'

'Carles,' Elisenda greeted him coolly.

'Any comments you'd care to make about the overturned conviction? Yet another failure by the Mossos.'

Àlex opened his mouth, but Elisenda hushed him. 'If you want to know anything, ask David to call me,' she replied.

The journalist recoiled. David Costa was Carles Font's boss at the local paper, whom Font was steadfastly undermining. David

Costa, a few years above Elisenda at school and a member of the same rambling club when she was in her teens. Carles Font, the shiny young incomer, eager to make his mark and then make his move. Destined no doubt for bigger and better things.

'Modern police,' Font commented. 'You're supposed to be working with the press.'

'And as soon as we can find a press that works with us, we will,' Elisenda promised. They stared at each other.

'Back to Vista Alegre?' Àlex finally spoke in Elisenda's direction, breaking the impasse.

'Sounds good,' Elisenda agreed, getting up.

They paid and left the bar, climbing the steep street to the right of the cathedral steps, winding through the tight mediaeval lanes to Plaça Sant Domènec, the large and enclosed cobbled square in front of the main university building, where Àlex had left the unmarked Mossos car he'd taken from the pool.

Opposite the university offices, the trees outside the Campus bar-restaurant were heavily in bloom, shading the handful of students seated at the tables with bottles of beer and glasses of water. A breeze blew in from the south, scented with orange.

'Days like this shouldn't be so beautiful,' Elisenda commented, angling her face to the sun. Àlex didn't reply.

As they walked past, Elisenda glanced at the stone steps descending sharply to the left of the bar.

The four thugs from the court were standing in a row three steps down from the top, staring with mortuary slab eyes at the two of them pass by.

She didn't tell Àlex they were there.

Chapter Eight

'*Bona nit,*' Elisenda answered to the middle-aged couple that walked past her, going the other way along Carretera de Barcelona. Thursday night cars flashed past on the busy main road, leaving the echo of a whumph in her ears for moments after they'd gone by. Ever since the city had got its university, Thursday night had been transformed from just another weeknight into Friday's dress rehearsal like it was the eve of a holiday. There's life in the old girl yet, Elisenda thought, remembering the milder Girona of her teenage years. She was heading back into the centre, past the rows of new apartment blocks in and around Parc del Migdia, which had been the old military barracks in the days of her childhood, and past the extensive roadworks for the new high-speed train line carving up the dividing line between the Eixample area and the now almost unrecognisable suburb of Sant Narcís. Apart from the traffic, little of Carretera de Barcelona was as it was when she was growing up in an old apartment near where the road began its journey, between the railway station and Plaça Poeta Marquina. As a girl, she'd always thought of Poeta Marquina, with its hundreds of deafening starlings nesting in the plane trees above the glass-sided Café Nuria, as the boundary where the city proper started. Now Girona sprawled out along the main road, throwing up buildings and modern squares and sculptures before it as it rumbled across its own past.

It was in one such new building in Parc del Migdia, on the outer fringes of her old new city, where she'd just had dinner. All she could recall now as she approached the station was her younger sister, Catalina, sitting on the terrace of her apartment overlooking the artificial lake, gazing at her watch for the umpteenth time.

'I'm really sorry,' Catalina had said. Also for the umpteenth time. 'He promised he'd do his best to be here.'

'Don't worry,' Elisenda had told her each time, clasping her hand on the white plastic table. 'I'm really not worried.' And she wasn't. It was nice to be able to talk to her sister without Sergi, Catalina's husband, dominating the evening.

'He'll be out entrepreneuring,' Catalina joked. 'He's good at entrepreneuring.'

'It pays for all this,' both women chanted, Sergi's favourite comment for every acquisition, and chuckled. Elisenda laughed along with Catalina, but her sister's face gave her away. She had the same very slight overbite that Elisenda found attractive in her sister but a flaw in herself. The same fine brown hair worn long and the same slender features. But Catalina had inherited their mother's easygoing nature, while Elisenda had been given their father's rebellious tenacity. Or stubbornness, as their mother called it.

'I'll do the dishes,' Elisenda offered. 'You're in no fit state to. Not in your condition.' Another of Sergi's more recent sayings.

Catalina looked down at her stomach and fluffed up the big, man's shirt she was wearing to hide her bulge. 'Seventeen weeks and look at me,' she moaned. She instantly closed her eyes and cursed herself. 'Eli, I'm sorry.'

Elisenda didn't look up from the plates. 'It's OK, Catalina.'

Catalina watched her sister clear the table, looking for the right thing to say. 'What do you mean, do the dishes? We've got a dishwasher.'

'That's why I offered.'

By the time Elisenda had left for the long walk home, Sergi still hadn't arrived and Catalina hadn't tried ringing him on his mobile. 'I'll be fine,' Catalina had said. 'You get off.'

Walking past her parents' old flat on Carretera de Barcelona, Elisenda looked up at the nineteenth-century stone building.

All the lights were off and the shutters half drawn. Her parents had left the home she'd grown up in and moved a few years ago to the family home in Monells where her grandparents had lived and where she'd spent her childhood summers. Leaving the apartment block behind her, she looked up one last time at her old bedroom window. She felt a sudden need to see her parents.

Quarter of an hour later, standing on the narrow pavement outside her apartment block in the old town, she looked up at the darkened windows and realised she wasn't ready for her flat. Not yet.

'That just means one thing,' she muttered to herself, walking in through the door of La Terra, the revered bar that occupied the ground floor of the old building where she had the top-floor apartment. Now given over to the next generation, La Terra was still her usual last port of call before home, especially after that evening's dinner with Catalina, her sister's pregnancy and the long walk home and the memories they'd provoked. Sitting alone in the cushioned alcove in the picture window, she took in a deep breath of her *licor de café* and stared in silence at the lights of the buildings reflected in the shallow waters of the Onyar trickling slowly through the city. A zephyr blew the window inward slightly, changing the spectral reflections of the room behind her. A vague glimpse of a young girl's face looked back at her. Elisenda glanced around but couldn't see who the reflection was of. Leaning forward, she pushed the window away from her and the reflection changed but the moment of quiet was gone.

–

In a small apartment just a few streets from La Terra, Pere Corominas, a researcher at the history archives, packed away his laptop and looked calmly at his phone. He had no messages.

It was Thursday night and the park beckoned as always.

But he had one more thing to do before he left.

He typed in the message *I will make sure everyone knows about you* and pressed Send.

Chapter Nine

The following day began with another effigy.

Another four effigies.

And Andrés Soriano.

'*Hijo de puta*,' he swore, cursing at the flow of water from his pipe slowing to a trickle, barely dampening the cobblestones at his feet. He hadn't checked the water tank in his cleaning cart before setting off from the depot that morning.

He also had an almighty hangover. Celebrating with the rest of the neighbourhood where he lived well into the small hours. Toast after toast like they'd won the *gordo*, the top prize in the state lottery. Just as good, Andrés Soriano thought, smiling gingerly through the searing cheap red wine headache.

But then he remembered that he'd have to hike all the way across the city to fill the tank up, and then all the way back to finish his work. It would be lunchtime by the time he was through. And in this heat. September, he remembered, and the summer showed no sign of giving up its hold on the city.

'*Hijo de puta*,' he growled again, raising his eyes to the heavens that he knew had it in for him. Which is when he saw the effigies swinging over his head, hanging like before from the Verge de la Bona Mort. Instantly recoiling, he quickly recovered and squinted up at them. Different this time. Not a face, but four little rag dolls. Complete bodies.

'What the fuck are you all about?' he muttered.

He looked in disgust at the hosepipe hanging limp in his hand. He couldn't even dislodge the figures with the jet of water like he'd done last time. Unless they were still there by the time he got back with a full tank of water. But there'd be more people around at that time. Can't go spraying the Catalans' precious statues, he thought bitterly.

A fifth figure appeared on his hung-over horizon, exacerbating his headache mood. That snooty lawyer. The one with the office down on Carrer de la Força, next to the city history archives, who'd complained to the council about the state of the streets in the old town. Or to be more precise, the streets in the old town cleaned by Andrés Soriano.

Walking through the Portal de Sobreportes underneath the niche where the Verge de la Bona Mort stood, Gerard Bell-solà looked up also, following Andrés Soriano's gaze. They exchanged a look, the lawyer pointing up at the effigies and walking on past the street cleaner without a word.

Andrés Soriano watched him go.

'*Hijo de puta*,' he murmured.

The lawyer had seen the effigies, too. That meant he'd have to report it back at the depot. Get someone to go up a ladder and get them down. Or worse still, do it himself. If he didn't, that shit of a lawyer would be sure to kick up a stink, and Andrés Soriano knew who'd be the one to end up on the carpet again.

Slowly, wincing at the pain in his head, he began coiling up the bright yellow hosepipe and storing it in the little cart before heading off across town for the second time that morning. Looking up, he gave one final curse to the four dolls hanging stiffly in the cloying morning heat and accelerated away.

Chapter Ten

Elisenda walked to Vista Alegre after the penance of her morning run. There was no breeze in the streets and an enervating humidity rose up from the river and coiled down from the haze-shrouded mountains.

'Roasting today, Narcís,' she commented to a figure seated at a desk in the open office she had to get through to reach her own unit.

'It is hot,' he replied stiffly.

The only man in Girona that Elisenda reckoned could make plain clothes look like a tightly-buttoned uniform, Narcís Pijaume was the head of the Local Investigation Unit, which dealt with lesser crimes within the confines of the city. It was a role Elisenda always thought was ideally suited to him.

'Air conditioning not on?' she asked, knowing the answer. It had been turned off at the start of the second fortnight in September, and off it would stay until the following spring. Cost-cutting and a devotion to the seasons where they really weren't wanted. Pijaume simply grunted.

Elisenda left him and went through to the outer office of the Serious Crime Unit to stand at the window for a moment. The family window, she and Àlex always joked, as it was the one bit of light that came into the rather dingy room. They reckoned the regional government must spend a fortune on light bulbs and electricity bills to lighten the unit's daily darkness, which Elisenda found oddly and poetically satisfying.

Finding it too quiet, she stuck her head back into Pijaume's larger office in time to see Josep brush in through the door,

40

staring at his mobile screen. He looked up and was as surprised as Elisenda was to see Pijaume on his own. 'Something we said?' she asked Pijaume, but he just shrugged.

'I've just sent my last two mossos out,' he explained. 'Drugs.'

'Things that bad?'

'Hospital Josep Trueta,' he went on. 'Drugs reported missing from the hospital pharmacy.'

'What sort of drugs?'

With a sigh, Pijaume picked up a file from his desk. 'Loprazolam,' he read, 'temazepam and pentobarbital.'

Elisenda whistled. 'Heavy duty. Just what we need. Someone selling those round the city.'

Pijaume grunted. 'Sedatives. At least we won't have to run much to arrest them.' He grinned in his curious lopsided rictus, where just the right side of his mouth and cheek lifted, half closing his right eye like an indecisive wink.

It was Elisenda's turn to shrug as she looked at Josep. Pijaume's occasional lapses into humour always left her feeling strangely uneasy. She went back into their unit's room to fetch her bag and came back out to find Josep waiting.

'Fancy coming to do battle with Jutgessa Roca with me?' she asked him. 'It'll be good for your soul.'

–

'Idiot bloody Jutgessa imbecile Roca,' she complained to Josep on the walk back to the station from the court buildings on Avinguda Ramon Folch. Josep kept quiet, concentrating on negotiating their way past the other pedestrians on Carrer Santa Clara and keeping his head down in more ways than one.

Elisenda had argued with Jutgessa Roca, now appointed the jutgessa d'instrucció, the examining judge who would be leading the case and handing out the orders for compiling the evidence, in favour of the Mossos pursuing a number of lines in their investigation. The judge hadn't. She'd decided that the gang-related killing angle was the one she liked. The one she wanted Elisenda's team to focus on.

'Meaning,' Elisenda had reasoned with her, 'that by ignoring the possibility of Masó's being killed by one of his victims, a group of vigilantes or a member of his own family, we could be letting other equally valid avenues go cold. It's far too early at this stage to narrow it down. We really need to keep an open mind.'

'Gang-related, Sotsinspectora Domènech,' the judge had replied. 'That is how you will conduct the investigation. I have every intention of putting an end to organised criminality in our city.'

'I'm quite willing to pursue the gang angle alongside other lines, judge.'

'If you've quite finished, Sotsinspectora, you will not.'

Jutgessa Roca closed the file on the desk in front of her and signalled that the meeting was over, so Elisenda and Josep came away from the meeting forced to report to the judge some days later with their evidence to support, or otherwise, a gang-related attack at the cost of all else.

'I really don't see your problem, Sotsinspectora Domènech,' the judge had told her without looking up as the two Mossos were leaving. 'Whether it's gang-related, vigilantes or whatever, whoever did this has done the city a favour. I'm sure not everyone is as eager to find the perpetrators as you are.'

Elisenda had turned to look at the top of the judge's head bowed over her desk. 'Can I quote you on that, Jutgessa Roca? He's still a victim, even if you think he's a deserving one. And I'm still a police officer.' She'd turned to go. 'And you're still a judge.'

'New police force, same old legal system,' Elisenda said now as they crossed the Pont de Pedra, the stone bridge crossing the Onyar from the new side of the city to the old. It was becoming her favourite phrase. Josep thought it best not to mention that the legal system was, in fact, changing too. It was just certain judges that weren't. 'I'm only glad I don't have the slightest intention of doing what she says,' Elisenda added.

She turned to look at Josep, walking in studious silence.

'What is it you're trying not to say, Josep?'

'May I say something, Sotsinspectora?' he finally asked. 'When I said you were hard on your informant, you told me to look him up on NIP. Doesn't that make him a deserving victim? Just to a lesser extent.'

'Good point,' she conceded with a sigh. 'This Masó case makes you question everything.'

'Yes, Sotsinspectora.'

'Just don't make any more good points for a while.'

They turned into Plaça Catalunya and skirted the tiny Plaça Vern. Office workers were finishing their morning coffees in the sun before heading back to their air-conditioned work. A woman dressed in linen and silk was changing the pictures in the window of an estate agent's office. At the ice cream bar, a large group of German tourists was placing a lengthy and complicated order with a frazzled waiter.

And at another of the café terraces, the four thugs from the previous afternoon's trial were seated, spread over two tables, staring at Elisenda. Staking out his territory, Chema GM had his feet up on the second table. Juan SP spat thickly into a large planter pot, the brightly-coloured begonias still in the sullen heat. The tables around them were empty, the clients unfortunate enough to be too near to them eyeing them warily. Elisenda approached them.

'Bit far from your comfort zone,' she said to them. They rarely strayed from the old town.

'Not a crime, is it?' Juan SP answered back. A third gang member, Manuel PM, sniggered.

Ignoring them both, Elisenda looked straight at Chema GM. 'Not yet it isn't.'

'Is that a threat?' Chema GM asked her.

'Not yet it isn't,' she repeated. 'Don't stray too far, boys.'

She and Josep carried on. Elisenda took her mobile out of her handbag and dialled.

'Àlex,' she said, explaining the situation, 'have a word with Seguretat Ciutadana. Get them to keep an eye on them.'

'*They're already on to it,*' he told her. '*I've seen them three times today. They were at the bar over the road from Vista Alegre earlier. I get the feeling it's me they're following.*'

'Right, get Seguretat Ciutadana to make their presence known. Harass them. Send them back to the old town.'

'*I can take care of it.*'

'I know you can. But we don't want that bunch giving us any headaches.'

'*I think it's too late for that.*'

Chapter Eleven

The bone cracked.

The sound of it washed along the cobbles of the old town, shining as black as a night sea, and tumbled back down from the steep stone walls of the ancient buildings.

There were no screams.

Cristobal HP saw to that, clamping the crook of his arm tightly around the man's nose and mouth.

Chema GM lashed out again, this time to the other leg, but it didn't break. The man had flopped with the pain of the first blow and his leg had absorbed the impact of the second, bending but not snapping. Angrily, Chema GM pulled Cristobal HP's arm away and pushed the heel of his hand into the man's face, enjoying the feeling of the cartilage in his victim's nose twist and crumble. He took a deep breath. His first Friday night of freedom in the labyrinth of alleys in the old town and it felt good. Cristobal HP let the man slump to the cobbles, shaking the blood from his sleeve but not daring to complain about it to Chema GM. Not when he was like this.

'Come on, man. Get his wallet,' Juan SP urged Chema GM.

'No,' the leader hissed, pulling Manuel PM back. 'This one's not for money. This one's for pleasure.' He looked down at the man on the ground and spat on the familiar, bloodied face before turning away. 'Come on.'

Over two hours after the beating, Juan SP was still asking the same question. 'Did you see? Did you fucking see? Fucking brilliant.'

Chema GM just sat on the low wall in Sant Daniel and nodded his head. He was suddenly tired. He noticed Cristobal HP lolling head-down over the wall, but couldn't be bothered to slap him across the back of the skull as he would normally have done. He smiled, a backyard predator's smile, his bared teeth dull and cold. He'd won at cards against the other three, taking the evening's meagre takings off them all. He always won at cards.

'Did you see? Did you fucking see?' Juan SP asked again, his words slurring.

'Fucking brilliant,' Manuel GM echoed. He took a drink from the cheap bottle of red wine that someone in the last bar they'd been to had sent over to them – to keep them sweet, they'd decided – and slumped back against the wall.

Juan SP took the bottle from him and yawned heavily, his head slowly sinking.

Chapter Twelve

'Àlex? Can you hear me? It's Elisenda?'

His eyes slowly flickered open, then closed again.

'Àlex?'

With one last effort, he opened his eyes. A small grunt came out of his dry lips.

'Happy Saturday, it's Elisenda.'

Àlex picked up his watch from the bedside table and yawned. 'Morning?' he said into the mouthpiece, sheltering the phone to avoid waking his wife. 'That's what you call this in Girona, is it?'

'We've got a body,' Elisenda told him, her voice loud in the phone pressed tightly against his ear.

He swung out of bed and gratefully put the soles of both feet flat on the cool tiled floor. 'Where?'

'Hanging from the cathedral steps.'

'How can you hang from the cathedral steps?'

'The balustrade at the top. Apparently, he's hanging naked from one of the stone balusters.'

'Naked and swinging from the cathedral steps. Sounds like any other Friday night in Girona.'

'We'll have none of your big-city wit,' Elisenda told him. 'Anyway, I'll be able to tell you for sure in a moment, I'm just coming to the top of Força.'

Elisenda rounded the corner at the top of the cobbled alley and looked up to her right. Way above her, two Seguretat Ciutadana were peering over the edge of the balustrade separating the small square at the top of the cathedral steps from the narrow road that curved sharply out of sight before looping down to the bottom. Below them, two more mossos were setting up a barrier at the foot of the steep stonewall drop. Between the two pairs, the naked figure of a man was slowly being buffeted against the heavy nummulitic limestone slabs on the sheer side of the wall descending from the ornate balustrade. The sun beyond the cathedral had still not fully torn itself away from the land.

'Àlex,' she said into her mobile, 'I think you'd probably better get here.'

–

'José Maria Guijarro Martín,' Àlex recited slowly. He and Elisenda were standing two-thirds of the way up the cathedral steps, looking over the side to where the naked man was hanging. His back rubbing against the wall had left pendulum trails of blood smeared either side of him like angel's wings on the light-coloured stone. 'Or Chema GM as he liked to be known.'

A caporal in the Policia Científica asked them to move on a bit while he videoed the scene. A second one was down below taking still photos, having worked his way down the steps from the top to the road at the bottom, where he was craning his neck back to get a few shots looking upwards. As the video operator filmed the scene, Elisenda and Àlex watched in silence as four uniformed mossos slowly started pulling on the rope to bring the body up to the balustrade.

'How long's it going to be?' Àlex asked the cameraman.

'Dunno,' he replied. 'It's an odd one, so it could be some time.'

'You're telling me,' Àlex said. All three of them looked at the figure. The rope wasn't around Chema GM's neck, but slung across his chest, under his armpits and apparently knotted at the back.

'Not suicide then,' Elisenda commented.

The cameraman grinned and went back to his work but Àlex stopped him.

'Any forensics?' he asked him.

The Científica looked bleakly at Àlex. 'Half the western world has walked up these steps since the low-cost flights started. The killer could have taken a pee on them and we wouldn't be able to tell who's who.'

Àlex grunted and let him get on with it.

Elisenda's phone rang and she walked a short distance away along the step to answer it so she wouldn't be captured on the video camera's microphone. She listened in silence, occasionally looking over at Àlex, and then darkened the mobile screen before rejoining him.

'And where Chema GM goes, three more are sure to follow,' she said.

Àlex turned to her sharply. 'You don't mean it.'

'Not quite. Two of them. Juan SP and Cristobal HP.'

Àlex whistled. 'Someone's had a busy night.'

'Haven't they just? One's down in front of Sant Feliu.'

'The church? That's two minutes from here.'

'Someone's just found the pair of them, apparently. The other one's on the Pont de Pedra.'

Àlex nodded, taking the news in. The Pont de Pedra, the stone bridge crossing the Onyar at the top of the Rambla.

'Seems they were both curled up against a wall,' Elisenda continued. 'People thought they were homeless sleeping rough. First Masó, now this lot. Someone will be benefiting.'

'We all will.'

They started climbing the steps and were almost at the top in the lee of the west façade when the sombre hush of the morning was rent by foul language.

'See Albert's arrived,' Elisenda commented to Àlex.

At the top, Albert Riera, the senior forensic doctor in the city's Institut de Medicina Legal, was kneeling over the body, screaming at the two poor uniforms unlucky enough to be in his line of vision.

'I know the training's bad,' the pathologist was yelling, 'and they evidently employ monkeys, but even you lot should be able to tell the two apart. Look at him.' With his latex-gloved right hand, he was waving a metal ruler about while the left was prodding the dead man's chest. 'You are a fucking waste of space.'

'And you,' Àlex's voice cut through the shocked silence, 'should learn how to talk to people.'

Albert Riera stood up. 'Our friend from Barcelona,' he said, drawing out the vowels of the last word in exaggerated mimicry of Àlex's Barcelona accent. 'We don't need you to tell us how we can speak to each other.'

Àlex made to reply, but Elisenda put her hand on his arm.

'What is it, Albert?' she asked the pathologist.

'You got me out of my bed to come and cut up a stiff.'

Àlex snorted and Elisenda tightened her grip on his arm. 'And?' she said.

'So when I'm called out to see a dead body, I expect to see a dead body. They're not too difficult to make out. No breathing, turning blue, smelling. Even you lot should be able to work that one out without a diagram.'

'Cut the sarcasm,' Àlex growled at him.

Riera pointed at the figure at his feet. 'This man isn't dead. He's drugged.'

Chapter Thirteen

Monday morning and the case of the four muggers was nothing to do with Elisenda's team. The fourth, Manuel PM, had been found, drugged like the other three, some distance from the city centre on Pont de Sarrià, the bridge spanning the Ter on the northern fringes of Girona. Not a series of murders as they'd first thought, so Elisenda's Serious Crime Unit had been stepped down and the investigation taken on by the Regional Investigation Unit, which dealt with the crimes in the city and region that the local investigation units didn't take on.

'Someone did have a busy night,' Àlex had repeated his own words when they'd found out where the last of the gang of four had been discovered.

'Strange,' Elisenda had agreed, 'why whoever drugged them should drop them off where they did. Two bridges and two churches.'

'And why they didn't finish the job.'

She watched him now on Monday morning walk into the Local Investigation Unit office deep in conversation with a sergent from the regional unit. The phone on her desk rang and she picked it up.

'*Elisenda,*' the voice on the other end spoke, '*it's Xavier. Can you come through a bit earlier?*'

She checked her watch. 'Sure.'

'*Just to find out what's happening with the Masó investigation. Could you make it now?*'

'Right,' Elisenda replied, her heart sinking. With a sigh, she picked up her folders and turned her mobile off. The politicians have got on his back, she realised, walking through to the Inspector's office.

Xavier – Inspector Puigventós to all but a few and head of the Regional Investigation Command – was on the phone when she walked in, so he signalled her to sit down. A few new photos on his wall, she saw. Dogs again. Always dogs. And always Catalan sheepdogs. His wife bred them and he adored both them and his wife. Indeed, his wife appeared in more than a few photos with one or another prize-winner. Smiling, really very beautiful, Elisenda thought, not for the first time, with straight jet-black hair and strong eyes. Elisenda looked away. She never really knew how comfortable she felt with such personal displays on an office wall. Her own room had two plants and three shop-bought framed prints. Outwardly personal but revealing nothing. Much like her, she considered, surprised at the realisation.

The inspector finished his call and hung up.

'Sorry about that, Elisenda,' he said, looking quickly at his watch. 'The other heads of unit will be here in a few minutes. I just wanted to ask how the Masó investigation was going.'

'Early days,' Elisenda replied warily. 'We're pursuing four lines of investigation. Rival gangs, internal rivalry, an attack by a victim and vigilantes. We're keeping an open mind on them all at this stage, although we are interested in Joaquim Masó, the victim's uncle.'

Puigventós considered for a moment. 'The last thing we want is vigilantes. Or for the press to get a whiff that we think it's vigilantes.'

'That's just one of our options,' Elisenda reminded him. 'We've checked Masó's old stamping ground, but there's no clear evidence yet of any sort of vigilante action. As I say, we're keeping an open mind.'

Puigventós grunted. 'Gang war wouldn't be entirely welcome either.'

Tell that to Jutgessa Roca, Elisenda thought.

'Could it be one of the new gangs coming in from the old Eastern bloc? South Americans? North Africans?' he asked, studiedly listing off every group currently being blamed for more or less all the country's ills.

'We've heard nothing, and there have been no reprisals yet, but we are following them up. There ought to be a vacuum, but as far as we can see, no one's filling it. From inside or outside the family.'

The inspector straightened some folders sitting on his desk. 'We want a quick resolution on this one, Elisenda. Clear it up and move on.'

'Wouldn't it be better for us to try and to make sure no one does fill the vacuum?' Not forgetting my under-funded unit only has one sergent, three caporals and me, she thought.

Puigventós sighed. 'Yes, I suppose it would.' He suddenly looked utterly fed up. 'But that doesn't further careers, sell newspapers or get votes, does it?'

He threw the previous day's newspaper across his desk. It was open on a full-page article demanding police action. Elisenda had read it the day before, but even after reading it over her third *cafè amb llet* of Sunday morning, she still hadn't been quite sure exactly what the police action the writer had been demanding was. She looked at the unprepossessing face of the author again. A priest. One of the old school she thought had died out with Franco, demanding a return to traditional values, which to him evidently meant the traditional values imposed during a forty-year span in the middle of the twentieth century that had blighted the lives of at least two generations. He was invariably wheeled out when an extreme view needed airing.

'Mossèn Eduard Viladrau,' Elisenda muttered, giving the priest his full title. 'Since when have we started worrying again what he and his ilk think?'

Inspector Puigventós was saved from replying by a knock on the door. Two men filed in, one was Pijaume, clutching a buff folder, the other a corporate clone with a neat and shining leather document case tucked under his arm.

'Inspector, Elisenda,' Pijaume greeted them, straightening his tie and placing the folder on the oval meeting table.

The second man's greeting was the mirror image. 'Xavier,' he said affably to Puigventós. 'Sotsinspectora Domènech,' he added, not looking at Elisenda. She fought back a smile. Sitting down and taking a gold fountain pen out of his jacket pocket in one smooth movement, he calmly unzipped his leather case.

Elisenda and Puigventós joined them at the table, Elisenda seated next to Pijaume, the inspector on the opposite side. Sotsinspector Roger Micaló, the other man, evidently realised that he'd sat down at what was the head of the table without thinking. Elisenda watched him calculate how to get out of it without either losing face or challenging Puigventós.

'Would you prefer to sit here, Xavier?' he simply asked, only the vague, fluttering movement of the fingers on his right hand showing his discomfort.

Puigventós just shook his head. 'Let's get down to business, shall we?' Pijaume smiled lightly at Elisenda. 'Elisenda and I have already discussed the Masó investigation, so unless either of you have anything to add, we can take that as finished.' He looked at the other two sotsinspectors, both of whom shook their heads. 'Fine. Narcís, if you'd like to lead with anything we should know.'

The Monday meeting, Elisenda mused, her mind wandering slightly. Led by Puigventós as head of the Regional Investigation Command, which reported to the Criminal Investigation Division in Sabadell rather than to Vista Alegre, and including, besides her, the head of the Regional Investigation Unit, which reported to Puigventós, and Pijaume, as head of the Local Investigation Unit, which co-ordinated with Puigventós but actually reported to the commander of the station. As if life wasn't convoluted enough, she always felt. Each meeting just fifteen minutes long to ensure that the various groups co-ordinated their investigations so that any crossover that might be of mutual help didn't go unnoticed. It was also meant to stop empire-building, Elisenda thought, instinctively glancing at Micaló. His gaze met hers for a second and he looked away. The head of the Regional Investigation Unit, he was one of that breed of political animal that Elisenda had come across so often in the Mossos, his career mapped out like a strategy of war, any actual policing an afterthought. Still, she thought, he'd be gone soon: he was in too much of a hurry to be hanging around Girona for any longer than was necessary.

She brought her concentration back when Pijaume mentioned drugs. It seemed more had gone missing from the hospital early that morning. 'Same as last week,' Pijaume went on. 'Sedatives. Strong ones.'

'The four men found drugged,' Elisenda asked. 'Do we know what was used?'

'My investigation, Sotsinspectora, I think you'll find,' Micaló interjected. 'Drugged, not murdered. Not a serious crime,' he added, emphasising the last two words.

'And were they?' Puigventós asked him. 'The same drugs?'

Micaló consulted a file ripped from the insides of his document case. 'Yes, they were,' he eventually answered.

'Thank you,' the inspector replied. He looked at Elisenda.

'These four survived,' she commented. 'Might not be so lucky next time. And what we don't know is if it's the thief who used the drugs on the victims or if it was a buyer who did it. Neither way is good, but if it is the first case and someone is stealing them not to sell but to target victims, that's even more disturbing. Whether people think they've got it coming or not.'

Pijaume nodded. 'I agree. I've put two caporals on to it at present, and the Científica are due at the hospital this morning. Until we see evidence of the drugs being sold on the streets, I think our priority is to track events through the actual theft and the four victims.'

'That's good,' Puigventós concluded. 'Everyone all right with that?'

The other three nodded, but Elisenda's mind was racing ahead. The moment she'd finished what she was saying about deserving victims, the image of Masó hanging from the derelict building came to mind. She stored it away for the time being, wanting to discuss it with Àlex before throwing it into the general arena.

'Roger,' Puigventós continued, 'anything you might like to add?'

Micaló consulted his files and said there was just one point he wanted to raise. 'There was an extremely vicious assault in the old town on Thursday night. A journalist. Carles Font.'

Elisenda sat up. 'Carles Font? I was talking to him last week.'

'He was very badly beaten up, but he recovered consciousness yesterday morning and made a statement.' Micaló paused and looked around the table. 'He claims that he was attacked by the four men who were later drugged.'

Elisenda looked at him. If he'd been going for drama, she thought, it worked. You might have told us this earlier, was her second, also unvoiced, thought.

'I will, of course, be devoting more than a pair of caporals to the investigation,' Micaló added.

Chapter Fourteen

'This is beginning to feel like my second home,' Elisenda commented to Àlex as he drove them both along the punctu-ated bustle of the Passeig d'Olot in the direction of Salt. They were heading for where the town petered out by the motorway flyover. On the way, she told him of the meeting she'd just left, about more drugs being stolen and about Carles Font being attacked by the four muggers shortly before they were drugged.

He took his eyes off the traffic for a moment and looked at her. 'More drugs? Does that mean we should expect more attacks like the one on the muggers?'

'And on Masó.'

Àlex glanced at her again. 'Masó? He wasn't drugged.'

'No, he wasn't, was he?'

Before he could reply, they turned into a narrow road flanked by 1960s red-brick and render apartment blocks and pulled up outside a pair of large and peeling corrugated metal gates leading into a scrappy courtyard between two buildings. They got out of the car and looked at a small door set into the gates that was wedged open with a half brick.

'Hardly a criminal empire, is it?' Elisenda muttered.

Àlex grinned and went on in. Catching him up, Elisenda saw a dusty white van in one corner of the yard, piles of papers yellowing and curled on the dashboard and a stack of boxes on the ground near the open side door, waiting to be loaded. Next to it, a heavy oil stain on the ground showed where another van was usually parked. Broken pallets were heaped up against a wall next to a door leading into an office.

Opposite the vehicle was an aluminium table and four mismatched chairs skewed next to it. Three of the chairs were occupied.

'Can I help you?' Joaquim Masó asked them. He didn't get up. He nodded to his two companions, who did. Without a word, the two men acknowledged the Mossos and walked away from the table towards the small metal door leading out. From their looks, they were evidently brothers but Elisenda didn't recognise either of them. They weren't part of the Masó family. In their early twenties, both were dressed in tight T-shirts and jeans, showing off their muscles. She caught the older one glance at Àlex and Àlex grin back, his muscles more pronounced under a loose white shirt. He looked at Elisenda and shook his head slightly to show he didn't recognise them either.

'Friends of yours, Joaquim?' Elisenda asked him.

'Business associates. Just chewing the fat, taking the sun.'

'Business associates,' Elisenda repeated. She'd interviewed him in the past about stolen goods, but had never been able to prove anything. 'Don't let us stop you.'

'They were just going.'

Elisenda sat down on the seat opposite Masó, and Àlex wandered over to the van to look through the doors.

'You'll find everything in order,' Masó told him.

'How's business then, Joaquim?' Elisenda asked him. 'I was expecting to find you out working.'

Masó shrugged. 'I get by. As much as anyone can these days.' He gestured to the empty space. 'My sister's boy is out with the other van.'

'Lucky you have your family to help.'

'I do business through my family, not with it.'

Elisenda was about to comment but Masó's mobile rang and he answered it. Someone wanting a delivery by the sound of the conversation, but Masó told them that he wasn't available.

'Must be doing well for yourself if you can turn work down,' Elisenda commented.

'Must be,' Masó agreed.

'Daniel,' Elisenda said. Àlex came and stood over the table. 'Sad news for you all, I understand, but I need to know where you were the night he died.'

Masó gestured around him. 'Here. I live upstairs. But you'll know that. And I was on my own. I keep myself to myself.'

'Do you know you're the only member of your family that wasn't with every other member of your family that night?' Elisenda said. 'No one can vouch for you? I'm almost inclined to believe you're innocent on the strength of that alone.'

The door rattled as someone knocked on it, sending metallic shock waves through the gates. Elisenda turned around to see Gerard Bellsolà walk in, his aged brown leather briefcase tapping against his short legs as he walked. She turned back to Masó.

'But now you've blown it.'

The lawyer greeted Masó and sat down between him and Elisenda. 'Sotsinspectora Domènech,' he said. 'May I ask what you're doing here?'

'Your client, I take it. I'm ascertaining what he was doing the night Daniel Masó was murdered. As I am with every member of his family to build up a picture to help us apprehend Daniel's killer.'

'I am aware of that, Sotsinspectora. I am acting on behalf of the Masó family to protect their interests. I would prefer all meetings with my clients to take place in my presence from now on, if you don't mind.'

'I'll bear that in mind,' Elisenda told him. She got up. 'But we've learned all we need to know for now, thanks.'

She and Àlex left the two men seated in their uncertainty and returned to their car.

'We have?' Àlex asked her.

'No, but we've found a few more questions.'

'Like why Bellsolà suddenly turned up?'

'Like that. And like how come Masó can have one van idle and still turn work down. You saw he's not exactly rolling in it.'

She waited while Àlex drove out into traffic on the main road.

'And like how come the rest of the clan haven't included him in the family alibi.'

Chapter Fifteen

Àlex dropped Elisenda off at Vista Alegre and drove to the Hospital Josep Trueta, on the northern edge of the city, and went in. Stepping out of the hospital lift, he immediately saw the room he wanted thanks to the two Seguretat Ciutadana standing outside, one a caporal, the other a mosso. He approached the caporal and showed him his badge.

'Any change?' Àlex asked him.

'None, Sergent. None whatsoever.'

Àlex grinned at him. 'Bored?'

'You can say, Sergent,' the caporal muttered. The mosso just grunted.

'Anyone tried to get in to see him?'

'No one. There's a doctor in there now checking.'

'You know they're a doctor?'

'Been here all night and most of yesterday. They do longer hours than we do.'

'Yeah, but they don't get the money we do,' the mosso chipped in. The two Seguretat Ciutadana laughed wryly at that.

Inside the room, Àlex found the doctor noting something down in a folder. She looked up as he walked in.

'Sergent Àlex Albiol,' he greeted her. 'Just checking up on our star pupil.'

She went back to her paperwork. 'Doctora Sans,' she introduced herself. 'Cristina.' She looked exhausted, her pen hand resting heavily on the stiff writing board of the folder.

'Been up all night looking after this beauty, I hear.' She just nodded and carried on writing. Àlex looked at Chema GM in bed, propped up on his right side, tubes coming out of his nose and mouth and drips going into his left arm. 'When's he likely to come round?'

'We can't say.'

'I hear the other three have all regained consciousness. How come he's still like this?'

'He ingested more of the drug than they did.'

Àlex nodded his head slowly. 'Chema GM drank more of the wine than he let his friends, in other words. That figures.'

'My job's to cure,' the doctor commented, clicking her pen shut, 'not to judge.'

'So's mine.'

'If there's anything else,' she asked, making to leave.

'Nothing. I'll just stay here a while if that's OK.'

Àlex watched her shrug, her tiredness glinting dully through, and waited until the door swished shut behind her before he walked over to the window to take in the view over the main road heading north out of the city. No one else came in. He walked over to the bed and stared at the patient. The sunlight streaming in through the blinds tore jagged strips of shadow over Chema GM's face and up the wall above him. There was no movement whatsoever from him. Àlex looked at all the machines and tubes and buttons and switches and took another step closer. He leaned directly over Chema GM's face and put his mouth to his ear.

'You should have died,' he said.

Chapter Sixteen

Elisenda tried Àlex's phone but it was switched off. He did that when it suited him, but then so did she so she couldn't get too uptight about it. And Àlex was one of those people who had to be cut just the right amount of slack for him to operate well. 'Unlike me,' she murmured wryly.

She saw David Costa already seated on a bench on Plaça Independència, the same place the rambling club had always met in their youth. He still looked the same as he did then, rather earnest with a sensible haircut and bookish glasses that made him look reliable and dull. Two pigeons were pecking at the pale brown earth by his feet.

'Elisenda,' he greeted her warmly, getting up to give her a kiss on both cheeks.

'Good to see you, David,' she replied, sitting down next to him. 'This brings back memories.'

'Happy ones, I hope.' He squeezed her hand and let go.

Elisenda closed her eyes, silently swearing. She thought his interest in her had died out years ago. Opening them again, she turned to one side and saw a mother, father and young daughter laughing as they walked past. She guiltily turned away when she caught the mother's eye.

David was watching her closely. 'Still missing Lina?'

She felt as though he'd gripped his fingers around her throat. It was a few moments before she could speak. 'I don't know, David. What do you think?'

'How long has it been?'

Elisenda looked at him in disbelief. 'Five years, David, that's how long it's been. That's how long it is since my daughter died. Do you think I might still be missing her?'

He reached for her hand to try and hold it. 'I see it's painful, Elisenda.'

She pulled her hand away. 'What was it you wanted?'

'Just to catch up, really. We haven't had a chat for ages.'

'I'm going now, David.' She stood up.

Costa shrugged. 'These four thugs. The ones who were drugged.'

'Not my case.'

He looked surprised. 'I thought it would be. Not a serious enough crime?'

'When does a crime become serious?' She'd asked herself the question often enough since being invited to set up the unit. Sighing, she sat down again, the police officer in her taking over. 'The Regional Investigation Unit are dealing with it. And if it were my case, I couldn't talk to you about it.'

'Not officially, no.'

'Or unofficially.'

'Unless you needed help.'

'You're not doing yourself any favours, David.'

'The four muggers,' he persevered. 'You must have some thoughts on them.'

'Why are you interested?'

'They attacked one of my journalists.'

'Carles Font. Someone you can't stand. Try again.'

'Come on, Elisenda, give me a break. This could be a big story. I need one. Precisely because of Carles Font I need one.'

'I'm sorry, David, I really can't help you. As I say, it's not my investigation.'

'Yes, but you have some idea.' He waited while a small boy ran past, shooing the pigeons before him. 'You're not going to tell me you've had no thoughts on it. Four vicious criminals, drugged, left in four different spots around the city. One of them posed like an angel.'

'Like an angel? Where did you hear that?'

'I have my sources.'

Elisenda considered the idea. He only looked like an angel because of the track of the blood as he moved, not part of the staging, probably not intended. She immediately discounted it but said nothing. 'Sources?'

'And Daniel Masó?' he added. 'Where does he fit in?'

'He doesn't. Different case, different team investigating it.'

'I know that. But it looks like tit-for-tat. One criminal gets killed, four others get punished.'

'Is that the way you see it, David? A reprisal?'

'Is that the way the Mossos' investigation is going? Or is it vigilantes?'

She could see him out of the corner of her eye, staring at her, gauging her reaction. She felt tired, the game summing up much of what she felt was the relationship between the Mossos and the media, between her and David. Supposedly mutually beneficial but often reciprocally distrustful. The tearing down of the barriers of the past creating new barriers in their place.

'You tell me, David.'

'People are saying the Mossos are floundering,' he continued. He looked almost hunted, she thought in surprise. 'And worse.'

'Worse?'

'Look at it, Elisenda. Daniel Masó killed and four muggers given a taste of their own medicine. You can't say you weren't happy at that.'

'I can, actually,' she replied, shocked to find herself doubting if she honestly could. 'A victim's a victim.'

'So you would have felt exactly the same about it had it been anyone else? This elderly man the muggers attacked, for instance. Or Carles Font, even.'

Elisenda recalled the phone call from Pep in Científica telling her the identity of the first victim and how neither of them had shown any great sympathy for Masó. 'Maybe I wouldn't have felt the same. But I'm a police officer. It's my job to find who did it and to see that justice is done. That doesn't change, no matter who the victim is.'

Costa snorted at that.

'You said worse,' she went on, irritated.

The journalist shrugged. 'Maybe the Mossos are doing more than just turn a blind eye. You said it yourself, it's your job to see that justice is done. Perhaps this is the only way the Mossos can do that.'

Elisenda stood up. 'This is isn't even speculation, David, and you know it'

'I'm just out there, Elisenda. Reporting the truth as I see it. As I hear it.'

'The truth? You're a good journalist, David. Maybe that's the victim you should be worrying about, not mine.'

Costa stood up and apologised. He asked her if she was free for dinner that Friday to make up.

'Afraid not,' she told him. 'Seeing my sister.'

'And Saturday?'

'I can't make it on Saturday, either, sorry.'

'One day next week?'

'David,' she said, the exasperation in her voice shining through.

Defeated, he kissed her on both cheeks and they walked off in separate directions, she across the square towards Pont de Sant Agustí, he towards Santa Clara. On her way to the bridge, Elisenda greeted the good-looking waiter serving the terrace tables outside Lizarran. She'd resigned herself to admiring him from afar for ages. Pity, as she could tell the attraction went both ways. Girona really was too small, she thought. Stopping to chat with him for a few moments, she turned to say goodbye when she saw David Costa on the other side of the square.

He was staring at her, his face blank with disappointment.

The sergent on the front desk stifled a yawn.

His first day back at work after a week's holiday in the Pyrenees and his mind was still in the mountains. He took a deep breath and looked at the paperwork. Everywhere you go in this country, he thought, there's paperwork.

The outer door opened and a young man came in and walked up to the desk. 'Who do I report a missing person to?' he asked the sergent.

'I'll ring through to the Local Investigation Unit,' the sergent replied. 'They'll take a statement.' He rang the internal number but no one answered, which meant that it was his job to take the details and pass it on. He found the right form on the computer and started typing.

'What's the name of the person who's missing?'

'Pere Corominas Vega,' the young man replied, giving the address when asked. 'He's my flatmate.'

'And when did you last see him?'

'Thursday morning, before he went to work. He seemed very agitated. He left home earlier than usual that morning. He'd been like that for a couple of days.'

'Has he got a girlfriend he might be with?'

The young man looked frankly at the sergent. 'He wasn't really one for girlfriends.'

The sergent nodded. 'Has he ever gone missing before?'

'No, never. And I've tried his work. He's a researcher with the city archive. But he hasn't shown up today. It's really unusual. He may have stayed away from home for a night or two if he'd met someone, but it's been four nights now. And he'd never miss work without letting them know. And he'd at least have rung me.'

The sergent finished taking down all the details and sent it through to the Local Investigation Unit mailbox. 'A member of the Mossos will be contacting you,' he told the young man.

'I'm sure your friend will turn up. And if he does, make sure you inform us.'

He watched him leave the building and checked and filed the statement he'd just taken. A copy had already gone through to the Local Investigation Unit, and he made a note to make sure they saw it.

Looking through other files, he picked up a single-page report from the low desk behind the front counter and looked at it. Someone had stuck four dolls on the Verge de la Bona Mort, he read, wondering, first, why anyone would want to do that, and second, why anyone would feel the need to report it to the police. Yawning again, the sergent entered the sketchy details from the typed report into the computer and carefully put the piece of paper in a new folder in a tray ready to be filed and forgotten.

Chapter Seventeen

Àlex's mobile rang on Friday morning.

'*Àlex? Laura Puigmal. I just thought I should let you know. Senyor Casademont died in the night of a heart attack.*'

Àlex sat down heavily. 'Can it be put down to the mugging?'

'*Are you asking me legally, morally or really?*'

'I take it there's no need to answer that one.'

'*I'm sorry, Àlex.*'

'We both are.' He put the phone down and stared into space, recalling the image on Monday of Chema GM surrounded by the nurses and doctors and machines that were busy saving his life. He was alone in the office. All the others were out, following up various angles in an investigation that they were starting to feel was political quicksand. He put through an internal call.

'Sotsinspector Micaló,' he spoke into the phone, 'you know that Senyor Casademont has died?'

'*Who?*' Micaló answered. '*And who are you?*'

'Sergent Albiol. Senyor Casademont was the victim of the four thugs currently in the Hospital Josep Trueta.'

'*And what is this to do with you, Sergent?*'

'What are you going to do about it? Their victim has just died of a heart attack brought on by the beating they gave him. An elderly man who had done no one any harm.'

'*An elderly man. You do realise that another victim of theirs is in hospital, Sergent. A journalist. His case takes priority.*'

'Because he's a journalist?'

'*Because he's alive. I don't like your tone, Sergent. And for your information, the four thugs, as you call them, are also victims. They deserve equal treatment and equal respect as your Senyor Casademont.*'

'And because they're more likely to make the papers than the death of a retired shopkeeper,' Àlex growled. He knew he was already pushing it too far but he couldn't stop.

'*I suggest you get off the phone now, Sergent Albiol. You are one of Sotsinspectora Domènech's team, aren't you? I'm not surprised she can't keep a control over her juniors. I will of course be making a formal complaint.*'

'You do that, Sotsinspector. I'm sure you'll find people on the force who share your priorities.'

Àlex hung up, shaking with anger. He knew he'd gone too far. Well, he thought, at least it meant that the family would probably be able to move back to Barcelona while he looked for a new job. He closed his eyes and opened them immediately, the argument and the threat of impending dismissal already compartmentalised and locked away in another part of his mind. He looked through the desk drawers for an aspirin.

–

Both fortunately and unfortunately for Àlex, Elisenda was in a foul mood when she got back to Vista Alegre an hour later.

'Is there anyone in this city who actually wants us to do our job,' she cursed, throwing her bag onto her desk. Àlex kept quiet. 'Another morning wasting my time with people who don't want us to find who killed Daniel Masó.'

Josep and Montse followed her into their unit, equally frustrated by a morning of prevarication and stonewalling. Montse sat down with a heavy thump. Josep stared at the screensaver in front of him.

All of which was fortunate for Àlex in that when Micaló rang through to Elisenda demanding a meeting, she was just ready to let off some steam before her long-delayed first coffee of the day.

'I am going to lodge an official complaint against Sergent Albiol,' was Micaló's first and last statement in the matter.

'One,' Elisenda said to him, 'I am the same rank as you, you do not summon me to your office. Two, Sergent Albiol is a good policeman, one of the best I've worked with. He feels passionately about police work and about the victims of crimes. Which brings me to three. You don't. And if you even attempt to threaten Sergent Albiol's career, I will come for you with everything I have. You and I both know you'll be gone from Girona on the next rung as soon as you can. I suggest you don't make any more enemies while you're still here. Now if you don't mind, I need a coffee before I lose my temper.'

By the time she got back along the corridor to her office, word had already got through to the Serious Crime Unit of her showdown with Micaló. Josep was sheepishly putting the phone down from a caporal in the Regional Investigation Unit when she walked through the door of the outer room. He and Montse exchanged a look.

'Àlex,' Elisenda said, looking straight ahead, 'my office.'

Àlex followed her into her room and closed the door behind him.

'Don't sit down,' she told him, 'you won't be long.'

'I'm sorry, Elisenda.'

She looked up at him and nodded. 'You're a city boy, aren't you, Àlex? You like the city?'

'Yes.'

'Good. Because if you ever pull a stunt like that again, I will make sure you get posted to the back of beyond. Up to the Pallars Noguera, where you will spend your evenings writing up reports about missing goats and describing electricity to farmers. Do I make myself clear? You cannot take the law into your own hands.'

'Yes, Elisenda.'

'Good. Now go and get me a coffee while I still have my good humour.'

'Yes, Elisenda.' He stopped and turned in the doorway. 'And thanks.'

'Coffee,' she said. She watched him go, half a smile playing at the edges of her mouth.

Chapter Eighteen

'Who is this guy?' Carme, Àlex's wife, asked him.

Àlex walked in from the kitchen carrying a glass of Rioja for Carme and an orange juice for himself. 'The boys have dropped off,' he told her. 'Finally.'

He sat down on the sofa next to his wife and looked at the television on the low bookshelves. The local TV channel, showing yet another talking heads programme. 'Isn't there anything else on?' he asked, although he knew it was pointless. Carme loved this sort of thing and had only recently discovered the local station, with its late-night menu of earnest and endless debate.

'You haven't answered my question,' she said. He'd barely registered it. 'Who's the guy on the right? Literally and politically.'

Àlex focused on the screen. Together, they listened to the head on the box calling for a return of traditional values, which appeared to mean the reintroduction of making contraception illegal, banishment of unmarried mothers and "corrective surgery" for homosexuals. Àlex felt, as he always did, that the TV station allowed him to spew this rubbish so they could quite rightly and comprehensively shoot him down. And so people would watch another otherwise dull example of televised radio.

'He can only be a priest,' Carme said. 'That or Franco's come back to haunt us.'

'Priest,' Àlex confirmed. 'Mossèn Eduard Viladrau. Circa 1950.'

Carme looked at Àlex. 'Can we go back to Barcelona now?' she joked.

He simply grunted. 'I can't take much more of this guy. I'm going for a walk around the block, if that's OK.'

'Sure,' Carme replied, taking another sip. She was getting used to his late-night walks last thing before bed.

Outside, Àlex walked quickly into the city centre as far as the river and entered a low-lit bar squatting darkly on a nondescript modern square. The barman, wiry and dangerous, stared cold-eyed at Àlex as he walked in. A man with two signet rings on each hand sat on a stool in silence, the thin young woman with him, her arms streaked with reddened track marks, talking too much. To the rear of the darkened room, a group of four men, older, more powerful, sat around an alcove table, their discussion frozen from the moment Àlex walked in.

Àlex stood at the bar next to the man with the signet rings. 'Beer,' he said at the figure behind the counter.

He looked around him and took in a deep breath of the stale, hostile air.

He felt alive for the first time all day.

–

The last of the plates and cutlery rattled into the dishwasher as the shuffle on Elisenda's iPod pushed Sopa de Cabra through the Bose speakers, filling her small flat with the hypnotic two-guitar riff from *Carrer dels Torrats*. Now disbanded, they were the Girona sound of her youth. A lifetime ago. Literally, she thought with a jolt, recalling David Costa and his thoughtless question about Lina, her daughter, who she placed in a corner of her mind when the pain of remembering her got too great. Her daughter, who died. Once again, she sealed up the seams of her thoughts to protect herself. Absently, she stared out of her top-floor apartment window at the Friday-night people joyfully interweaving back and forth across Pont de Sant Agustí and washed her wine glass from dinner. The song reminded her of a night long ago at La Sala del Cel, the huge club out along the river, dancing with some guy from school whose name she couldn't remember.

'You're showing your age, girl,' she said out loud.

Looking at the people on the bridge below and then focusing on her own reflection in the night-blackened window, she dropped the damp cloth into the sink.

'And now it's Friday night and you're at home washing up one wine glass and talking to yourself.'

She waited until the song ended before switching the system off with the remote, slipping on smarter jeans and a pair of rope-soled coffee-coloured *espardenyes* and warily checking all the rooms in her flat. They were empty. She turned the lights off and went out of the door.

A group of young people, stopped off for a coffee between dinner and a late-night bar, was just leaving the window seat in La Terra as she walked in. She recognised some of them and said hello before taking one of their vacated seats overlooking the same bridge as before. She laughed to herself. Same view, just fifteen years younger, she thought.

The waitress brought her a glass of red wine and Elisenda chatted for a while to two guys who took a couple of cushioned places on the tiled bench at the other end of the window seat. She watched them go and ordered a *licor de café*.

She considered the Masó case. Considered the four thugs. She considered again how that investigation had gone to Micaló's team, her own team left with just the one major case. That worried her. How long before the politicians in the Mossos decided her unit wasn't cost-effective? Wasn't justifying its existence? Serious crimes strangled at birth because no one knew what a serious crime was. Just as there was more to the Masó case, so was there more to the corridors and closed rooms of the Mossos.

'Connections,' she mouthed at her reflection in the blackened window. There are connections everywhere, she thought.

'But what are they?' A couple nearby stared at her muttering to herself and looked away. Masó and the muggers. Small-town crooks and small-time criminals. Both now victims themselves. And Joaquim Masó, on the outside, looking in.

With one last look at the river and the bridge, she finished her drink and went to pay at the bar before climbing the narrow stairs back up to her apartment when her mobile rang. She looked at the caller number and sighed. It had been a long day.

She listened to the voice at the other end and hung up, immediately dialling another mobile number.

'Àlex?' she said when he replied. She could hear street noises in the background. 'Meeting tomorrow morning at eight. The station's just called me. Chema GM has just died in hospital. The case is ours now.'

She hung up.

'This changes things,' she murmured.

Chapter Nineteen

'Tell them to turn those damned sirens off,' the Seguretat Ciutadana sergent yelled, 'and get that ambulance to shut it too.'

Scarcely able to take his eyes off the scene in front of him, Mosso Paredes walked out from under the arches on the Rambla and went towards his patrol car, which was slewed on the paving stones in front of L'Arcada's terrace of empty aluminium chairs and tables. Despite the early hour, a crowd was already gathering on the Rambla, stopping the ambulance in its journey the wrong way along the promenade. Two other Seguretat Ciutadana mossos were struggling to pull up a barrier to stop nosy civilians from sneaking around under the arches to get a glimpse of what was going on. A third was trying to clear a path for the ambulance through the onlookers, ignoring the flash of a mobile phone camera in his face.

Taking a deep breath, Paredes rang through to the station to deliver the message telling all cars to turn their sirens off.

He had never seen so much blood.

Not even that Masó guy hanging out of the window had shed so much blood. He'd been sick that time, he recalled. That sotsinspectora from that new bunch in the Serious Crime Unit had told him to go get a brandy. He hadn't, just in case his own boss saw him, but at least he hadn't been sick this time. Barely ten days' difference between the two events and already he was used to it. He wasn't sure how he felt about that.

He steeled himself and went back under the arches.

The man, he thought it was a man, was lying propped up against the inside angle of the arch, facing inwards to the shops away from the Rambla, hidden from view until you were almost on top of him. Despite himself, Paredes retched at the sight, but was still able to keep it down. The blood hadn't spread far but had congealed on the man's body. Just a few small rivulets ran in thin trails along the cracks in the stones. He'd been cut open, Paredes thought. A dark reddish brown lump of fat and gristle emerged from his stomach, dribbling down over his groin, blood soaking into his tan-coloured trousers. Whoever had done it had pushed something into the man's mouth, it too dripping blood down the man's chin and into the fabric of his shirt. His heart, Paredes immediately thought with a shudder. He finally saw the man's right hand. It was clutching hold of something. Paredes crouched down to take a closer look. It looked like a small plastic square had been fastened to the victim's hand by brown tape wound tightly around it.

'What is it, Paredes?' the sergent asked him. Paredes jumped. He hadn't heard the sergent approach. He looked more closely.

'It's a DVD case, Sergent Ayats.'

'Don't touch it until the Científica get here,' Ayats told him.

'Right, Sergent,' Paredes replied. He'd had no intention whatsoever of touching it.

Ayats stared at the man on the ground for a moment and hurried out from under the arches, dodging the tables and chairs on the terrace. He saw a Científica car. 'I need you in here now,' he shouted through the swelling crowd. Another Seguretat Ciutadana patrol car was pulled up alongside Paredes' car, its two occupants helping push back the throng of spectators and trying to set up a fence with some yellow municipal barriers they'd commandeered. Two other members of the Policia Científica were removing their equipment from the boot of another car. 'You two,' he called to them, making sure everyone around could hear, 'I want videos of the crowd. Anyone caught obstructing the Mossos or the medics will be prosecuted.'

While the onlookers retreated slightly under the threat, the first two Científica followed Ayats back under the arches.

'*Hòstia puta*,' the younger of the two cursed when they rounded the thick stone arch.

Both newcomers stopped and stared at the figure lying on the ground.

They made Paredes move to one side and the younger one, a mosso, began recording the scene on video while the other, a sergent, knelt down next to the man on the ground. 'We're going to need our colleagues in here,' he told Ayats.

'Paredes,' Ayats ordered, 'get the other two Científica in here.' Paredes got up, relieved to be getting away from the sight in front of him. The heat of the day was just beginning and the smell rising from the man on the ground was worming its way into his nostrils. 'And come back with them,' Ayats added.

'Yes, Sergent,' Paredes muttered.

The young mosso re-entered the arches after running his errand in time to see the Científica sergent pick up part of whatever was lying on the man's stomach. Paredes put his hand over his mouth.

'I recognise him,' one of the new Científica members said. The sergent peered at the man's face, not yet touching whatever it was protruding from the victim's mouth. Ayats and the video cameraman crowded in for a better look.

Ayats let out a low whistle. 'We all do.'

Paredes leaned in and saw a face he recognised emerge from under the streaks of blood and tissue covering it. He also saw the sergent carefully pull the piece of flesh from the man's groin.

'What is it?' Ayats asked them.

'Well, it's not part of this guy,' the sergent said.

'Is he dead?'

'He's dead all right.' The sergent unbuttoned the victim's shirt to reveal his unharmed stomach. 'But this isn't his.'

Another of the Científica poked the piece of flesh wedged tightly in the victim's mouth and looked up at Ayats. 'It's an abortion,' he said simply. He looked at it closely. 'A pig, if I'm not mistaken.'

Paredes' breakfast finally gave up its struggle to stay inside.

Chapter Twenty

'Where were you last night when I rang?'

Àlex shrugged. 'Out walking. Clear my head.'

Elisenda nodded. 'Sounded busy.'

'Girona. Big city, bright lights.'

'Less of your Barcelona sarcasm.'

Àlex simply grinned back at her. She understood, though. A glass of *licor de café*, she thought, and one of the window seats in La Terra. That's how she cleared her head. After calling him last night, she'd gone back and spent another hour nursing a second glass and staring at the lights reflected on the river.

'They're connected,' she suddenly said to Àlex. Her eight o'clock meeting in her office. Just Elisenda, Àlex, two coffees and a buff folder. The only other member of the team in the office on a Saturday was Pau, working on a computer in the outer office.

'They?' Àlex asked. 'Daniel Masó being one, I take it. And the other?'

'Chema GM,' Elisenda replied. She took a mouthful of milky coffee.

Àlex stared back at her. 'Masó and Chema GM? How are they connected? There's no record of Guijarro Martín doing any work for Masó. He was the classic small-town yob. Masó was an organised criminal. He would have seen Chema GM as a liability.'

'Not in life,' Elisenda corrected him. 'In the way of their passing. So sadly missed by all.' Àlex looked surprised at her last comment. 'That's the point,' she went on, noticing his reaction.

'At best, no one is going to miss them. More to the point, most people are rejoicing that they've gone.'

'So are you coming down more in favour of the vigilante angle? Especially now with Chema GM?'

'Vigilante, victim. I'm not saying it's necessarily villagers with pitchforks, but there's just something in it all that tells me there's more to it than we've been seeing. Two career criminals who've made the city's lives a misery. Both killed in highly elaborate ways. Both bodies staged theatrically.'

'Or one gang killing. As retribution or takeover. As Puigventós and Roca see it. And one reprisal. Or unrelated vigilante attack. And, anyway, Chema GM wasn't dead. We don't know if he was supposed to die. The other three in his gang didn't.'

'I don't think that's the point. There's something in the way of their death, or staging, that's common. And that's what we're not seeing.'

Àlex didn't look convinced. 'Masó was killed with a knife, Chema GM was drugged. We're still not certain that Chema GM was meant to die. And there's a big difference between slicing someone's face with a knife and putting drugs in a drink. I don't see how the same person could have done both. The first, at least, sounds like a gang killing.'

'The first was opportunist,' Elisenda said. 'Masó was there, the killer had a knife. Or Masó did. They argued. Masó came off worse.'

'But the second was planned. Elaborate.'

'Precisely. It was inspired by the first, but more cautious, planned, not spur of the moment. The killer was emboldened by having killed Masó, but not enough to carry out the second killing face-to-face. And the dressing-up of it after was every bit as elaborate as Masó. That's where the connection lies.'

'If you think they're connected because they're staged, doesn't that rule out Joaquim Masó?'

Elisenda opened the folder in front of her. 'These are the strands we've been working on. Significantly, no other gangs appear to be involved or trying to muscle in. I'm beginning to think we can rule that avenue out. The vigilante or victim angle hasn't thrown up any realistic names, but I think it's still worth pursuing. And I think an internal Masó issue is still of interest, particularly Joaquim Masó. I think we should pull him in for more formal questioning at this stage, if only to see what falls out of the tree.'

'You say connected,' Àlex said. 'Why would Joaquim Masó go for the muggers? Different business, different part of town. And if it is him, would he stage the victims like that? It seems too elaborate for someone like him.'

'We know very little about Joaquim. He's been on the fringes of the family all his life. If he is starting to move into it, we have no idea at the moment how he will operate. He might prove to be even worse than Daniel.'

Àlex grunted. 'Please don't say that.'

'It's a good point, though. We need to rule it in or out. And I still say we need to look at the whole idea of deserving victims, too. There's just something about the staging that tells me we should be casting our nets wider.'

'So how do we run the two investigations?'

'Officially,' Elisenda said, 'separately. I'm taking on the Chema GM case with Pau. You're running the Masó case with Josep and Montse. That's how Puigventós and Roca want it, so that's what they'll think they're getting. Unofficially, we'll be co-ordinating the two investigations, looking for crossovers. Either way, we're not actually going to mention any connection until we've got evidence there is one.'

Àlex nodded. 'Okay, I see that.'

'And there's also the press to contend with. At the moment, they're leaving us alone. No one cares much about a dead loan shark. But the moment we make it official there's a link between the two investigations, we'll have them on our backs.'

Àlex sighed. 'Don't you miss the days when the press did as they were told?'

'No. And neither do you.'

They heard a noise outside and Pau knocked on the door and came in. 'Can I have a word, Sotsinspectora? I've just been talking to a guy in the Regional Investigation Unit. They've found a body on the Rambla. He was covered in blood, but he had no wounds on him.'

'So where was the blood from?' Elisenda asked.

'From animal abortions. Pigs.'

'And he was on the Rambla?'

'Lying hidden under the arches by L'Arcada. They reckon he had a DVD taped to his hand.'

'Still think there's no connection?' Elisenda asked Àlex. She turned to Pau. 'Did the guy in the Regional Investigation Unit say who it was?'

'Yes, it was that priest. The one on TV. Mossèn Viladrau.'

Chapter Twenty One

Meir Perlman enjoyed his work. It suited him. The conscientiousness, the attention to detail, the solitude. A visiting researcher from Israel, he knew everything there was to know about Girona's medieval Jewish history – the city within a city, the persecution, the expulsion – but little about conveying that passion to a listener. Even when the listeners were two history lecturers from Columbia University, the one with her husband, the other with his wife and teenage daughter, paying a courtesy call to the Jewish History Museum, a centre of Jewish learning a thousand years ago, now a museum devoted to the history of its long-gone community.

Meir was out of the comfort of his museum and spending the afternoon showing the small group the Call, the old Jewish quarter. He was trying to engage what he would have thought would be a rapt audience in the story of Nahmànides, the thirteenth-century rabbi of Girona after whom the museum was named, but even he could see it was a losing battle. He'd caught the male professor checking his watch twice while they'd been standing by the Portal de Sobreportes. He was even more out of his area of expertise in the presence of the male professor's teenage daughter, who alternated between staring intently at Meir and letting her gaze rove idly around her.

'What's that?' she suddenly asked now. 'Up there.'

All six of them looked up to where the girl was pointing. A small statue set in a niche high above the ancient arch leading out of the city. The Verge de la Bona Mort, Meir was about to explain to them. Until, like the girl, he saw something hanging down from the figure.

'It's a bat,' the female professor muttered.

'You're right,' the teenage girl commented, 'a joke one. You can see the string hanging down from the statue.'

All five heads swivelled to Meir as though seeking an explanation. Not for the first time, he was lost for words. He wasn't entirely sure if he was supposed to do anything about it. Fortunately, two Mossos d'Esquadra in their blue and red caps walked through the arch just at that point. He'd tell them, he decided, so he wouldn't have to worry about it. Or be embarrassed in front of the visiting academics. He just wanted to get back to his archives.

Chapter Twenty Two

'No apparent physical wounds, no apparent asphyxiation. Approximate time of death between midnight and four a.m. That's all I'm prepared to say for now. You can wait for the full post mortem if you want any more.'

Albert Riera turned back to his examination of the priest's body in the harsh halogen glare of the arc lights set up under the arches, helped by his assistant, a quiet young man with that odd air of harassed calm that anyone who worked on a day-to-day basis with the forensic doctor ended up adopting.

'Was he drugged?' Àlex asked him.

'I don't know, sergent. Why don't you stick your tongue down his throat and see if you can taste anything?'

'All right, Albert,' Elisenda told him before Àlex could reply. 'That'll do.'

She looked around. The scene had been well secured despite its being in such a public place. Beyond the temporary plastic walls of the crime scene, crowds of people were milling about on the Rambla, conjecture building on speculation. Rumour on fantasy. Even with that, they probably couldn't imagine the scene in front of Elisenda's eyes now.

Riera had removed all of the dead animal parts from the victim's torso, but the pig's abortion in the priest's mouth had been wedged too tightly for him to remove easily until they were back at the lab. His assistant was bagging each piece, blood running down his arms as he struggled to fit them into the narrow ends of the bags. The animal blood had caked on the priest's body and clothes, which clung to the lumps of meat as the assistant lifted them clear. Horrified, Elisenda couldn't tear her eyes away. Despite the mask over her nose and mouth, the stench had found its way into her throat and rasped with every breath she took.

Sergent Ayats from Seguretat Ciutadana was still at the scene, he too enthralled. Elisenda thanked him for securing the site so quickly.

'Never seen anything like it,' Ayats told her. 'Hope I never do again.'

Elisenda hoped so too.

A sergent from the Científica cut the tape binding the DVD to the victim's hand once Riera grudgingly gave his permission and bagged it.

'When can I see what's on that?' Elisenda asked him.

'Monday. We won't be able to check for prints and so on until Monday morning, but I'll make sure you get it as soon as possible.'

Riera stood up. 'Right. No useless fucking judges here as it's Saturday, so I'm releasing the body.' He signed the documents and handed them to his assistant for him to deal with getting the body removed and taken back to the Institut de Medicina Legal. 'Post mortem probably on Wednesday,' he told Elisenda. 'Can't do it any sooner, so don't ask.' He lifted up the edge of the canvas shielding the scene from the outside world and vanished through it.

'Prick,' someone muttered. It wasn't Àlex for a change.

Elisenda called Àlex over and they stood away from where the priest was lying, out of the twin circles of white cast by the two arc lamps.

'Okay,' Àlex told her. 'You've got me with the connections.'

'Yes, but what are they? And where does this leave the investigation? Where does it leave Joaquim Masó? Why would he want to kill the priest?'

'Distraction? Put us off the track of his nephew's murder? He killed once for benefit, then found he wanted to make up for being outside the family his whole life?'

'Can you see him doing that?' They both stared at the priest, considering. 'These are punishments. Get Pau to check up on Masó's past. See if there are any links with Viladrau that would make him want to kill him. And get Masó in. I still want to talk to him.'

'Do you think it's him?'

She gestured towards Mossèn Viladrau's body. 'There's something more going on here. This is someone with a message. Or a mission. But we do need to keep up the pressure on Joaquim Masó to be sure.'

–

'My client was at a family celebration.'

Elisenda looked at Bellsolà across the table in the interview room and at Joaquim Masó seated next to him. Masó was learning to adopt the remote smirk of the rest of his family when being interviewed.

'This is the same family celebration at which his presence was not previously stated by any other member of his family,' Elisenda commented. She could feel Àlex getting increasingly agitated next to her.

'Their omission is no evidence of his absence. I now have signed statements by a number of those present at the event saying that my client was in attendance on the night of his nephew's death. It was a family celebration, Sotsinspectora Domènech. He is a Masó family member.'

'Isn't he just?'

Masó whispered something to Bellsolà, who relayed it. 'My client wishes to state that the nature of his business activities led some of his family members to believe that the mention of his presence at the function was not necessary.'

'Not at the top trough in the sty, in other words,' Àlex said. 'Not then, anyway.'

Bellsolà made a note on his pad. 'I would suggest you watch your words, Sergent Albiol.'

Elisenda took over again. 'Where were you on the night that Chema GM was attacked?'

Masó and Bellsolà briefly conferred before Masó spoke. 'With family. At my brother's restaurant.'

'You appear to spend a lot of time there. And I suppose I can take it they'd all be prepared to sign statements to that effect?' Elisenda nodded her head and moved on. 'Where were you last night and the early hours of this morning?'

Masó looked triumphant. 'At dinner in Girona. With my wife. You can ask the waiters. And it wasn't a family restaurant.'

'And after that?'

'In bed with my wife. I'll give you the details if you want. You might like it.' Masó winked at her and leaned forward. 'Why would I want to kill any of them? I don't even know the priest or the other four.'

Bellsolà hurriedly told him to keep quiet but Elisenda pressed forward. 'But you do know Daniel Masó. Someone from whose death you appear to be benefiting.'

'My own nephew?'

Bellsolà silenced him again and spoke to Elisenda. 'You have proof that my client is benefiting from his nephew's death, I take it, Sotsinspectora Domènech? Because if you don't, I suggest you consider withdrawing that statement.'

Elisenda pointed at the mound of Masó family statements heaped in front of Bellsolà. 'Those tell me he is.'

Bellsolà put all the papers together and shoved them into his briefcase. 'Then if that is all you have, and if you have no intention of charging my client, I am terminating this interview.' He signalled Masó to get up.

Elisenda looked at them both and nodded. 'You can go for now. But we will speak to you again.'

The two men left and Àlex clenched his fist on the table. 'He's still in the frame. He's benefiting from this.'

'But is he behind it? He might be the effect.' Elisenda stood up and pushed her chair under the table. 'But that doesn't make him the cause.'

Chapter Twenty Three

Elisenda finished cleaning her flat on Sunday morning and sensed a shadow dance across the kitchen. She turned from the window and stood watching for a few moments but the shadow didn't return. Changing her clothes, she went out and bought a newspaper at the kiosk on the Rambla and stopped for a coffee under the arches on Plaça del Vi to enjoy an hour to herself before her lunch date. The summer still showed no signs of taking its leave.

And then the moment was gone.

The press had latched on to the story. The front page and the editorial. Both criticising the Mossos. Both revelling in lurid conjecture. The usual bizarre blend of verbatim facsimiles of the Mossos' own lifeless press releases and the opinionated rejoinders of the paper's writers. But that wasn't the worst of it. The worst of it was the editorial by David Costa, of all people, raising the spectre.

"An organised criminal, a thug and a Francoist terrorised our beautiful city at will for years and the Mossos d'Esquadra stood by and did nothing," she read. "Now the tables have turned, will they continue to do nothing?"

"Police dragging their heels on the first two cases, unwilling to devote resources to the deaths of two men in investigations they feel the public will find unpopular."

"Are these deaths linked? We at this paper think so. The citizens in their homes think so. The politicians on the Town Council think so. So when will the Mossos start to think so?"

And the killer closing paragraph: "While this paper does not condone acts of violence and vigilantism, the question begs to be answered, what are the citizens of this city to do if the Mossos d'Esquadra will not – or cannot – stem the flow of crime in Girona? If the police will not do their job, then perhaps the citizens of this city will have to do it for them."

Elisenda threw the paper on to the chair on the opposite side of the table and sat back, frowning. The first time she'd read it, she'd taken her mobile out and gone so far as to scroll up David Costa's phone number, but thought better of it. She was too angry to ring. And she was even angrier that he was, in part, right. There was a link between all the events, even if the powers that be at the Mossos refused to see it. But what alarmed her was his comment on vigilantes, no doubt stoked by her conversation with him. The V word, she thought, the last thing they needed. And if it wasn't vigilantes before, it might well be now, with every self-appointed neighbourhood watchdog whipping up prejudice and resentment. A malfeasant's charter, courtesy of the press. She swore under her breath.

Checking her watch, she realised she was going to be late, so she picked up her bag and the paper and went inside to pay before cutting through the tightly shaded Carrer Abeuradors to get to the Rambla. She was first to arrive, so she picked a table on the terrace at Arts and opened the newspaper to another page while she waited.

'Sorry I'm late,' Laura Puigmal said, getting there ten minutes later and squeezing past a large group of Israeli tourists who had spread beyond the two aluminium tables they'd pushed together.

Elisenda folded her newspaper and stood up and smiled. 'No problem. I was enjoying the shade.' She and Laura kissed on both cheeks.

'This is the coolest part of the city,' Laura agreed, pulling her linen blouse away from her chest and softly blowing down it to get cool. 'I've never known it this hot in October.' She pulled an orange-cushioned wicker chair around so they were both facing out at the Sunday throng crowding slowly up and down the Rambla. Dwindling now as people began drifting home for lunch, the confusion of morning strollers looked reluctant to give up the shelter of the pollarded plane trees lining the boulevard.

Laura ordered a Bitter Kas when the waiter crossed over the wide paving of the Rambla, and Elisenda asked for a tonic. He came back with their drinks together with a plate of cheese, sent over on the house by the owner. Elisenda smiled a thanks at him and grimaced at the smell of Laura's Bitter Kas. It always looked and tasted to her like childhood medicine.

'Are you still all right for lunch?' Elisenda asked Laura. 'I was thinking of the new one over by Pou Rodó.'

Laura pulled a face. 'I don't know. Have you read the reviews?'

'Just this minute.' She showed Laura the page in her newspaper she'd been reading. 'That's what makes me want to go.'

Laura scanned the write-up of the city's newest restaurant and laughed. 'You really want to go after reading that.'

'Precisely because of that. You should always show your opinion of critics by going against them.'

They looked again at the review. A large picture of the reviewer glowered out at the top of the page, next to her name. It was obviously a photo of herself that she liked, but Mònica Ferrer always looked like she'd just eaten half a dozen of the dishes she was berating and swallowed them down with a glass of vinegar. Capable of ruining the best reputation – and business – with her Sunday column, she had evidently saved up all week to unleash her sulphuric sarcasm on her latest destruction of a new restaurant. Elisenda only knew her by sight but she knew that Laura had gone to the same exclusive girls' school as the journalist.

'If Mònica Ferrer says we shouldn't go there,' Elisenda concluded, 'then I think it's our duty to go.'

Laura shrugged. 'Why not?' She nodded at Elisenda's paper and asked her if she'd read David Costa's article.

'Afraid so. It's as I thought. The Mossos are going to be painted as the villains whatever happens.'

'Maybe, maybe not. I think he's simply stoking the fire to see which way public opinion fans it.'

'He's not the only one.'

Laura turned to face her. 'I gather Jutgessa Roca's the examining judge. She sees taking on the Masó family as good for her career.'

'I'm updating her on Wednesday. Try and make her see there's more to this than just the Masó family.'

'I'd keep all angles covered if I were you. She'll take your case down one path and then come up smelling of jasmine if it all goes wrong.'

'What are people saying at the Fiscalia?'

'Not a lot of sympathy for anyone, really. Three thugs who had it coming, poetic justice.'

'There's nothing of poetry or justice in any of this,' Elisenda commented.

'No, I suppose not. Just politics.'

'So the Fiscalia sees all three cases as being connected then?'

'Don't the Mossos?'

Elisenda pulled a face. She finished her tonic and called for the bill. 'Let's go and eat bad food.'

Chapter Twenty Four

Impatient for the DVD to be released to her team on Monday morning, Elisenda couldn't help feeling bewitched listening to Pau. Recently returned to the city after a posting to Barcelona, he spoke Catalan with the closed vowels of his Girona upbringing and Spanish with the broad Seville accent of his immigrant parents. At the moment, he was dipping from one language to the other, even his hand movements and posture changing with each vernacular shift.

'Come on,' he said now in Spanish to the figure slouched in the chair opposite him. 'You fall asleep in Sant Daniel, you wake up on a bridge half a dozen kilometres away. How'd you do it?'

'I didn't do it,' Manuel PM objected.

'So who did?' he said, the palms of both hands raised centimetres from Manuel PM's nose.

'Think I'd tell you?'

'Think he actually knows?' Pau said in Catalan to Elisenda, both hands resting lightly on the table.

She sat in silence. If she was honest, she was too enthralled with Pau's exaggerated way of chopping and changing language to answer. It was like a linguistic bipolar disorder, she thought, wondering for the first time what effects it must have on an individual's psyche. She was already beginning to learn that the newest member of her team had a way of seeing things that she and the others often didn't.

'I'm not saying a thing without a lawyer,' Manuel PM said.

'We're not questioning you as a suspect,' Pau replied, 'but as the victim of a crime. We're here to help you.'

'Like hell you are.'

Manuel PM sat back even more heavily in his metal chair. Released straight from hospital into the prison set amid a grid-iron of dreary apartment blocks on the northern outskirts of the city, he had spent most of the meeting in the interview room sulkily staring at the wall behind Elisenda and Pau.

Elisenda leaned forward and spoke for the first time. 'You're right, of course. I couldn't give a toss what happens to you. We just want to ask whoever killed Chema GM why they didn't do a proper job on you while they were at it.'

Pau looked at her, even more stunned than Manuel PM but trying not to show it.

'I don't have to sit here and listen to this,' the prisoner replied.

Elisenda looked at the two-tone brown walls and the bars on the window set high up in the wall. 'Well, I don't see you going anywhere in the foreseeable future, so I reckon you do have to sit here and listen to this.'

'I'm not telling you anything.'

'No, you're not, are you? You're not the brightest spark. Even Chema GM's hotter than you and he's lying in a freezer.'

It was Pau's turn to sit in silent thrall. Manuel PM sniffed, his lips tightly shut, his right thumbnail scratching back and forth into the table top. He looked up, defiant. 'Not so smart, since he's the one that got killed.'

Elisenda shrugged. 'That was just luck. Unless it was you that bought the wine, spiked the bottle.'

'Someone gave us the bottle.'

'Bet it wasn't sealed, though. You could have slipped something in it.'

Manuel PM thought back. 'No, it was already open when we got it from the barman.'

'Where was that?'

'Place in Sant Daniel. By the river.'

'So the barman did it?'

'No, he just gave it to us. Said it was from another customer.'

'Who'd buy you a bottle of wine?'

Manuel PM shrugged. 'Didn't see. Someone keeping on our good side.'

'No, doesn't wash,' Elisenda said, shaking her head. 'Odd you didn't drink much of it.'

'I drank as much as Cristobal and Juan.' Elisenda noticed he'd dropped the initials.

'The three of you, then. You made sure Chema GM drank the most. You were afraid of him. Wanted him gone.'

'Fuck off, that's not true.'

'Masó give it to you?'

'Masó? They don't come anywhere near our part of town.'

'So when did you get the drugs?'

'I didn't get any drugs,' Manuel PM objected, slowly shrinking in his chair. 'Someone gave the wine to us.'

'Joaquim Masó?'

'Like he'd give us wine.'

'Not a friend of yours, then?'

'Joaquim Masó? He's a headcase. Not even Chema wanted to cross him again.'

'Again?'

'He saw us. The day Chema was killed. Told us to keep out of his way.'

Elisenda whistled. 'You don't want to go up against the Masó family.'

'Not the family. Just him.'

'So how did you get Chema GM out of the bar?'

'We didn't drink it in the bar. We drank it over by the river.'

'See anyone?'

'No one to see.'

'Not much call to go that way,' Elisenda agreed. 'Not much traffic.'

'Just a van,' Manuel PM said, some of his bravado coming back. 'Quiet. No one bothers us.'

'Van delivering to the bar?'

He shrugged. 'Just parked there. One of those big Citroens. White.'

'Any name on it? Anyone in it?'

'No, nothing.'

Elisenda gathered up her bag and got up. Pau followed. 'Well, that's about it. You haven't told us much.'

Manuel PM sneered up at her.

'Unless, of course, you count the bit about the van,' she added, walking to the door leading out of the cloying hopelessness of the interview room. 'And the wine. And Joaquim Masó.'

–

'Can you tell everyone to wait in my office?' Elisenda asked Pau when they got back to Vista Alegre. 'I'll be there in five minutes.'

Pau nodded and went on in. Elisenda checked her mobile for any messages from Científica about the DVD but there was nothing. She knocked on the glass door separating Pijaume's office from the main room and waited until he invited her in.

'Anything I can do for you, Elisenda?'

'Drugs, Narcís.' He looked taken aback. 'Do you know if any more have gone missing from the Hospital Josep Trueta? Or any of the other hospitals?'

'Not that I'm aware. Let me check.' He tapped something into the computer on his desk. 'No, nothing. Those are the only two incidents we have on record.'

'Have any of them shown up around town?'

'No record of any being dealt. That doesn't mean they're not being sold. Just that we haven't found anyone doing so.'

'None found on anyone else? In anyone else?'

He tapped a few more details in. 'Nothing. Why do you need to know, if I may ask?'

'We're simply trying to find out the link between the drugs and the victims of these attacks,' she told him. She saw him shaking his head at something on his computer and asked him what was wrong.

'Someone appears to be throwing things on to the statue of the Verge de la Bona Mort?' he told her. 'Some dolls and a toy bat.'

'And someone's reported it? That means there's at least one person in Girona with less of a social life than me.'

Pijaume switched the screen off. 'And a lot more time on their hands,' he added, with his twisted smile.

The rest of her team were waiting for Elisenda in her office. She asked Pau to sum up the interview with Manuel PM for the others. When he'd finished, Elisenda could see a faint optimism in the others that had been missing for some days. Ruefully, she recalled her fears of a few days ago that her unit didn't have enough work to justify its existence. Now it had too much for a team that comprised just one sergent, three caporals and her.

'We'll have a clearer picture once we've seen this DVD,' she told them, 'and then we'll divide up the areas of the investigation, but first things first, we need to follow up the sighting of the white Citroen van and any possible link between the four muggers and Joaquim Masó. Pau, can you follow up the white van? Check for any reported stolen around the time the four muggers went walkabout, and if there are any, see if they've turned up again.'

'Are we convinced the van is significant?' he asked.

'We need to follow it up. If it is, it means our man, or men, drugged them, put them in the van, drove them around town until the early morning, dropped three of them off seemingly at random and then hung the last one over the balustrade by the cathedral.'

'How?' Josep asked. 'And why?'

'Why indeed?' Elisenda murmured.

'Do we know if these are the only attacks?' Pau asked. 'Daniel Masó, the muggers and Mossèn Viladrau, I mean.'

Elisenda looked at him. 'We aren't supposed to be seeing any links between the attacks, remember.'

'I know we aren't, Sotsinspector, but there are. My question is if there are any more.'

'That we're not supposed to be seeing, you mean?' Elisenda asked him. The others laughed wryly.

'If there are,' Pau said, 'a clearer picture might emerge.'

Elisenda looked at him thoughtfully. 'Worth looking at. Montse, can you look for any other attacks in the last month that appear like they could be related?'

'And missing persons,' Pau added. 'That might be significant.'

Elisenda looked at him and back at Montse. 'Missing persons, too.'

They were interrupted by a knock on the door. It opened and a mosso from the Científica came in.

'Sotsinspectora Domènech, I have the DVD for you. We've completed our tests on it.' He left the DVD in a transparent envelope on the table and backed out of the room.

Elisenda thanked him and looked at the parcel on her desk.

'So, what was worth killing Mossèn Viladrau for?'

Chapter Twenty Five

The picture of a young woman filled the screen.

Dressed in a long coat over jeans. The gap at the top of the buttoned-up coat revealed a red roll-neck sweater. She was standing on a square, in front of a statue of a nude male, posing for the camera and laughing.

'Well, that wasn't what I expected,' Elisenda commented.

'Is that Rome?' Josep asked.

Àlex shook his head. 'Florence. That's by the Uffizi.'

The camera zoomed inexpertly in on her face. She had a shock of long, dark hair falling in curls over her shoulders, a slender nose and a gap between her front two teeth that showed when she laughed. She was saying something but her words were lost amid the noise of the camera and the hubbub of the busy square. Elisenda turned the volume up as loud as it would go, but the woman still couldn't be heard.

'Looks like autumn,' Montse said. 'Not that recent, either.'

Pau agreed. 'Look at the people around her. What they're wearing. Got to be at least twenty years ago.'

The picture went off, coming back after a blank screen to show the same setting but with a man standing in front of the statue.

Elisenda sat forward in her seat. 'Mossèn Eduard Viladrau.'

He was some years younger, but it was definitely the priest.

The woman's voice could now be heard, speaking in Italian. She was evidently holding the camera as her voice was being picked up on the microphone. She was calling him Eduard and telling him to stand nearer the statue.

'So who are you?' Elisenda asked.

Another voice spoke. A man's. The woman could be heard thanking him and the camera was lowered, showing hectic pictures of the ground and upside-down shots of the square before settling to catch the woman walking up to Viladrau to pose next to him. Linking her arm through his, the woman leaned in and the priest kissed her on the lips, holding the kiss for some moments.

'You dirty little bugger,' Elisenda muttered.

Pau laughed out loud. 'He used to come to our school and talk to us of purity. And godliness.'

'He still does,' Àlex murmured, heartfelt after all the evenings at home watching the man rant at modern amorality.

'This is Girona,' Josep spoke up. 'How come he could have done this and no one knew of it?'

Elisenda counted back. 'This has got to be well over twenty years ago. He was in Rome for a long time. He went there after Franco died because he was too much of an embarrassment in the early days of the democracy, so the church packed him off to the Vatican. He only came back about fifteen years ago.'

'So all this was going on when he was away,' Àlex added.

'Well, someone found out about it,' Josep commented, nodding at the screen.

The image went off abruptly and a new one appeared. A still shot this time. The interior of an apartment. The same woman was standing in front of the camera, her body in profile, her face looking straight at the camera. Wearing nothing but a pair of white underpants, her arms folded across her breasts. She was heavily pregnant.

'I don't believe it,' Montse said.

'I do,' Elisenda replied. 'Now.'

The image cut to a photo of the woman with a baby, then Viladrau with the baby, smiling at the camera. Other photos of a boy's childhood appeared, most alone or with just the woman, only the occasional one with Viladrau. Then more images of the man and boy together, on a beach, in the mountains, increasing again as the boy got older.

'That's here,' Pau said. 'That's up in La Garrotxa.'

'The woman and boy stayed in Italy,' Elisenda guessed. 'When he first came back, Viladrau only saw them when he went to visit. Then they joined him. She and the son are in this country.'

Another video section. Grainy, washed-out images, brown with age and occasionally over-exposed, but no sound. It looked like an old cine film, digitised.

Another woman this time. Even younger than the first one in the square in Florence had been.

'That's Barcelona,' Àlex said. 'Up by Collserola.'

'How long ago?' Elisenda asked.

'I don't know. The seventies?'

The cine camera was evidently propped against a stone and Viladrau appeared in flickering shot. Younger, but still recognisable. The woman standing next to him looked barely half his age.

'Still a dirty little bugger,' Àlex commented.

'If that's here,' Josep asked, 'how did he get away with it?'

'If it was the seventies,' Elisenda replied, 'very easily. Franco in power. The church stronger than it had been for centuries, the regime closing ranks, no one daring to say anything and no free press to report it.'

The filming ended and was again followed by a series of still photos. Not snapshots this time, but documents. A plane ticket to London, dated September 1975. Elisenda sat back and sighed, her eyes closed for a second, she knew what was coming. Another photo, this time of a brochure. A family planning clinic in London. Then a letter with the same letterhead as that of the clinic. An appointment. For the young woman.

'Oh, Christ,' Àlex said.

He and Elisenda exchanged a glance. The pigs' abortions placed on Viladrau's body, they both recalled.

'He made her have an abortion,' Elisenda said.

'Why London?' Montse asked.

'It was illegal here in those days.' Àlex explained. 'But not in London.'

Elisenda leaned forward, gripping the desk. 'So while Viladrau and his like were denying every other woman in the country the right to choose to have an abortion, he was probably denying that poor young woman her right to choose not to.'

They turned back to the screen.

The final image was of a death certificate, also dated September 1975. The name on it that of the young woman in the appointment. The cause of death, suicide.

The five Mossos in the room sat and stared in silence at the blank screen. There were evidently no more pictures, but no one wanted to switch it off.

'How did he get away with it?' Montse finally whispered, echoing Josep's question of a few minutes earlier.

Elisenda leaned forward and took the DVD out, holding it up.

'He didn't.'

–

Àlex was the first to speak. 'They are punishments.'

'I think so,' Elisenda agreed. 'I will take this to Puigventós and Roca, but whether they'll be willing to see a connection between all three is another matter.'

'They've got to see they're linked,' Pau said.

'Jutgessa Roca's got her own agenda. She'll want to keep the Daniel Masó killing separate so she can take on the gangs. And I imagine Puigventós won't want to see a serial killer on the streets. He'd sooner see Masó as a gang killing, even Chema GM as well, and Viladrau as separate to play the whole thing down. The one argument they've got is that Masó was killed in a knife fight and these two both appear to have been drugged.

We'll know more about how Viladrau died on Wednesday. In the meantime, we need to know how we're going to carry on.'

She looked at everyone in the room individually.

'This does not go out of this unit, but we are seeing them all as linked and we will be investigating them as such. Whether that's the official line or not.'

All her team nodded their agreement.

'What about Joaquim Masó?' Àlex asked.

Elisenda considered for a moment. 'Viladrau's death would seem to put him out of the picture, but we can't rule him out completely. Pau, can you check for any historical links between the two of them, see if there's anything that would make Joaquim Masó target him. It might be some spree that killing Daniel set Joaquim on that would include the priest or it might be some massive attempt to distract. Also, what are the links between him and the muggers? Either way, I still get the feeling Joaquim Masó's falling out of the frame.'

'Montse, I want you following up Daniel Masó. Watch what happens to his business, if Uncle Joaquim does appear to be taking it over, also any victims making a noise. Besides that, I also get the feeling that not much has been done about these stolen drugs. Get out to the Hospital Josep Trueta and nose around. Someone there might know something.

'Josep, you'll be concentrating on the muggers. Get out to the prison and interview the other two, see if they noticed anything about the van. If there was anyone in it. They're not the shiniest pins, but between them they might come up with something they remember. Don't let them know it's the van we're interested in, though, or they'll clam up for the sake of it. And then I want you to have a word with the barman who gave them the bottle. See if he remembers anything. And check up on known victims of theirs.'

Àlex shifted in his chair. 'That leaves Viladrau.'

Elisenda laughed wryly. 'I'm leaving the priest to the most secular of us all. Àlex, we want to find the woman, she might know something. And the son. And check out family members of the first woman, the one who died, see if any of them know what happened and might have wanted Viladrau dead. Also, look for any other women who have been victims of his.' A thought occurred to her. 'Just for reference, is anyone here religious?'

The other four looked at each other in silence, but only Pau put his hand up.

'Okay, just so I know. Besides that, Àlex and I will be here to help in any of the lines of investigation when you need it. Pau, I want you collating everything we find, looking for patterns and connections.'

'And if I find any?'

'Then it raises two more questions,' she concluded. 'Do we dare go to Puigventós with this?'

'And the second question?'

'Do we dare not?'

Chapter Twenty Six

Elisenda knew before she'd even closed the door to Jutgessa Roca's office and crossed the five hostile paces to a straight-backed wood and leather chair that Roca wasn't going to give her the warrant she needed. The unhurried tilt of the judge's head and the wait before she raised her gaze from some papers on her desk to look at Elisenda told her that.

'You have not yet convinced me to my satisfaction that we are not dealing with gang criminality,' the judge told her.

'No, I don't suppose I have.'

'Until you can give me further evidence to substantiate your bizarre idea that this is anything other than an organised crime matter, Sotsinspectora Domènech, there is little more I have to say on the subject.'

Elisenda stared at the judge as she spoke and noticed as always how the end of her narrow nose dipped momentarily when she said certain words. She had to fight a terrible impulse to put her finger on it to stop it moving.

'We feel that the Masó killing is related to the subsequent sequence of attacks on the four muggers and Mossèn Viladrau. We need to focus our efforts on tackling the cases as a single matter.'

The judge snorted. 'You are the only officer that sees that. They are separate investigations, Sotsinspectora Domènech, and they are to remain separate. I will be recommending that the various cases be distributed to other units within the Mossos to prevent you from empire-building. Now if there's nothing else.'

Elisenda spoke slowly to keep her cool. 'We also need to find the identity of a woman who appears in the DVD left on Mossèn Viladrau's body. I've made an application.'

The judge picked up the official forms that were lying on her table. 'A warrant to subpoena the bishopric to disclose the name and whereabouts of an unknown woman you allege to be linked sentimentally to Mossèn Viladrau. What on earth for?'

Elisenda watched the judge let the papers fall to the desk and calmed herself with a deep breath. 'Because if we're to stop these killings, we need to gather as much information about the individual attacks as we possibly can. We need to speak to this woman to find out what she knows and for the protection of everyone in the city.'

The judge looked at Elisenda and sighed. 'Far be it from me to tell you your job, Sotsinspectora, but wouldn't it be better to find the people carrying out these attacks, not harassing the victims. Have you no respect for the church's wish for privacy?'

'We aren't harassing anyone, Jutgessa Roca. Everything we are doing is aimed at bringing the attacker to justice and making the city safe. That involves questioning anyone who is relevant to our investigation.'

'Well, it smacks to me of harassment, Sotsinspectora Domènech.'

Elisenda sighed. She'd had enough. 'Are you going to give me the warrant? Yes or no?'

'No, Sotsinspectora Domènech, I am not. I have already told you. I cannot sanction your wilful harassment of the victims of these terrible crimes. Now, if you don't mind, I have other more pressing matters.'

Elisenda stood up. 'So do I, judge. It's called upholding the law. I see I'll just have to do it without your help.'

Outside the modern court buildings, Elisenda walked down to the river and leaned against the railings to stare down at the meagre river below to calm herself. She could see the mottled brown-skinned carp idling in motionless formation facing the quiet flow of the water, catching whatever food drifted their way. It struck her that so many of the people she relied on for her investigation appeared to be taking the attacks in the same way. Waiting in the flow for events to come to them, their mouths gaping expectantly.

A familiar sound overhead broke through her thoughts and she looked up. A small red and white plane came from behind her, flying across the city, heading for the coast. She watched it slowly disappear over the ancient rooftops and waited until the earnest sound of the engine died in the distance.

Turning her back to the river, she crossed Plaça Independència and hurried along Carrer Santa Clara, back towards Vista Alegre.

—

'I've been looking for links,' Pau told her once she got back. 'There's nothing that connects either Joaquim or Daniel Masó with Mossèn Viladrau. There's nothing that links the Masó family to the four muggers. They've never worked together and there are no records of any antagonism between them.'

'Until now that Joaquim Masó appears to be pushing his weight about.'

'I've also been trying to find other patterns, but I still can't find any link between the victims. I mean actually between them. Not one mutual victim or individual who might have a grudge against them all collectively. No one who owed Masó money reported being attacked by any of the four muggers. No one who was mugged by them appears to have any beef with Viladrau, and so on. Nothing fits into place in that sense.'

'Okay, let me know if anything does come up. There's something else I want you to have a look at.' She explained how Àlex had come up against barriers every time he had asked the church authorities for help in finding out the woman's identity or whereabouts. 'I'm certain that someone in the church knows who she is, or at least has some idea where she might be.'

'And you want me to use my faith to gain entry?'

'Yes,' she said bluntly. 'Just as I want you to use the fact that you are a Mosso to do what it takes to prevent anyone else from becoming a victim of this person. Are you comfortable questioning someone in the bishopric about Viladrau's whereabouts?'

'Yes, I am,' he answered her, without hesitation.

'Good.' She felt hugely relieved. 'You're the best organiser in the unit. I don't want to have to question your loyalties.'

'You don't.'

Before Elisenda could reply, Montse knocked on the door and leaned in.

'Sotsinspectora,' she said, 'there's something you should see.'

—

'Damn,' Elisenda muttered for the third time.

She scrolled down the page on the computer, taking in all the comments and suggestions.

'We've just found it,' Montse explained.

It was a social network site. A forum. Someone had set up a page about what was going on in Girona, describing the attacks on Daniel Masó, the four muggers and the priest. As usual, the Mossos came in for a lot of criticism.

But none of that was the problem. The problem was that the site had become a message board for anyone who felt like it to give their suggestions as to who deserved to be the next victim. And they did. In their droves. Elisenda read the names of local politicians, businessmen, lawyers, teachers who'd marked their students down, classmates who were outside the favoured cliques, shopkeepers, shop customers, anyone who had in any way slighted anyone else. Petty malice and self-justifying vindictiveness lobbed out from behind the safe anonymity of a keyboard and screen.

'Technology bringing out the best in people,' she muttered.

'There's more,' Montse told her.

She took over the control and scrolled down the many suggestions. A number of names appeared several times.

'Bellsolà gets mentioned a lot.' Pau observed. He was about to comment further but Josep caught his eye and he kept quiet.

'There,' Montse said, stopping the wheel on the mouse. Elisenda leaned in for a closer look at the confusing strips of blue and grey comments made by successive contributors.

She finally spoke. 'Oh good.'

Someone had suggested her name as the next victim.

Chapter Twenty Seven

Pau cadged a lift off Josep to Plaça del Vi rather than put up with the parking and traffic in the city centre.

'What's that?' Josep asked as they pulled up past the entrance to the bishopric office. He was pointing at a small face carved in stone staring at him from the corner of a building.

Pau looked up. 'En Banyeta.'

'What's it supposed to be?'

'The legend goes that he was a usurer who was found turned to stone one day. They say that if you rub noses with him, you'll be excused all your debts.'

'It's about three metres off the ground. You can't.'

'That's the point.'

Pau watched the Seat drive off and took a deep breath before entering the bishopric. The temperature inside the ancient building was much more chilled than the stifling heat outside and the sweat on his forehead instantly cooled to what felt to him like pinpricks of ice. A woman in a white cardigan and a helmet-stiff hairstyle showed him to a waiting room. He'd rung ahead to request a meeting, but he imagined he'd be kept waiting by the bishop's heavy timetable. As it was, a door opened within a scant ten minutes and a man walked out to greet him.

'Caporal Yáñez?' the man asked, before introducing himself as Mossèn Arnau. 'I am the bishop's acting secretary.'

'Thank you, Mossèn Arnau. I made an appointment to see the bishop.'

'Ah, yes, I'm terribly sorry, Caporal, but I'm afraid the bishop is unable to see you today. He has a very full agenda.'

'I understand that, Father. I appreciate that God's work respects no worldly timetables.'

The priest bowed his head ever so slightly to one side and smiled. Pau could see he'd scored a hit with that. He was also grateful that the man was speaking Catalan. Pau knew that he came across much more softly-spoken and reverential in Catalan than in his parents' Spanish.

'It is good to see that the word of the Lord does not fall on deaf ears among our policemen and women,' Mossèn Arnau commented. 'Please come this way.'

The priest ushered Pau through the double doors into the room out of which he'd emerged and showed him to a pair of elderly but expensive sofas in a large office dominated by a walnut desk. The one discordant note was the beige-grey of a computer monitor in the middle of the desk.

'How may I help you?' the priest asked Pau once they were seated.

'I'm afraid it's rather a delicate matter, Father.'

Mossèn Arnau held up a slender, manicured finger. 'Mossèn Viladrau.'

'Yes, Father.'

'A woeful circumstance, which reflects badly on the church.'

'Mossèn Viladrau was also a victim, Father. He suffered a brutal attack.'

'That's as may be, but we in the church today have to address the sins of the past. We must not be seen to be condoning the unsavoury actions of a previous time in the history of our faith. Despite their being the unsavoury actions of a very small number of our members during that time.'

'I agree, Father. And by that same token, neither can the law be seen to be condoning the unlawful actions of a vengeful society in exacting retribution in this manner on those who have lost their way. It is our duty to bring whoever is committing these acts to a higher justice, both worldly and otherwise, and to protect other, perhaps more innocent, people from suffering similar attacks.'

The policeman and the priest sat in silence for a few moments, considering the other's words. 'So how may I help you?' the priest finally asked.

Pau turned to face him. 'I need to know the identity of the woman who bore a son to Mossèn Viladrau, Father, and where I might find her. For her protection and that of others.'

The priest sighed and smiled gently. 'I am not alone in the church in believing that we should confront our sins, but I am not in the majority either. There are those who feel that it is better for the church to protect itself from public scrutiny.'

Pau remained silent. He knew the next few moments were going to be key.

The priest finally rose from his seat and walked towards the door. 'I should show you out, Caporal Yáñez,' he said.

Slowly, Pau got up. 'Thank you, Father,' he said, barely hiding the disappointment in his voice.

Mossèn Arnau waited for him at the twin doors. Before opening them, he looked at Pau and spoke. 'You should possibly consider a house owned by Mossèn Viladrau in Santa Pau,' he said, quietly reciting an address.

'Thank you, Father,' Pau replied, but the priest simply nodded and pulled the doors closed between the two of them.

Pau had to resist punching the air in triumph until he was outside on the street in front of the diocese bookshop. He rang Elisenda but got her voicemail so he called the station instead and got through to Montse, who told him that Elisenda was at the Institut de Medicina Legal.

Pau hung up and set off on foot for the pathology institute, past the Town Hall, crossing the road where it narrowed at the corner of the square with Carrer Ciutadans. Glancing up, he saw the grotesque little face carved in stone that Josep had mentioned earlier, and carried on walking down to the arches on the Rambla. He stayed underneath them as it was much cooler there than out on the promenade itself. He peered out at the dappled shade as he walked under the arches. Summer had most definitely not given up its hold.

Halfway along, a young Spanish couple visiting the city asked him the way to the Jewish Quarter, so he walked on with them to the end of the arches and showed them the alleyway that led to the start of Carrer de la Força. Turning away, he looked back to where Mossèn Viladrau was found that Saturday morning and instantly started, as though physically struck by a blow. Hurriedly, he retraced his original steps back the way he'd come from Plaça del Vi, looking back over his shoulder until he found the section of the interconnecting arches that he was looking for.

He found it.

And stopped instantly.

And stared at a small scene high on the wall to his left.

And remembered his schooldays in Girona.

He rang Elisenda's number and this time he did leave a voicemail.

'Elisenda,' he spoke after the recorded message. 'I've worked it out.'

Chapter Twenty Eight

'You're not worried, are you?' Àlex asked Elisenda.

He'd silently left the post mortem for a moment and she'd told him about the website that Montse and Josep had just discovered. They were standing in the corridor, speaking in whispers.

'Àlex, I'm sandwiched between a housewife who hangs her washing out too noisily and the guy who hoses down the streets at night. I don't think I'm going to lose too much sleep.'

'Maybe not.'

'Not about that, anyway. What I don't like is the fact that the thing has been set up in the first place. We haven't got a clue where that'll lead us. I've asked Pau to refer it to UCDI in Sabadell, see what they can do about it.' She gestured with her head to the room where Riera was carrying out the post mortem on Mossèn Viladrau. 'What's the verdict?'

'Apart from Riera being a prick? Viladrau died of a massive drugs overdose.'

'The ones that were stolen?'

'They don't know yet. I'd say they were.'

'Me too.'

The door opened and Riera's assistant called them both in. Riera was standing back from the stainless steel table on which the priest lay, now truly eviscerated. Elisenda looked for a moment at the man's body and then looked away. It was hard to feel any sympathy for the priest for what he'd done, but she knew she had to see him as a victim.

Riera greeted Elisenda reasonably enough, as she'd expected. His manner once inside the pathology lab was always calmer and more respectful than it was outside. He also tended to suffer her more gladly than he did others. He reeled off the facts he'd so far gleaned without any emotion. His last meal, the approximate time of death, the cause of death.

'Death would have been almost instantaneous. It was a very large dose of the drugs. I'll have more details by the beginning of next week.' He sounded doubtful. 'The animal parts were laid out post mortem, as was the pig's abortion inserted into his mouth.'

'What is it, Albert?'

'The abortion. It was wedged firmly into his mouth, rather than simply placed the way the other parts were. As though the killer had wanted him to choke on it, even though he would already have been dead at that point. I don't quite understand why.' He brightened. 'Still, that's your job, not mine. Off you go.'

He turned back to the priest's body and Elisenda gave Àlex a half-smile before leaving the three men to their dissection of the fourth.

Outside, Elisenda walked down to the riverbank where she'd stood in the morning and breathed in lungfuls of air untainted with the medicine of the dead. The fish below seemed to be gasping in sympathy. She thought of the abortion wedged in Viladrau's mouth and Riera's doubts. She turned her mobile on and listened to her messages, surprised at the last one, Pau's stark statement. She rang him and found out he was just over the river, at the bottom of Carrer Argenteria.

'Stay where you are,' Elisenda told him. 'I'll be with you in two minutes. I need a coffee. Get the taste out of my mouth.'

She hung up and headed for Plaça Independència and the Rambla. She didn't want to get her hopes up, but she reckoned that if Pau's analytical mind claimed he'd worked it out, there was a pretty good chance he had. She quickened her pace despite the unusual autumn heat. Underneath the arches on Plaça Independència, two friends of her parents' stopped and greeted her. Further on, the good-looking waiter from Lizarran smiled and said hello as she walked past. Damn, she thought, a curse on small cities.

She crossed the river and found Pau waiting for her the other side. He led her straight to the arches on the Rambla.

'Don't I get a coffee?'

He grinned back at her and replied in his brashly extrovert Spanish. 'You'll be buying the coffees when you see this,' he said. 'Sotsinspectora,' he suddenly added in Catalan, instantly more subdued as he remembered who she was. Elisenda had to stifle a laugh.

'This way,' he carried on, leading her to where Viladrau was found. He showed her the large angle between the side archway connecting with the next section of arches and the one at the front giving on to the Rambla. 'Mossèn Viladrau was found propped up in this corner.' He suddenly remembered something. 'Ah. I've also got an address where the woman in the DVD might be. A priest at the bishopric gave it to me. Unofficially.'

Elisenda stopped and looked squarely at him. 'You will do anything to get out of paying for coffee.'

'Anyway,' Pau went on, pleased but embarrassed, 'he was placed in this corner because it's the biggest one of any of the arches, so therefore the most secluded and the easiest place to hide someone.' He walked back in the direction of L'Arcada, with Elisenda following. 'Look up there,' he said, pointing at a small figure carved into the corner of the vaulted ceiling.

Elisenda had to squint to make out in the gloom what Pau was getting at. It was a curious stone carving of a man's head with a long beard and bat's wings. 'The Vampir de la Rambla,' she said.

'You remember the legend?'

'If you want someone to fall in love with you, you bring them here and get them to give you something,' Elisenda said, recalling the legend every child in Girona is taught at school.

'Right. In effect, it's traditionally where lovers declare themselves.'

Elisenda looked back at the part of the arches where the priest had been found. 'So you're saying that Viladrau was "declared" here.'

'Precisely. As not being celibate, as having a worldly love, in other words. And as being a father, also in the worldly sense.'

'I'm not sure,' Elisenda said slowly. 'And the gift?'

'Either the son. If we think it's supposed to symbolise a gift to Viladrau. Or the DVD if we think it's a gift from the perpetrator to the city.'

Elisenda looked back up at the dark sculpture set into the wall, considering. 'It's pretty tenuous.'

'There's more.'

He led her back to Plaça del Vi and the Town Hall, where he took her to the corner of Carrer Ciutadans and pointed up at the face that Josep had seen.

'En Banyeta,' Elisenda said, unsure what he was getting at.

'Masó,' he said simply.

Her head snapped back up to the head carved into the stone. 'A usurer.'

'A loan shark in today's world.'

'The nose,' Elisenda said. 'You rub his nose, the slate's wiped clean.'

'Masó's nose was cut off. All debts gone.'

'He's part of it. I knew he was.'

'And his body was found on Pla i Cargol,' Pau reminded her. 'Just up there on the right.'

Elisenda looked at the caporal. 'I think I owe you coffee.'

'That's not all. The perpetrator is using local legends to out people. Or to punish them.'

'Legends? Or sculptures?'

'Legends. Don't forget the four muggers.'

'How do they tie in?'

Pau stood back and looked straight at her. 'The Bou d'Or.'

Chapter Twenty Nine

'What exactly is the Bou d'Or?' Àlex asked Pau.

The whole of the unit was in Elisenda's office, seated on a hotchpotch of chairs brought in from the outer room. Pau had just finished explaining his legends theory to the others.

'The Bou d'Or,' Pau explained, 'is a local legend about four gamblers out one night in Girona. The Bou d'Or itself was the name of a bridge and a quarry to the north of Montjuïc. The story goes that there was an ancient ruined house on the site that had a hidden treasure inside a stone coffer embedded in the walls, but there were so many tales told about the house that no one dared open the coffer.'

'I thought the legend was that the treasure was a huge golden ox, which is where the name comes from,' Montse, the other Gironina, said.

'Actually there are quite a lot of versions of the legend,' Elisenda interrupted, 'but one of them ties in neatly with the way the four muggers were found. You ask five people in Girona, you get six different versions of the legend.'

Àlex turned to Josep, the other non-native of Girona, and raised his eyes. 'Now why doesn't that surprise me?'

'Because we are a complex and individual breed,' Elisenda told him.

'The story,' Pau carried on, 'is that the four gamblers were moaning about their losses when they met a sinister stranger. He told them that he could take them to a place where there were untold treasures and they could take as much of it as they wanted.'

'That's Girona for you,' Àlex muttered.

'Watch it,' Elisenda warned him.

Pau waited until the room was silent and continued. 'So the stranger led the four men outside the city walls through thunder and lightning to the house with the stone coffer and when they got there, he took them to a well at the back of the ruins. Inside the well was a spiral staircase, and the stranger told them they had to climb down it to get to the treasure. The four men started going down the staircase, but the steps just kept on going deeper and deeper, and all the time, the stranger kept shouting at them to keep going, until finally one of the gamblers called out "Lord help me, when will these steps end?"

'The moment he said the Lord's name, there was a loud bang and the four men were suddenly shot out of the well and sent flying through the air, each one to a different place. One landed on the Pont de Sarrià, one on the Pont de Sant Francesc, the third ended up clinging to a bell in Sant Feliu church and the fourth, the one who'd spoken, finished up at the cathedral, holding on to the angel. The legend says that the man who implored God had saved the four of them from being led down to Hell and that the sinister stranger was the devil.'

Pau's story was met with silence as the others took it in.

Josep was the first to speak. 'Pont de Sant Francesc?'

'That was the original bridge where the Pont de Pedra stands now,' Pau explained.

Àlex looked at Elisenda. 'It does fit.'

She ticked them off on her fingers. 'Manuel PM on the Pont de Sarrià, Cristobal HP on the Pont de Pedra, the Pont de Sant Francesc as was, Juan SP by Sant Feliu and Chema GM, the leader, by the cathedral. Not exactly the same as the legend, but as near as dammit.'

'Especially given the practicalities of dropping the four muggers off at the various sites,' Pau pointed out. 'He was never going to be able to get the last two to the bell in Sant Feliu or to the angel on the cathedral roof, but the point was simply to leave them in the right places for it all to fit the legend.'

'This is where the white van becomes even more important,' Elisenda added. 'Our man must have used it to ferry the four victims around to the various sites.'

'Our man,' Àlex commented. 'Where does this put Joaquim Masó?'

Elisenda sighed. 'Where indeed? Do we think he'd be the sort to carry out this type of serial attack? It seems a pretty extravagant way of covering up killing Daniel to take over his business.'

'I think it rules him out,' Àlex said. 'This comes back to what you've been saying all along, Elisenda, about something more going on.'

'I agree,' Montse added.

Elisenda considered for a moment. 'We put him on the back burner,' she decided. 'I think we need to be focusing on the character of the victims and the links between them and the legends. Someone with a grudge specifically with them.'

'Or with what they stand for,' Pau commented.

Elisenda looked at him and nodded.

'Do we have any news on the drugs?' Àlex asked.

'I'm trying to get as much as I can out of Sotsinspector Pijaume, but they don't seem to have any leads on it. Montse's checked out the hospital but no one knows anything, and none of the drugs stolen has been found anywhere other than in the four muggers and Viladrau.'

'Not Daniel Masó?' Àlex asked.

'No. That's the problem. I'm convinced that Daniel Masó was an opportunistic killing by the same perpetrator – and we're now more or less certain that it is linked thanks to Pau – and it was his killing that gave the perpetrator the idea for finding other victims to punish, so he then stole the drugs to use in the subsequent attacks. The problem is getting anyone outside this room to see that.' She looked at the others in turn. 'Anyone have any other questions? Do we all agree with Pau's theory?'

Everyone in the room nodded silently.

It was Àlex who broke the quiet. 'How do you know all this stuff?' he asked Pau. 'I could name about two legends from Barcelona.'

'I'm the son of immigrants. When I was at school, I had to be more Catalan than the Catalans. So I had to know more about Girona and Catalonia than anyone else. That's how I felt, anyway.'

'Okay,' said Elisenda, 'and all that brings us back to the same two questions as always. Do we dare go to Puigventós with this?'

'And do we dare not?' Àlex added.

Chapter Thirty

Catalina came out of the changing room and stood before Elisenda. 'How do I look, Eli?' she asked.

'Huge.'

Catalina looked down at the summer-coloured maternity dress billowing over her legs and sighed deeply. 'Could they make these dresses any more frumpy?' She shrugged and went back into the changing room. 'I'll buy it then, shall I?'

'I would.'

Elisenda sat on one of the armchairs on the ground floor of Zara, in the Eixample district, and watched the steady shuffle of shoppers around her as she waited for her younger sister to get dressed. She was still trying to switch off at the end of her working day, her thoughts tumbling with the links between the murders and the legends. She'd used the word "serial" without thinking, but it was now preying on her. As was Pau's comment about what the victims stood for. They'd also checked out the website again before leaving work. Row upon row of narrow comment and hate-filled suggestion filled her eyes.

Thinking about it now, she sank further into the shop's armchair. A young Philippine maid pushing an expensive pram around the store caught her eye, her gaze never rising above the level of the baby, and more usually focused steadfastly on the floor. She was with a woman that Elisenda's mother would have described as being "of a certain age and a certain standing". Evidently the grandmother of the baby, she had one of those forty cigarettes a day voices and trim figures that showed she was of the generation that had thought smoking was a good way of keeping their weight down. Ultimately, it probably was, Elisenda thought gruesomely. She was ordering the maid about, dismissively telling her to go and look for some piece of clothing or other in a smaller size. For a brief moment, Elisenda had a sudden and unbidden insight into what led others in the city to vote for the attacker's next victim. She shook her head, refusing to allow herself to think that way. The images of Viladrau and the two young women were still preying on her mind but she was determined not to see the victims as anything other than victims, despite the revulsion she felt at the priest.

When Catalina emerged from the changing room with her shopping, Elisenda was surprised to see her greet the older woman.

'You didn't recognise her?' Catalina asked Elisenda outside when she commented on it. 'That's Laura Puigmal's mother.'

'You are kidding.'

'No. The baby is Laura's older sister's kid. Another lawyer. Married in turn to another lawyer.'

'That's social mobility for you.'

They walked slowly on through the shaded streets of the Eixample to a junction and waited for the pedestrian lights to go green. The lights changed and the two walls of pedestrians closed on each other in the middle of the road, the cars throttling impatiently either side of them. A young man, his shirt unbuttoned that bit too far, his kempt hair that bit too solid, was walking a Rottweiler through the crowds from the other pavement when he hit the dog across the rump with the braided leather end of the lead. There was no reason, the dog was calm, he evidently just felt it looked good. Most people tutted, no one said anything.

'I wish someone would do that to him,' Catalina hissed to Elisenda as the young man passed them. She suddenly turned to her sister and put her hand to her mouth. 'That's the point, isn't it? This person you're after.'

When they got to the other pavement, Elisenda turned to look at her. 'This person I'm after?'

'The one on this website. It's the one you're after, isn't it? I was going to tell you about it. I wasn't sure you'd seen it.'

'Don't worry, I've seen it.'

'It's what they want, isn't it? Us wanting someone else to take revenge. Hit that man because he hit his dog.'

They walked on in silence for a moment before Elisenda replied. 'That's precisely it. And that's why everyone's supporting him, not the Mossos. He appeals to the most vindictive, impotent side of us. Of all of us.' Me included, Elisenda hated to have to admit, recalling Viladrau, the muggers and Masó and her ambivalent feelings towards what had happened to them.

'Where does it end?' her sister asked after a few moments' thought.

'Where? When he goes too far. The moment he chooses the wrong victim, people will turn against him.'

'You have to hope for that, then.'

'No, we don't. That's when it'll get worse for us. The public won't suddenly start supporting us. They'll demand to know why we haven't done enough to catch him. Forgetting they've all been fanning the flames from the start.'

'I'm sorry I said what I did. About the dog. I didn't think.'

'Don't worry.' Elisenda smiled and hooked her arm through Catalina's.

Carrying on along Carrer Maragall, they crossed Gran Via in silence and came out in front of the modern extension to the Hospital Santa Caterina. Throughout the sisters' lifetime, the ancient building had been a hospital, but it had recently been turned into local offices for the Generalitat, the Catalan government. The Mossos d'Esquadra even had a small station in the old heart of the new creation.

'Eli—,' Catalina began to say as they walked past the ramp leading up to the tourist office and the bookshop, but she was interrupted by a man standing in front of them.

'Good evening, Elisenda,' the man said.

Elisenda turned away from her sister to see Inspector Puigventós.

'Xavier,' she said. 'Good evening.'

'Out for a stroll?'

'While the weather's still hot. You haven't met my sister, have you?'

'I'm afraid not,' Puigventós replied gallantly, kissing Catalina on both cheeks.

'Are you going into the Generalitat?' Elisenda asked him.

He turned and looked scornfully at the new extension. 'Not if I can help it. Loathsome monster. Such a beautiful old building and they attach this abomination to it.'

'You really think so? I have to admit I don't dislike it.'

'We shouldn't be imposing the modern world on the past. I just hope we don't ever get transferred into the station in there. I'd have to come to work blindfolded.'

The sisters laughed and took their leave, pressing on across Plaça Catalunya towards the Rambla, just like pretty much everyone else in the city seemed to be doing, unwilling to let the summer go.

'Seems a pleasant guy,' Catalina commented.

'Yes, I suppose he is, really. What was it you were going to say? Before we saw him?'

'Nothing.'

They found a table on the Rambla and ordered a red wine for Elisenda and a Bitter Kas for Catalina. Half the world they knew strolled past, some greeting one or the other or both, some looking away when they spotted Elisenda, all clinging on to the wardrobe and spirit of the dying days of summer.

'Where are you taking me for dinner?' Catalina asked.

'Somewhere with plenty of room between the tables.'

Chapter Thirty One

Elisenda examined Catalina closely. 'Are you sure you're not our mother?'

Her sister lifted up the edge of her plate to scoop up a spoonful of ice cream and chocolate sauce and put it in her mouth, followed by the last piece of crepe. They were at one of the tables in the front room at the Creperie Bretonne rather than the antique train and bus seats bolted to the concrete floor in the back. The waiter had unknowingly gone along with Elisenda's tease about plenty of room between the tables. Especially once Catalina had declared the tight confines of the creperie was where she wanted to go for dinner.

'It's a craving,' she'd argued, which pretty much closed the deal as far as Elisenda could see.

'I should have cravings again,' Elisenda decided. 'That was good.'

'You see. Pregnant women. We can say what we want. The only nine months that's ever going to happen.'

Which is when Catalina had asked Elisenda for the umpteenth time since becoming pregnant when she was going to settle down and start a family again.

Which is when Elisenda asked her if she was their mother.

'We just care for you,' Catalina replied, licking her spoon and looking straight at Elisenda, a sad smile playing around the edge of her mouth.

'Please don't, I can care for myself.'

Catalina ran her finger around the lip of her plate to soak up the last of the chocolate. 'I always feel guilty talking about my baby. I want you to be happy again.'

'I am happy, Catalina. And don't feel guilty. I want you to talk to me. This is your baby. Your time.'

'I want you to have a baby again. We're both on our own.'

Elisenda watched her sister diligently lick her fingers. 'No, Catalina. I lost Lina. I'm not going to have a replacement child. I'm moving on, it's time the rest of you did too. Now can we change the subject?' She suddenly felt exhausted.

'We just want you to be happy.'

'Please, Catalina, stop.' She finished her wine and took a long breath. 'Anyway, our mother went on demos against Franco and protested long and hard for our generation of women's rights so that I could grow up to be sad and lonely with a job. This is the least I can do to repay her.'

'Oh, Eli, I know I worry too much. You're the least sad and lonely person I know.'

'Aren't I just?'

'Except in your own head.'

Catalina got up and squeezed out from behind the table to go to the toilet, leaving her last statement hanging in the air.

The silence left by Catalina was filled by a man and a woman at the next table.

'As far as I'm concerned,' the man was saying, 'Viladrau and everyone like him should be strung up from the lampposts.'

'An eye for an eye?' the woman responded. 'Bring back the death penalty?'

'Yes. For certain cases. Bring it back.'

'You can't be serious.'

Suddenly depressed, Elisenda had to tune out before she was tempted to join in. She got up and went to the bar to pay to stop herself from doing just that.

Outside, the sisters strolled back to the Rambla to find a band playing traditional music and dozens of people dancing in the warm night.

'Thursday,' sang Catalina. 'I'd forgotten this was on.'

Elisenda hung back and watched the musicians and the dancers while Catalina went on and joined in with them. One of the free concerts offered every Thursday through spring and autumn, heralding the summer, holding off the winter. Elisenda watched her younger sister sway gently to the hypnotic, strident keening of the bombards and clarinets amid the merrily waltzing and twirling couples and groups of friends. People who had grown up with both sisters went up to Catalina and greeted her warmly, waving hello to Elisenda when they saw her. I used to join in, Elisenda thought. Before I lost my daughter and came back to Girona a police officer. She remembered Catalina's comment in the restaurant and peeled herself away from the arches to go out on to the Rambla. She needed to be moving.

Weaving in and out of the various groups of people dancing in more or less raucous confederation, Elisenda wandered out of the coloured light cast from the wooden stage and on to the terrace cafes, still busy at this time of night at this time of year. Give it a couple of weeks, she thought. She turned and looked back at the stage, able to stay out of the light and out of the sensation that she was somehow doing wrong in not joining in. She could see Catalina from where she stood, looking the happiest she'd appeared in ages. A white, blue and red Seguretat Ciutadana patrol car pulled up near Elisenda on the narrow road alongside the Rambla.

Coming from over to her left, in a break between tunes, she heard heavily-accented Spanish. She looked over and saw a group of young immigrants, some seated on a bench, others standing in front of it, all talking to each other in quiet voices now the music had paused for a moment. Latin American by their accents, Elisenda realised, Cuban she thought. Some of the many who had come over to Catalonia and were working as waiters or porters or cleaners, unable to get work back home, unable to get a job over here for which they were more than qualified.

131

At the bench next to them was another group of people talking. Different accent. Elisenda recognised the young Philippine woman working as a maid for Laura Puigmal's sister or mother, out with friends from her country, all probably doing similar jobs here, their evening out spent on a bench as they earned too little to do much else. Nice to see the old traditions carrying on, Elisenda thought to herself wryly. In the past, Thursday had always been the one day of the week that servants were allowed off. The modern world evidently didn't stretch to everyone in it.

Elisenda found herself staring at the young Philippine maid. And staring.

And feeling like someone had punched her in the stomach.

Reaching into her bag for her mobile, she dialled Vista Alegre and asked for an address and a number.

She hung up and dialled a second number.

'Àlex,' she said. 'I think I know who the next victim is.'

Chapter Thirty Two

Elisenda tried the three numbers again. The landline switching to the artificial sing-song voice of the answering service after half a dozen rings, both mobiles coming back with the caller not available message.

'Damn,' she muttered, tapping her knee nervously as she sat back into the rear seat of the patrol car she'd flagged down on the Rambla.

She checked her watch. Gone two in the morning. After calling Vista Alegre, she'd tried calling the numbers they'd given her, with no luck. So she'd put Catalina into a taxi and got the patrol car to take her to a house in the quiet streets and swimming-pooled villas of Palau. No hurry, yet, just a need to be sure. The domains of the great and the good had been dark and shuttered, the villa she sought empty, the two Seguretat Ciutadana who'd driven her there circling the quiet black lawn.

Àlex called her from Vista Alegre with no news.

She got back in the car with the two uniforms and considered her next move. There was nothing to suggest an attack was imminent, she just wanted to make sure the potential victim was safe while they planned what they would do with the notion.

'Odd night, this,' the caporal riding shotgun said, cutting across her thoughts.

'Why's that?' she asked him, her mind only half on what he was saying.

'Someone's been nicking full rubbish bins from outside restaurants,' he told her, chuckling. The driver, an otherwise taciturn mosso with a Barcelona accent, joined in.

Elisenda looked straight at him and leaned forward. 'Put the light show on, we're in a hurry.'

At Vista Alegre, Àlex told her that the person they were looking for had been seen in the old town around midnight, but there'd been no further sightings. He'd sent a patrol car to wait outside the villa in Palau and other uniformed Mossos on foot to check possible routes to the house from the old town. The rest of her unit was with them, woken in the small hours and called in to search the ancient streets.

'It was seeing the Philippine maid again,' Elisenda told Àlex. 'The whole idea of the servant thing. It reminded me of the last time I saw Laura. We went for a meal together and made a joke about bad food. And then there were the bins.'

'I don't get it,' he replied.

'I'm not sure I do. It only struck a chord with me because it reminded me of a story I'd heard. A local one about a servant who did something wrong and was taunted with food, but it's not one I remember when I was growing up.'

And then the call came through, telling her what she feared.

She closed her eyes and cursed, holding the dead phone to her shoulder. She looked up at Àlex and nodded and they left her office, turning out the lights.

Dawn was already breaking by the time they got to the Mercat del Lleó, the city's main covered market, just a short ride from the police station. Bleary-eyed Seguretat Ciutadana were shepherding people out of the building and setting up tape barriers. A crowd of early-starters was lingering behind the line, avidly sending rumours rippling back and forth through their shaking heads. A Policia Científica van turned up as Elisenda and Àlex went in through the main doors.

It was the smell that hit them first. The smell and the quiet of a building that should have been thriving at that time in the morning.

They were told by a uniformed sergent with a white paper face mask on that the first stallholders to open up had noticed the smell, but they hadn't thought any more of it. Not until one stallholder had arrived, last as usual, and thrown the aluminium shutters up on the confined space of his stand, releasing the full force of the contents of all the rubbish bins that had been stolen in the night. By that time, the first of the day's shoppers had already started trickling in.

The audience the perpetrator wanted.

Elisenda and Àlex accompanied the sergent to the market stall, one that had a commanding view down the central aisle, feeling the stench getting stronger the nearer they got. They were glad of the paper masks that the sergent had given them, although the bitter sweet smell still seeped through the fibres and into their nostrils.

'Rotten food,' Elisenda remembered a little more. 'The story says she was pelted with rotten food.'

They came to the end of the aisle and stood before the market stall, taking in what lay before them.

It was a woman. The woman Elisenda expected to see. Held in place by padlocked chains coming from both wrists to the metal stanchions over the stall. Held in place too by the kilos and kilos of rotting fruit and vegetables and meat dumped into the small space between the narrow counter and the rear of the stand, enveloping her from legs to waist, trapping her. Her face and upper body were covered in peel and rind and skin, her hair a sticky tangle hanging limply down over her forehead. Her eyes and mouth gaped open, her head pulled back by the forced grimace, defiant in death. Bruising around her eyes, the skin mottled and discoloured. Her mouth torn open by staring fish heads and uneaten culinary invention. A cloud of flies swarmed up angrily from the wasted food, thrown out in the rubbish from the city's restaurants, and quickly settled back on the putrid mass, its decomposition speeded up by the last heat of summer and the temperature it created in itself in the confined space.

'For Christ's sake,' Àlex muttered. Elisenda turned to him to see his fists clenching, a muscle in his cheek twitching. She was momentarily shocked at the chill anger she saw rise in him.

'Who is she?' he asked.

Elisenda stood aside to let the first of the Policia Científica pass, recording as much of the scene as they could before the forensic doctor arrived.

'Mònica Ferrer,' she told him. 'Restaurant critic with the local paper. Never read her column?'

Àlex shook his head.

'I make a point not to,' Elisenda said.

'Is she really a deserving victim?'

Elisenda looked at the familiar but sullied features of the woman in front of them.

'She's rapacious, sarcastic, arrogant, self-important and petty-minded. She was born into one of Girona's wealthiest families and has never created one single thing in her life, only criticised. She's said to have closed down more restaurants in the city than the health department, botulism and the recession.'

She turned to Àlex.

'But no,' she said, 'she didn't deserve this.'

Chapter Thirty Three

He didn't know it, but Octavi Marsans' first-year history students called him The Showman. Had he known it, he would have been delighted. His voice rolled and boomed now like a bad impersonation of a bygone classical actor, worming its way into every crack and corner of the packed and stifling lecture theatre, curling around the toes of the pretty young women seated in silent confederation at the front and sniffing through the idle and salacious doodles of the anonymous and unfavoured young men at the back. The ten o'clock lecture on a Friday morning. Hard-core hangovers and morning-after pills. The local students making arrangements for Friday night's perfection of Thursday night's dry run. The ones from out of town, most in time-warp hostels, the lucky few with a shared and liberal apartment, ready for the off with packed bags of dirty washing at their feet, dutifully going home for the weekend, back to boyfriends and mothers, to be cleansed of the guilty sins of a Thursday night.

And at the front, Octavi Marsans. Tanned and lined, in his trademark cream linen jacket over a pale T-shirt and loose linen trousers. The look that had made him a minor cult figure on a late-night talking heads show on the local TV station, exquisitely and articulately to cue crushing an obscure book by an obscure rival or savaging the latest Hollywood abomination.

'Before we begin,' he declaimed to the hall now, 'I beg of you to indulge me. Just remind me how the Catalan flag came into being. The four red bars on the yellow background. The story behind its birth. Just for my benefit. I'd like to know.'

'No shit,' muttered a voice at the back. Not enough to reach the front, although the muted giggles rippled up and down the cheap seats, but studiedly low enough not to travel the full distance. In the middle rows of the steep bank of benches, the good and the plain, the conscientious and the shrinking, looked uncertainly at each other, hoping another would take up the challenge and answer. After all, it was easy. One everyone knew. Including the bright young things in the front two rows, seated side-saddle, one ankle crossed over the other, exchanging attractive and knowing smirks. It was one of their number who answered. Roser Caselles, daughter and granddaughter of lawyers and firmly ensconced in the top flight of the city's list of most eligible young women.

'Guifré el Pelós,' she said confidently. 'Emperor Lluís el Piadós dipped his four fingers in the blood of Guifré el Pelós, Count of Barcelona, when he was wounded in battle against the Normans and ran them down Guifré's gold shield. That's how we get the flag.'

Octavi Marsans looked at her and smiled, and then embraced the rest of the room in his largesse. 'Guifré el Pelós,' he echoed. 'Very good.'

Almost as one, the room nodded.

'Guifré el Pelós,' he repeated, drawing them all into his warm conspiracy. Nodding once more, he took a long step forward and bellowed. 'Wrong, wrong, wrong, wrong, wrong.'

Almost as one, the room fell into shocked silence. Roser Caselles' perfectly plucked and shaded eyebrows creased in panic over blue and gaping eyes. Almost imperceptibly, her friends either side shrank back from Marsans and away from Roser. The wag at the back sniggered, but again, not so loudly as to risk being heard at the front.

'That would have been quite hard, don't you think, Senyoreta...'

'Caselles,' Roser answered faintly, 'Roser Caselles.'

'Senyoreta Caselles, considering Lluís el Piadós died some twenty years before Guifré was born.' He held his long, manicured fingers up beside his head, hushing anyone else who might have wanted to add to the debate. 'And before anyone else cares to join in, neither was it Carles II el Calb who did the dirty with the fingers. He was merely substituted in the legend the following century as he at least was around at roughly the same time as Guifré. But that still doesn't make it true. And neither is the flag the standard of Otger Cataló, founder of our country. And it's not the seventeen bars of Comtessa Ermessenda and Comte Ramon Berenguer II found on their tombs in Girona cathedral either. Nor is it any of the legion of myths and fabrications that some of you might feel like flinging out at me right now. This is a history lecture. History. Not legend. The four red bars on the yellow background were most probably simply the evolution of the heraldic emblem of the Counts of Barcelona through the Counts of Provence and Foix, the kings of Mallorca and then the kings of Aragon. After Pau I of Catalonia, it was known as the royal flag of Catalonia, then the flag of Aragon, and after that it was batted back and forth between the two. It was not until the nineteenth century and the Catalan Renaixença that it became identified as our national flag.'

He paused, covering the room with his eyes. 'And if you go to Aragon, they'll no doubt tell you that it's not even our flag at all.'

Now entirely as one, the room let out its collective breath in a protracted and nervous giggle. Octavi Marsans smiled. His existence had been utterly and irrevocably confirmed. Pity about the girl in the front row, though, he thought for a moment, as she had most definitely been on his radar of impressionable, beddable young beauties. He looked frankly at her now, her expression one of eagerness to atone. Most satisfactory, a suddenly aroused Marsans realised, unleashing the full wattage of his electric smile on her. For atone she would, of that he had no doubt.

He flapped his fingers in front of himself to call silence. 'As I say, people, this is history. It is not legend. It is not fairytale. It is not politics.' Another pause. Even the back-row wags were silent. 'It is rarely even fact. It is history. We are historians. We do not deal in facts. We deal in symbols. We deal in collective memory. We deal in identity. So yes, Senyoreta Caselles, you are quite right. It is the legend of Guifré el Pelós. But it is not the legend of Guifré el Pelós because it is fact. Or because it is true. It is the legend of Guifré el Pelós because we all say it is. Because we all believe it is.' Another pause, also perfectly timed. 'Well, ninety-nine per cent of us, at least. Those of us in this room, the historians among us, know it not to be true. Which is by no means to say that it is false.'

Marsans paused, his eyes flickering around the room, taking in every student.

'I said that as historians we dealt in symbols. But what is a symbol? Yes, we know it comes from the Greek *symbolon*, which literally means "thrown together", but what exactly was it? The *symbolon* was a token, a means of identification, that was divided into parts, each one representing the greater whole. A certificate, if you like, that helped the holders of each part to recognise each other and be recognised. To the members of the group for whom it had a meaning, the symbol showed the presence of the larger context. In terms of national identity, it formed a bond between contemporaries and a link between generations, and it is precisely this power of symbols that was central in their construction of the national identity. Which is why we must never let anyone outside this room know the truth of the legend of the Catalan flag.' He scanned the rapt faces and grinned to make sure the room saw he was letting them in on the big joke.

'Because if we lose the symbols,' he concluded, 'we lose what binds us. We lose what it is that makes us a nation. Our collective memory. And if we lose our collective memory, we lose our identity.'

He looked around him. The students seemed unsure as to whether they were supposed to applaud or not, so they simply nodded. Even the wag at the back was silent.

'I've spoken,' Octavi Marsans said.

Chapter Thirty Four

Josep turned the car ignition on long enough to open his window. In the passenger seat, Elisenda opened hers.

'It's stifling,' she commented, checking her watch. Nearly lunchtime. Ignasi Perafita, Mònica Ferrer's husband, had finally been located in Barcelona and was being driven to Girona by Mossos car. She and Josep were awaiting his arrival outside the couple's villa in Palau. The wealthy suburb was lifeless. Children at school, parents at work or lingering over the shops in town. Elisenda knew the husband would have been told the bare minimum. That his wife had died in suspicious circumstances. Little more.

It was Pau who had known more about the story that Elisenda had only vaguely recalled.

'The Majordoma,' he'd told the rest of the team a few hours ago. 'It's a newly-created legend. She was Sant Narcís's, Girona's patron saint's, housekeeper. She's supposed to have been an extraordinary cook, but also a terrible gossip and a show-off, which annoyed Sant Narcís, so he took her gifts away from her and she became the laughing stock of the city. She'd wander the streets in a daze and not react when people threw rotten food at her.'

'Hence the food from the stolen rubbish bins and the way she was posed in the market,' added Elisenda.

Pau had also shown them the latest developments on the website, which was going more and more into overdrive with rumours and speculation about the latest victim.

'There's the odd one or two saying that what this person's doing is not right,' Pau had commented, 'but the vast majority are applauding the attacks still.'

Elisenda scrolled down the page, scanning comment after comment, some congratulating the attacker on his choice of victim, others joining in with more suggestions both of victims and of what should be done to them, others sarcastically thanking the Mossos for doing nothing about it all. She only found two that criticised the attacks, and their posts were shot down by other contributors in very blunt terms.

'Makes you proud to be a member of the human race, doesn't it?' she muttered to Pau.

'Doesn't it just? I'm afraid you come up a few more times.'

She shrugged. 'To be expected. So what else do you have to show me?'

He clicked on a hyperlink that she'd seen added to a few of the posts and the screen instantly showed the top of a photo. Pau had to scroll the page down to bring the whole of the image into view, but Elisenda knew immediately what she was going to see.

'Great,' she said when it finally filled the screen.

In front of her was a photo that had evidently been taken of Mònica Ferrer in the market before the Mossos had got there. The lurid colours of the flash photo, probably from a mobile phone, looked almost as distressing as the actual scene had been. The victim was in the same position as when Elisenda and Àlex had arrived in the market, but the starkness of the image seemed to accentuate the way her face had been frozen as in a scream and her hair and clothes filthy from the rubbish that had been dumped over her. Pau clicked another link to show three more pictures, two of them the same shot from the slightly different angle afforded by the narrow entrance to the stand, the third a close-up of her face.

Worse still were the metres and metres of savage and mocking comments unwinding down the screen and the rash of glib and easy jokes that always erupted at times like these.

'Okay,' Elisenda said. 'I've seen enough. Have you heard from UCDI?'

'I've got an e-mail here,' Pau told her. He switched to his account on the computer and showed her. 'We've been assigned a team to investigate the site.'

Elisenda quickly read the e-mail from a Sergent Gispert in the Computer Crime Unit in Sabadell telling Pau of the steps he'd be taking. 'Good,' she commented. 'Keep on top of it.'

'They're here,' Josep suddenly said, breaking her reverie. 'Not a Mossos car, though.'

Elisenda looked up to see a red Audi Roadster turning into the palm-lined drive, the electronic gates opening to allow it through. An unmarked Mossos Seat followed it and parked at the kerb behind Elisenda and Josep.

She and Josep exchanged a look and got out of the car. A sergent from their station got out of the Seat and explained that Perafita hadn't wanted to leave his car in Barcelona. 'Caporal Escofet accompanied him to Girona.'

The three of them walked up the steep drive to where Mònica Ferrer's husband was climbing out of the driver's seat. Escofet was already out of the car. She rolled her eyes at the other three Mossos. Perafita strode up the steps to the front porch without waiting for them and opened the door, quickly turning off the intruder alarm. Elisenda told the two Mossos that they could go back to the station and she and Josep followed Perafita into the house. They went through a vestibule dominated by a huge sculpture of a pair of clasped hands in dissonance with gilt-framed watercolours on the walls and into a living room that displayed an impersonal moneyed comfort.

They found Perafita pouring himself a brandy into a large balloon from a bottle of Torres 10 on a marble-topped sideboard.

'We're very sorry for your loss,' Elisenda told him.

'What are you doing about it?' He sat down on a spotless cream leather sofa and took a sip of his brandy, staring frankly at her. Elisenda and Josep sat on an identical sofa opposite him.

'We have a specialist unit investigating the case,' she told him. She began to explain something of the circumstances in which his wife was found, but his mobile rang and he held his finger up at her for silence before answering it. As the call dragged on, a lengthy discussion about his business interests, Elisenda caught Josep's look of disbelief.

When Perafita hung up, Elisenda asked him about his movements the previous night. 'Purely routine,' she assured him when he asked her why.

'I caught the redeye from Madrid to Barcelona,' he told them. 'I got into the airport too late to drive home, so I stayed at a friend's flat in Barcelona.'

'Will they be able to corroborate that?'

He gave them the name and details of the friend, when Josep asked him for the exact time of the plane he caught from Madrid.

'I told you. The redeye. In the end, it didn't leave until gone midnight.'

Josep nodded. 'We have confirmation from the airline that you were, in fact, on the shuttle flight that left at eighteen fifty-five.'

Perafita spluttered for a moment and insisted the airline had got it wrong.

'More than enough time to get to Girona, in fact,' Josep pressed home.

'Where were you between midnight and four a.m.?' Elisenda asked him.

He sighed and took a long sip of brandy. He finally looked at Josep for sympathy. 'We're all adults. I returned to Barcelona early to spend the night with a friend.'

'I take it not the friend you stated earlier,' Elisenda said.

'A lady friend.'

'And will she be able to corroborate that?' Josep asked.

'I imagine she will, caporal, but I would appreciate your discretion in this matter.'

'I'm sure you would, Senyor Perafita,' Josep replied, closing his notebook.

They left him to his brandy and cream leather wealth and walked down the drive to their car.

'Not exactly the grieving husband,' commented Josep.

'I see why everything Mònica Ferrer ate left such a bad taste in her mouth,' Elisenda agreed, sliding through the gate that was already closing on them. 'Follow up everything he told us. Make sure it ties in.'

Chapter Thirty Five

The restaurant owner brought over a small earthenware dish of cod with honey and romesco to the table in the corner.

'It's a new dish I'm trying out,' she explained.

Àlex tried a mouthful and looked at her. 'It's beautiful.'

She stared into his eyes. 'Thank you.' She picked up a fork and tore off a small piece from the same dish and tasted it. 'It's not bad.'

Àlex put his fork down and thanked her for seeing him. 'I appreciate you're very busy, Anna.' Most of the tables were occupied in the small restaurant that appeared to be hewn out of the city's rock, the thick stone walls of the centuries-old building effectively shielding them from the unwonted heat outside.

'You were asking about Mònica Ferrer,' Anna said. She pushed her long brown curls away from her face.

'She was here last night.'

Anna laughed. 'Like I'd miss her. She came to see if we'd improved since the last time she came to point out where we were going wrong. Her words.'

'Do you remember anyone approaching her table?'

Anna thought back, absently tearing off another piece of cod. 'No. I don't remember anyone talking to her. People tend to steer clear of her.' She put her hand to her mouth, suddenly looking guilty. 'What a terrible thing to say. I'm sorry.' She called over a waiter and asked him if he remembered anyone talking to the critic. He thought and shook his head.

'Was she behaving peculiarly in any way?' Àlex asked them, but they both said that she wasn't. The kitchen bell rang and the waiter left to serve a table.

'She usually sits… sat at a table,' Anna told him, 'and made notes on a pad next to her when she ate. She didn't really engage with anyone.'

'Can you remember what time she left?'

'Just a second.' Anna went over to a concertina file behind the bar and checked through some papers. She brought back the credit card receipt to show Àlex. 'She paid at eleven seventeen last night. She left pretty much straight after that.'

Àlex made a note and handed the receipt back to her. 'I'm surprised restaurants kept letting her in.'

Anna shrugged. 'We were all over a barrel. Looking like you're afraid to let her in is worse than a bad review. We live in a strange world.'

Àlex closed his notebook and thanked her for her help. 'Call me if anything else occurs to you.'

'I'll be sure to call you.'

—

'Follow it,' Elisenda told Josep.

They'd driven back into the city after seeing Mònica Ferrer's husband and had just joined the traffic on Avinguda Pericot when a Seguretat Ciutadana car ripped past them with its lights and sirens on. They'd already heard a commotion somewhere ahead of them. The patrol car led them along Pericot past Carrer Emili Grahit and turned into the gridiron streets of the Eixample, zig-zagging to the heart of the district, where they found one of the side roads cordoned off.

Josep pulled up amid a slew of police vehicles and they got out. Elisenda could see Pijaume in the midst of uniformed and plain-clothes Mossos, directing their movements with an orchestral calm. She sometimes forgot how good an organiser he was. He was having to shout to make himself heard above the multi-toned keening of several shop alarms.

On the ground near Pijaume, restrained by two Seguretat Ciutadana, a man was lying face down, his face pressed sideways into the asphalt, his hands cuffed behind his back. A metre or so away from him, a sledgehammer lay untouched on the ground like a malevolent icon.

'How can I help?' Elisenda asked Pijaume.

The other sotsinspector looked around. 'Thank you, Elisenda. Can you ensure that the suspect is duly processed and placed in a van, please? Uniforms are checking all the buildings and looking for any victims inside.' He had to shout above the whoops and whistles emanating from the shops along the street. 'My unit is trying to find the keyholders so we can turn these alarms off.'

Elisenda and Josep helped with the suspect and oversaw the sledgehammer being bagged, as the sound of the sirens steadily subsided with the arrival of owners and employees of the various businesses. In a lull, Elisenda was able to see that a number of them, seemingly taken at random, had had their display windows smashed.

'What happened, Narcís?' she asked when the scene was slowly coming back to normal and all the alarms had been silenced. The audience of onlookers started to fade away.

He straightened his tie and brushed his hand over his hair. 'It appears that the suspect went along the street breaking the windows of certain businesses.'

Elisenda looked more closely. She saw a bank, an estate agent and a chain café with their windows caved in. Then two local shops untouched, followed by another bank, its plate glass front shattered. The other side of the street showed the same pattern.

'Banks, property and multinationals,' she muttered.

'Precisely. It appears there was talk of it on the internet earlier this morning, so he seems to have taken it into his head to carry it out.'

'This website,' Elisenda mused out loud. This is where it was leading.

'Apparently, the majority of people simply watched him do it.'

'Man with a sledgehammer. Who wouldn't?'

'Many applauded.'

Elisenda nodded, picturing the scene. It didn't surprise her. The new villains of the age taken to task by an individual. 'Just what's happening to this city.'

Pijaume looked at her. The street was back to normal, most of the Mossos cars gone, cleaners already starting to put everything back in place, workers shoring up the gaps with plywood. 'Have you got time for a coffee?'

'Of course.' Curious, she told Josep to go on to the station without her and led the way round the corner to a small, old-fashioned café with melamine tables along one wall and a zinc bar along the other. The top of the bar was illuminated by the lighting inside a row of aluminium and glass food displays holding metal trays of meatballs, potatoes, Russian salad, kidneys and every other dish the two of them had ever grown up with. Every available piece of wall space was covered in Barça posters and team calendars dating back years. The owner, an ageing beach Lothario with slick hair and a trim moustache eyed Elisenda in open appreciation while taking their order for coffees. Elisenda decided he'd been conditioned to do that since some time in the early 1970s. Or condemned.

'You were on the scene quickly,' Elisenda commented, explaining why she'd turned up.

'I was in the clinic a couple of streets over. More drugs supposedly gone missing, but it turned out to be nothing more than a clerical error.'

'Can I ask how far you've got with the drugs, by the way? We need to know.'

'Little progress, I'm afraid.'

Elisenda simply nodded.

'These are strange times,' Pijaume continued, watching the owner vigorously polishing the milk spout on the coffee machine while their coffees were being made. 'There's something I've been wanting to say to you, Elisenda.'

The café owner brought them their coffees and Pijaume waited while he filled up their cups with steaming milk from the stainless steel jug. Elisenda kept quiet, wondering what was on Pijaume's mind.

'I think they've given you a poisoned chalice,' he explained. 'With this investigation. It could go the wrong way for you, Elisenda, however it turns out.'

'Damned if I do, damned if I don't, you mean?'

'Precisely. I just think you should be careful. Whatever you achieve with it, you're going to tread on someone's toes.'

'Catch the bad guy, half the public won't like it?'

'And half the Mossos.'

Elisenda looked surprised at his comment. 'Don't catch the bad guy and the other half of the public won't like it.'

'Or the other half of the Mossos.'

'And the press won't like it either way,' Elisenda concluded.

Pijaume sat in silence for a moment and sipped at the hot coffee. 'Still, this person's certainly made our job easier,' he commented, looking closely at Elisenda.

Elisenda looked up at him from her coffee cup. 'He's killed four people.'

'Yes, but what four people. A moneylender, a hooligan, a hypocrite and a destroyer of reputations. The courts haven't been able to hand out justice to any of them for years. And neither have we.'

'Narcís, I don't believe you're saying this.'

He shrugged. 'These people have ridden roughshod over us all for years. Now they're finally getting caught out.'

'So you excuse him his crimes? Would you be as happy for Viladrau to get away with his crimes? And Masó?'

'I'm not saying that.'

'Viladrau, Masó and the muggers should go down for what they've done,' Elisenda went on, 'but so should whoever it is who's killed them. One man's crimes can never justify another's. And now there's Mònica Ferrer. Are you saying she did enough to warrant what happened to her?'

'Are you saying she didn't? Compared with the other victims? A violent criminal dies violently. A hypocritical priest gets shown for what he is. A critic who does nothing but humiliate is humiliated in death. Where do you draw the line?'

'I know where I draw the line, Narcís. I draw the line the moment anyone becomes a victim. It's where others draw the line that worries me.'

'Can you honestly say that? Can you honestly say you don't feel more sympathy for the critic than the priest?'

Elisenda's mobile phone rang, buzzing angrily across the table top. She and Pijaume both looked relieved.

'I have to take this,' she said.

Pijaume looked at his watch. 'I should be getting away. Please don't take what I said the wrong way, Elisenda. I can't condone any of this, but I do think you need to be careful.'

Elisenda nodded as they separated outside on the pavement. 'I know you do, Narcís, thank you.' She sighed. 'And you're right to raise these questions. I know I do every day. It's becoming increasingly hard to know where each of us stands on this.'

She watched him go and went back to her phone call. 'News, Montse?' she asked.

'*We've found something,*' Montse told her. '*A guy called Pere Corominas. He went missing a month ago.*'

Chapter Thirty Six

'Where are you now?' Elisenda asked Montse, moving out of the way of an elderly couple moving slowly along the narrow pavement.

'*I'm at Vista Alegre*,' the caporal replied. She explained about Corominas' being reported missing by his flatmate. '*He works as a researcher at the university foundation on Plaça Jordi de Sant Jordi. I'm on my way there now to talk to him.*'

Elisenda looked at her watch. 'I'm about five minutes away from there. I'll meet you outside.'

She hung up and walked briskly through the Eixample back towards the centre. Crossing Gran Via, she thought of her conversation with Pijaume and was reminded of the incident she and Catalina had witnessed of the man hitting his dog. It brought to mind something that had happened years earlier and that she'd forgotten. A car on Plaça Catalunya had been left parked straddling two spaces and Elisenda had silently applauded a guy ringing the police to have it towed. When she'd walked back some time later, though, it was still there and someone had scored a number of deep scratches down the side of the car. She'd been horrified, but when she'd told her friends about it at the time, they'd all laughed and said the driver had deserved it for being inconsiderate. It struck her now how everyone was capable of welcoming someone else taking revenge, or justice, on everyone else's behalf. It simply differed in the degree.

She suddenly realised that Montse was standing next to her, saying her name, as she stood outside the smooth walls of the university foundation building. She'd been miles away. She wasn't sure if she'd even registered walking along Carrer Santa Clara to get there.

'Sorry, Montse,' she said. 'I was just going over the attacks in my head.'

'No problem, Sotsinspectora,' the younger woman replied. It was another hot day but she looked cool despite that. It was one of those rare occasions when Elisenda envied Montse her short hairstyle. Elisenda held her own hair up against the back of her head for a moment to let what little air there was cool her neck.

'So tell me about this guy,' she said.

'Name's Antoni Sunyer,' Montse told her. 'He's worked here as a research assistant for just over a year now, since graduating. Originally from Olot, but studied history at university in Girona, which is where he met Pere Corominas. He and Corominas have shared a flat in the old town since they were students together. Corominas also studied history and works as a researcher with the municipal historical archives. He's from way up near Ripoll.'

'Parents still alive?'

'Both of them. I've spoken to them on the phone. I get the feeling it's a bit of a free and easy relationship. They don't seem that concerned he's missing. Looks like parents and son were a bit alternative. They dropped out and left Barcelona over twenty years ago to live off the land.'

Inside the building, they were shown by a smartly-dressed receptionist to a suite of small offices where Sunyer worked. Seated at a desk covered in folders and pen pots and pieces of paper riddled with brightly-coloured fluorescent markings and below a wall papered with clutter, a young man with a wispy black beard and moustache that didn't quite meet in the middle turned to face them.

'Antoni Sunyer?' Montse asked him. 'Caporal Salas and Sotsinspectora Domènech.' They both held up their badges for a brief moment.

'You'd better sit down,' Sunyer said, his voice nervous. He fetched a couple of straight-backed chairs from another desk and pulled them nearer his own.

'Thank you, Antoni,' Elisenda said, gazing at him. He smiled shyly. He was very slight and, despite the beard – or perhaps because of it – looked younger than he probably was.

Sunyer turned to Montse. 'Are you Montse?' he asked her. 'Who I spoke to on the phone?'

'That's right. We're grateful you could see us at such short notice.'

The young man shrugged. 'I'm pleased something's being done to find Pere. I'd pretty much given up on the Mossos looking for him.'

Montse looked at Elisenda, who spoke. 'We're not part of the team looking for Pere. We're pursuing another investigation and we think that his disappearance might be related.'

'Another investigation?'

'Would you mind telling us exactly when you last saw Pere?' Elisenda carried on. She didn't want him connecting their reason for questioning him with the recent troubles in the city.

'I've already told the Mossos.'

'I'm sorry, Antoni, but we need to know,' Montse added. 'For our own investigation.'

Sunyer sighed and told them what he had told the sergent at Vista Alegre and the two officers from the Local Investigation Unit when they'd come to see him. He told them about how Pere had not turned up for work on the Friday or been home since. How all his clothes were still in the flat, as was his laptop, and how he had seemed agitated for a couple of days before he went missing.

'Agitated?' Elisenda asked. 'In what way?'

'Snappy,' Sunyer replied, choosing his words carefully. 'On edge like something was worrying him. It's been so long now, I can't really remember how he was and everything's distorted in my memory, but he was unhappy about something. I do know that.'

'You don't know what was causing it?' Montse asked him but he shook his head. 'Girlfriend problems?'

Sunyer shook his head again. 'He's gay. And he's much too free a spirit for steady partners. Pere's more into cruising than courting.'

'The Devesa?' Elisenda asked. The park on the northwest edge of the city.

Sunyer nodded. 'He'd never had any problems there. But as I say, he did seem worried about something the last few days I saw him.'

'Have you spoken to his parents?' Elisenda asked.

Sunyer grunted. 'I've tried. They live in this weird world where modernity degrades us. Pere was always repeating it. They both worked in banks in Barcelona and just decided one day to give it all up and go and raise goats and chickens up near Ripoll.'

'And children,' Elisenda added.

'Pere was born up there,' he said, nodding. 'He grew up in some weird shit. Running naked through the woods and survival in the wild. He couldn't wait to get away. Mind, he's not as different from them as he likes to think.'

'In what way?'

'Traditional. He needs the city and his laptop and his mobile, but he believes in tradition. Popular tradition. Just like his parents.'

'Have they been down here since he went missing?'

'No. They're really not that worried. Tried telling me he's a free spirit and he's gone in search of himself.'

'But you don't think so?'

Sunyer shook his head vigorously. 'He enjoyed his job too much. He lived the way he wanted. He didn't need to go and find himself.'

'And he was unhappy about something,' Elisenda concluded.

'Definitely.'

Elisenda thanked him and she and Montse left him to his paper and coloured pens and clutter.

Outside, a blast of heat hit them all the harder after the near-glacial air conditioning of the building. Elisenda turned to Montse. 'What do you think?'

'I'm not so sure,' Montse replied after a moment's thought.

Elisenda agreed with her. 'I'm not convinced he's a victim.' They set off slowly in the heat for Plaça Independència and the bridge over the river to the shade of the Rambla. 'Not one of our victims anyway.'

Chapter Thirty Seven

Sunday. Elisenda left Monells behind her and struck out along the dusty, baked track towards the neighbouring village of Sant Miquel de Cruïlles. Through the heat haze, she could see the eleventh-century monastery rising gently above her on a low bluff in the distance. She checked her watch. She just had enough time for a solitary walk before her sister and her husband turned up later for lunch. Her parents were pottering around the house, which was as good an excuse as any Elisenda needed to get out.

'I forget how good these are,' Elisenda's mother had commented when Elisenda had arrived at their house, taking a second bite into a *xuixo*, the rich confectioner's custard squeezing out of the thick, torpedo-shaped doughnut. She licked the tip of a slender finger and dabbed at the sugar left on the plate.

'You had one yesterday,' Elisenda's father objected.

'Not from La Vienesa.' She turned to Elisenda. 'I trust you brought more.'

'Sunday with the family,' Elisenda said with a sigh, leaning back against the ancient garden chair and stretching her feet out in front of her in the shade of her parents' garden. She still couldn't quite get used to coming here and not finding her grandparents. Too many childhood memories of summers and Sundays crowding in. Her parents bringing cakes from La Vienesa just as she had done today. Her grandmother rarely setting foot outside the kitchen, the garden a functional affair tended by her grandfather, not this verdant luxury of palms and olive trees and the recent addition of a small swimming pool. The rest of the building the same, the three-hundred-year-old village house skilfully restored and modernised inside and out without any damage to its soul.

On the marble table in front of her, amid the scattered plates and coffee cups, her tablet stared back at her, ruining her mood. She'd checked it over coffee after she'd been to La Vienesa, on Plaça del Vi, to buy *xuixos* for when she got to Monells. Feeling good at seeing her parents for the day. At getting away from the microscope of Girona.

It hadn't lasted.

It had been over a week now since Mònica Ferrer had been found. A long week. And it had been crowned by yet further escalation on the website that was getting people talking. And acting.

'We're getting all these minor incidents,' a sergent in Pijaume's unit had told her. 'People taking the law into their own hands. Egged on by the comments on the forum. And by what they see happening.'

And now the website was taking it that bit further. In the tranquil shade of her parents' garden, she recalled the latest development.

A top ten of voters' favourites had been added to the website. Two top tens, in fact. One for individuals, one for groups. Each one being voted on like a genuinely malevolent talent show. The individuals were the usual choices: politicians, local celebrities, the footballer who'd scored an own goal the previous week. The groups included South Americans, North Africans, Spaniards, cheap tourists, the unemployed, long-term patients, anyone it was felt didn't contribute. It was almost a relief that the city council got voted in. And the Mossos.

After the incident with the smashed windows, she'd asked Pau about progress on tracing the website.

'I've had this from Gispert in Sabadell,' he told her. He showed her a printout of a map showing what looked like air routes stretching across the world. 'It shows the trail of IP addresses used to hide the central server.'

'Are they close to finding it?'

'Nowhere near, he reckons.'

She poured herself a cup of coffee and swore under her breath. Her parents, silent throughout, exchanged a look.

'Saw old man Bellsolà this week,' her father told her, breaking the silence. 'He says he's retiring next year.'

'Can he take his son with him?' Elisenda said, looking up.

'Reckons the son's going to be taking over his practice.'

'As well as his own? It'll be huge.' Elisenda shuddered at the thought of yet more cases being handled by Gerard Bellsolà's firm of lawyers. As if her job wasn't hard enough. Bellsolà senior was fabled as a slippery character, and his lawyer father before him had been quite an element by all accounts, but the present incumbent of the family amorality that Elisenda had to put up with was the crowning glory of three generations of natural legal selection. And he had a son, Elisenda remembered. She'd seen him once, dressed like a ten-year-old version of his father, his hair plastered in pungent cologne in a fashion that had died out at least a couple of decades earlier. So that was Girona's future taken care of, Elisenda mused grimly. So much for the lessons of the past.

'No bad thing,' her father commented through her fug. 'Someone to take over.'

'Any more coffee?' Neus asked, just that bit too quickly. She could see what was coming, Elisenda too preoccupied to recognise the signs.

'I don't want to work forever,' Enric persisted. 'I need someone to take over when I do decide to retire.'

Elisenda turned to face her father, the message getting through. 'Don't,' she warned.

'No, Enric,' Neus agreed. 'Don't.'

'You were a good lawyer,' he told Elisenda.

'I was never a lawyer. I studied law, I never practised it. There are other ways of upholding the law. I chose mine.'

'You could have been a good lawyer. And there's more future in law than in the police.'

'No, there's my future in the police. I ceased to believe in the legal profession at university. I began to despair of it in the Mossos. I'm happy with what I do. Ten years ago, a woman like me couldn't have got anywhere in the police. No woman would have even contemplated it. And now we can, and we can make a career of it. That's my future, papa, please don't try to change me.'

'And what will happen when you want another promotion? What if they send you to the other end of Catalonia? Who'll take over my practice then?'

'Pere. You've always said how good he is.'

'Not family,' Enric commented.

'Not important.'

'Maybe not to you.'

'Enric,' Neus barked, shocked.

Elisenda stood up. 'Stop this now, papa, or I'm going.'

Neus held her daughter's hand. 'And I tell you now, Enric, I will go with her if you don't stop this selfishness.'

Enric looked up at his wife, surprised, and then at his daughter. 'I'm sorry. I just want what's best for you.'

'What's best for me changed five years ago, papa.'

Neus gave Elisenda's hand the slightest of squeezes and let go.

—

Without realising, Elisenda had walked through the village of Cruïlles and was passing a flowing gold and green field of rape-seed on the dusty track back to Monells. She wiped the sweat from her face and listened for a moment to the cicadas' lazy chirruping across the dry fields. She heard another sound. A child singing. She stopped and stared intently along the path and over the fields but could see no one. She couldn't tell which direction the singing was coming from. It was a traditional song, one she'd learnt at school. And taught in turn. The singing stopped as abruptly as it had started and she waited a few moments before carrying on along her way. Without her fully noticing, she quickened her pace in time with the noise of the insects, a bead of sweat running down her spine, sticking her T-shirt to her back. A startled dust-coloured cicada half-hopped half-flew in front of her before jumping out of her path into a clump of sun-wizened grasses.

The image of Mònica Ferrer in the market stall came into her head, moving in and out of focus in pace with her stride. The story that Ferrer's husband had given them had been corroborated by a woman in Barcelona, the wife of one of his business associates. An affair that had been going on for over six years. And not his only one, they'd discovered. One small tragedy on top of a greater one. She couldn't help feeling more sympathy for Mònica than she'd ever felt for her in life. She'd also caught herself wondering what it was that made Mònica suitable for punishment but not her husband, before shaking the thought out of her head.

'Damn,' she swore, breaking into a full run, perspiration quickly pouring down her head and legs and arms, her feet in her rope-soled canvas *espardenyes* sliding over the loose, sharp stones on the track. Finding her stride on the pitted surface, she quickly settled into a steady pace, her head barely moving, her elbows tucked into her sides, conserving energy. Two cyclists stared at her as they went past in the other direction.

She also pictured Riera on the morning of the critic's post mortem.

'He's learning,' the forensic doctor had told her bluntly. 'She died of asphyxia, in the market stall. Probably sedated and taken to the murder site, where the food was placed in her mouth. If this is the same man, he's learned the right dose.'

Elisenda remembered Mònica Ferrer's body suspended in the stall. 'So that's what his aim was? For her to die like that. Not from the drugs.'

'I would say so. And I would imagine that's what he intended for Viladrau too. He's refining his technique. He's learned to keep his victims alive to take their punishment.'

'She would have been aware of what was happening to her?'

Riera looked closely at Elisenda. 'Very much so.'

Back in Monells, Elisenda slowed down to a breathless walk and skirted her parents' house to the small, porticoed main square where she bought a bottle of water from Ca l'Arcadi and sat outside in the shade for a few minutes to cool down. Over at the far end of the square, the band was just setting up for the Sunday-morning *sardanes*. Elisenda checked her watch. If she'd had time, she would have hung around and joined in one of the circles. It seemed ages since she'd danced in the square. Or anywhere else for that matter. With a sigh, she got to her feet and walked up the slight cobbled incline to her parents' house.

Rounding the corner, she saw Sergi, Catalina's husband, pulling the heavy Corten steel driveway gate shut behind his new car, a bright white BMW with vents and stripes and more lights than he would ever know how to use. Top of the range, Elisenda thought to herself. Of course. She put a spurt on and squeezed through just as her brother-in-law finished closing the stylishly and deliberately rusted gate.

'Hi, Elisenda,' he greeted her.

She kissed him on both cheeks and helped him carry a wicker basket of shiny fresh aubergines into the house. 'From your parents' garden?' she asked.

'Yeah, they can never eat them all.' His parents' garden was, in fact, several hectares of land up in the volcanic Garrotxa region near Olot, a good hour or so northwest of Girona. Making money ran in Sergi's family.

She went on through the house with Sergi following her and out into the back garden, where Catalina was being held tightly by their mother in the shade of a luscious oily magnolia.

'Hey, Catalina,' Elisenda greeted her, first hugging her carefully, then standing back. 'Let's look at you.'

'How do I look, Eli?' Catalina asked her.

'Like you swallowed a really big olive.'

Chapter Thirty Eight

'That requires at least three homicides over a period of time that can be judged as intentional or premeditated,' Puigventós declared.

The Monday meeting with Puigventós, Micaló and Pijaume, and Elisenda was surprised to find herself backed úp against a wall. She'd raised a spectre of her own. The word "serial", which had been circling above her thoughts since Viladrau was murdered, and more so since the Ferrer killing.

'We have four victims,' she argued. 'Daniel Masó, Chema GM, Viladrau and Ferrer.'

Puigventós disagreed. 'Intentional or premeditated. There is no evidence to suggest that the mugger was intended to die.'

'We have the evidence of prior and subsequent actions. The other three victims confirm that his death was both premeditated and intentional.'

'Two, Elisenda, two. Masó is not a part of this investigation. Both Jutgessa Roca and I believe that his killing is gang-related. The manner of his death was completely different from the other three killings.'

Elisenda looked to Pijaume for support, but he was focusing his gaze steadfastly on the table in front of him. Out of the corner of her eye, she caught Micaló leaning in, ready to attack.

'Why on earth would you want to see serial killers on the streets of Girona, anyway?' Puigventós insisted.

'Girona doesn't have serial killers,' Micaló scoffed.

'I don't. I want to find a way to stop any further killings. To do that, we have to face up to the truth about what's happening so we can anticipate and catch this killer.'

'Why do I get the feeling you're trying to snatch all the high-profile investigations for your team, Sotsinspectora Domènech?' Micaló asked. 'Something to do with a lack of any real success since you formed it, perhaps?'

Puigventós put out a finger to shush the other sotsinspector. 'I see the connection between the muggers, the priest and the critic,' he told her, 'although not all of those are intentional. But I just don't see the Masó link. That to me is gang-related. I want the investigation kept separate.'

Which is when Puigventós delivered his own killer verdict.

'So I'm giving the Masó case to Sotsinspector Micaló's team. You have more than enough on your plate with these other murders, Elisenda. I would sooner you concentrated all your unit's efforts on them.'

'I think that's quite sensible, Xavier,' Micaló commented. 'Thank you.'

Elisenda simply stared at Puigventós and nodded. She had no intention of looking at Micaló.

And neither did she have any intention of paying any attention whatsoever to Puigventós' instructions. As far as she was concerned, the Masó murder was very firmly a part of her investigation, whether Micaló's unit were supposed to be handling it or not.

'There's one other matter, Elisenda,' Puigventós continued. Out of the corner of her eye, she caught Micaló sitting back, relaxing. 'Your relationship with David Costa.'

'Relationship? He's a childhood friend. Nothing more.'

'He's a journalist. The press has no place in a police investigation. I don't want to see you cosying up to the media any more.'

Elisenda was aghast. 'No place? We have a press office. We're supposing to be breaking with the image of the past. So we use the press when we need to.'

'I'm serious, Elisenda.' Puigventós shuffled his papers into order and stood, the discussion called to a close.

Micaló carefully placed his selection of buff folders into his leather document case and looked straight at Elisenda. The other two men had already got up and moved away from the table, their backs turned. 'I will fuck you,' he mouthed at her and stood up.

Elisenda watched him walk to the door. 'Sotsinspector Micaló,' she called to him. He turned. 'I doubt very much I'll notice.'

—

Outside Puigventós' office, Pijaume asked Elisenda if she would come with him. 'There's something I want you to see.'

Intrigued despite her annoyance, she followed him to his office.

'I do have to ask you about the drugs, though, Narcís. I'm sorry but I just can't see any progress being made.'

Pijaume put his hand to his temple. 'I'm doing everything I can, Elisenda. You must understand I have to prioritise.'

'Prioritise? You can see what's going on in the city. Do you want me to talk to Puigventós about taking it over?'

'No, Elisenda,' he snapped. 'I do not. Please can I just show you what I asked you in to see? I simply thought you might want to see this.' He turned his computer screen to face her. 'There's a young man called Toni Clavell who drives up and down the streets in Santa Eugènia, making a nuisance of himself.'

'Okay,' Elisenda said, unsure why she needed to see it.

'This surfaced on the internet yesterday.'

Pijaume clicked over an icon and heavily pixellated images came up on screen. Blurring in and out of focus and jumping a lot, they were evidently shot with the camera on a mobile phone. A group of people, of all ages by the look of them, even though their faces were partly hidden by scarves, were steadfastly striking a car with hammers.

'That's Clavell's car,' Pijaume explained.

They both watched as the crowd systematically beat dents into every part of the car's metalwork. Cheers went up when the remaining windows and lights were broken. None of it was done in anger, but in a joyous mood like a village celebration in the main square. Elisenda could see small children running gleefully in and out among groups of onlookers chatting over pushchairs and prams and elderly people laughing and clapping. By the end, the car had been systematically destroyed in calmness and delight.

A man walked up to the screen, his face masked by a scarf and sunglasses, and spoke quietly to the camera. 'This is justice now. If the Mossos and the courts and the politicians won't give us justice, we will get it for ourselves. This is what we have learned.'

The image froze there. The man staring out at Elisenda and Pijaume, who could do little more than stare back at his sightless dark glasses in silence.

'Nice to see a sense of community still alive,' Elisenda muttered. Not so nice to see how things were escalating, she thought to herself. 'As long as that's the extent of any copycat attacks, I suppose we should be grateful,' she added. She seriously doubted it would be.

'I just thought I should show you.'

Chapter Thirty Nine

Aurora Torrent scrolled through the social network website, dismayed to see her name appearing three times. She looked at the cryptic user names of the people proposing her as the next victim and was able to work out two of them: students on her second-year history course that she'd marked down. She couldn't work out who the third person was, but she had a rough idea of half a dozen or so she suspected.

She was at her desk in the faculty offices at the university, tidying up paperwork and idly surfing through the website that everyone was talking about. A chime on her computer announced an incoming e-mail, so she tore herself away from counting her colleagues up for opprobrium to check her inbox.

And cursed.

And read on.

And cursed and cursed and cursed again.

She turned to look out of the window over the rooftops of the old town and held back the tears. The vents of the air conditioning blew directly into her face, drying her moist eyes. The heat shimmer outside the window looked unreal in the damp cold of the forced air blowing through the office, as though it belonged to another world far distant from the one where she sat.

She looked back at her mail. It was from the publisher's in Barcelona, rejecting her proposed book on iconography and identity. The one for which she'd been in discussions for months. The one that had looked so certain just a day or two earlier, that had appeared to be drawing inevitably to acceptance. It was the second blow in almost as many days. The first being the organisers of a congress to be held the following spring in New York rejecting her paper on the same subject. She had planned it all so carefully, the one timed to aid the other.

The door banged open and she looked up to see the last figure she would want to see at a time like this strut into the room.

'Good morning, Aurora,' the figure said.

'Octavi,' she replied. She minimised her e-mail screen to make sure he saw nothing.

'Anything wrong?' Marsans asked her. 'You look like you have hay fever?'

'I'm fine,' Torrent answered, rather more forcefully than she intended.

Marsans shrugged and took his jacket, which he had been carrying slung over his shoulder in the damp heat outside, and put it on over his tightly-fitting pale yellow T-shirt as protection against the air conditioning inside. Sitting down, he switched his computer on and pulled a memory stick out of his battered leather satchel.

Aurora Torrent watched his fluid, confident movements. Barely surprising, she thought, that he had a reputation for having taken so many of his impressionable female students to bed with him. She watched him pick up the phone on his desk, his slender fingers beautifully manicured, and wanted to throw something heavy at him. He dialled an internal number.

'Enriqueta,' he said into the phone, 'Octavi here.' He laughed at the reply of the woman on the other end. Torrent sneered involuntarily. 'You couldn't possibly organise a plane and hotel for New York for next March, could you? That's right, the congress at Columbia. That's marvellous. Thank you so much.'

Torrent didn't trust herself to speak for a moment or two after Marsans hung up but simply stared at his profile hunched casually over his computer. Finally she spoke. 'You're going to Columbia?'

He turned in his seat to face her. 'That's right. You are as well, aren't you?'

'No. No, I'm not.'

'Really? I thought you were. Changed your mind?'

'Something like that.' She could fell her eyes pricking with tears. 'Are you giving a paper?'

'Yes. On symbology and collective identity.' She gasped but he didn't appear to register. 'I have a book coming out next year on the subject.'

'That's what I was going to do.'

'Is it? I didn't know.'

'Of course you knew, Octavi. You knew perfectly well.'

'I'm sorry, Aurora. I know your field of research overlaps somewhat with mine, but I didn't know exactly what you were going to be doing in New York.'

'And a book. I was going to write a book on it. On iconography and identity.'

'My field is symbology,' Marsans said. 'It's a much broader canvas.'

The phone on his desk rang before Torrent could object any further. 'Enriqueta,' he said into the mouthpiece. 'My, that was quick.'

Torrent was about to turn away to her computer screen but Marsans suddenly flopped back heavily in his chair so she carried on watching him, intrigued. His left hand, resting on the desk, began to tremble slightly. 'The Mossos d'Esquadra?' he asked. 'Did they say what they wanted? Just that I'm to ring back. They didn't give you any idea what it was about? No. Thank you. Thank you, I will.'

He put the phone down and stared out of the window, running an elegant finger along his bottom lip.

'They've finally caught you out,' Torrent said to him with some glee.

'Yes,' Marsans replied absently, picking up the phone again.

Torrent turned back to her computer and the social network website. She was pleased at first to see that Marsans' name came up at least three times as many as hers did, but that quickly changed to dissatisfaction when she realised that that was simply because he was better known in the city than she was.

As Marsans slowly dialled the number he'd been given, Torrent added her own anonymous suggestion that her colleague be the city's next victim.

Chapter Forty

'I thought Puigventós wanted them kept separate,' Àlex said when Elisenda told him how she was going to organise the investigations.

'He does,' she replied. 'And we are. And if anyone says we're doing otherwise, I will teach them a marvellous new trick with a *xuixo*.'

Àlex grinned and changed down to overtake a foreign camper van struggling up an incline. They fell silent again and Elisenda watched the countryside slip by in a blur out of the passenger window. They had already skirted the lake at Banyoles and were taking the minor road to Santa Pau and the address given to Pau by Mossèn Arnau, climbing almost imperceptibly through the lush pastures and dense beech woods of the volcanic Garrotxa region. It really was very beautiful and bucolic, Elisenda thought. She was already missing the city.

'This is so green,' Àlex suddenly commented in awe, echoing her thoughts.

'Is that a good thing?'

'In small doses,' he finally decided, 'but you wouldn't want to live with it.'

'You're from Barcelona. You have an ambivalent relationship with scenery.'

'I ran into Senyor Casademont's son over the weekend,' Àlex told her. 'They'd been in Begur. The family has a house there. He says he and his wife took his mother with them to give her some time away.'

Elisenda sighed. 'I know the Casademont shop. We used to buy things there when I was a kid. You liked Senyor Casademont, didn't you?'

'Yes, I did. He'd worked hard all his life. I object to scum like Chema GM taking everything away from him. And I like his son, too. He's just an ordinary, honourable man who shouldn't have to cope with his father dying the way he did.'

'Do you get the feeling that whoever's doing all this is someone ordinary? Honourable even. Someone we don't want it to be.'

'You're not saying it's Casademont's son?'

'No, but it's not necessarily going to be a Daniel Masó or a Chema GM either. Or a Joaquim Masó.' Elisenda told Àlex about her conversation with Pijaume and about the incident with the dog that she and Catalina had witnessed. 'He asked me where I drew the line and I had to question what I thought. Everyone crossing the road that evening wanted someone else to have a go at the guy who hit his dog.'

Àlex shrugged. 'Why for a dog?'

'You're not sentimental about animals, are you?'

'No animal is as important as a human, if that's what you're asking. If he'd hit another person, maybe someone would have done something about it.'

'Maybe, maybe not. It's one thing to be outraged, it's another to do something about it. And who's to say you're right if you did do something? What would you have done in those circumstances? Hit him?'

'I don't know.'

'And if he'd emptied his ashtray on to the pavement? Would you have emptied a rubbish bin over his car?'

'No.'

'And would you applaud if someone else did it?'

Àlex glanced sideways at her. 'Probably.'

'So might I. Once. So, ultimately, we're saying we'd accept someone else doing what we wouldn't do.'

'These are all hypothetical, Elisenda.'

'Not any more. Not with what's happening in the city. What about a critic? Would we humiliate a critic?'

'Possibly.'

'But we wouldn't kill one. It becomes a question of degree. You can humiliate someone who deserves to be humiliated, but only up to a certain point. Punish someone who deserves to be punished. But only up to a certain point.'

'That's why we exist, Elisenda, the Mossos. And the courts and the prisons and the legal system.'

'Precisely. We get someone else to do it for us. That's what society is. The problem is that now someone else is deciding how it's done and who it's done to. Someone outside that society. And it questions everything we think we believe.'

'Viladrau,' Àlex said. 'We both know we find him reprehensible. Deep down, we would have welcomed his being found out.'

'Yes, but not his being killed. They're guilty, they should be brought to justice. They shouldn't be victims of another crime.'

'I agree with you, Elisenda.'

She sighed. 'Do you? I don't even know if I agree with myself anymore.'

'We all know where we draw the line.'

'I'm not sure we do. Not anymore. This person is challenging that. The problem is I have the feeling they're going to challenge it a great deal more before this is all over.'

She looked at the road ahead.

'You need to slow down here and start looking for a parking place. You can't take cars into the village unless you're a resident. We don't want to drive in and have to explain what we're doing.'

Àlex found a space to park on a road curling down along the side of the small valley. The village was a short walk through narrow streets over on the opposite slope. They crossed on foot and turned left, in among the brightly flowered balconies crowning the shaded porticoed arches of the main square. In a dark doorway, an elderly man in a black beret sat smoking a cigar on an ancient straight-backed chair, a grey-whiskered dog lying quietly at his feet. Àlex greeted him but he simply stared back at them. A party of green and brown hikers emerged wearily from the village shop-cum-café, wordlessly unwrapping huge baguette sandwiches. The crumbling castle loured silently over them all.

Elisenda led Àlex along a winding lane until she found a small doorway in among a row of narrow homes huddled together in the shadow of the steep stone fortress. The door itself was old but not original, going by its neighbours. No doubt salvaged from a grander building, Elisenda thought, looking at the fine tracery of the wrought-iron grille set into the dark and aged wood. It had the air of an expensive renovation.

Elisenda was about to use the imposing metal knocker in the shape of a hand clenching a ball when the door opened and a woman in a nylon housecoat came out carrying a bucket of grey, soapy water.

'All right if I go on in, senyora?' Elisenda asked. The woman simply looked at her and nodded before walking out into the middle of the cobbled lane to empty the bucket into a stone drain.

Elisenda glanced at Àlex and pushed the door open fully.

Inside was one large room, as she'd expected, with a stone staircase to the right leading upstairs and a door at the rear to further rooms at the back of the building. She trod lightly on the ornate glazed ceramic floor tiles, some of them brighter than the others, new casts of a traditional design to plug the gaps.

Àlex patted her on the shoulder and pointed to the stairs. She nodded and let him pass, watching him climb slowly. The original steps had been covered with La Bisbal green and yellow tiles and edged with mahogany. Viladrau had obviously not skimped on the details, she decided. She watched him pause for a moment and listen before carrying on his ascent.

There wasn't a sound in the house.

Moving quietly through the downstairs room, which was dark and furnished sparsely but expensively with a mahogany coffee table and two brown leather armchairs, she began crossing it towards the door at the rear. The room would have been where the animals were kept in times gone by and was now used as a cool atrium in the summer months. She shivered. The temperature was considerably lower than outside.

Silently, she turned the handle on the door and opened it slowly into a kitchen. Despite herself, she let out a low whistle. Everything in the kitchen was new, yet designed to look original in a way that original had never been in this sort of house. Light brown earthenware floor tiles, a central cooking island of ceramic and walnut with a double oven and eight gas rings, walnut cabinets around the walls. A Serrano ham hung from a small hook in the ceiling, the flesh a rich crimson where slices had been carved from it. The end of a baguette was sticking out of an old-fashioned cotton bread bag hanging on a hook. She felt it. A day old at most, the white flesh where a generous chunk had been ripped off still white and springy. Two plates, both used, stood next to the sink. A fine-stemmed wine glass stood alongside them, red flakes of dried wine peeling off inside the bottom of the bowl like sunburnt skin. An empty bottle of Vega Sicilia stood next to it. Vega Sicilia, she thought. Enough to feed all the beggars scrabbling for the faithful's change outside any church in the country for a week. It was a kitchen of firmly terrestrial delights.

Beyond the kitchen, she opened another door and walked quietly in.

A man seated on a deep and faded brown leather sofa turned to look at her.

'Well, isn't this a nice surprise?' she said to him.

Chapter Forty One

'Professor Marsans?' the young plain-clothes policeman greeted him affably in the foyer to the Mossos d'Esquadra station in Vista Alegre. 'Thank you for coming.'

'Um, delighted,' Marsans replied. He had steeled himself over a *café amb gel* in the bar on the corner before walking through the glass doors into the police station, but he hadn't let the ice melt properly in the thick black coffee and it was sitting heavily in his stomach. Killing time in the bar, he hadn't known what to expect but he had to admit, it wasn't this educated cordiality. Like all his contemporaries, he'd distrusted the old Spanish police since his days of student demos and sit-ins, a distrust that had deepened throughout his adult life of staff room politics and posturing, and the Mossos had done little or nothing to change that attitude as far as he was concerned.

'My name is Caporal Pau Yáñez,' the policeman in front of him continued, 'and I'm a member of the Serious Crime Unit. Would you be so kind as to follow me?'

Mystified, Marsans followed the quietly-spoken officer out of the reception area and along a corridor. The policeman stopped in front of a door and ushered Marsans in.

'I'm afraid we're going to have to use an interview room,' Pau told him, 'but it will be comfortable enough.'

Marsans went into the room and sat down on a straight-backed chair at the table in the centre of the room. Pau took another chair and placed it at the end of the table at a right-angle to Marsans. He placed a folder he'd been carrying, unopened, in front of him.

Marsans stared at it. 'May I ask what this is all about?'

The policeman looked taken aback. 'You have spoken to my superior?' he asked. 'Sotsinspectora Domènech?'

'I haven't spoken to anyone. I rang as I was asked, but there was no one available to take my call. I was simply asked to come here to meet you.'

Marsans looked on in surprise as the policeman shook his head and sighed.

'I'm terribly sorry, Professor Marsans. There's evidently been a mix-up. It's entirely our fault. You were supposed to be put through to either Sotsinspectora Domènech or me. I really cannot apologise enough.'

Marsans fluttered his fine fingers nervously.

'I should explain,' Pau continued, gathering his thoughts. 'I've no doubt you're aware of these unusual events that have been occurring in the city over the last few weeks. With Mònica Ferrer and Mossèn Viladrau.'

'Yes, of course,' Marsans replied cautiously. He was finding the room rather stuffy.

'Okay, first of all, I have to ask you to take everything I'm going to say to you now in the strictest confidence. These are police matters and they must be kept entirely out of the public domain. I'm afraid we would have to ask you to sign a written undertaking not to disclose anything of what we discuss.'

Marsans hesitated before replying. 'I imagine that would be all right, Caporal...'

'Yáñez,' Pau reminded him. Pau turned his gaze away for a moment and placed his hand on the folder, sliding it over to the space between them. 'Anyway, Mònica Ferrer and Mossèn Viladrau. We have noticed some correlation between what happened to them and certain traditional stories related to the city.'

'Go on,' Marsans said, leaning forward slightly.

'In the case of Mossèn Viladrau, as you might know, he was found underneath the arches on the Rambla.' Pau pulled a photo of the Vampir out of the folder. 'We see a connection with this.'

Marsans considered it. 'In what way a connection?'

'I take it you'll know the local legend that you reveal your love under the Vampir.' Pau explained a little about what was on the DVD, leaving out the story of the young woman dying after the abortion, and described how the priest was found near the carving of the Vampir de la Rambla.

'Declaring love,' Marsans muttered slowly, unsure.

'Declaring love in a very perverse sense. The idea of love being discovered.'

Marsans thought for a moment. 'It's a little tenuous, but I suppose it could be construed as that.'

Pau pulled some more papers out of the folder. 'I take it you're aware of Mònica Ferrer's murder?'

'Poor Mònica.'

'And you've seen the photos on the internet?'

Marsans said that he hadn't, so Pau showed him the picture of the critic propped up among the rotten food in the market stand. 'We see this as reflecting the legend of the Majordoma.'

Marsans looked at the photo and considered. 'Yes, I see how this would match the story. Rotten food was supposedly thrown at the Majordoma because she was rather arrogant.'

'We know it's a modern legend, Professor. Newly-created. We were hoping you would know if that was significant.'

Marsans looked uncertain. 'Not that I'm aware.'

Pau pulled a typed sheet of paper out of the folder and placed it in front of the lecturer. 'I'll just let you read this.'

Marsans read the report on the four muggers and how each one had been drugged and then left at a specific location. The report then went on to explain how the spot where the men were found tied in with the Bou d'Or legend.

'It's only one of the versions of the legend,' Pau said, repeating what was written on the paper, 'but it does fit.'

Marsans put the piece of paper back down on the table. 'I hadn't realised the full extent of this. I remember that one of them died, but I didn't realise the rest of it.'

'We've been trying to keep it out of the papers, which is why it really is very important that you don't disclose any of this.'

The professor tapped the piece of paper. 'This is very good research. Very thorough. But why are you showing me?'

Pau patted the papers and photos into a neat stack and considered his answer. 'It's one thing that we recognise the link between these incidents and local legends and statues, but what we don't know is how to anticipate what the perpetrator might do next. I asked Sotsinspectora Domènech, my superior, if I could approach you as this is your area of expertise. We want to know if you can see more of a link than we can. If there appears to be any sequence to the incidents. Basically, so we can attempt to predict the attacker's next move.'

Marsans took the papers from Pau's hand and laid them out in order. His voice was more confident. 'Of course, these are legends and carvings about which we know very little. There's no way we could determine any chronology with them. As you say, the Bou d'Or legend has constantly been updated and changed, primarily by word of mouth, so we don't really know the exact source, age or meaning. And the origin of the vampire carving is largely unknown, let alone its original sense. While the Majordoma legend is of very recent creation.'

'I appreciate it's difficult for you to see a link here and now, but we'd be very grateful if you could consider what I've shown you in case more of a connection does occur to you. We really do need to try and find some way of predicting what to expect next.'

'I will,' Marsans said, 'but initially, I must say I don't see that it's going to be possible to map out any timeline given the nature of the use of legends and carvings. I don't know how much help I'll be.'

Pau appeared to be taking a decision for a moment and then took another series of papers and photos out of the folder. Marsans looked at him quizzically.

'There may be more.' Pau showed a photo of Daniel Masó hanging from the balcony. 'We think this might have been the first incident.'

Marsans studied the picture and asked what the link was.

'He was found near Carrer Ciutadans with his nose cut off.'

Marsans looked up at Pau. 'En Banyeta.'

'That's what we thought.'

Chapter Forty Two

Elisenda looked out of the French windows at a peaceful view across a shaded garden of beech and holm oak towards the volcanic mountains in the distance. Through the door the other side of the kitchen, the rest of the downstairs in the house in Santa Pau had proved to be an expansive living and dining room, with more new but classical leather and mahogany and a wide picture window overlooking the valley.

She sighed and turned back to the man seated on a dark brown sofa.

'We knew to expect you, Sotsinspectora Domènech,' the man told her.

Alex walked quietly into the room and was as surprised as Elisenda had been to see the man waiting for them

'Ah, Sergent Albiol,' Gerard Bellsolà continued. 'Find anything on your illegal search upstairs?'

'We smelt burning,' Elisenda commented, shrugging the lawyer off. 'How did you know to expect us?'

Bellsolà didn't answer her question. 'I simply waited here to inform you that my client is no longer here...'

'Your client? You find yourself in the oddest of places.'

'...and to inform you that you can expect to receive an official complaint for your harassment of my client.'

'Or doing our duty as police officers by interviewing the next-of-kin of a victim of a crime to attempt to stop any further attacks, as I prefer to call it.'

'I'd like you to leave now, Sotsinspectora.' Bellsolà got up from the sofa and picked up his briefcase from the huge coffee table in front of it.

'I will find out who this woman is,' Elisenda told him. 'To protect her and her son.'

'Good day, Sotsinspectora.' Bellsolà waited until Elisenda and Àlex had begun to leave and followed them out, locking the door.

Àlex glowered as the lawyer scuttled off along the cobbles and muttered to Elisenda. 'This is a bizarre case, when a victim's family is as reluctant to be found as the perpetrator.'

Elisenda watched Bellsolà disappear towards the small village square. 'Is it her that doesn't want to be found, though? It seems a lot of people are reluctant for us to do our job properly.'

–

The drive back to Girona after the failed attempt to find the woman in the DVD had lost much of its pastoral charm. Àlex's mobile was in the coin tray between the two front seats and started ringing, the vibration sending it skittering around the smooth plastic hollow, breaking the silence.

In the passenger seat, Elisenda picked up the phone and looked at the caller ID. Laura Puigmal. 'Hi, Laura, it's Elisenda,' she answered. She looked across at Àlex, staring at the road ahead. 'No, sorry, he's driving at the moment. Can I help?' She listened for a moment before speaking again, her face steadily more serious. 'Thanks for letting us know, Laura. I'll tell him now.' She hung up and replaced the phone in the coin tray.

'What is it?' Àlex asked.

'You aren't going to be pleased.' She paused while he over-took a small flatbed lorry carrying twisted skeins of rusting scrap metal. 'The three muggers that are left were all released on bail this morning.'

Àlex was silent for a moment. When he spoke, his voice was surprisingly calm. 'And we wonder why someone's taking the law into their own hands.'

Elisenda didn't have the energy to reply to that.

'Do you ever get the feeling we're making it all up as we go along?'

Àlex took his eyes off the road for a moment to glance at her. 'Because we're a new police force, you mean? To all intents and purposes, anyway.'

'We're having to create everything anew.'

'And that's a bad thing? Look at what came before us. We can't do much worse.'

Elisenda nodded slowly and sat in silence for a moment, staring at the white lines in the middle of the road being engulfed by the car's steady pace.

'Did Josep find out any more from the muggers?' Àlex asked after a few minutes.

'Nothing. They reckon they didn't see a thing. One of them didn't even react when Josep asked him about the white van. He hadn't even noticed it.'

Elisenda's mobile rang this time and she picked it up from next to Àlex's in the coin tray. Pau's name was displayed on the screen.

'Got some news for me, Pau?' Elisenda asked him, switching the phone to loudspeaker.

'*The white van, Sotsinspectora, it's only just come up now because it wasn't reported stolen until after the weekend. I'd been looking for incidents before the day of the attack on the muggers and the owner claims he hadn't realised it was missing until Seguretat Ciutadana told him it had been found.*'

'Where was it found?'

'*Out past Salt, on a piece of land after the motorway flyover. Completely burnt out. One thing, Sotsinspectora, the owner's Joaquim Masó.*'

'Joaquim Masó?' Elisenda repeated, stunned. 'Good work, Pau,' she added and hung up.

She looked at the green-blue sheen of the lake in Banyoles coming into view ahead of them. 'Welcome back into the fold.'

Pau had more news for them when they got back to Vista Alegre.

But first Elisenda asked him to pay a visit to Mossèn Arnau, the priest who'd given them the address of the house in the mountains.

'Bellsolà knew we were on our way,' she explained. 'I want to know how. See what you can find out from Arnau.'

Pau then showed them an e-mail from Octavi Marsans, in which the lecturer both wholeheartedly and evidentially endorsed their legends theory.

'Excellent,' commented Elisenda, flicking through the pages and pages of notes the lecturer had sent to them.

'I did mention Daniel Masó as well,' Pau told her, a little nervously. 'About the way he was staged.'

'What did Marsans say?'

'It's all there in his report,' Pau said, gesturing at the papers. 'He agrees with us. What he doesn't do is give any indication of who the next victim might be or even what legend might be used next. He said it was impossible to predict given the uncertain backgrounds of the stories and the different interpretations that there are of them.'

'Pity,' Elisenda muttered, 'but not surprising. I've been thinking of all the legends and I really can't find any order of any sort.'

'There's really no way to narrow them down?' Àlex asked.

Elisenda shook her head. 'This is Girona. He's not going to run out of material any day soon.'

She and Pau looked at each other, aware of the implications of what she was saying.

Pau turned to face Àlex and started listing them for his benefit. 'El Tarlà, the jester who entertained the people during the plague. Hanging by his arms over the streets. The lioness's arse. Kiss it and you return to Girona. The witch on the cathedral walls. Turned to stone because she threw pebbles at religious processions. Charlemagne's sword. Charlemagne's chair. The snake at Pericot fountain. The flies from Sant Narcís's tomb. Shall I carry on?'

'No,' Àlex told him. 'Please.'

Elisenda stared at Pau. 'Sant Narcís's tomb. The next major event is Sant Narcís's Day. That's it. That's the next victim. He won't let an opportunity like that go by.'

Pau looked straight back at her and began to nod slowly in agreement.

'Why?' Àlex asked her. 'What's the legend?'

'One of the times the city was laid siege by the French. A swarm of flies is supposed to have come out of the saint's tomb in the cathedral and driven the French away. That's why he's the city's patron saint. With the Sant Narcís festivities coming up, it has to be the next attack.'

'So who would the victim be? Someone French?'

'Someone our man thinks is besieging the city,' Elisenda replied. 'A tourist?'

Pau looked at them both. 'Or an immigrant?'

Elisenda closed her eyes and swore. 'Please not that.'

'You have to go to Puigventós with this,' Àlex told her. 'But you'll never convince him.'

Elisenda picked up Marsans' notes. 'At least I can take this to him. Give him some reasons why we think another attack's going to coincide with Sant Narcís. And argue our corner to have Masó included in the investigation.'

Pau and Àlex shared a glance as Elisenda made to leave the room to see Puigventós.

'There's just one other problem,' she added. 'Sant Narcís's Day lasts ten days.'

–

'Do you have any idea what you're asking, Elisenda?' Puigventós complained once she'd finished relating the theory of the legends and the credence that Professor Marsans had given to it and explained how she felt that there would be an attack to coincide with the saint's festival. She hadn't yet mentioned anything about Masó. 'We're talking mobilising all the Seguretat Ciutadana, the other criminal investigation units, cancelling all leave, back-up from the regional support unit. For ten days. Right across the city. And all without panicking the public.' He shook his head and stared out of the window. 'On the basis of a few fairy tales.'

'I think the attack's likely to be either on Sant Narcís's Day, the evening before or the day after. Those are the three key dates. We really need to concentrate our efforts on those three days. That's all.'

Puigventós gave her a bleak look. 'That's all?' He skimmed through Marsans' notes again. 'If this goes wrong, Elisenda, you will make us a laughing stock.'

'I know that, Xavier.'

He stared directly at her for what seemed an age. 'Yes,' he finally consented. 'But I will add that I'm not entirely happy you've brought in help from this Professor. It's not at all standard practice. I hope you can trust him.'

'There's one other thing. We showed some of the details of the Masó case to Professor Marsans. Like us, he saw a connection between the murder and a local legend.'

Puigventós sighed. 'Please, Elisenda.'

'I still feel it ties in. I firmly believe we're looking for the same perpetrator. The similarities and the arguments are too strong for it not to be linked.'

'Look, Elisenda, I really have to disagree with you on this. We can't start seeing serial killers in every crime that happens in Girona. Things are bad enough without seeing mass murderers in the streets.' The inspector considered her. Disconcerted by his gaze, Elisenda finally realised that it was simply a case that Puigventós just didn't want to contemplate the idea of any form of serial murders in the city for fear of the panic, the press and the scrutiny. And for his own career, the thought occurred to her. Far easier to have a series of isolated murders than the thought of someone who was prepared to kill targeting individuals in a cold and systematic way. And all the political fallout that that would entail.

'If you do believe this is the case,' Puigventós continued, 'which I personally do not for one moment think is so, then I feel it would call for greater help and co-ordination between units. Or even from outside. I am coming under increased pressure to consider other alternatives in tackling these murders, Elisenda. Sotsinspector Micaló has his friends.'

He looked closely at her. She resisted closing her eyes and sighing.

'My unit doesn't need any help from outside,' she breathed.

'I agree. So the Masó investigation remains with Sotsinspector Micaló's team and I will sanction all that you need for Sant Narcís's Day.' He shuffled some papers on his desk, telling her the discussion was closed. 'Within reason.'

Chapter Forty Three

The hooded figures ran from the white fire.

Sparks from the flame spattered their backs, guttering from life on their bowed heads, raining on the hard cobbles in front of them. A further flame erupted, balling up into the sky and lighting the ancient university building before folding up into itself, casting the stern walls into a brief cavernous dark. A new burst broke the respite of the night and threw raging shadows over the buildings and faces, each one looking on at the man in the middle.

Two giant wheels. Connected by a crossbar. Flames briefly licking at the wooden spokes and steel rim, fire spitting out from them. The noise deafening. Metal scarring stone, sparks crackling clothes, hoarse voices raised.

And the man in the middle.

One of the hooded figures looked up, his face shining in the night flare, the white skull glinting. A young girl looked up at him and put her hand to her mouth. Taking it away again, she quickly looked at her brother, younger than her. His eyes were wide open. She laughed.

The boy in the hood pulled his skull mask down to take a drink of water from a plastic bottle and slapped one of the other figures on the back before running back towards the flames.

Elisenda watched it all.

The *correfoc*. The fire run. At the end of Sant Narcís's Day. Fireworks and flames dancing through the streets to frighten the families and taunt the teenagers. The man in the middle of the wheels controlling them, turning it this way and that to push the crowds back. His helpers, dressed as demons, cavorting through the throng, pulling people in, keeping them out.

Elisenda looked around at the laughing people, the university square filled with grandparents and toddlers, parents and youths.

It was the worst Sant Narcís holiday she could remember.

She began down the steps leading away from the square, the noise barely receding behind her, latecomers rushing up in front of her.

She rang Pijaume at Vista Alegre, there to co-ordinate all the Mossos who'd lost their time off for the festivities, all the ones drafted in, all the ones Elisenda had seen in the city throughout the day. All the ones who were there because of her.

Pijaume told her again that nothing had happened. Not even a false alarm.

She hung up. So much of her wanted that to carry on. For nothing to happen. And another part of her was shocked to realise that she was afraid nothing would happen. Because of all the problems that would cause her.

She sighed and called Àlex.

'Where are you?' she asked him.

'*At the old fogeys' dance. Nothing.*'

It really had been the worst Sant Narcís she could remember.

The briefing of the evening before, a little more than twenty-four hours ago, and then again that morning. The faces of the Mossos in front of her increasingly hostile, increasingly sceptical.

Through the day, she'd roamed the city, watching the festivities from outside the glass, listening to the scantly concealed triumphalism of the other units when she spoke to them at the craft markets, the museums and the puppet shows.

'It's worse than trying to find a needle in a haystack,' one uniformed caporal told her at the foot of Carrer de la Força as they watched a walking tour go by, the earnest guide describing the city's past persecutions of its Jewish community to the new people of the city. 'We don't know who or what we're looking for.'

'Just being here is helping prevent anything from happening,' Elisenda encouraged him, trying to convince herself.

She met Josep and Montse at the archaeology museum, Josep watching the visitors shuffling in and out, making the most of the open doors day, Montse leaving to check out the cathedral and Sant Narcís's tomb again.

'I almost wish something would happen, Sotsinspectora,' Josep whispered to her as they watched two elderly couples slowly organise themselves in through the museum doors. 'I know I don't mean that, but we're coming in for a lot of stick from the other Mossos.'

Elisenda knew what he meant.

She'd just come across Micaló on Plaça Independència.

'I'm surprised to see you here,' she'd told him.

Micaló looked about him before answering in a low voice. 'I wouldn't miss this for the world, Domènech. Watching your career crumble in front of your eyes. You're a dead woman walking.'

He'd hurried off before she'd had a chance to reply. She wasn't sure she could even have been bothered.

'We'll see,' she murmured, more to herself than to his retreating back.

She left Josep and headed for the Rambla, criss-crossing the bridge between the old and new towns, watching and listening. Pau joined her in the Jardins de la Francesa, checking the exterior of the cathedral, dodging the mood of the festive strollers, before he carried on along the city walls and she went back down to the cathedral steps. At the bottom, she looked up at the Verge de la Bona Mort statue over the mediaeval gateway.

'Always gives me the creeps,' a voice rasped behind her. 'Blessing the condemned.'

She turned to see Joaquim Masó staring up at the statue with her.

'You just have to live a blameless life, then.'

Masó adjusted a thick gold bracelet on his heavy wrist. It looked new. 'No complaints about my life right now. Out enjoying my city.'

'Your city?'

'Before all the darkies take it over. Already too many in Salt.'

'I could arrest you for that. Odd your family didn't include you in the alibi when Daniel was killed.'

'They didn't think they had to. Not then. I wasn't part of the business.'

'And now?'

He grinned wolfishly at her and walked silently away towards Carrer de la Força. Elisenda watched him go.

'So you're the future,' she muttered.

When night fell, she made her way with what seemed like everyone else in Girona to the funfair in the Devesa park, the raucous lights and sounds of the rides and stands and sideshows funnelling up through the tall plane trees and bouncing back down again. She checked her phone constantly and nodded at all the pairs of Mossos she saw patrolling the edges and the heart of the fair until it was time to follow the *correfoc* through the streets of the old town.

Now the fireworks were over and she was walking down the steps from the university square, heading for the *barraques*, the open-air rock concerts on the square at the northern entrance to the city, played out before a horseshoe of beer stands and annual wildness.

Àlex called and told her where he'd meet her.

'I used to love the *barraques* when I was a teenager,' she shouted in his ear above the din when they met up.

Àlex looked at the groups around him, drinking beer from plastic cups and listening to the band on stage. 'It's good. This is my first Sant Narcís.'

'I'm sorry it's like this.'

He gently nudged her shoulder with his. 'Don't be. We're doing the right thing.'

'I saw Joaquim Masó earlier today. He's going up in the world. Check up on him, find out more about this van thing. Personally, I think he'd be too streetwise to use his own van, but we need to follow it up.'

'Unless it was a hurried job. Retaliation for Daniel. Or marking out his territory.'

Elisenda had to shout louder as a new song started up on stage. 'Or distraction. His or ours.'

It was past three in the morning when Elisenda finally gave up and headed for home. Night patrols would be out, but she had a feeling nothing would happen now. Àlex had already left to hook up with a Seguretat Ciutadana car roaming the streets of the new town. They parted, both knowing the fallout the next day would bring.

Crossing the river, she walked up Carrer de la Força to the cathedral, not yet ready for home. An incipient headache did its best to push its way through her temples. In front of the cathedral, at the top of the steps, she counted more Mossos than revellers. Just two couples sitting on the stone wall opposite the front doors laughing in low tones and a group of teenagers talking quietly.

Elisenda said goodnight to one of the pairs of Mossos and headed back down the road sloping past the cathedral steps to the square in front of the Audiència Provincial law courts and out under the Portal de Sobreportes.

The other side of the arch, she heard a child's voice. A girl. Singing the same song she'd heard in Monells the other day. She looked around but could see no one. The few flats there were all shut up, no lights on, the window shutters down.

She thought the singing was coming from ahead. From Carrer Rei Martí, the narrow lane that fell steeply to Sant Pere de Galligants, where she'd spoken to Josep in front of the archaeology museum so many hours earlier. Her flat was down to the left, but she carried straight on, through the high stone walls of the dark street. The child's voice seemed constantly to move away from her and she quickened her pace to try to catch it, quickly becoming engulfed in the black shadows of the ancient buildings that closed in on either side of her on her descent through the medieval darkness.

The singing stopped for a moment and she froze, listening.

It started up again, faintly, borne on the wind. She couldn't tell if it was from in front of her or from behind. From above or below. Other sounds rustled and scratched around her, confusing her. Turning, she went back the way she'd come, back to the little crossroads by Portal de Sobreportes, led by the singing until it suddenly stopped again. Finally, this time.

Leaning against the cold stone walls, she tried to hear it one more time, but it was no longer there. She felt a tear run down her cheek for the first time in years and she bowed forward, what little she'd eaten all day thrusting bitterly back up through her throat and mouth and nose.

Chapter Forty Four

'Look at me, papa.'

His daughter needn't have called out to him. Foday Saio hadn't taken his eyes off her for one moment. He watched her run down the grass bank at the edge of the little park outside the city walls.

'Did you see, papa?' Her voice was breathless with fun when she ran back to him.

'I saw you, Patricia.'

He put his arms around her and kissed her lightly on the cheek.

She ran off again to play with a boy and a girl, the boy older than Patricia's four years, the girl about the same age. Joining in the peals of laughter in perfect Catalan. He wondered at his daughter. Her Catalan so much better than his or her mother's. Theirs was fluent, but they still sounded foreign. Foday more so than Isata as she was able to work and so mixed with people more. She had two jobs. One at the Hospital Doctor Trueta, where she worked evenings as a cleaner, the other early in the morning, cleaning a factory near their home in Salt. She was always tired. Foday was always restless.

'That's not how you say it, papa,' Patricia would correct her father when he spoke Catalan. He always thought it strange that his four-year-old daughter should be teaching him so much, not the other way around, as it should be. But she'd been born here. Had started nursery, then school, here. Catalan more natural to her than her parents' Mende. More use to her in her life here. Her parents' old life in Sierra Leone over for good.

Out of the corner of his eye, Foday saw the other two children's parents staring at him. They half-smiled at him when he looked over and quickly turned away, embarrassed. He knew it wasn't his colour they were staring at. It was his arms. He slowly slipped them both between his knees and hung them down in front of him, hidden by his thighs where he sat.

'Look at me, papa,' Patricia called again. He looked up at her and smiled. He didn't wave.

At the end of each arm was a stump. The hands amputated, the wounds still ragged. Not cleanly removed, but hacked, chopped off by the men who had come to his village one day when he was barely ten and killed his parents and his older brother. The civil war was long over but he knew they'd never go back. He felt safe now. At least he had felt safe. Lately, he always felt like someone was watching him. He felt it now but could see no one.

The other children's parents were joined by an older couple. The grandparents. Patricia was just beginning to question the idea of grandparents. It was something she couldn't understand. She found it funny. The four adults smiled at Foday as they slowly walked past, the children running in and out of the grown-ups. He smiled back.

'How far away's the funfair?' he heard the boy ask.

'Not far,' the grandfather replied.

Foday stayed seated. He couldn't afford to take Patricia to the funfair, so they now had the little park to themselves, except for some teenagers who were draped over a bench on the other side of the gardens, engrossed in their own hormones. It was the day after Sant Narcís's Day, but all the schools were closed for the week and many people had finished work after lunch.

He sensed rather than saw a movement behind him, but when he looked over his shoulder in the direction of the gateway through the city walls, there was nothing there. He looked the other way, towards the trees, but saw no one.

He turned back. Standing on the ground behind him was a green bottle with no label. The sort you take to the old-fashioned bodegas and get filled up with cheap wine from a barrel and then topped with a plastic stopper.

He looked at the bottle and turned towards it.

Chapter Forty Five

'This is not the usual sort of perpetrator. It's cold, it's calculating and it's a reaction to whatever wrongs this person imagines they see. This is someone we wouldn't imagine doing these things, someone doing things that are completely out of character. And that's why we have to try and predict what they're going to do next, because we're not going to catch them any other way.'

Elisenda had spent the last ten minutes in silence, soaking up Inspector Puigventós' channelled frustration and the pressure that he was under, and she had no intention of surrendering the floor back to him until she'd said what she wanted to say.

The afternoon of the day after Sant Narcís's Day and nothing had happened. No attacks, no rituals, no humiliations. With the exception, perhaps, of Elisenda's as she walked the long corridors from her office to Puigventós' room. Past the scornful looks of the Mossos who'd lost time off. Past the smug, open door into Micaló's office. Past the sympathetic looks of her own unit.

Pijaume had stopped her in the corridor. 'I'm sorry, Elisenda,' he'd told her.

'Thank you, Narcís.'

'If you're not going to catch them any other way, Sotsinspectora Domènech,' Puigventós came back at her, the anger still present in his voice, 'perhaps you should consider relinquishing the investigation to a more experienced officer. Someone who will make an arrest.'

'This is not about making arrests, Inspector.' The tension of the last two days was simmering behind her eyes. 'This is about putting an end to the attacks. We can't just trawl in known criminals or people close to the victims. You might as well throw twenty names in the air and arrest the first one that hits the floor. There's much more to this.'

'You're saying it's not a criminal?'

'It could be. It could be you or me.'

Puigventós was not satisfied with that. 'Weeks, Elisenda. These attacks have been going on for weeks, and you don't have one arrest to show for it.'

'I know they've been going on for weeks. I am the one that's been telling you they've been going on for weeks. But I've been obstructed from the word go by the reluctance of everyone around me to see that the Masó attack is part of this. The attack on the four muggers was originally assigned to another team, Jutgessa Roca has been obstructive every step of the way and Gerard Bellsolà always seems to know where I'm going to be next.'

She sat back heavily, as too did Puigventós, his own tiredness evident.

'I believe in your unit, Elisenda,' he finally said with a deep sigh. 'And I have faith in you, in your abilities. But we need an arrest. The chain of command needs an arrest. I am coming under pressure, and the way the investigation has been handled over these last two days has not sat well.'

'I simply repeat what I said before. I am not going to make an arrest for the gallery, and the only way we're going to end these attacks is by looking at what exactly this person is trying to say and anticipating an attack by them.'

'I don't know, Elisenda. I can only protect you for so long.'

Elisenda nodded her head slowly. 'I didn't realise I needed protecting.'

'There's been a complaint. By Gerard Bellsolà, for harassment.'

'Harassment? Trying to question someone who's so reluctant to speak to me, she or the church calls in a lawyer?'

Someone knocked on the door and opened it before Puigventós had a chance to tell them to go away.

It was Montse.

'I'm sorry to disturb you, Inspector Puigventós.' She turned to Elisenda. 'Sotsinspectora, there's been an incident.'

Chapter Forty Six

'Why teenagers?'

Elisenda and Àlex watched as a Científica team went centimetre by centimetre over the fine dust of the little Fora-muralles park in the shade of the city walls, barely ten minutes' walk from Vista Alegre. Seguretat Ciutadana had already strung up tape around the trees and benches to keep out a growing throng of spectators.

Pau was standing a short distance away from Elisenda and Àlex, near a bench next to which eight teenagers were laid out on the ground in thermal blankets. All eight were awake and looking around, dazed, evidently not knowing what was going on. Albert Riera and his assistant were slowly examining each one.

'I take it the Sant Narcís legend doesn't contemplate teenagers,' Àlex commented, trying to lighten her mood.

'Does anyone?' Elisenda dug the toe of her shoe under the fine coffee earth and shook her head. 'All we can do is try to predict where this person will go next.'

'We predicted this one. We know what type of victim he's going for. People he thinks have it coming.'

'And who half Girona thinks have it coming.'

'Teenagers?'

'Plenty of people who are scared of them,' Elisenda considered. 'But I don't see where it fits in with Sant Narcís.'

A sergent in the Científica came over to them, holding something in his hand. All Elisenda could see of him under his white suit was dark brown eyes and an uneven, straggly moustache that made him look rather sleepy. She recognised him, though, and knew he was anything but.

'We found this next to the bench where most of the victims were found, Sotsinspectora.' He held up a plastic evidence bag with an empty wine bottle in it.

'How soon can you let me know what was in it?'

The sergent shrugged, the white suit crinkling. 'It's Sant Narcís. Skeleton staff at the lab. I'll hurry it through, though.' He was not one of the Mossos who'd lost his day off thanks to Elisenda.

Àlex watched him walk off. 'What's Pijaume doing about the drugs?'

'Very little as far as I can see.' Elisenda rang Pijaume's number but hung up when she got no reply. 'Voicemail again.'

Standing by Riera and his assistant, Pau called them over. A Seguretat Ciutadana caporal was standing next to him.

Riera turned at the sound of Elisenda and Àlex walking over. 'Sotsinspectora,' he acknowledged her. He turned back to the figure lying bewildered in front of him. 'Kindly keep the fucking noise down.'

'This is Caporal Vinyamata,' Pau introduced the uniformed Mosso. 'She was first on the scene when the call came in.'

Elisenda greeted Vinyamata and asked her what had happened.

'A phone call from one of the victims, Sotsinspectora, on her mobile. Saying they'd drunk some wine and felt ill.'

'Where did they get the wine?'

'They found it. By the time I arrived, they were all at this end of the park. Two were sitting down, one was on the floor. The others were staggering about.'

All awake, Elisenda thought, the drugs in the wine too diluted to knock all eight of them out.

Àlex looked at the scene. 'Eight victims? How would that have worked?'

She looked thoughtfully at him. 'It doesn't gel, does it?'

Over Vinyamata's shoulder, she could see a man among the crowd of onlookers who appeared to be getting very agitated. He was waving his right arm insistently at them. There was something odd about the way it looked.

'See what that's about, Pau,' she asked her caporal.

Elisenda turned her attention back to Vinyamata as Pau walked over to the man, but she was immediately pulled up by Pau's reaction to something the man said. The caporal looked like he'd been stung. He quickly pulled the tape up to usher the man and a little girl through and signalled Elisenda to come over.

'This gentleman is Foday Saio,' Pau told her. 'He has something I think you should hear.'

Elisenda smiled at Foday and asked him over to a bench, away from the group of teenagers and the hustle of the Científica. The man's daughter held on to him by clutching the edge of his trouser pocket and walking alongside him

'What exactly was it you saw, Foday?' Elisenda asked him once they'd sat down. Pau and Àlex stood nearby with Vinyamata, listening. The little girl was standing between her father's legs, holding on to his knees and staring wide-eyed at Elisenda. Her name was Patricia, Foday told her.

'It was nothing I really saw,' he explained. He spoke good Catalan, but slowly, considering his words. 'I sensed a movement. Behind me.'

'And where were you sitting?'

Instinctively, he pointed with his arm. Elisenda saw that he had no hands. 'Over there. Near the archway. Patricia was playing on the bank and I was watching her.'

'And then what happened?'

'There was a bottle on the ground behind me. Someone must have left it there in a moment. But I don't drink, so I didn't touch it.'

Elisenda looked at Foday and nodded. He was supposed to have been the victim, not the teenagers. Sant Narcís's besiegers.

An immigrant, as Pau had predicted. As she had, too, but hadn't wanted to think it. She couldn't help looking at the ragged ends to his arms and wondering what he'd had to go through before coming to Catalonia. And now this. She asked if she could talk to Patricia and he consented.

'Is this your favourite place, Lina?' she asked the little girl.

'My name's Patricia.'

Elisenda touched the girl's cheek. 'I'm sorry, sweetheart. Of course it is.' She held on to her hand. 'I bet you can see forever from up there, Patricia.'

'I can see over papa's head.'

'What could you see over his head when he was sitting on the bench?'

Patricia thought for a moment before answering. 'A very old man.' She pointed to Pau. 'Like him.'

Elisenda looked up at Pau and smiled at Patricia. 'That's really good, sweetheart.' Pau was in his mid-twenties. 'And how old am I?'

'You're very old.'

Elisenda laughed and squeezed the girl's hand. 'You should always be honest, Patricia.'

Foday looked at Elisenda and half-shrugged. 'Even I'm very old,' he told her.

Elisenda thanked them both. 'You've been extremely helpful. Thanks for coming forward.'

They all stood up and Patricia jumped up into her father's arms. He caught her with his forearms and she slid down and caught hold of the flap of his trouser pocket again. The Mossos watched them go.

'Imagine not being able to hold your own daughter's hand,' Vinyamata said in a low voice.

'Imagine,' Elisenda echoed.

Chapter Forty Seven

Siset hated Sant Narcís.

Everyone spending their money on funfairs and roast chestnuts and junk, so no one was spending their money on his dodgy DVDs.

None of the piss-poor yokels from neighbouring villages he'd never heard of buying his hash.

The city crawling with Mossos. Everywhere you looked. Stifling private enterprise. And no one nicking anything he could buy to sell on because of all the noise and light and fucking people everywhere.

And now he was spitting a tooth out of his burst and swollen mouth.

Gingerly, painfully he looked up. They'd gone. He slowly got to his feet and threw up immediately, spluttering the last bitter remnants of the thick red wine and thin red ham he'd cadged for breakfast down the narrow front of his ripped shirt. The bile stung his throat and tore savagely through his shattered nose and he was sick a second time. Kneeling down again, he steadied himself against a dry, stunted bush and waited until the pain settled down to a calmer, number ache. This wasn't his first time. He knew how to cope.

He couldn't even blame that bitch policewoman Domènech.

He thought at first it was something to do with her. With her making him look like a grass that time. But they didn't say a thing about that.

'You give me sixty per cent of everything you make on your DVDs,' the man had said to him, 'to pay back the money you owe me.'

'I don't owe you anything,' Siset had replied.

It was the last thing he'd said for a while.

When the other two had done, the man came back into his face. 'To pay back the money you owe me,' he repeated, 'because now you owe me.'

'I've never owed you,' Siset said.

Which is when they broke his nose.

'And,' the man went on, 'you buy all hash to sell from me from now on. Clear?' The man kicked him in the knee to make sure it was clear. It was.

A born pragmatist, Siset got to his feet again and looked at the rough track snaking back down the hill to the city. The three men in their car had long gone and he was left with the scrub and the cicadas and the heat. And the pain.

So he had a new business partner, he thought to himself grandly.

He'd never worked with the Masó family before, unless you counted him owing Daniel Masó money ever since he'd overstretched himself with the South American dealers. And even though it now appeared he owed even more money on that debt, perhaps working with Daniel's uncle Joaquim would be a step up, he thought, putting one foot painfully in front of the other along the dirty brown path leading back down the slope to the city.

Chapter Forty Eight

'Welcome to the modern world,' Elisenda muttered.

Àlex grunted and watched as Pau scrolled down through the website.

A tide mark was clearly visible where the news of a bunch of teenagers being found was swept away by the rumours of an immigrant being targeted. Comments about the young of today and their lack of respect and poor dress sense making them welcome victims were steadily superseded by views on what the politicians called 'the new Catalans', the unprecedented mass immigration the country had experienced in the last decade. Some, a minority but at least a sizeable one, criticising a racial attack. A smaller number, at the opposite end of the scale, demanding more savage acts. Appallingly, many more in between not outwardly applauding it but quietly condoning it under a falsely reluctant veil of justification.

'That's what our man is feeding on,' Elisenda commented. 'The pettiness of people who'd describe themselves as normal.'

'And this is the point,' Pau interrupted, 'where word gets out that Foday Saio doesn't have any hands.'

The three of them read silently through the posts. The comments about immigrants being bad enough, why we had to put up with disabled ones. The strain on the health service. The blame for his disability evidently lying at the victim's door. The only thing worse being his willingness to come here and go on the dole. The miserable jokes about having no hands.

'Turn it off,' Àlex told Pau. Elisenda turned to look at him and saw a nerve in his cheek fluttering. She could feel her own face flushing with anger.

'Take your pick, then,' she said. 'What would we prefer our fellow humans to consider suitable targets? Immigrants or the disabled?'

Pau switched to another screen. 'You need to see this, too.'

Pijaume and one of his sergents came into the room and stood and watched with them.

A number of strands had broken off from the main one. Two in particular were of interest. The first was a series of calls for direct action. Half-heartedly criticising the killings, most of the contributors then went on to urge others to take part in actions on the groups being voted for elsewhere on the site.

'A Halal butcher's in Salt was attacked last night,' Pijaume informed them. 'Its windows smashed.'

Elisenda shook her head and turned back to the computer. The second thread was more uplifting. A small band of people calling for each other to protect vulnerable groups from the first bunch. As they read, more contributors added themselves to the list of those wanting to help.

'Some hope, then.'

Elisenda's phone rang and she answered. 'Puigventós,' she mouthed to Àlex and Pau and went into her room, closing the door.

He wanted a meeting. To discuss the racial angle.

'I agree,' Elisenda replied. 'But I'm following something up right now. Can we make it later?'

He agreed and she hung up. She couldn't face another meeting with him. Not right now. She wanted to get the latest attack clear in her own mind before another onslaught from the senior ranks tried to push her this way or that.

Taking another look at the printout of the map of IP addresses that UCDI had sent Pau, she picked the phone up again and got through to Gispert in Sabadell.

'I just wanted to know the latest developments on this website,' she told him. 'I've been looking at the map you sent my caporal.'

'*That's simply a snapshot of the relay at a given moment, Sotsinspectora,*' Gispert explained. '*Whoever this guy is, he knows his stuff. He's using headless fast-flux DNS to hide his trail.*'

'Which means?'

'*Which means that he's swapping the IP addresses about every sixty seconds and that there's no single command centre at the top that we can shut down. The map you can see will change after sixty seconds, then again another sixty seconds later, and so on. It's going to be very hard to stop him, but we will be able to.*'

'How many days will that take?'

'*Days, Sotsinspectora? Try months. Weeks if we get lucky.*'

She asked him to keep Pau informed and hung up. 'He might understand what you're saying,' she muttered.

She heard a knock on her office door. Through the glass panel, she could see a uniformed mosso. She called him in and he entered, nervously fingering a pair of evidence bags in his hand.

'Sotsinspectora Domènech?' he said.

Elisenda looked closely at him. 'Paredes,' she said. 'Francesc.'

Paredes looked relieved she'd recognised him, although he carried on fiddling with the two plastic bags like an elderly lady with an unwieldy handbag. 'Do you have a moment, Sotsinspectora?'

'Take a seat,' she invited him, intrigued.

He sat down, placing the bags on his lap, and paused before speaking.

'I've heard around the station that you were looking at the attacks that have been happening. About how they're supposed to be similar to some of the city's myths.'

'Go on.'

'Well, perhaps it's nothing, Sotsinspectora, but there have been a couple of incidents that I don't know if you've heard of. Involving the Verge de la Bona Mort. The little statue up above Sobreportes.' Paredes opened one of the bags on his lap and took out a doll. 'I found this hanging from the Verge on my morning shift a short while ago.'

He handed the doll over to Elisenda, who turned it over and over, looking at it. It was of a matronly woman in simple medieval dress, the sort you could buy in souvenir shops. She understood the significance. 'The Majordoma. When did you find it?'

'The day before Mònica Ferrer was found. I only kept it because of an earlier incident. I was walking through the arch when some guy from the Jewish museum pointed this out, hanging down from the figure.'

The mosso opened the other evidence bag and pulled out a small black object before holding it up for Elisenda to see.

'A joke bat?' she said. She recalled Pijaume showing her something about a bat.

'It was just before Mossèn Viladrau was found. I didn't really think anything about it at the time, but when someone told me you were looking at a link with these myths, I wondered if it was significant. The priest found near the vampire and the critic found in all the rubbish in the market. So I checked in the records and I found that there'd been another one reported.'

Elisenda leaned forward over her desk. 'What was it?'

'Four rag dolls. The morning before the four muggers were attacked.'

'Were there any others reported?' Elisenda asked him, her mind on Masó. And on Corominas, she thought, surprised that his name had sprung to mind.

'None, Sotsinspectora. Just those three.'

'Pity,' Elisenda muttered, disappointed.

'I've got the name of the guy who reported the first incident, though. It was in the report. A street cleaner. He might be worth questioning.'

'You could say that,' Elisenda agreed with him.

Chapter Forty Nine

Elisenda looked at the name appearing on her mobile screen and pressed the red button to reject the call. Inspector Puigventós again. She put the phone back in her bag. Standing next to her, Àlex got a call on his phone almost immediately. He looked at the name on the screen and held it up to show her. Puigventós. He shrugged and rejected the call.

'I'm sure the Policia Municipal will take us on,' she reassured him.

He grunted and turned back to look at Mosso Paredes gingerly climbing the ladder from the uneven cobbles to where it was lodged untidily below the little statue of the virgin.

'If this person really has been leaving figurines on the Verge de la Bona Mort,' Elisenda had reasoned to Àlex after speaking to Paredes, 'then why wasn't there one for Foday Saio?'

Which was why a nervous Mosso Paredes was bleakly ascending the unsteady ladder, held absently in place by his partner. Shakily taking his latex-gloved right hand off the top of the ladder and gripping firmly with his left, Paredes carefully felt with his fingertips between the pigeon spikes.

'There is something here, Sotsinspectora,' Paredes called, not looking down.

Elisenda half-turned to Àlex. 'It'll be a fly,' she told him.

Holding on to his find with his right hand, Paredes slowly shuffled back down the ladder with his left hand jerking from rung to rung. At the bottom, he walked over to them and held out his hand.

It was a fly. A stuffed toy. Of a type sold by the souvenir shops in the city.

'The wind must have blown it back on to the ledge,' Paredes said. 'It was caught on a spike.'

'Well done, Francesc,' Elisenda told him, holding an evidence bag open for him to put the toy into. 'Thanks for coming to me with this.'

She and Àlex left the two Seguretat Ciutadana to return the ladder to the elderly porter in the Audiència Provincial, who was fussing over its return like a prodigal son, and walked to where their unmarked car was parked at the foot of the cathedral steps.

Elisenda placed the evidence bag in the boot and looked up, distracted for a moment by the sound of an engine. She watched a small plane stutter across the thick air of the sky and only looked down once it had passed from view. Àlex watched it too but turned away before she looked at him.

'A fly?' he asked once they were in the car. He started the engine and slowly drove through the Portal de Sobreportes to turn sharp left down Pujada de Sant Feliu.

'Sant Narcís,' Elisenda explained as they wound their way through the narrow streets towards the busy Pont de Pedret junction north of the old town. Her phone rang again but she ignored it. 'The legend says that when the French were besieging Girona in the thirteenth century, a swarm of flies emerged from Sant Narcís's tomb and warded them off, saving the city.'

'So the fly symbolises protecting the city from attack.'

'Precisely. That's why you see these toys and chocolates in the shape of flies everywhere. And given the time of year, it was inevitable that the attacker should use the legend. We're just lucky it didn't come off.'

'Why an immigrant? Why not a French target? A French company? Just someone French?'

Elisenda considered that for a moment. 'Our man sees the influx of immigrants as the city under siege, I suppose. One that we need protecting from.'

'He calls this protecting? God help us.'

They drove across the Pont de Pedret and passed the evidence of the patron saint's day celebrations: empty *barraques* to the left, roadies working on the stage, the beer huts all shut up until the evening. Ahead of them, the sound of the funfair filtered through the trees as they passed a short queue of people buying roast chestnuts at a makeshift stand. They drove on in silence past the Devesa and its hardcore daytime funfair-lovers and cut along Carrer Ferran Puig to head for the stop-start grind of Carretera de Barcelona. Àlex spoke first.

'Is there any significance to his disability? The hands?'

'I don't think so. There's nothing in the legend that I can think of, but we can always ask Professor Marsans. As far as I know, it's entirely to do with the city under siege.'

'Pity. It would almost be better if it weren't about invaders. About immigrants. Less contentious. Fewer headaches for us.'

'He's making us choose our victims again.' She stared out at the traffic. Her phone rang. She sighed and checked the screen absently, but then answered once she saw the caller's name.

Àlex listened in silence until she ended the call and switched her mobile to vibrate before putting it back in her bag.

'News?' he asked.

'Pau. He's outside the bishopric. Mossèn Arnau, the priest who gave him the address in Santa Pau. It appears he's on holiday. In Santiago de Compostela.' Over on the other side of the country, she might have added.

'Great,' Àlex commented. 'When's he back?'

'That's the rub. He's not. He'll be going straight from there to his new posting. In Rome.'

'Is there anyone in this city who actually wants us to find this killer?'

'Not yet.'

Àlex pulled off the main road and drove into a characterless complex in the industrial estate to the south of the city. They went inside the low, modern building they'd come to visit, both of them gladdened by how much the air conditioning was turned up after the cloying humidity of the day outside.

A receptionist showed them to a small meeting room and asked them to wait. The walls were decorated with glossy blow-up photos of waste treatment plants and refuse lorries and cheerful men and women in protective clothing sorting through conveyor belts of junk. A pitcher of water and half a dozen glasses stood on the table, and Elisenda poured a glass for herself and another for Àlex. They both swallowed them down in one gulp and Elisenda poured them a second glass each. The door opened and the receptionist came back in followed by a short, sulky-looking man in sweat-stained corporate overalls.

'Andrés Soriano,' the receptionist announced, backing out of the room, leaving Soriano standing undecided just inside the doorway.

Both Elisenda and Àlex stood up.

'Thank you for seeing us, Senyor Soriano,' Elisenda said to him in Catalan.

'I don't know what they expect me to tell you,' Soriano complained in Spanish.

'I'm sure you'll be of great assistance,' Elisenda told him, switching into Spanish. 'It's good of you to offer us your help in this matter.'

'Well...,' Soriano replied, shrugging nervously and pulling himself up to his full height.

'If you'd care to take a seat,' Elisenda invited him.

The three of them sat down at the table and Elisenda poured Soriano a glass of water.

'In your own words, Andrés,' Elisenda continued in a low voice. 'We'd just like to hear what exactly it was you found on the Verge de la Bona Mort that morning.'

'I reported it.'

'Yes, and we're glad you did. We just need you to tell us what you remember.'

Soriano shrugged and hawked noisily to clear his throat. 'It was a pigeon.'

'A pigeon?'

'Yeah, it took a shit on my overall so I looked up and saw it.'

'The pigeon?'

'The dummy. On the statue.'

Elisenda looked uncertainly at him. 'I understood you found four dolls on the statue.'

'That's right, but that was when the water wasn't working. The tank was empty and I had to come back here and fill up.'

Elisenda and Àlex exchanged looks, confused by the street cleaner's meandering account.

'Tell me about the four dolls,' Elisenda persevered.

'They were four dolls,' Soriano said with a shrug, 'hanging down from the statue. Rag dolls like when you were a kid, that's all.'

'What did you do with them?'

'Threw them away. I reported it to you lot because that lawyer was there, miserable bastard, but I just chucked the dolls in my bag. Went out with the rest of the rubbish. Like I said, rag dolls. Nothing special.'

Elisenda started to rise out of her chair, realising they weren't going to get much more out of him. 'Well, thank you, Andrés,' she said.

'Pity you threw them away,' Àlex commented.

Soriano shrugged. 'Yeah. Didn't think they were important. Just like the other one.'

Elisenda looked straight at him and sat back down. 'Other one?'

'I told you. When the pigeon took a dump on me.'

'There was a second incident?'

'No. Those four were the second incident. The one with the pigeon came first.'

'When exactly was this?' Elisenda asked him patiently.

Soriano sucked his teeth, thinking. 'Middle of September? Somewhere round there.'

Elisenda looked at Àlex and back at Soriano. 'And it was a pigeon you saw on the statue?'

'No, the pigeon shit on me. It was a face I saw.'

'A face? Can you describe it?'

Soriano leaned over and took a piece of paper from a pile in the middle of the table and a pen from a holder next to it.

'I can draw it for you.'

'And this was in mid-September, you say?' Elisenda insisted.

Soriano nodded, concentrating on his picture. 'I remember now. It was the day before we had the fiesta in the street where I live.' He looked up at Àlex, who he imagined would be more sympathetic. 'I got plastered. Celebrating. It was when that bastard Daniel Masó got carved up. Some night.' He looked at Elisenda. 'Excuse the language.'

Both Elisenda and Àlex craned forward and watched as he clumsily sketched a crude moon-shaped face. They looked at each other as the big, staring eyes and tall, pointed ears took shape in the drawing. When he'd done, he proudly held it up and showed it to them.

'En Banyeta,' Àlex murmured.

'Daniel Masó,' Elisenda added.

Chapter Fifty

Àlex turned the siren on and headed right for Salt instead of left for Girona.

Pau had called the moment they left the industrial estate. *'There's a standoff outside an Arabic baker's in Salt,'* he told Elisenda.

Heading straight there, they found a short section of road in the brittle honeycomb of streets near the town hall cut off at either end by Mossos cars and vans. A steady swell of noise seeped around the blue and white vehicles blocking the view, pulling Elisenda and Àlex in. The uniformed mosso at the channel funnelling Mossos in and out recognised them and let them through.

'Two groups,' the uniformed officer, who'd introduced himself as Sotsinspector Pascal, told them. He pointed to a string of three shops in a row, all of them foreign-owned. Between the baker's and a Bangladeshi restaurant was a Halal butcher's, its windows boarded up. 'The people outside the shops are there to protect them. The other group over there,' he pointed to a crowd gathering at a corner where a lane led into the street, 'are what they're trying to protect them from. And we're trying to protect them from each other.'

Elisenda thanked him and walked over to the group of people outside the shops. It was made up of local people and immigrants, mothers with small children and blue-collar workers standing in calm defiance next to students and pensioners. She couldn't help feeling heartened at the sight despite the situation.

'We're taking a stand,' a Catalan woman told her. Clutching her hand, a small boy was holding a placard almost as big as he was, calling for respect between races. Other children and adults were holding similar hurriedly-made signs. 'We won't allow this to go on.'

'Neither will we,' Elisenda assured her. 'Please try to remain calm, even if you're provoked. And please leave the Mossos to find a solution to this.'

Some of the crowd standing vigil grumbled at Elisenda's words, but most acquiesced. She went back to where Àlex was standing next to uniformed Mossos watching the mob on the corner.

'There's more of them gathering,' he told her.

A stone rose in a high parabola from the heart of the mob and thumped against the plywood covering the butcher's damaged shop front, narrowly missing an elderly man. A cheer went up from the mob and the crowd holding vigil parted for a panicked moment to come back together in a tighter group.

Sotsinspector Pascal and half a dozen of his officers approached the gang on the corner and ordered them to disperse. Voices from behind the front row jeered and swore. A second stone was thrown, landing harmlessly in the street. Pascal sent his Mossos in to look for the stone thrower but they were pushed back by the crowd. He appealed for calm, but pulled his Mossos back when the jostling became more aggressive.

Elisenda looked back at the shops and saw that the crowd outside them was swelling in a larger proportion to the stone-throwing mob. She wasn't sure that was necessarily a good thing.

The sotsinspector spoke to a sergent, and two of the Mossos vehicles at one end of the street moved aside and two vans came through. They pulled over and a group from the regional support unit in riot uniforms slowly emerged to form up. Not carrying shields or batons yet. The mob jeered more.

'Please, not this,' Elisenda muttered.

She and Àlex made a move to go back to speak to the people standing vigil, but Pascal came over to them holding his phone out to her, an apologetic look on his face.

'Inspector Puigventós is on the line,' he told Elisenda. 'He wants to talk to you.'

Elisenda took the mobile and explained where she was, but Puigventós cut her short.

'*I don't care, Elisenda. I want you back at Vista Alegre immediately.*'

She handed the phone back to Pascal and shrugged.

'Sorry.' She gestured to the gathering storm. 'Good luck.'

Chapter Fifty One

'I'm not happy with this, Elisenda, not happy at all.'

Elisenda sat in Puigventós' office and let the bluster wash over her. At least she had something she could offer him, regardless of whether he was going to like it or not.

'I asked you for a meeting hours ago,' he went on, 'and you have completely ignored all my phone calls. We need to discuss this new racial angle before it really gets out of hand. We cannot allow racial tension to take hold. Especially now with events in Salt and the Sant Narcís celebrations at their height.'

'I couldn't answer your calls, Xavier, because I was in the middle of interviews which have cast substantial new light on the attacks.'

She placed four evidence bags on his desk. The joke bat, the figure of the Majordoma and the fly were in three of them. The fourth contained a sheet of paper. Puigventós sighed and looked at the bags, his interest piqued, but not enough to be swayed quite yet.

'The racial angle, Elisenda,' he reminded her. 'We can't sweep it under the carpet.'

'We're not going to. But neither are we going to focus solely on it.'

Puigventós snorted. 'You might not. But you'll be the only one if you do. We need to speak to the community leaders. Calm things down before there's any retaliation by one of the immigrant groups. We're only lucky the intended victim wasn't the one that got hurt.'

'Good job it was only teenagers, in other words.'

Puigventós looked straight at her. 'An attack on young people or a race crime, Elisenda. Which would you rather see the city facing?'

'I'm sure the young people now in hospital see it the same way.'

'You feel no sympathy for the intended victim?'

'Of course I do. Enormous sympathy. He lived through a civil war, his family was killed, he was mutilated. He had to leave his home and start again in a completely different culture in a completely different language. And then this is the way he's treated. And I shudder to think what the killer had planned for him. And what would have happened to his little girl. I feel far more sympathy for him than for any of the other victims. And that's what galls me. I'm doing exactly what the attacker wants me to do. I'd prefer the victim to be a young person rather than an immigrant. A fit person rather than a disabled one. I resent being forced to question everything that makes me human.'

She looked at the evidence bags on the table and realised she had to forget about them for the moment. 'I understand we have to tread carefully with this, Xavier, and we have to make sure no one in the city sees it as open day on immigrants. This website is already doing enough to stir up trouble without that. But I think we also have to be careful not to go too far the other way. We have to focus on the attacks as a whole, not on the racial aspect of one of them. Not if we don't want to give someone the excuse to make it worse. Or if we want to come out of this undamaged. Evil as this last attack is in every single way I can think of, it is not an isolated racially-motivated crime. It's part of some awful bigger picture that the perpetrator is trying to tell us.'

Puigventós rubbed his forehead and exhaled deeply. 'Possibly it is, Elisenda, but is that going to help us keep control of it all?'

Elisenda stretched her back on the uncomfortable chair and looked back at him. 'If it's any consolation, there will be a new attack that will target another group or another individual and all the ghouls and twitters and rants will move on to the next one.'

'We just have to hope for that to happen soon,' Puigventós replied. 'And yes, I do know what I'm saying.'

Elisenda kept quiet. She couldn't swear in all honesty that she entirely disagreed. She picked up the first of the evidence bags on the inspector's desk and showed it to him.

'The developments I was telling you about.'

She showed him the bat first and then the figure of the Majordoma, explaining the visit to her office by Mosso Paredes and when each one had been found. She then showed him the fly through the clear plastic of the bag.

'We found this one this morning. On the statue of the Verge de la Bona Mort like the other two.'

Puigventós took the bag from Elisenda and turned it over and over, peering at the giant stuffed toy fly inside. 'Sant Narcís.'

'Precisely. It was announcing the attack on Foday Saio. An invader in the perpetrator's eyes.'

Puigventós dropped the bag back on the desk. 'And the piece of paper?'

Elisenda looked at it but left it lying close to her, away from the inspector. 'Mosso Paredes also told me of another find that had been reported. Unfortunately, we don't have the evidence but we've been able to speak to the man who found it. He's a street cleaner. The morning of the attack on the four muggers, he found four dolls hanging from the statue. He threw them away, but it's clear to us that they'd been put there to announce the attack on the gang of muggers.'

'Pity we don't have the dolls,' Puigventós said absently. He looked in turn at the three evidence bags that Elisenda had already shown him and spoke quietly, almost to himself. 'So this latest attack can't really be seen as racial, but as another incident motivated by other reasons.' It seemed to please him. 'And the four dolls equating to the four muggers was the first sign, followed by these three?'

'No.' Elisenda pushed the final bag towards him. 'This was the first one. The street cleaner found this in mid-September. He also threw it away but he was able to do this drawing.'

Puigventós flattened the plastic across the piece of A4 paper and looked at the sketch. 'What is it?'

'En Banyeta. A moneylender. There's a carving of this face on the corner of Carrer Ciutadans with Plaça del Vi. The legend goes that if you rub your nose against his, you'll be excused all your debts.'

The inspector looked up at her sharply.

'It was found on the morning that Daniel Masó was found dead. A moneylender who bled to death with his nose cut off.'

Elisenda sat back in her chair, surprised at how shaky she felt, and watched Puigventós. He looked from bag to bag, coming back each time to the fly. The announcement of the attack on an immigrant. She felt she could see the connections being made in his mind. And more importantly, the acceptance of Daniel Masó as part of a horrific series of killings being weighed up against the dread of Foday Saio being targeted solely for his race. For a fleeting moment, she wondered if she'd ever become politician enough to make the rank of inspector.

'The Masó case is part of your investigation,' he finally judged. 'I'll inform Sotsinspector Micaló.'

Chapter Fifty Two

Elisenda left Puigventós' office and crossed the front desk to find Gerard Bellsolà and Ignasi Perafita waiting. The critic's husband didn't seem any more distraught than he had the day his wife was found.

'Can I help you?' she asked them.

'No thank you, Sotsinspectora Domènech,' Bellsolà told her, turning away. 'We're here to see someone rather more senior.'

'May I ask in relation to what?'

Perafita looked at her in disdain. 'In relation to my wife's murder, evidently.'

'My client doesn't want a failed attack diverting attention from the pursuit of his wife's assailant.'

'I can assure you that is not the case,' Elisenda told them.

'And you can rest assured it won't be the case,' Perafita answered. 'I will not allow a so-called attack on an immigrant to take precedence over finding the murderer of a local woman from the higher spheres of our society. Which is why I would sooner see a more senior officer than yourself leading the investigation. A male officer.'

'I understand your concern Senyor Perafita, but I am leading this investigation and I will leave no stone unturned to find the killer and put a stop to these attacks.' She turned to walk away. 'Whatever secrets that may bring to light.'

At the end of the corridor, she looked back to see Micaló emerge from his office and head towards where the two men were waiting.

'More senior,' she muttered, carrying on to her unit's offices.

Pau had something for her.

'I've been going back over arrest sheets and complaints forms and I've found these.' He showed her three incident reports. 'Foday Saio made official complaints in September about vandalism to his front door. He had paint thrown on it twice and chunks taken out of it with a hammer another time. And that's not all.'

Elisenda glanced through the forms Pau had given to her. She saw that in the last incident, Foday claimed that members of the Masó family had been responsible for the damage.

'The Masó family just won't go away, will they? Find out what you can, any other incidents, what action has been taken by Pijaume's unit. I'll speak to Foday and see what he says.'

'There's something else. I've been checking up on Pere Corominas, the guy that's gone missing, and I've found a blog that he's been posting. There's been nothing new posted for two months now, but it was always sporadic, so that doesn't really mean anything.'

He showed it to Elisenda and she saw that Corominas would write six articles in two weeks and then nothing for three months at a time. 'Anything we should know about?'

'Most definitely.'

Pau found a number of articles on the history and legends of Girona and showed her a rabidly scathing one on modern legends and how they erode what Corominas called the real culture of the city, with particular reference to the Majordoma. He then brought up a series of entries about going back to nature and living wild in the woods.

'How are they related?' she asked Pau.

'This is someone who feels strongly about the city and its history, and someone who is able to live wild for periods of time. He's also someone who fell out of view at the same time as the killings started. Taken together, I think they make him someone who could be of interest to us.'

'In what way is he missing, in other words,' Elisenda muttered. 'Good, find out what you can, and avoid going through Micaló or Pijaume if at all possible. We'll have to dig him up ourselves.'

Pau scrolled through Corominas' blog and clicked on one more article.

'But this is the one you really need to see,' he told her.

Elisenda read what was on screen: "Before my lifetime, Franco garrotted Catalan heroes wanting a free Catalonia. The garrotte. At that time, the Spanish state's execution of choice. Tied to a post by the neck, and a handle turned behind you, tightening while you agonised in death. And all for wanting freedom. Well, now the tide has turned. We are nearer regaining our freedom than at any time in the last three hundred years. For all those who would prevent us from regaining our freedom, from reaffirming our identity, from reclaiming our culture, perhaps the time has come for them to feel the garrotte."

Elisenda read it a second time in her disbelief.

'God knows what planet he's on,' Pau commented.

'One we need to find.'

Chapter Fifty Three

'Brought her along to fetch the coffee, have you?'

Joaquim Masó laughed at his own joke but the two younger men seated either side of him at the café table simply stared at the two Mossos with dead eyes.

The bare, dusty room at the motorway end of Salt was empty. The two old guys staring at each other across a slow trail of dominoes had cleared out the moment Àlex and Montse had walked in. The black and white slabs of their game still lay on the table separating two half-drunk glasses of beer. The café owner had shrunk behind a faded plastic bead curtain into the kitchen behind, leaving the insistent tinny blare of a one-armed bandit to stand guard over his business.

'Very funny,' Àlex told Masó. 'You'd better explain it to your friends.'

'I wouldn't worry about them. They don't miss much.'

Àlex looked from one to the other, the brothers he and Elisenda had seen in Masó's yard, and grinned. 'I'm glad you have faith in them.'

The younger of the brothers reacted slightly, turning to see his older sibling's reaction, his jaw clenching. Àlex was pleased to see he'd got a rise out of him. He now knew the younger brother was the weaker one. The older one was the one to watch.

'What can I do for you, Mossos?' Masó asked. His words were aimed at Àlex, but his eyes didn't move once from leering at Montse's breasts.

'We're here to help you,' Àlex told him. 'Your stolen van. We're here to do everything we can to resolve it.'

Masó grunted.

'We were just wondering why you didn't report it missing,' Montse added.

'You let it speak?' Masó said to Àlex, still staring at Montse's chest.

Montse took a step forward, but Àlex touched her arm lightly. 'You know, it really isn't in your interest to talk to a Mosso like that.'

'You're threatening me?' Masó looked right and left at the two brothers and sneered at Àlex. 'Me?'

'We're simply here to help. Besides, you don't really think dumb and dumber here will be any use, do you?'

The younger brother swore in Spanish and jumped up, reaching past Montse towards Àlex, but instantly found himself pinned on the table in front of Masó, Montse's right hand pulling his arm up behind his back, her left grinding his face into the coarse wood.

Àlex turned to the older brother and smiled affably. 'Your go.'

'When I'm good and ready.'

Not Masó family, Àlex suddenly realised. The few words he'd said told Àlex that. He spoke unnatural, first-generation Catalan with a Barcelona accent, obviously the son of immigrants from elsewhere in Spain. They were the typical bargain-basement toughs he'd known all his life, bullying on street corners, stealing car radios, snatching tourists' bags.

He turned back to Masó.

'Your van. Why didn't you report it missing?'

'I settle things my own way. I don't need your lot involved. For all the good you do, anyway.' He looked bluntly at Àlex. 'I've learnt to take the law into my own hands to get what I want.'

'I would advise against that.'

'Yeah, you probably would. But no one's ever going to take the Mossos seriously.'

Àlex stared back at Masó and signalled to Montse to let her captive go. She released him and he looked first at his brother and then at Montse, rubbing his arm. Sullenly, he sat back down in his chair.

'Impressive,' Masó said. 'Strange seeing women in the police, even if it is only the Mossos. Not like the old Policia Nacional. They'd never have stood for having women tagging along with them. It's unnatural.' He turned to look Montse in the eyes for the first time. 'You never know. You might be the next victim. He's going for freaks.'

Àlex laughed, moving immediately after at a speed that left the two brothers shocked motionless. With his right hand, he scooped Masó up by the neck from his chair and slammed him into the back wall. Masó struggled for breath, his feet scraping the ground as he scrabbled to support himself.

'I would suggest you take us very seriously,' Àlex whispered in his face. 'And I would also suggest you tell your friends to stay seated if you want to breathe again.'

Masó fluttered his fingers to tell the brothers not to move.

'And my third suggestion is that you never talk like that to one of my officers ever again. You are now in my sights, Masó. You will regret that.'

Àlex let him drop to the ground and turned away, following Montse out of the café to their car.

As she drove away, Montse spoke. 'You didn't have to do that for me, Sergent. I can take care of myself. It just plays into the hands of people like that when you stand up for me because I'm a woman.'

'I know you can, Caporal. I wasn't defending you because you're a woman. I was defending you because I'm a sergent and you're a caporal and you are in my care. I won't have scum talking to a fellow Mosso that way.'

Montse nodded, still unsure of how she felt. She'd heard of Àlex's cold rages but had never witnessed one before.

'They were from Barcelona,' Àlex commented as Montse turned on to Salt's Carrer Major, heading back towards Girona. 'The two brothers.'

Montse nodded. 'Strange. The Masó family have never allowed outsiders into their businesses.'

'It is curious. But I think we can say the vacuum left by Daniel Masó has been filled.'

Montse waited at the traffic lights to leave Salt.

'Probably worse than before,' she added.

Chapter Fifty Four

Josep was arriving as Elisenda was leaving the unit.

'I'm off to see the wonderful and helpful Jutgessa Roca,' she told him. 'To try and get a warrant to search Pere Corominas' flat. Pau will explain.'

'Good luck,' he replied, his head hung low.

Pau showed him Corominas' blog, eliciting the same shocked response as Elisenda's. 'And it looks to be going viral,' Pau added. 'The number of hits has doubled since I found it this morning.'

'He's gone missing,' Josep pointed out. 'Or underground. Must have created a buzz.'

A sergent from the Local Investigation Unit came into the room, followed by Pijaume, asking him to check up on any evidence of the missing drugs being reported found. Josep shot Pau a look and they turned back to the computer. Switching to the website, they saw that activity on it was going into overdrive as news of the confrontation outside the immigrant businesses in Salt seeped out.

'More divided than before,' Pau commented.

Curiously, a victim surviving an attempted attack seemed to have brought out the compassion that murder hadn't. Many people continued to suggest new victims and many posts encouraged the actions of the mob in Salt, but increasingly more voices were raised against them, calling for the protection of potential victims and for the people of the city to reject the attacker and the results of his actions.

'Still not ideal, though, is it?' Josep said, pointing to a thread that was just beginning to gather pace. A stand-up comedian from Barcelona was appearing in Girona on All Saints' Day, in two days' time, and it was polarising opinion. As they watched, more and more posts called for him to be targeted. 'Why a comedian?'

'He's a *monologuista*,' Pau answered. 'A lot of people see that as foreign.'

'Or they just don't like new. Montse and I were thinking of going to see him before all this lark kicked off.'

Elisenda returned an hour later with a piece of paper and a look of disbelief. 'Jutgessa Roca actually gave me something I requested,' she told Pau and Josep. 'This is a warrant to search Corominas' flat and check his phone records.'

'How did you manage that?' Pau asked.

'I told her it was nothing to do with Daniel Masó. She still wouldn't give me a warrant ordering the bishopric to assist with the investigation, though, so all's well with the world.'

Before they had a chance to leave, Pijaume clicked on the local TV station's website. 'Inspector Puigventós is on,' he explained.

They watched as Puigventós appealed for calm in the events in Salt. 'I want to reassure everyone that the thwarted attack on an immigrant member of our community is not a racially-motivated crime. It is part of a wider series of heinous attacks taking place in our city, and it should be viewed as such.'

Elisenda hung her head. 'Well that should do the trick.' Sow even more panic than there already was about a serial killer to avoid racial tension. Some trade-off. She also recalled Puigventós' comment on using the media.

'What's happening to this city?' Pijaume asked.

'The report of the bat on the Verge de la Bona Mort,' Elisenda reminded him. 'Are there any reports of any other incidents?'

'Not that I'm aware. In relation to what?'

'It's to do with these attacks.'

Pijaume shook his head and told her that there had been no more reports in the last few days.

-

Across town, Antoni Sunyer let Elisenda, Pau and Josep into the flat he shared with Pere Corominas and sat in the small living room while they went through the bookshelves. He'd pointed out which books were Corominas', with more in his bedroom.

'We'll cause as little disruption as possible,' Elisenda promised him.

'I'm glad to see something being done about finding Pere.'

Pau and Josep went into Corominas' bedroom while Elisenda stayed to speak to Sunyer. She asked him about his flatmate's political beliefs.

'Pretty radical. Although he does blow hot and cold about a lot of things. He'll get worked up about some issue and then forget it all a week later. One day we should all live off the land, the next he's buying a new iPad, that sort of thing.'

She thanked him and joined the other two in the bedroom. Dark like many of the flats in the old town, the airless room faced the tiny patio to the rear of the building. The room looked second-hand, with a single bed in the corner by the old wooden-framed window, an ancient wardrobe against one wall, another wall taken up by a length of wood on two trestles, which acted as a desk, and two battered grey metal filing cabinets. A laptop stood open on the desk. Pau was checking the files on it, Josep was going through one of the filing cabinets.

'Research for his degree,' Pau told Elisenda when she asked what he'd found. 'On iconology and culture. And there's a lot of other material that looks like he's compiling local legends.' He checked another folder. 'Yeah, there's what looks like a draft of a book on the city's folk tales.'

'This guy gets more and more interesting. Check as much as you can, then bag it up and send it to UCDI.'

'If he was going underground, why didn't he take his laptop with him?'

'He had another computer? We'll check. Anything in the files, Josep.'

'Same as on the laptop, by the sound of it. It's all legends, myths and stories. Personal stuff apart from that. Bills, credit card, bank statements. Nothing out of the ordinary so far.'

They heard the doorbell go, and Elisenda went back into the living room to see Sunyer open the door. A stylish young woman came in and kissed him on both cheeks but was then shocked to see Elisenda. Sunyer explained who she was and what she was doing there.

'Still no news on Perc?' the woman asked.

'I'm afraid not,' Elisenda told her. 'And you are?'

'Roser Caselles. I'm a friend of Antoni and Pere.'

'She's doing first year history,' Sunyer explained. 'Pere and I both studied history and we met Roser at summer school in July. Is it all right if she stays?'

'Of course. One thing, Antoni. You mentioned Pere bought an iPad. Do you know where it is?'

'It's not here. He never let it out of his sight. He used it more than his laptop.'

Elisenda thanked him and went back into the bedroom to find Pau and Josep discussing a stand-up as they searched. Pau explained to her about the number of people on the website suggesting him as the next victim.

'It's because he's a *monologuista*,' Pau said. 'It's not our tradition. They've only become fashionable because of American TV programmes like Seinfeld.'

'That doesn't make him a target,' Josep argued.

'It does to some people. It is cultural imperialism in a way.'

Elisenda opened the wardrobe and began searching through Corominas' clothes. 'You're not keen on observational humour, Pau?'

'Not because it's observational. It's because it's not ours. We don't have a tradition of that sort of humour. Not like other cultures.'

'It's not about tradition,' Josep insisted, 'it's progress. The same as music. Tastes develop from one generation to the next. We can't all watch the same tired old comedians telling jokes that our parents did. It has to move on.'

'Are you going to see this guy, Josep?' Elisenda asked.

'Montse and I were thinking of going, Sotsinspectora, but I don't think we will now, with all this going on. We'd thought some of us from the unit could have gone together.'

'Not me, I'm sorry,' Pau replied. 'Not my scene. We should stick to what we do.'

Elisenda closed the wardrobe and looked at her two caporals intent on their work. Odd that off-the-wall thinker Pau should resist change and dour Josep should embrace it. No one was ever entirely as you thought they were.

Chapter Fifty Five

On the slow road from Ripoll, Pere Corominas' father hummed the same tune he always did when he drove, *Mediterraneo* by Joan Manuel Serrat. Next to him, his wife inhaled a large sprig of fragrant lavender on the van's dashboard and let her mind idle, staring at the mountains and valleys out of the window.

Pere Corominas' father was still quietly humming when they finally pulled up outside a yard in Salt. There was no one else in the small road. No elderly men sitting on straight-backed chairs commenting on the world passing them by, no women with shopping trolleys coming back laden from the shops, no men idling jobless in the sun.

A door opened and three men came out.

'Where is it?' the first of them said.

From a hidden compartment in the back of the van, Pere Corominas' father pulled out a neat rectangular parcel and handed it to one of the other two men, who put it into a canvas holdall. More followed until the bag was full.

The first man counted out a pile of twenty-euro notes and handed them over. 'I will need more.'

Pere Corominas' father shrugged. 'We had an agreement with Daniel. This is how much we sold him. We never sold him more.'

'Very nice, but I'm not my nephew. And you work for me now.'

'No, we don't.'

At a signal, the older brother gave Pere Corominas' father an open-handed slap across the left ear, leaving his head filled with a numb rushing noise, like sea water flooding in.

'Yes, you do,' Joaquim Masó told him.

Chapter Fifty Six

Elisenda's stomach complained as she and Àlex watched a pair of Seguretat Ciutadana walk slowly past the Verge de la Bona Mort. They were the second team to check on the statue in the last five minutes and the result of Puigventós' reluctant acquiescence earlier that day to step up patrols around the gateway over which the figure sat. He'd drawn the line at round-the-clock surveillance when Elisenda had asked for it.

'At least today,' she'd argued. 'All Saints' Eve. We have to expect another attack between today and tomorrow.'

'The attack on Foday Saio was only yesterday.'

'Failed attack. That's why he'll try again today. He won't want to let All Saints go by. We need the surveillance tonight on the statue.'

Puigventós' reply was one word. 'Budgets.'

He had also drawn a line at setting up CCTV. It was the one time in her life Elisenda regretted not having cameras plastered all over the city like they had in some other countries. What he had agreed to was for patrols to pass by the Verge de la Bona Mort every fifteen minutes through the night to check on her.

'It's not much but it's something,' Elisenda had told Àlex when they'd left the station.

In theory, they were both off duty, but they had wordlessly come together in walking from Vista Alegre through the old town to the foot of the cathedral and the virgin's niche. It was All Saints' Eve, and the city was wearily heaving at the tail-end of the Sant Narcís celebrations, due to go out to fireworks and wondrous exhaustion on Sunday. They'd had to dodge the throngs taking advantage of the open-doors evening at the city's museums. Elisenda had to admit that it was unlikely anyone would dare try to get something on to the statue with half the city milling around.

'I still don't see how he gets the figures up there,' Àlex commented, looking up at the statue. They were standing outside the front door to L'Arc, opposite the Portal de Sobreportes, the music from the bar tumbling out on to the street every time the door opened.

'Like a lasso, I'd say. To catch on the pigeon spikes. That's why the fly didn't land the way he wanted. He doesn't get a second chance once it's caught.' She stared at the Verge. 'Would we have been able to stop Mònica Ferrer's murder had we known of the effigy, do you think?'

Àlex paused before replying. 'Possibly. But you can't think that way, Elisenda. We have to use it now to stop another killing.'

They watched a group of families standing by the stone gateway immediately under the Verge, the younger children running round and round the cluster of two generations of adults. The older children wanting away to the funfair, wheedling at parents and grandparents to be allowed.

'Nothing's going to happen any time soon, is it?' Àlex muttered. 'You hungry?'

Some of the fast food restaurants in town had come under fire on the website. Two had closed for the evening and others had hired security, and all the other restaurants in town would be full, so they cut through the darkened alleys to find somewhere Elisenda knew that was more down to earth. Far from the light and noise of the area around the cathedral, they came to a darkened door in an anonymous old building. The street lights were fainter here, separated from one another by a more distant void. Nonetheless, there were still plenty of diners in the know buzzing around the faded wood and iron entrance to the small restaurant. Elisenda invited Àlex to enter first and he shoved against the stiff door and went in.

'For Christ's sake,' Elisenda heard him curse the moment she shut the door behind them. There was barely enough room to squeeze in through the entrance and she had to wait while a young couple went past before she could see what had annoyed him.

It was the photo of Mònica Ferrer. The one taken on someone's mobile phone in the market. A printout of it on cheap paper had been pinned up on the wall behind the counter, the legend "ha ha ha" scrawled across the bottom in red felt-tip.

'Take that down,' Àlex told the owner, a grizzled old guy who Elisenda knew rarely smiled or even spoke with any civility as he served up huge and tasty meals at ancient prices. People came for the food, not the charm.

The owner carried on pulling a bottle of white wine out of a fridge to give to the waiter, his middle son, and shrugged. 'She had it coming.'

'No one has that coming to them,' Àlex continued, leaning forward over the counter, unwilling to let it go.

The owner looked directly back at him. 'Ferrer did. My daughter's restaurant went out of business thanks to her. She deserved everything she got and more.'

Àlex leaned across the counter. 'You are no different from the person who did this.'

'Get out.'

'I will. But you will take that picture down first or I will arrest you.'

'Take it down,' Elisenda told him quietly.

Outside, Àlex apologised to Elisenda.

'No need to,' she told him. 'You were right to say something.'

They walked back through the streets and passed through the crowds at the foot of the cathedral steps and out underneath the Verge de la Bona Mort.

'I'm still hungry, mind,' Elisenda complained.

In the end, they stood among the throng on Elisenda's street and ate a savoury pancake from the stand a few doors down from her building that sold crepes through its front window. They stood in the middle of the cobbles away from the other groups of standing diners so they could speak. Elisenda told Àlex of the search at Corominas' flat and the discussion about the stand-up.

'I don't find them that funny, either,' he told her. 'Same old rubbish under another name. But I don't see why people get so worked up about it.'

'I think they see it as a foreign culture creeping in and taking over.'

He gestured with his crepe at the crowd around them. 'So what is it that makes a crepe acceptable and a burger not? They're both foreign. Everyone's selective when it comes to deciding what's allowed and what's not.' He took another mouthful. 'Did the kids at the Foday Saio scene tell us much?'

Elisenda shook her head as she tried to push the smoked salmon back into her crepe. 'They're teenagers. Too many hormones to see anyone else. The only half-decent sighting is by Foday's daughter and she thinks anyone over the age of twelve is very old.'

'Even so, this guy's good at going unnoticed.'

'Visually and forensically,' Elisenda agreed. 'The Científica have found nothing at any of the sites.'

'Like he's part of the legends himself.'

Elisenda shuddered. 'I refuse to see him that way.'

Àlex took Elisenda's finished serviette from her to throw in the bin. 'We will catch him, Elisenda.'

She just nodded, staring at the smiling people around them. Everyone was tired at the end of a hotter Sant Narcís than anyone had ever known and they were all moving with a partied-out slowness through the cloying streets. She realised she was sweating in the night air and she could see Àlex's face glistening with perspiration.

'This weather's ridiculous,' she told him.

'Girona. When it's not humid, it's raining.'

Elisenda grimaced at him and looked up at the tramway of sky she could see through the narrow buildings either side. The night was blackening and closing in on them by the minute, feeling its way down the ancient walls. The air was thick in her nostrils.

'There's a storm coming.'

Àlex looked at his watch. 'Time for me to go home, then. Before it breaks.'

Elisenda wished him goodnight and watched him head off for the footbridge across the river to the new town before she turned away and walked towards her apartment.

'No, can't face it,' she muttered to herself outside the front door to her building.

La Terra was packed, so she carried on to Carrer de la Força and up the steep road to the bottom of the cathedral. Some people were seated at the tables outside L'Arc, making the most of a warm evening, but most of the tables were empty as others started moving inside, all of them with one eye on the heavy, descending sky. Elisenda chose a table on the edge of the terrace and sat down with a *licor de cafè* to watch the Verge de la Bona Mort.

'Cigarette?' a man's voice asked.

A young guy in dirty jeans and a stained T shirt was moving from table to table trying to cadge a cigarette. He came to Elisenda and stopped in front of her, blocking her view of the statue. His eyes were glazed and he was unsteady on the uneven ground.

'Cigarette?' he asked her.

'Sorry, I don't smoke.'

She watched his eyes flicker from her to the ten-euro note she'd placed in the red saucer the waiter had left with her bill. She caught his eye and shook her head very slightly. Unfazed, he walked off to the table behind her to ask for a cigarette. He was having no luck.

Elisenda looked back at the statue in her niche.

There was nothing hanging from it.

The first rain drop landed thickly on her table, quickly followed by another, then more, reverberating on the aluminium, throwing up dust and oil from the cobbles in a sweet haze. The crowds walking up and down the cathedral steps scattered, some climbing, some descending, all heading for the nearest shelter. The first dull thud of distant thunder rolled slowly in from the mountains west of the city.

She grabbed her drink and the saucer with the note and followed everyone else running in from the terrace through the crowded doorway into the bar, her hair and arms already soaked, her shirt and trousers sticking to her body. Inside, she turned back but couldn't see through the hordes at the door. She was the only one in the bar not laughing at the sudden downpour.

–

Àlex stood alone at the hostile bar and looked around.

He hadn't gone home, either.

He examined his fellow patrons. Evidently, most of Girona's lowlifes enjoyed a funfair, too. Just four cloned yobs playing table football noisily, slamming the small wooden footballs on to the centre of the table in nervous, self-aware bravado.

He finished his orange juice. Too quiet tonight, he decided, the adrenaline not rising, so he paid up and left.

Outside, the storm had hit. Sant Narcís's revellers had scattered and the streets were all but empty. Just the sorry sound of the last-gasp waltzers and ignored dodgem klaxon in the park underpinned the thudding of heavy raindrops on the soaked streets and sizzling of car tyres. Thick black water ran in torrents along the gutters, collecting a summer of oil and grease and dust from the road and funnelling it down storm drains and up and over the pavements where the gratings backed up.

Making his mind up, Àlex ran for the arches of Plaça Independència, along the river. This was where the city was, he discovered. Drenched partygoers were resolutely shaking out their soaked hair and laughing under the stone porticoes of the square, the steam rising in a swirling haze from their heads. Others stood in the doorways of the welcome dry of the bars or were already seated with a drink at the covered terraces, staring pleasurably out at the rainstorm.

Àlex stood with the rest of the crowd for a while, but it was obvious the rain wasn't going to let up any time soon, so he wound his way through the damp throng to a solitary taxi at the rank outside the ornately ineffectual post office building. He ran for it and climbed in. It was a driver he recognised, a dignified, greying man who'd taken up driving a taxi after forced retirement and the lonely boredom of living alone.

'I haven't seen you for a time, Senyor Pere,' Àlex said. 'Sorry for jumping in like that.'

The driver turned round in the front seat before pulling out on to Gran Via and looked at Àlex, who gasped. The centre of his face was marked with the X of a heavy white plaster holding his nose in place. His right eye was bruised, a cut below it healing.

'I've only just started working again,' Pere told him, his voice thick. 'My insurance won't pay for me to be off any longer and I need the money.'

'What happened?' Àlex asked him.

Pere turned back and edged out into traffic through the rain-sodden stalemate, looking at Àlex in the rear-view mirror as he spoke. 'Couple of yobs. They got in before I knew what was happening. They held a knife to me, made me take them up to Sant Daniel, out at the end of the valley, and did this to me.'

Àlex couldn't think of anything to say, but simply looked at Pere's eyes in the mirror and turned away to look out at the shop window lights reflected on the wet pavements, his lips tight in anger.

'Who was it?'

Pere stopped at a red light and looked up into the mirror. 'We both know who it was.'

Chapter Fifty Seven

One of the things Octavi Marsans loved the most was the feel of his black silk kimono on his bare legs in the morning. And the soft noise it made, like the susurration of an ambitious door sliding open just for him.

Going into the trim kitchen, he switched the designer espresso machine on and pulled two pods out of a drawer and two cups and saucers from a cupboard. That was another of the things he loved the most. The morning after bedding one of his students. Clearing away the detritus of the meal he had expertly whipped together the night before, in carefully planned spontaneity after an evening spent late going over her course work and the suggestion that he cook for her. Listening to her take a shower, recalling the shape of her body and the compliance of her moans, waiting for her to appear in his kitchen wearing one of the oversized man's shirts he put out for her, just enough of her slim legs revealed to him. Rituals and traditions, tradition and ritual. We are nothing without that, Octavi Marsans thought to himself. He looked out of the kitchen window in his steep, rambling house at the top of the old town. A dense curtain of grey had descended over the city, not as savage as the previous night's deluge, but relentless in its steady insistence.

He prepared the DVD he'd left to record the previous night in the player in the kitchen. Last month's recording. Now even more topical than ever. He remembered he'd been superb, putting down his opponent effortlessly, playing on the spectres of the past to score easy points. His image came up on screen now, in his usual linen suit and pastel T-shirt, looking much calmer and cooler under the moody lights of the city station's one TV studio than his adversary, a sweating and spluttering Mossèn Eduard Viladrau. Now more famous than ever since his bizarrely-staged murder. Fame that would only do Marsans' own reputation good. Marsans looked at the priest now, rabidly defending the indefensible, calling for increasingly wilder and more regressive reforms, setting himself up like the cheapest of stooges for Marsans' withering putdowns. Marsans couldn't help smiling at the display. If the city were talking about what had happened to the priest before, they'd be talking about it even more now. And about Marsans' performance.

'Is that coffee?' a voice said behind him. 'Smells good.'

He turned to see Roser Caselles come in, wearing the shirt, her exquisite moneyed legs tapering down to the cold marble floor. Without a word, he poured her a coffee and placed it on the kitchen bar for her in good view of the screen.

'Thanks,' she said. She looked at the TV. Marsans was going in for the kill, pummelling the hapless priest with his usual argument that tradition did not mean conservatism, ritual was not rite, collective identity was not selective memory.

'I recorded this, too,' Roser added. 'I imagine the whole city did.' She knew how to play the game by Marsans' rules. He nodded, as though it was only right that she should, his gaze turning irrevocably away from her and back to his own image on the small screen.

His mobile rang. A number he didn't recognise. He picked it up and walked towards the door into the living room with it.

'Would you excuse me, my dear?' he asked Roser, not waiting for a reply.

Chapter Fifty Eight

Stabbing with a fork at her breakfast bowl of pineapple and strawberries, Elisenda closed the door to the smaller of the two bedrooms with her foot and wandered back past her own solitary tousled bedroom to the living room. Overlooking the large terrace that had a view out over the river and beyond to the Devesa and the mountains, the living room was separated from the small kitchen by an open archway. She sat down at the wooden table by the French windows in the kitchen and looked out. The apartment was empty. She thought of Pere Corominas' parents and how calm they seemed at the disappearance of their son and she thought of herself. She put her fruit down unfinished.

Outside on the terrace, her begonias in a medley of ceramic pots that had been tricked into constant flowering by the never-ending summer were wilting under the incessant rain. Craning her neck to one side, she could see down to the river below. The level had risen and the water was flowing more loosely than usual. The river had been widened years ago as far as the other side of Plaça Catalunya to prevent the flooding that used to see water over a metre high in the old town, but heavy rain could still surge under the Pont de Pedra and between the houses on either side of the Onyar where the river narrowed through the city. As a child, she'd once seen a whole tree, uprooted kilometres away upriver, trapped and flailing under the old stone bridge. She'd stared at it for ages from under her mother's umbrella, wondering why the adults wouldn't free it.

For once, the rain had charmed the city. She'd checked with Vista Alegre first thing, to be told that the downpour had kept the mob in Salt indoors. The racial tension hadn't gone away, but it hadn't been allowed to flourish either.

Her work mobile, on the table in front of her, rang and she picked it up.

'*Sotsinspectora? It's Josep. I've just had a message forwarded to me from Sotsinspector Pijaume. Someone's reported a tile left in the city history museum.*'

'Why's he told us that?'

'*The tile's of the Verge de la Bona Mort. The curator found it this morning. She thought it was just vandalism, but Sotsinspector Pijaume felt it might be worth informing us. It was on El Tarlà.*'

Elisenda stood up quickly.

'Thanks, Josep. Can you get hold of Àlex and tell him to meet me at the museum?'

She turned to look at the rain falling over the river.

'Got you, you bastard.'

—

'It's him,' she told Àlex twenty minutes later. She'd made another phone call of her own in the meantime. 'With all the activity around the statue, he's changed how he announces his attacks. If he can't take the sign to the Verge de la Bona Mort, he'll take the Verge de la Bona Mort to the sign.'

'You're sure?'

She pointed at the small ceramic tile hanging from around the neck of the life-size doll in the museum. 'Why else would that be there? Who else would know to do this?'

They were waiting for a Científica team to arrive, requested by Elisenda the moment she saw the tile. The curator stood nearby, anxiously watching the figure hanging above them.

'So what's the story?' Àlex asked her. 'El Tarlà?'

'During the plague, the old town was quarantined and a local man kept people's spirits up by playing the clown. This model is supposed to depict him. It's normally kept here but it's brought out in the summer and at Carnival.'

Àlex looked up at the doll of the jester hanging by his arms from a bar above where they stood and then back at her. 'You think it's going to be the stand-up.'

'It's got to be. Look at the way his appearing here has divided opinion on the website. Our man would see him as a natural target.' She pointed at the doll. 'And this can only mean it's him.'

'So what next?'

'We're going to set a trap. But first, we need some help.'

–

'It's more specifically about the Argenteria part of the old town,' Marsans told them.

The moment he'd ended Elisenda's call, he'd ushered Roser Caselles out of his house and hurried down to the museum. In his eagerness, he'd eschewed his usual wannabe pastel cool and thrown on jeans and a waterproof jacket. Now he, Elisenda and Àlex were standing under El Tarlà, studying the tile.

'May I ask why you needed me to ask me about it? The significance?'

Elisenda considered before she replied, unwilling to tell him more than was necessary. 'It bears a relation to these attacks that have been taking place in the city. We told you we saw a link with local legends, which is why we asked for your help. What we hadn't told you is that the Verge de la Bona Mort has been used as a way of announcing them.'

Marsans looked back at the tile and nodded, surprised.

'I know the basics of the legend,' Elisenda continued, 'but the more we know about it, the greater the chance we have of anticipating what the killer might do.'

The lecturer deliberated before answering. 'As with every legend, versions and variations abound and the celebration and telling of them is refined over time to the point where it's impossible to give a precise description. As I say, we know it centres on Argenteria. The original date it's celebrated is August 28th, but it's also used during Carnival nowadays. That's the problem. The more you try to find the origin of a legend such as this, the more you find divergences between stories and with popular perception.'

'Meaning our man could be using one of any number of interpretations.'

'Precisely. You know the story about the man playing the fool in the plague to cheer the citizens, I take it. Well, as for the tradition, in a nutshell, a treasurer would keep the image of the patron saint in their home and lead the procession on the eve of the celebration through the streets to Sant Feliu church. Then a vote was held, and the fool was announced on a scaffold, who was then adorned grotesquely and led through the neighbourhood, accompanied by a drummer. He was later replaced by this doll, which was hung by the arms outside the treasurer's house and turned loops over the bar while the drummer stood underneath playing.'

Elisenda took it all in. 'Thank you, Professor Marsans, this will help us narrow down how we tackle what we do next.'

'You must understand, Elisenda, that there are so many vari ants of every part of what I've just told you. It's extremely difficult to pin these legends down with any great accuracy.'

Elisenda thanked Marsans and a uniformed mosso accompa- nied him out of the museum. When he'd gone, Elisenda turned to Àlex.

'I think we should focus on the most popular perception of the legend to catch this guy.'

'So what's our next move?'

'We're going to have a word with this comedian.'

Chapter Fifty Nine

'Those two do know they're on expenses, I take it?' Elisenda asked Pau, watching Josep and Montse tuck into tapas at a terrace on Plaça Independència.

The rain had finally stopped, giving way to a warm evening, illuminating the buildings with a fading tungsten light. She smelt the air. It had the scent of a late summer storm that washed away the louring humidity and refreshed the streets of the city, sloughing off its damp lethargy.

The stand-up raised his head and appeared to glance in their direction but then turned back to his plate of seafood. He was feeding himself well before his gig in an hour's time.

Elisenda and Àlex had met him off the Barcelona train. He'd looked alarmed at first, but then became interested as they explained their presence. After that, he'd agreed quite readily to help them, eager no doubt for more unusual material to make his stand-up stand out.

'You'll never be out of sight of at least four Mossos the whole time, Carles,' Elisenda had told him. His real name was Carles Pont, but he followed the tradition, new and old, of a stage name, in his case Xarlu.

'Same old rubbish,' Àlex had muttered.

Xarlu paid for his meal and left. Elisenda saw Àlex and a member of Pijaume's team follow him. Two other plain-clothes Mossos were standing on the corner past which he'd walk. She didn't think the time before his performance would be key, but they were taking no chances. It was after his show that she felt the attacker would make his move, if he was going to.

His performance over, the comedian returned to Plaça Independència and crossed the river to Carrer Argenteria, following the route Elisenda had carefully rehearsed with him. Mossos were positioned along the way and in all the bars where he was to take a drink. Seguretat Ciutadana in plain clothes had been drafted in, and Pijaume had offered help from his unit. Micaló was nowhere to be seen.

Xarlu stopped for a glass of wine on Argenteria, giving any would-be attacker an opportunity to spike his drink, and went on from there along Carrer Ballesteries to Carrer Calderers, stopping for a drink in a bar on both streets. Fans stopped him for a chat and to have their photo taken with him. Others offered him drinks. None stood out. He looped round the quieter edge of the old town as the first rumble of thunder tumbled in from the mountains and entered a low-lit bar.

'Now that's interesting,' Elisenda muttered. She knew Pau and one of Pijaume's team would be waiting in there. She phoned Pau and told him to make himself scarce.

'That's Antoni Sunyer and Roser Caselles who've just followed him in,' she told Àlex. 'They're friends of Corominas.'

Àlex left her and went into the bar. They wouldn't recognise him, unlike Pau, and he stood next to them at the bar, where he watched their movements. They were already talking to Xarlu. They'd evidently been to his show and were gushing about some of his routines. Àlex had to admit the stand-up was self-effacing in the onslaught of praise. When they asked him if he wanted to go for a drink with them, the stand-up glanced at Àlex, who shook his head slightly.

Checking his watch, Xarlu left Sunyer and Caselles to go on to the next bar. He was coming to the end of the route. Àlex and the other Mosso stayed in the bar with the two fans, while others in the team took up the shadowing, and when the two friends left the bar, they followed them up into the lanes near the cathedral.

Which is when Elisenda called his mobile.

To ask if the stand-up was with Sunyer and Caselles.

'No,' Àlex told her. 'He left the bar. I assumed the team outside followed him.'

'*They did, but he went into Trasfigueres one end and didn't come out the other. I've got Mossos searching there now, but I wondered if he'd hooked up with those two again.*'

'No, I've got them in my sights.'

Elisenda told Àlex to stick with them and hung up.

She called the other members of the various teams into the search through the tangle of alleyways and cursed.

The black cloud descended over the city and the skies tore apart, lightning searing the ancient stones, the thunder moments later punching through the narrow streets, crowding into the secret corners. The rain fell, pulling Elisenda down into the cobbles beneath her feet.

Chapter Sixty

The sound of drumming.

Unnatural, incessant, echoing a beat under the rain.

It drew a caporal from Pijaume's unit outside the protection of the city walls to the path running along their base, the compass of the drum now deafening over the roar of the rain. He saw a rubbish bin had been pulled away from its stand and placed under a turn in the high walls, a spout of rain pouring off the stones and beating a frenzied attack on the empty plastic. Instinctively, he peered up through the downpour for the source of the water. A sheet of lightning lit the sky and he fell to his knees, scrabbling for his phone.

—

Two Mossos finally moved the rubbish bin and the thrumming in Elisenda's head subsided. They'd found the stand-up. He'd been left hanging by his feet from a rusted iron bar projecting from the city walls at their highest, loneliest point. The water that had beaten the plastic bin had beaten Xarlu too. A torrent spewing out through a gap in the walls onto where he was hanging, the surge of water relentlessly hitting his upturned face, his hobbled hands and feet giving him no respite from the flow. He'd drowned like that. In terror and panic and despair.

The rain running harshly down Elisenda's face were the tears her anger was able to stem. She watched as two Mossos pulled the body up, supervised by Albert Riera. The victim's face was bloodied and bruised from his struggle against the stones to escape the rainwater. He'd trusted Elisenda and she'd failed him. She knew that would never leave her. Only Pau and Josep stood close to her, Àlex and Montse back at Vista Alegre, the other Mossos keeping a distance.

When Xarlu left, she left too, to return to the station and the scrutiny.

'I am not relinquishing this investigation,' she told Puigventós in his office. 'I will catch this person and I will make them pay.'

'I can't support you indefinitely, Elisenda. An innocent man has died because of us, because of you.' His anger was growing colder, more political.

Elisenda refused to bow her head. 'You think I don't know that?'

'One more chance, Elisenda, that's all I will give you.'

'That's all I want.'

Àlex met her in her room. 'They've got the perfect alibi,' he told her. Antoni Sunyer and Roser Caselles. 'Watched by two Mossos the whole time the victim was being abducted and murdered. At no point did they manage to put anything in his drink. I don't see how they could be a part of this.' Àlex had brought them in straight away when he'd got news of the stand-up's murder and he and Montse had questioned them turn and turn about until dawn, but his own evidence and their answers seemed to take them out of the equation. They were simply fans.

'They know Corominas. They study or have studied history. They spoke to Xarlu.' She stared at her desk, knowing there was nothing they could keep them on. 'Let them go.'

'They also know Marsans.'

'Check that out. And keep an eye on them.'

She was relentlessly drawn to the website. News had broken of Xarlu's murder, creating the greatest divide they'd seen since the killings had started. She and Àlex read the threads that were battling for supremacy. The ones taking a stance against cultural imperialism but drawing the line at killing for it against the ones who didn't. The ones who loved Xarlu against those who hated what he stood for and, between those, the ones who stood for or against his fate. The young against the old, the traditionalists against the progressive, the reasonable against the righteous and every shade in between. Those whom people chose to protect and those to threaten.

The online edition of the newspaper had also got the story, the print one too late. But it also carried some notion of a Mossos operation gone wrong. 'Someone's talking,' Elisenda muttered. She got out of the site.

'I think we're seeing a shift,' she told Àlex. He looked surprised at the sudden shift in her. She gestured at the computer. 'Not in this. In the killer. I think perhaps we're looking too closely at the individual victims. The first ones, Masó and the muggers, I think who they actually were is important. Viladrau too. And Mònica Ferrer. But Foday Saio? He was a victim of civil war, an exile. We of all people should understand that. The attacker chose Foday Saio, but he could have chosen anyone who's moved into Girona from outside.'

'And the stand-up?'

'That's even more discordant. He's done nothing. He symbolises change, but he doesn't symbolise any great evil, he doesn't know anyone in Girona for them to hold a personal grudge. He simply reflects the El Tarlà legend. The jester on the scaffold, the hanging overhead, the drummer below. All the elements of the story are there, just wrapped around the crime to suit the killer.'

'What are you trying to say? The victims themselves aren't what matters anymore?'

'In a way. It seems to be moving away from the personal to the political. The victims are simply the vehicle. The message is the legends and the Verge de la Bona Mort.'

'So where does that leave us?'

'I don't know. But we have to use it to help us find this person and stop them.'

Àlex knew to leave her and to get on with his job of being her sergent, but first he needed a coffee. He'd been awake for twenty-four hours. Crossing the front desk, he ran into Micaló, who turned when Àlex approached.

'Sergent Albiol. You should possibly inform Sotsinspectora Domènech that a member of the city council has just been assaulted in the street. He's been taken to hospital.' He lowered his voice. 'If your superior had done her job properly, none of this would be happening.'

'I'll be sure to let her know,' Àlex told him, reeling in his anger before the audience Micaló had ensured was there.

He left the building and walked to a café where he'd be sure not to find any Mossos. He wasn't in the mood to have to defend his unit. He looked for somewhere to sit. A man at a table by a pillar was looking up at him and it was a few moments before he recognised him as Senyor Casademont's son. He seemed to have aged disproportionately since Àlex had last seen him. He felt a renewed flare of rage at the memory of the thug who'd attacked Casademont's father lying amid all the resources the health service had to offer while the victim's family had been left largely to fend for themselves. He thought, too, of the latest victim and of the pressure Elisenda was under.

'Take a seat here if you like, Sergent Albiol.'

Àlex sat down at Casademont's table. 'Please, call me Àlex. How are you?'

Casademont simply shrugged. 'I'm selling the business.'

'It's been in your family for years.'

'I've had enough.' His face was pale, the lines sunken and heavy. 'We're getting out of Girona. My family's always had a house in the Baix Empordà. We don't like living here any more, so we're moving out to live there. Me, my wife and my mother.'

'You've lived here all your life.'

'Yes.' He stared at the table in front of him.

'If there's anything I can do,' Àlex said. His words sounded empty even to him, but he could think of little else to say.

'Thank you, Àlex. You've been a good friend to my family.'
Casademont looked at his watch and stood up. 'Time to go.'

Àlex got up from his chair and the two men embraced. Àlex watched Casademont leave the café and took his phone out of his pocket.

'Senyor Pere,' he said when the taxi driver answered his call. 'There's something I want to ask you.'

Chapter Sixty One

David Costa emptied the big bag of croissants from the baker's downstairs onto a plate, the warm oil staining the brown paper with a smooth sheen, and put the *cafetera* on the stove. He was beginning to know his way around the modern flat in the new white-baked streets encroaching on the tall trees and dark dust of the Devesa. When the coffee was ready, he put everything on a tray and carried it through into the rented anonymity of the living room, where he found Carles Font sitting at the dining table, his crutches leaning against the back of his chair.

Carles Font, Costa thought. Strange times make for strange bedfellows.

On the table, Font's laptop was open, the screen casting a pallid glow over the journalist's gaunt face. His recovery from the beating he'd received was slow and he was on sick leave from the paper, sending the occasional article to the news room. Besides other things he was working on.

Costa considered the laptop. The story Font had told him. About the guy in Barcelona who'd helped him with a story he'd done some years back. Who'd helped him now, setting up a long trail of servers and accounts and relays that the journalist couldn't begin to understand but was happy to trust to the guy in Barcelona. The very secretive guy in Barcelona who was as interested in protecting his own identity as he was in borrowing other people's.

Costa sat down next to Font and poured the coffee. Font pressed a key on his laptop to bring it out of sleep mode. The social network website that had the whole of Girona yapping at their neighbours and colleagues with petty expectant vengeance shone out of its slumber. Font tapped in a series of commands and got into the administrator page.

'Who do we have?' Costa asked him.

Chapter Sixty Two

Ignasi Perafita was waiting for Elisenda at the front desk. This time without Bellsolà.

'I'm next,' he told her. 'I demand police protection.'

Elisenda sighed, trying to switch back to the present. For the time being, cramming her guilt at Xarlu's death into a corner of her mind that she knew would ambush her for the rest of her life. She placed it carefully next to her daughter.

'Is there anything that makes you think you're next? Have you had any threats?' All Mossos were alert for tiles of the Verge anywhere in the city now that the statue itself was no longer the vehicle. She knew there were no sightings of one at present.

'I just know, Sotsinspectora Domènech. My wife was murdered. I am bound to be on this killer's list.' His aggressive self-centredness bubbled above his fear.

'There's nothing to suggest you're a potential victim, Senyor Perafita. If you are concerned, I advise you to take precautions, but the Mossos are simply unable to offer individual protection for everyone who thinks they may be targeted.'

'Do your job, you stupid bloody woman,' Perafita raged, storming out. 'I will make an official complaint.'

Join the queue, Elisenda thought.

She caught up with Josep and he drove her to Salt in silence. Both of them knew that the investigation had to continue. Neither knew what to say. No one did. She found Joaquim Masó where she expected to, in an old-fashioned bar at the foot of a grim 1960s apartment block. Grizzled men smoked poor cigars and clacked dominoes onto rough wooden tables to the sound of an ancient transistor radio sputtering the odds of the evening's football matches. Masó watched Elisenda approach and told the two brothers to sit at another table.

'I hope you're going to be more polite than your sergent,' he told her. 'It's the Sunday after All Saints. I've been to the cemetery to show my respect to my loved ones and now I'm relaxing among friends.'

'Very traditional. I applaud you.' She looked at the two brothers on an adjacent table, staring coldly back at her. 'Although I see you don't really subscribe to the family tradition of only employing your own.'

'Tradition moves on. I'm just quietly getting on with my business. No crime against that.'

'Your nephew's business.'

'Mine now.'

'And now it's my business. I just came to tell you.'

Masó took a drink from a glass of beer. 'I don't think so. You're too busy chasing after this other guy to worry about me.'

'Don't count on it.' Elisenda got up to leave.

'Give my regards to young Pablo Yáñez, won't you.'

Elisenda nodded at that and left, her face not giving away her surprise at his last remark.

Deep in thought, she and Josep drove on to an apartment in Salt. Foday Saio opened the door to let them both in. Patricia was quietly drawing at a low coffee table. His wife was out, working.

'I just wanted to ask you about the complaints you made about vandalism, Foday,' Elisenda told him. 'Have you been threatened by the Masó family?'

'They tried to make me borrow money from them to repair the door after the second time, but I wouldn't. That's when they did more damage. But it's stopped now. Since Daniel died.'

'Please tell me if anyone from the Masó family threatens you again,' Elisenda told him. 'I'm sorry you became a victim of these people.'

Foday held up his arms, showing Elisenda the puckered, lighter skin at the ends where his hands should be.

'Some men did this to me when I was a child. Here, one man threw paint at my door and another man tried to make me drink some drugged wine and failed. No one will ever make a victim of me again. The Masó family cannot hurt me.'

Elisenda looked at Patricia engrossed in her drawing and wished it were true.

Josep told Elisenda that he and Pau had seen another change on the website. 'Fewer individuals are being suggested as victims. We think people aren't so willing to name specific people now the killings are escalating. So they're naming types of people to be attacked.'

They were driving from Salt along the fast dual carriageway towards Ripoll, able to speak now they were leaving Girona behind. The leaves on the beech trees were changing. Any other time, it would have been a beautiful sight.

'Hence this councillor,' Elisenda considered. Despite no evidence of any wrongdoing by the council in general and the councillor in particular, the city council had been targeted for attack on the website and two unknown men had set upon a junior councillor in the street earlier that morning when he was walking to work. Cuts and bruises and under observation at hospital, but nothing serious as far as she knew.

'The Mossos are also near the top of the list,' Josep told her.

'The question is, is public opinion responding to the killer, or vice versa?'

'Public opinion is responding to public opinion. Some of them are doing what other people are telling them.' He fell silent for a moment. 'It feels like the killer is taunting us, like he can anticipate what people are going to do. What we're going to do.'

'Or he knows.'

They turned off before Ripoll and arrived at a farm sheltered in a wooded valley. Elisenda got out of the car and stood for a moment, scenting the autumn mountain air. It felt almost too pure, too heady.

She got two very strong sensations from Pere Corominas' parents who, greying in kaftans, invited her and Josep into their kitchen.

The first was dope. She could sense it in the thick darkness of the smoke-stained kitchen and in the parchment-dry Saint John's Wort tied in bunches over the range to ward off sickness. And she could sense it in the two people seated opposite her, separated from her by a far greater gulf than the kitchen table could ever provide. It was in their clothing, their words and their movements.

The other was a complete lack of grasp on reality.

'He's finding himself, that's all,' the mother insisted.

The father looked at Elisenda pityingly. 'He'll come back when he's ready.'

'Do you know where he is now?' Elisenda asked the question again. 'We need to find your son.'

'He'll be among nature,' the father told her. 'Revitalising.'

'When did you last see him?'

Corominas' mother asked her what month it was now and Elisenda knew she was going to get nowhere. 'Do you mind if we take a look around?'

'Not without a warrant,' the mother instantly replied.

Outside, Elisenda scanned the outbuildings and barns. She wondered what lay hidden in them. In the car, she called Pau and asked him to apply to Jutgessa Roca for a warrant to search the farm.

'What did you make of them?' Josep asked her when she hung up.

'That was one of the few times since I've been in the Mossos that I've had no idea whatsoever what was in someone's head.' They bumped along the track back to the main road. 'But I do know they're hiding something.'

Chapter Sixty Three

'Bet you're glad that funny guy got killed.'

Elisenda got her breath back from her run around the outside of the city walls and looked at Xiscu. Pujol was lying stubbornly at the end of his leash on the cobbles in the Monday morning air.

'How do you work that out?'

'Because no one's talking about the crippled black guy any more.'

'Go home, Xiscu. Get some rest.'

When she got into the office, she saw from the latest comments on the website that he was, in his awful way, right. The circus of applause and opprobrium had moved on to the next victim. The problem was that the next victim had been part of a Mossos operation. There were all sorts of rumours on the website and speculation in the media, but no facts. Yet. She reckoned her own stay of execution with Puigventós was down to the sudden drop in racial tension, which had risen and fallen like sea foam, but that would change the moment she was named. Scrolling back through the history, she saw that after the attack on Mònica Ferrer, most people were still pretty much sympathising with the attacker but then the comments started to turn against him. First with Foday Saio, now with Xarlu. There was still a hard core that applauded any act he carried out, but the tide was definitely ebbing. She also saw that as the support for the attacks decreased, so the criticism of the Mossos rose in inverse measure. An upsurge was steadily beginning to rise against the police. She hoped it wouldn't become a riptide. Even with that, it almost made her life easier than when everyone was whipping up hatred of everyone else.

A gentle voice behind her made her start.

'You're doing the right thing, Sotsinspectora,' Pau told her.

'It doesn't feel like it, but thank you, Pau.'

Embarrassed, he showed her an e-mail he'd had from Sergent Gispert. 'He's identified three individuals in Barcelona that he thinks would be capable of a set-up like this,' Pau explained. 'The Central Investigation Unit in Sabadell will be questioning them.'

'Good. Keep me informed.'

'I've also got a name for the woman in the Viladrau DVD. Valentina Cioni. She's an Italian national. From what I can gather, the church have got her back to Rome, where they've cut her loose without any support.'

Elisenda sighed. Yet one more victim. 'Don't waste any more time on it. It's not such an important avenue now that other events have escalated. I don't think she could help us much anyway.'

'May I say, Sotsinspectora? You are doing the right thing. You're anticipating the attacks. You're getting nearer.'

'I haven't stopped him. And I got someone killed, Pau.'

'You didn't, Elisenda. You're getting into his mind. How he thinks. That's the only way we'll stop him.'

'The only problem with that is that he also gets into my head. And I'm not sure I want that.'

Her mobile rang. She listened in silence and hung up, looking at Pau.

'And it's about to be put to the test again. They've found another tile.'

Chapter Sixty Four

'So what's this one, then?' Àlex asked.

'El Cul de la Lleona,' Elisenda told him. The Lioness's Arse.

Àlex looked at the statue of a primitive lion climbing a pole.

Two Seguretat Ciutadana had already been on the little square in front of Sant Feliu church when Elisenda and Àlex had arrived. The two uniforms had been walking through the streets of the Mercadal part of town and had crossed the Pont de Sant Feliu footbridge over the river to the old quarter when they'd come across the tile, hanging around the stone pillar to which the statue of the lioness was clinging. They'd recognised straight away what it was and called Vista Alegre immediately. They should do. One of them was Mosso Paredes.

'Francesc,' Elisenda said to him, 'you're making a habit of this.'

He'd smiled in embarrassment and helped the Policia Científica string a length of plastic tape in a wide, irregular arc around the statue. Four more Seguretat Ciutadana turned up and tried to edge an audience of mystified Japanese tourists further away, just as Pau and Montse arrived in an unmarked car. The four of them from Elisenda's team were standing outside the plastic cordon, waiting for the Científica, now bolstered by four more members, to tell them they could go through. Elisenda called Paredes over and asked him if he'd seen what was on the tile.

'The Verge de la Bona Mort,' he told her. 'Like before. And there's something drawn on the back of it, but I couldn't see what it was.'

Elisenda thanked him and he went back to controlling the increasing number of onlookers, a small crowd gathering to watch, many holding up mobile phones and digital cameras in intent supplication.

'What's the significance of the lioness? Àlex asked. 'I know that if you kiss her arse, you're supposed to come back to Girona, but what is it we're supposed to be expecting this time?'

'Have you ever done it?' Elisenda asked him. 'Kiss her arse?' He shook his head. 'The point is, if you do, you see that she is in fact a he.'

One of the Policia Científica came over to where they were standing and lifted the plastic tape, calling Elisenda and Àlex through.

'So many people have been up and down the ladder and around the base, there's precious little left to contaminate,' she explained. She wanted to show them the tile. All three craned their necks to look up at it, hanging by a length of wire looped around the pillar above the lioness's head.

'I see what you mean about her being a him,' Àlex muttered.

A simple shape had been drawn on the unglazed clay on the back of the tile in thick black marker pen.

'A fly?' Elisenda exclaimed in surprise.

She and Àlex moved away again, back to where the others in their unit were standing, and watched the Científica do their jobs, filming, photographing, recording, searching.

'Why a fly again?'

'Because the last one with a fly failed?' Pau asked.

'The lioness and a fly.' Elisenda shook her head. 'They don't go together in any way I know.'

'So what does it mean?' Àlex asked the other three, all Gironins.

Elisenda stopped to consider. 'If it were just the lioness, I'd say it meant one of two things.'

Pau interrupted. 'Pujada del Rei Martí?'

269

'That's one. The other one's the Font dels Lleons. According to legend, the fountain of lions is called that because wolves used to go there to drink.'

'Wolves or lions?' Àlex asked.

'In popular tradition in Girona, wolves and lions were always confused.' She pointed to the statue of the lioness. 'That's probably really a wolf. No one knows. Some people thought at first it was a monkey. Either way, we know it's not a female lion.'

'So who would the victim be?'

She looked back at the statue. 'The way this attacker's mind works, I think his victim will be gay. Man or woman, I don't know.'

'Gay?' Montse asked. 'Because everyone thinks the lioness is a she and it's a he? I don't get it.'

'Be thankful you don't,' Elisenda told her. 'No one normal would. But this guy's anything but normal. Not in how he sees his victims.'

Montse shook her head in disbelief. 'I see it but I don't.'

'That's exactly what I'm trying to hold on to.'

All four stood in silence and looked at the statue. It was Àlex who broke the still. 'And what about Pujada del Rei Martí? That's the road just up by the Verge de la Bona Mort.'

Pau was the first to respond. 'There used to be a carving on a lintel above one of the doors. It's now in the art museum, but it's supposed to relate to a legend about a wolf snatching a young boy during a procession and killing him.'

'It killed a young boy?'

'That's why my money's on the Font dels Lleons,' Elisenda said. 'I just don't think he'd attack a child.'

'He's attacked a disabled man.'

'Even so. I just feel even he would draw the line at a child. In which case, the victim's more likely to be up at the old drinking fountain.'

'And gay.'

'I hate it as much as you do,' Elisenda replied, 'but I'm pretty certain. I can't see who else the attacker would think fits in with the statue. He's making us choose which victim we'd prefer again. A homosexual or a child. That way, we all lose.'

'I think we should check the Pujada del Rei Martí,' Àlex said. 'Especially if it's near here.'

'I agree.' Elisenda told Pau to get hold of Seguretat Ciutadana to check the street. 'There are some houses that are semi-derelict, waiting to be renovated. Concentrate on those.'

She told Montse to call Josep at Vista Alegre and get him to pick her up to go out to the fountain. 'It's at the end of Sant Daniel. Way up the valley, after the road ends. Tell him to use a 4x4 from the pool, but you're still going to have to hike to get there.'

Elisenda watched the other two members of her team move away to make their phone calls and she turned to Àlex.

'The question is where the fly fits in.'

Chapter Sixty Five

'Was that a snake?'

Montse watched the dry undergrowth shiver as something slithered into it. 'Don't worry, it'll be a grass snake. They're harmless.'

She saw Josep stare intently at the low bushes next to the trickle of the stream as they tramped past. 'It had stripes.'

'A striped grass snake.'

'Do they exist?'

'Probably. Who knows?'

'God, I miss Hospitalet.'

Josep and two Seguretat Ciutadana had picked Montse up near the statue of the lioness and driven as far as the 4x4 could take them along the Vall de Sant Daniel, to the north of the city walls. They'd passed the monastery and gone on to where the road had become too narrow and strewn with boulders and logs to pass, so now they were making the last stretch of the journey on foot. Josep had complained all the way.

'I thought everyone in Hospitalet had a romantic vision of the countryside,' Montse told him.

'We have a romantic vision of the moon. It doesn't mean we want to go there.'

Montse signalled for them to stop. The faint path they'd been following opened out into a clearing, revealing the incongruous sight of a once ornate stone drinking fountain backed up against a natural rock outcrop. Josep walked on slowly into the mottled shade of the ancient fountain and looked around. Montse joined him and stood in silence, listening to the soothing sound of the cicadas calling out to each other amid the last of the summer's leaves. Many more leaves had fallen, carpeting the stone ground in shades of amber and garnet. Water trickled down from the fountain spout, its meagre flow augmented by the recent rain. Montse knew the water to be undrinkable.

There was no one there.

Josep spoke to Montse in a low voice. 'I'd have thought if we were going to find anyone, it would have been here by the fountain.'

A plane flew high overhead. They could hear it but were unable to catch sight of it through the forest encircling them. The whisper of the water flowing unevenly from the spout and the chitchat of the cicadas reclaimed the woods after the noise of the plane had died away. It would have been a beautiful afternoon were it not for their mission.

Josep peered off into the trees. A couple of paths besides the one they had followed could just be made out through the undergrowth. 'Logically,' he said, 'if he managed to carry someone this far on foot, he can't have taken them very much further. If we do find anyone, they can't be far away.'

They agreed that Josep and the two uniforms would take a path each, Montse would carry on looking beyond the rock at the rear of the fountain.

'Go for fifteen minutes,' Montse told them. 'If you don't find anything, you're unlikely to. This person was supposedly carrying a dead weight.'

They separated, Montse and Josep touching fingertips as they parted. Josep found himself taking the path to the right of the small clearing. Gorse and brambles scratched at his trouser legs, snaring them and flicking away as he broke on through. In the exasperated still of the air beneath the leaf-filtered sun, he was sweating heavily under his jacket. He took it off and slung it over his shoulder, swatting ineffectually at the flies buzzing around his face.

Almost immediately, he came across a second path that veered off from the first. He decided on impulse to take it. He thought he'd give it five minutes and turn back if he'd found nothing by then. Concentrating on his footing, he suddenly paused for a moment and took half a step back. Something he'd almost missed. Off to the left, he saw what he first thought was a large rock, but what he quickly realised were the remains of an old stone hut.

Reaching the hut, he saw it was abandoned. Some of the stones had crumbled and part of the roof had fallen in. The lock on the door had long since rusted away and the wood was rotting at the top and bottom, leaving gaps large enough for small animals to get in. Footprints and the smell told him they frequently did. He put on latex gloves and gingerly pushed at the door. It resisted stiffly for a brief moment before lurching inwards, coming to a rest against the raised earth floor. The light that came in through the gap in the roof lit up the shambles of the tiles and splintered timbers lying across the ground. Against the far wall, an ancient wooden chest stood rotting, its lid oddly cleared of the debris from the roof with the exception of three large stones placed at regular intervals along the top. And hundreds of little black objects scattered like raisins on a cake.

Josep stared at the chest for a while and went back outside to ring Montse. 'I think I've found something.' He gave her directions to the hut and went back in. As his eyes grew more accustomed, he made out more of the black crumbs lying by the right-hand corner of the chest, where the wood had rotted through. Stepping carefully forward to the far side of the room, he moved the three stones off the lid and placed them on the floor. It was only at the moment he put his hands under the lid to lift it that he registered that the black objects were dead flies. In their hundreds.

The lid was up before his brain had time to send the message back to his hands and a swarm of tiny orange and black flies rose in a bitter cloud from inside the cask. He pushed away, fighting the flies off, knocking the lid back against the wall, propping it open.

Behind him, Montse came in as he was backing away from the chest, his hands flailing at the flies. She went forward to help her colleague when she saw inside the old storage box.

'My God,' she said, dragging Josep back outside into the pale autumn sun.

Her hand shaking, she took out her phone and dialled.

Chapter Sixty Six

'This place is so lonely.'

Elisenda brushed a thorn aside and considered Àlex's comment. It was a lonely place. She remembered Sunday morning rambles along this same path with her parents when she and Catalina were children, but they never went beyond the lion fountain.

When Montse's tremulous call had first come through, she'd caught herself feeling almost a sense of relief that she'd be making the trek out to the disused drinking fountain in the woods rather than roaming amid the precarious floors and walls of a medieval terraced house looking for a dead child. That had gone now they were walking with four Científica along a shaded path to a dead body.

Behind her, Àlex stumbled and she caught him. A penknife fell out of his waistband and clattered to the stones on the path. Hurriedly, he picked it up and put it back.

'Rules are there to be broken,' Elisenda commented.

He looked sheepish. 'Hangover from my uniform days.' Many Seguretat Ciutadana kept a penknife in their waistband, even though it wasn't standard issue and was frowned upon.

The noise of snapping twigs and foul language from behind them made them turn. Another party was making its way along the path, with Albert Riera and his assistant sandwiched between two Mossos. The language was Riera's.

'Out of the way,' the forensic doctor told them as he drew level.

'Please,' Àlex replied, more in reflex than thought.

'Just get out of the fucking way.'

Elisenda stood in front of him. 'Doctor Riera, I would be grateful if you didn't talk to members of my team like that.'

Riera stopped up short and looked at Elisenda in surprise. 'I am in a hurry.'

'I don't care. If you are going to talk to anyone in my team like that, then you are talking to me like that.' She leaned forward. 'And if you ever do that again, I will have words with you. Do you understand?'

Riera stared straight at Elisenda. 'Thank you, Sotsinspectora, I will remember that. Now, if you don't mind, I have work to do. Our victims come before our personalities, as I am sure you will understand.'

Elisenda stood aside to let him pass and they carried on walking, past the fountain, and along the path to the hut. There, one of the Científica handed her and Àlex an overall each and they put them on over their clothes. Elisenda recalled the cold cruelty of a killer who could leave a man to drown in rainwater and calmly place a rubbish bin below to recreate a drum. She could already feel the sweat trickle down her spine as she steeled herself for the scene that she knew would knock the breath out of her.

–

Elisenda took a sip of water from a plastic bottle and she and Àlex watched a Científica team, their white suits ghostly in the diffuse sunlight, set up a small generator and a quartet of arc lights to shine on the hut. The sun still had some way to go before it would sink behind the trees, but the light was so gloomy in the dense wood that it was becoming harder to discern shapes. They were waiting to be told when they could go back into the hut. There was little to say.

The judge and the court secretary were standing to one side, away from them. Not Jutgessa Roca mercifully, as this was far too dirty and far too far from the city centre for her to come, but the two court officials still kept themselves to themselves. Elisenda was more than happy with that. And they certainly weren't too worried about entering the hut a second time to allow the body to be removed. They'd already signed that piece of paper. Anything to avoid going back inside the stifling cabin with its lonely occupant. For once, Elisenda didn't blame them.

Riera came out of the hut and walked over to her and Àlex.

'Elisenda,' he said. They were still treading carefully after their argument on the path.

'Albert. What have you got for me?'

'I'm not an expert in this field, but we think that the flies that are still active are calliphoridae, blow flies. And there are beetles, too. Silphidae. I've come across them before, obviously, but as I say, it's not my field.'

'What does that mean?'

'Well, you'd need an expert and they'd have to check temperature and so on recently, but given the flies and the state of decomposition, I'd say that the body must have been there between one to two months. That's as specific as I can be at present.'

'Thank you, Albert, I appreciate it.'

He made to go back to the hut, but turned again to face the two Mossos.

'What's happening to this city, Elisenda?'

'I think I'm beginning to get an idea, Albert.' They looked at each other for a moment and the forensic doctor returned to the hut, pulling his mask up over his face again.

'I don't envy him in there,' Elisenda muttered as she and Àlex watched him being swallowed by the dark of the small stone building.

Àlex made a calculation. 'One to two months. Between the end of August and the end of September. And it's been very hot since the summer, so I'd put it nearer one month than two.'

'End of September, then. Meaning it took place around the time of the Masó killing.' Elisenda tapped her empty water bottle against her leg, issuing a hollow dull sound. 'I just don't see how it all fits together. Why stage this for now? Why not reveal the victim at the same time as the attack? At the same time as the attacks on Masó and Chema GM?'

'The fly,' Àlex said simply. 'The fly drawn on the back of the tile. To coincide with Sant Narcís.'

'So where does Foday Saio fit in? Two victims to mark Sant Narcís? And it can't be in response to the attack on Foday failing as this was obviously carried out long before.'

They watched two more Policía Científica enter the hut, evidently summoned by someone inside.

'Besides which,' Elisenda continued, 'what is this attack suppose to be reflecting? Sant Narcís and the flies? Or the lioness? He's mixing the legends.'

Àlex nodded to where a white-suited figure was emerging from the hut and walking in their direction. 'I suppose we have to wait and see who this victim is to find out where they fit in.'

The figure in white, one of the Científica, paused before reaching Elisenda and Àlex and removed her mask, gulping in a deep breath. She was holding a pair of objects in two transparent evidence bags.

'Sotsinspectora Domènech,' she said. 'Doctor Riera has lifted the body. He thinks that the victim was dead before he was put in the box. We found the victim's wallet underneath the body.' She held up one bag, which contained a stained leather wallet. 'This was inside it.'

She lifted the second bag for Elisenda to see. Inside was the victim's national identity card, kept sadly clean by its plastic coating and the protection of the wallet.

Elisenda simply stared at the name and the picture on the card.

'Thank you,' she said.

Chapter Sixty Seven

Carles Font's injuries were healing, but David Costa still turned up most days to make them both breakfast and keep the website ticking over. They were almost like old friends.

Costa had seen straight away that Font had been the one to set up the website. He had recognised his style, his turn of phrase, even his punctuation. Font had expected the editor to go to the Mossos with it, or at least lose him his job. Instead, he had come to Font with a proposition. Work together on the website. Guide it, say what they were unable to say in the newspaper, promote sales of the newspaper. And it had worked. Circulation had trebled since the attacks had started. The fact that the website had drawn out the worst and most vindictive in people was neither here nor there to either of them. They were reaping the benefits of increased sales and augmented repute in a mutually rewarding relationship. Font would make his name and eventually move back to Barcelona. Costa would garner favour with the paper's owners and get rid of his young rival on terms that suited them both.

Costa went into the living room with the breakfast tray and set it down on the table before sitting down next to Font. Font's laptop was already open and logged in to the administrator page. They checked the latest posts and saw that the tide continued to turn. Both journalists were glad they'd foreseen the gradual shift and had reflected it equally gradually in their articles.

The news of the body in the woods had broken the previous night, but since no identity for the victim had been confirmed, all the postings so far were speculation. A neighbour who'd suddenly gone quiet, a boss who hadn't turned up to work. Wishful thinking and gleefully shocked anticipation of who the dead man should be.

Font typed in a couple of postings to add to the voices raised in horror at the turn of events, and a third to keep up the antagonism towards the victims.

'We ought to shift focus, perhaps,' Costa suggested. 'Bring in more people to blame. Float them, see what the mob says.'

Font took a bite out of a croissant, brushing away the crumbs that had fallen onto the keyboard. 'The Mossos? They're an obvious target.'

'Yes, I think we should up the ante against them. Maybe even make it more personal.'

Font considered for a moment. 'There's Micaló. He's not popular with other Mossos, it might stir them up.'

'Not so sure,' Costa replied, breaking the end off a croissant and chewing it slowly. 'There must be other more high-profile Mossos we can target.'

Font snapped his fingers. 'Domènech. Of course. She's the one in charge of the investigation.'

Costa considered that for a moment. 'Yes, if you think so. Domènech. But we need a hook to hang her on.'

'Imply her involvement in the comedian's death. We could never get away with that in the paper.'

'Yes, if you think that's a good idea.'

Font opened a new account and began to type a bitter posting about Elisenda. Costa stared at his own dark reflection on the laptop screen and at a faint smile playing around his mouth.

Chapter Sixty Eight

'Actually, it's not called Font dels Lleons because wolves used to go there to drink. That's just a popular myth to try and romanticise it because of the name. It's simply called that because the fountain originally had a shield carved into the rock featuring the twin lions of Bishop Lorenzana.'

'Nineteenth century?' Elisenda asked.

'Eighteenth,' Marsans corrected her. 'He was the bishop of Girona who had the chapel to Sant Narcís built in Sant Feliu church, partly using stones from the area where the fountain was subsequently built. The fountain was probably put there to mark his part in the chapel's construction.'

'Why lions?'

'He was from León. As simple as that. The vast majority of legends that pass into popular culture really are exceedingly mundane in their origins.'

Elisenda looked away from the lecturer and out through the window of his office, but she wasn't registering the view over the city walls. It had been a curiously unreal limbo since the discovery of the murder victim the previous afternoon. Elisenda had gone to the university that morning to clarify the legend of the lioness so that she could get the perpetrator's thinking straighter in her mind. And to get away from Vista Alegre to think. She still couldn't see the connection with the fly and Sant Narcís. The post mortem was scheduled for that morning, rushed through thanks to Albert Riera's surprisingly co-operative insistence. And to the slow panic of the Mossos and the authorities finally breaking down the resistance of formality and procedure. She looked at her watch. Riera knew to ring Elisenda the moment he had news from the post mortem, if only to confirm the victim's identity. Àlex and Pau were going through the attacks on Masó and Chema GM to try to find a chronology that included the latest body they'd found. The rest of her team were sifting through the evidence of the more recent attacks, looking for anything they'd missed first time round. And Puigventós had called a meeting for later in the morning.

She sighed heavily and turned away from the window.

'So there's actually no relationship whatsoever with the statue of the lioness,' she finally said. 'That's interesting.'

'Why?'

Elisenda considered for a moment how much she wanted to say. 'Because the first thing I thought of when the tile was found at the lioness was the Font dels Lleons. And that's evidently what the attacker thought too.'

'Perhaps he knew you'd think that way.'

Elisenda looked back out of the window. Studded amid the evergreens and lawns locked within the city walls, the leaves on the deciduous trees were finally beginning to turn red and gold, escaping the deceit of summer's reluctance to leave. She shook her head very slightly. She wanted to get into the attacker's head. She didn't want him in hers.

Marsans turned to look beyond the walls. 'It's a beautiful view, isn't it? I love rambling in these hills.' Elisenda sensed him moving closer to her, almost touching her as he stood alongside to gaze out of the window. 'This is a dreadful thing that's happening to our lovely city.'

'We've been checking Pere Corominas' phone records, Professor Marsans. He made a number of calls to you.'

Marsans moved back very slightly before replying. 'He often calls me with doubts about his research. He can be really quite needy.'

'His views on the lessons of history are pretty radical.'

'Pere is a very intense young man, but also rather skittish. His views have a tendency to metamorphose before your eyes.'

'You also know Antoni Sunyer and Roser Caselles, friends of his.'

'Students, past and present. You're not suggesting they have anything to do with Pere's disappearance? With what's going on?'

The door into the office opened and Elisenda turned to see a woman walking in. She was clutching a small sheaf of papers in her left hand, the printed sheets crushed in her grip, her knuckles white. Her eyes were red, as though she'd been crying.

'How could you?' the woman said.

Marsans turned to face her slowly. Watching him, Elisenda registered a fleeting expression of alarm on his face.

'I'm most awfully sorry, Aurora, I'm afraid I don't know what you mean.'

The woman shook her fistful of paper at Marsans. 'This. How could you?'

Elisenda turned fully, her eyes scanning back and forth between the two. Marsans was next to speak, relying on his charm to defuse the woman's anger.

'But where are my manners? Elisenda, may I introduce my colleague, Professora Aurora Torrent. Aurora, this is Sotsinspectora Elisenda Domènech from the Mossos d'Esquadra. She's investigating these simply terrible events that have been occurring in the city.'

Torrent brandished the papers. 'I've just received this, Octavi. It's an abstract for the lecture you're giving in New York.'

Marsans turned to Elisenda. 'I have been invited to give a lecture at a conference at Columbia University. Professora Torrent had assumed she would be doing so too, but her proposal was rejected.' He turned to Torrent. 'I'm sorry, Aurora, but this does rather smack of professional jealousy.'

Torrent almost lunged forward and Elisenda had to calm her. Elisenda looked at Marsans. 'If you wouldn't mind, Professor Marsans, perhaps Professora Torrent could explain.'

'I was invited,' Torrent went on after she'd gathered her thoughts, 'but then the invitation was revoked. They claimed another person was giving a paper that was too similar to my own. Then I found this.' She thrust the papers at Elisenda. 'It's the programme with the abstracts. Professor Marsans is the person giving the talk that is too similar to mine.'

'You know as well as I do, Aurora, that we work in parallel fields. There's bound to be an element of similarity in what we do.'

'This isn't similarity. This is plagiarism. There are phrases lifted directly from my own work in the subject. Conclusions that I reached. Research only I undertook.'

'Plagiarism? That's a very serious allegation, Aurora. You'd better have extremely good proof of it.' Elisenda could hear the undertone of casual triumph in his voice.

Torrent turned to Elisenda. 'I don't have proof because I hadn't published any of it yet. I had a book deal and this paper at Columbia with which I was going to make my research public. But this work by Professor Marsans has led to both being cancelled.'

'Where is your research?'

'On my laptop.'

'Could anyone have accessed it?'

'No. I never leave it here. I conduct my research at the city archives.'

Marsans spoke. 'Then how can you claim that I plagiarised your work? I've never seen it. I've never had any interest in seeing it. You said yourself you never leave it here. I quite simply would never have had the opportunity.'

Torrent looked at him. 'You have your little disciples scattered about the city, doing your bidding. Which one did you get to do this?'

'This is just fanciful nonsense, I'm afraid.' Marsans started getting some papers together. 'Born of unfettered jealousy, Aurora.'

He walked in a self-consciously casual lope across the room to the door and left. Elisenda quickly scanned through the abstract of Marsans' lecture, barely having time to finish it before Torrent snatched it out of her hands.

'I wouldn't expect you to understand it,' the academic told the police officer.

Chapter Sixty Nine

Elisenda found herself at the Portal de Sobreportes, staring at the Verge de la Bona Mort. The Madonna held her gaze with the same sightless beatific smile she had given to centuries of condemned and innocent.

Elisenda took a deep breath. To her left, the Audiència Provincial, soon to be moved to a new building nearer the centre. To her right, what every child in Girona knew to be the largest Rococo staircase in Europe. In front of her, the medieval gateway into the city, its Roman foundations still visible. Beneath her feet, what was once the Via Augusta, leading straight to Rome.

And above her, the Verge de la Bona Mort, giving no secrets away.

She sighed and closed her eyes.

The day of curious limbo had been irrevocably turned into one of numb activity once the identity of the murder victim had been confirmed.

Pere Corominas.

She now had to view him as a victim, not a suspect, tearing down all her recent suppositions to leave her searching for new ones. Tearing down the walls of her investigation to leave her without a suspect, without a focus. And tearing down the barrier against her guilt at Xarlu's death that the search for Corominas had provided.

Until that point, she'd moved on auto-pilot. She'd left the two professors to their squabbling and gone back to the station. Assigning tasks, reading and re-reading Pau's summaries,

287

listening, looking, structuring. And listening to her own gut feeling. The one that shocked her.

Something else was nagging at her.

'His mobile phone is missing,' Pau had told her.

'Stolen by the perpetrator.'

'No. One of the Científica thinks she saw it at the murder scene. Now it's not in his effects. It's gone missing since the body was found.'

'Thinks she saw it?'

Pau looked apologetic. 'Thinks she's certain she saw it.'

Pau had also told her that Jutgessa Roca had refused their application for a warrant to search the Corominas family farm. 'She said it was no longer necessary.' And he'd discovered that Pere Corominas was already being discussed on the website. Some contributors sympathising with the new victim, a hard core still virulently behind the attacker, others who had opposed the attack on Xarlu now backtracking and applauding the treatment meted out to a gay man.

'I guess people choose their own morality,' Elisenda had commented, her voice tired.

And there'd been the meeting with Puigventós and the other two sotsinspectors. More painful limbo. She'd looked at her watch, not as surreptitiously as her upbringing would have predicted, and listened to Micaló waffle on about targets and societal segments and customer-oriented crime prevention. Pijaume had glanced over to Elisenda and given her a look of bored disbelief. She'd looked away. Only minutes earlier, they'd argued.

'Nothing is being done to trace these drugs,' Elisenda had complained.

'I am fully stretched,' Pijaume had told her.

'Please, Elisenda,' Puigventós had said, signalling her to keep quiet. She'd looked at him, controlling her anger.

She tuned in for a second only to realise that Micaló was still talking and tuned back out. Corominas. She could now see how the killer's mind might see Corominas as being a suitable victim simply by being gay. And she could also see how the same appalling mind might see a connection between a gay man and the ambiguous sexuality of the statue of the lioness. What she couldn't see was the connection of the drawing of the fly on the back of the tile. She knew it was to signify Sant Narcís and the flies emerging from the tomb, but nothing she knew of in the life or legend of the saint pointed to an attack on a gay man or a link with the lioness legend. Nor could she understand the timing. He had to have been murdered at roughly the same time as Masó and Chema GM and the body left until now to be discovered for the flies in the tomb to have a meaning. But in the meantime, the killer had attempted an attack on Foday Saio, an immigrant, also to coincide with the Sant Narcís holidays. That incident did at least tie in with the legend of Sant Narcís repelling invaders, in the attacker's mind anyway, even if this latest one didn't, but she couldn't see the reason for the two attacks. She also wondered what fate he'd had in mind for Foday and shuddered.

She'd been to see Foday Saio the previous night. There'd been one too many ghosts at home when she'd got in from the scene of Corominas' murder, so she'd picked a book off her shelves – one she'd loved as a child but had no reason to keep any more – and driven out to Salt. Foday had answered the door to the tiny flat and asked her in, surprised.

'I just wanted to go over what you remember seeing,' Elisenda had told him.

Patricia rushed up to her at the door, but then hung back, clinging to her father's legs.

'Hi Patricia,' Elisenda greeted her, bending down. 'I thought you might like this book. It was one of my favourites when I was a little girl. It's about a dog called Quin Desastre who's always getting into trouble.'

The little girl thanked her and ran off to the living room with the book. Foday ushered Elisenda into the same room, where

Patricia was already ensconced on a small red sofa immersed in the illustrations, and went to the kitchen to make coffee. Elisenda watched the little girl engrossed in the tale, letting out a loud belly laugh every now and then. She smiled, remembering the stories and how her own daughter had, in turn, loved them.

'Do you like the pictures?' Elisenda asked her. Patricia nodded. 'If you look carefully, you see lots of little things going on that you didn't see the first time. Like the day you were in the park with your daddy. Can you remember anything like that, Patricia?'

The little girl looked at the picture book and frowned. 'I saw a very old man. He had white hands and he was carrying a bottle.'

White hands, Elisenda realised. Latex gloves.

Foday came in carrying a tray with two coffee cups and a steaming glass of hot Cola Cao for his daughter. Elisenda looked up at him and he signalled for her to carry on.

'Did you see what colour his hair was?' Elisenda asked Patricia.

'No. He had a cap on. It was blue. And he was wearing a coat. It went all the way up his face.'

Elisenda smiled at her but she knew she wouldn't learn any more from her. The one eye witness they had was too young to know what she'd seen and the attacker was evidently too clued up to show much of himself. She asked Foday if he'd remembered anything else, but he hadn't.

'Has the Masó family come back?' she asked him.

'No. I reported the vandalism to the police all three times, but they did nothing about it.'

Elisenda was shocked to hear that and apologised. It should have gone on record and been followed up. In the ensuing silence, they both looked at Patricia laughing at the book.

'Do you have any children?' Foday asked.

Elisenda looked back at him and placed her cup on the coffee table, surprised at how steady her hand was.

'I had a daughter but she died.'

Foday hung his head. 'I am sorry, Elisenda.'

'You weren't to know.' She smiled at him. She felt like talking. The first time in years. 'She's called Lina. Short for Catalina. I named her after my sister.'

'How old was she?'

'Six. I got married and had her when I was still a student. Much too young. Her father and I didn't even make it to two years before we split up.'

She shrugged and looked up. Foday looked so upset at having said anything that Elisenda felt she had to tell him more. Show him it was all right.

'My ex-husband had a small plane. Five years ago, he was flying Lina to Mallorca for the summer holidays. One of those summer storms blew up and they never made it to the island. Nothing was ever found. No debris. No... Nothing. So Lina flew away from me one morning and she won't be coming back.'

Foday asked her if she wanted to stay for dinner but she declined, saying she had to get home. She kissed Patricia and left, standing outside the building for some minutes to get her breath back. She looked down. Now her hand was shaking.

Chapter Seventy

Carles Queralt swore for the third time at the four giant brightly-coloured letters squashed down on the pavement like they'd been dropped from high in the sky. There's always money for modern tat like those new statues, he thought, but never anything to solve the city's parking problem.

'Try the disabled spaces again,' Anna, his wife, told him.

'Are you blind or what? You can see I've been trying them.'

In the back seat, their son Jordi started to whimper.

'Now see what you've done,' Anna told him, shifting round in her seat to calm the boy. 'Happy now.'

'I'm never fucking happy,' Carles muttered under his breath.

Anna rubbed her fourteen-year-old son's legs and made shushing noises, but he was already starting to cry. Carles looked at his son in the rear-view mirror and tried to smile at him.

At the lights, he turned left around Plaça Catalunya in one last attempt to find a space amid the cars parked in brightly-coloured battery. In front, separated from him by two cars, a grey Volkswagen reversed slowly out of a disabled space and drove off. The first car in the queue drove off after it, but the second turned into the space. Carles banged the steering wheel with his fist.

Before starting off again, he watched the driver get out of the car and lock the door. He was alone. There was no one else in the car. And he looked perfectly able-bodied to Carles.

He opened his window and shouted. 'That's a disabled space.'

The other man shrugged. 'What's it to you?'

Carles started undoing his seat belt and opening the door.

'Please don't get out,' Anna asked him. Jordi began crying again.

Carles ignored his wife and got out.

'I said it's a disabled space.'

The other man waved him away with one hand. 'I'm in a hurry. I've got to get to the bank.'

'I'm in a fucking hurry, too. And my son is disabled. I need this space.'

'I was here first.'

Carles advanced towards him. 'It's a disabled space. You have no right.'

He carried on walking to the other man, his hands already raised. Through a dark tunnel, he could hear the drivers in the cars behind him start to sound their horns. He could even hear his son's mewling under the harsh sound.

The last thing he heard was Anna screaming.

Chapter Seventy One

Elisenda opened her eyes and turned away from the Verge de la Bona Mort, setting off almost at a jog up the cathedral steps towards Vista Alegre.

There were two surprises waiting for her when she got back to the station. The first was Sergi, Catalina's husband, waiting for her by the front desk.

'Have you got time for a coffee?' he asked her.

'Okay.' She led him to La Llosa, wondering what he wanted, and sat down at a table away from the bar, ordering coffees for them both from the waitress.

'What is it?' she asked him after they'd been served.

'Catalina. I think she's depressed.'

Elisenda stared back at him. 'Sergi, of course she's depressed. She's pregnant. She's scared.'

'Of what?'

'Of the birth. Of the days after the birth. Of going home without an instruction manual. Of the next twenty-odd years.'

'I'll be there.'

'You're never there.'

He was still stirring his coffee, so Elisenda took the spoon from his hand and laid it down in the saucer.

'I work hard. For her.'

Elisenda realised this was probably the longest exchange she'd ever had with her brother-in-law. It felt less comfortable than browbeating murder suspects and hopeless judges. She suddenly felt sorry for him. 'Don't listen to me. I'm having a long day.'

He just sat and watched his coffee going cold. 'No, you're right. I should spend more time. I know you and I aren't close. But I do want what's best for Catalina.'

'Yes, I suppose you do. But I think you want what you think's best for Catalina. You should listen to her more.'

'Would you talk to her?' He finally took a sip of his coffee and grimaced when he realised it was cold. 'She listens to you.' He suddenly looked at his watch. 'I have to go.'

Surprised, Elisenda watched him get up.

'I'll call her, Sergi,' she told him. 'But it's not my job, it's yours.'

The second surprise was brought to her by Pau when she walked back into the unit's offices. It was a piece of paper covered with times and dates and explanations for each one.

'You're going to need this,' he told her.

She didn't have time to ask him what it was about before a uniformed caporal came through to ask her to go with him to see Inspector Puigventós. Pau simply pointed at the sheet of paper he'd given her as she followed the caporal out through the door. Pijaume had watched her exchange with Pau and smiled encouragement at her before turning back to his computer. Along the corridors towards Puigventós' office, Elisenda hurriedly read through the notes Pau had given her, not entirely understanding what they meant. There was a name at the top of the page that she didn't recognise.

The Seguretat Ciutadana caporal knocked on Puigventós' door and opened it to let Elisenda in. She was surprised to see Micaló in the room with him. She entered and the caporal pulled the door shut behind her. Puigventós invited her to take a seat. Micaló pointedly ignored her arrival.

Puigventós spoke first. 'There's been a development, Elisenda.'

'With your investigation,' Micaló added. 'In your absence.'

Elisenda nodded, looking at Puigventós. She waited until one of them spoke again, to give her an idea of what was going on. Of how to defend herself, since she knew that that was about to become necessary.

It was Puigventós who continued. 'A man has been arrested this morning, Elisenda. After an incident. We believe that it is related to the events that have been occurring in the city.'

'Incident?' It was the only word Elisenda could get out.

'A man attacked another man on Plaça Catalunya this morning for parking in a disabled space,' Puigventós explained. 'It appears the attacker has a disabled son, while the victim was not disabled. He also has a history of violent assaults. On his first wife, two counts of threatening behaviour in bars when he was younger and another traffic-related incident. Sotsinspector Micaló's men took him into custody and he began boasting about the attacks taking place recently. About how the city and everyone in it had it coming.'

'Boasting? Or just invoking?'

Micaló snorted. 'Boasting, Sotsinspectora Domènech. Boasting.'

'It does appear so, Elisenda,' Puigventós agreed. 'When he was brought into the station, he made continuous references to the other attacks and claimed that this latest victim would now at least be able to use disabled parking spaces in all honesty from now on. The man he assaulted is in a coma. The prognosis isn't good, apparently.'

Micaló joined in again. 'And my team has made the arrest, Sotsinspectora Domènech. Not your unit with all its budget and hype and political allies, but a proper policing unit with targets and goals and infrastructures.'

'We're sure it's not just someone who snapped in a given situation? A copycat?' Elisenda asked Puigventós. 'Was there a warning of a tile or anything on the Verge de la Bona Mort to announce it? Any staging of the victim?'

Puigventós looked down at the papers on his desk, embarrassed.

'Please accept that your conducting of the investigation is going nowhere at best,' Micaló told her. 'We feel that now is the opportunity to hand the investigation over to a more serious unit. To my unit.'

Puigventós looked for a moment as though he were about to apologise to Elisenda. She just felt tired at the constant rearguard actions she was forced to take. 'This is a mistake, Xavier,' she told him. 'What's the man's name? The attacker?'

Again, it was Micaló who got his answer in first. 'Carles Queralt.'

Elisenda glanced down at the piece of paper that Pau had given her just a few long minutes ago. The name at the top was Carles Queralt. She quickly reread what Pau had written for her and looked up.

'And you feel the investigation should be given to you?' she directed at Micaló.

'Yes, Sotsinspectora Domènech. I trust you can accept that.'

She held up the piece of paper. 'Then I suggest you do your homework first.'

'What is it, Elisenda?' Puigventós asked her.

'A caporal in my team has cross-checked the dates and approximate times of the attacks against Carles Queralt's movements. It appears that he was at a sales conference in Madrid at the time of the Daniel Masó killing. A credit card receipt for petrol shows he was three hundred kilometres away in Zaragoza on the night of the attack on Mònica Ferrer. And it would seem that the entire family was in Lourdes throughout the whole of the Sant Narcís festivities, which is when Foday Saio and Xarlu were attacked and the tile announcing the death of Pere Corominas was placed.'

Micaló snatched at the piece of paper.

Elisenda looked at Puigventós and stood up. 'Now if that's all.'

Chapter Seventy Two

That night, Elisenda had dinner alone in the upstairs room at L'Arcada, overlooking the Rambla. Quite literally alone in terms of diners. The first Tuesday after Sant Narcís and no one had any money or desire to dine out until the weekend at least, so she sat in a window seat, attended by two waitresses with nothing else to do. They chatted to her while they served, but she wasn't in the mood for company and they soon left her to her thoughts.

She thought of Sergi's visit to Vista Alegre that afternoon and wondered if she should have asked Catalina if she'd wanted to come for dinner. If she was honest, she wouldn't really have been in the mood for conversation, so she decided she'd ring her sister later. She immediately thought of Pere Corominas' supposedly missing phone. It hadn't turned up and the Científica who reckoned it was under the body in the hut now doubted she had actually seen it at all. Elisenda sighed and picked at her dinner without tasting it.

She considered her day. After her meeting with Puigventós and Micaló, the inspector had asked her to stay.

'I understand your frustration with Sotsinspector Pijaume,' he'd told her.

'He's doing nothing about these drugs,' Elisenda complained. 'It's hampering my investigation.'

Puigventós looked uncomfortable. 'He does have extenuating circumstances, Elisenda. In his private life. I'm afraid his wife is ill, but I really can't tell you anything more as he has asked for it all to remain confidential.'

'Seriously ill?'

'Seriously ill.'

Elisenda sighed, her anger deflating with her breath, and sat back heavily in her chair. 'I'm sorry, Xavier, I didn't know.'

It was while she was in Puigventós' office that news came through that the man Carles Queralt had attacked had died in hospital. That's two more families destroyed by what was happening in the city, Elisenda thought now.

She finished her meal and went home. The first thing she saw when she got in was the empty space on the bookshelf where she'd taken the book to give to Patricia. She couldn't help staring at it until she suddenly leant down and closed the gap. She looked around her flat and decided she couldn't face an evening in. She might not feel like company, but neither did she feel like solitude. She turned the lights off and went back downstairs to La Terra and a *licor de café* in a lonely window seat, the dark of the imagined river below soothing her thoughts.

One of her first jobs the following afternoon when Pau arrived at Vista Alegre with Josep was to thank him. He showed her the latest website postings. Now that it was known that Queralt wasn't responsible for the other attacks, many people were showing some sympathy for his making a stand against the other man's lack of consideration, extending it to anyone who parked badly or drove selfishly.

'It's sparked off another attack,' Pau told her. 'Someone else was seen parking in a disabled bay and walking off briskly. Evidently able-bodied. Two men attacked him and broke his jaw.'

Elisenda considered for a moment. 'Except of course, he wasn't the disabled person.'

'Precisely. He was on his way to fetch his disabled mother. She lives nearby and he was picking her up to take her to hospital for a check-up.'

'And in the meantime, people are still jumping to the wrong conclusions, only now they're acting on them.' She paused for a moment. 'There's something I wanted to ask you. How come you know Joaquim Masó?'

Pau looked surprised. 'I don't really. His wife's from the same village as my parents. I've sometimes seen him down there in the summer when we visit my grandparents.'

The door into their unit's office opened and Pijaume walked in, a pained look on his face. He waited until Elisenda and Pau turned to face him. 'I'm very sorry, Elisenda, but would you have any aspirins in here?'

'There are some in that drawer over there, Sotsinspector,' Pau answered, pointing to the next desk over from his.

'Are you all right, Narcís?' Elisenda asked him.

He didn't hear her the first time, so she had to repeat herself. 'Just a headache. I'll be fine.' He looked in the drawer and pulled out a packet of painkillers. He squeezed two out of the blister pack and turned to go. Elisenda noticed that his left ear was red and swollen.

Pau carried on speaking. 'I've been going through various forums.' The computer screen in front of him displayed a list of names, dates and comments. 'I've been checking out local history websites, online journals and newspaper articles written over the last year, and I've compiled a list of people who've written anything that could be of interest to us.'

'Inciting collective indignation at collective paranoia?'

'My darling, you are so cynical for one so young and lovely,' he replied in his curious and camp over-the-top Spanish. He would never dream of – or get away with – saying the same things in Catalan. Like most people, Elisenda just took it in her stride, too taken aback to take offence.

Pau reverted to Catalan, probably unaware he'd even switched languages and personality. 'Not just the more inflammatory ones,' he went on seamlessly, 'but anything that relates to collective identity, local tradition, local fears. I used keywords to search through them all, so it threw up all sorts of things, from the very learned to the really rabid.'

'Any patterns?'

'Much as you'd expect. Professor Marsans comes top of the table. You couldn't call his articles incitement by any means, but they are provocative. In a very broad sense of the word. One of Marsans' colleagues turns up a few times, a Professora Aurora Torrent.'

'I've met her. I can't see her lugging four muggers around in the back of a van. She'd be worried about catching something common.'

'A few other names. Carles Font, the journalist who was attacked. Doctor Riera's there, but he seems to moan about everything anyway, and Mossèn Viladrau, of course. He was a victim, but we forget some of the things he used to come out with. And there are two other names.'

Elisenda looked at the names he'd highlighted. Inspector Puigventós had written a couple of articles in the last year about globalisation and local disintegration, and Jutgessa Roca had published an article on immigration and the legal system.

'Please let it be her,' Elisenda said in Spanish, mimicking Pau's accent.

Pau grinned. 'Of course, then you get the forums, where a lot more names come up. I've only included people who contributed regularly or anyone who wrote anything really close to the mark, but I think they'd be worth following up.'

Elisenda clicked her tongue. 'Is there anyone in this city who actually likes anything post-medieval?' She looked at the roll-call of names flickering on the screen. 'Of course, it's highly possible the person we're looking for hasn't contributed to any of these forums. They might just have been influenced by them without actually taking part. See if you can check out the forums and journals for names of subscribers.'

'It'll be huge. And anyone can read the newspaper articles. We simply couldn't cope with that volume.'

'Do what you can, then. Prioritise people on the list, and then get Josep or Montse to break it down and organise them into people for questioning. Informal questioning.'

'There's one other thing you should see.'

He took out two texts from a folder that he'd already printed on two sheets of paper. A couple of sections were marked with a fluorescent pen. Elisenda scanned them quickly, checking the name at the end of the articles, and then reread them more slowly before putting the pages down.

'So how did he know that?'

Chapter Seventy Three

Elisenda noticed the time displayed on Pau's computer and realised she was running late. 'Got to go,' she told him. 'I'm meeting Professor Marsans.'

Before going, she took another look at the two pieces of paper she'd just been reading and decided to make a call.

'Siset,' she said when the phone was answered. 'I will have words with you.' She told him when and where he was to meet her and hung up.

Marsans was already waiting in the café when Elisenda got there. She apologised profusely but he was perfectly calm about it.

'I've only just got here myself,' he assured her, no doubt untruthfully.

The waitress brought them both a coffee. A table of two holidaying foreign couples opposite Elisenda dithered over the menu, new takes on old dishes, neither meaning much to the four visitors flown in on budget wings. A snapshot in time, she thought, both of them and of the city. Girona's newfound favour as a city break. She wondered what they saw.

'And so the city changes,' Marsans commented, as though reading her thoughts.

'Changes. In the legend, the Majordoma repented her ways and devoted the rest of her life to caring for the weak. Mònica Ferrer wasn't given that chance. And the paper has a new restaurant critic. An anonymous one. Far more savage than anything Mònica Ferrer ever came up with.' She rubbed her eyes. 'I'm sorry. I should offer you my condolences.'

He looked surprised. 'Condolences?'

'Pere Corominas. You knew him.'

'Of course. Poor Pere. He showed such promise, but he was a troubled young man. He could have done great things.'

'You didn't share his distaste for newly-created legends?'

'Not at all. The creation of modern myth is fascinating for a historian. The chance to see popular history at its inception. Although it is a double-edged sword. The way in which legends are born is intriguing, but it can be merely pandering to those with no sense of the past and to ideological tourists seeking a culture sound bite.'

'Maybe that's the point our man's making,' Elisenda replied.

Marsans shrugged uncomfortably. 'Who knows?'

'Who indeed?' Elisenda replied. She'd originally arranged to meet Marsans when Corominas was still alive, still a suspect, to find a way into what Corominas might be thinking. Now she felt she was back to square one, picking Marsans' brains to get a renewed angle on the mind of the killer. 'We're more interested in the significance of the victims. In the later attacks, the victims appear to become more generic. A type of victim rather than a specific victim. You deal with symbols. These people are perhaps symbolic. Hate figures.'

'Hate figures? A disabled man? A gay man? A comedian?'

'His idea of a hate figure is different from yours or mine. Have you looked at this website lately? There are some who see them as worse than an extortionist or a petty criminal. Or a corrupt priest. He's provoking us. Making us decide where we stand. Where we draw the line. He began with victims that pretty much everyone thought had it coming.'

'Including you, Elisenda?'

She shrugged. It was her turn to be uncomfortable. 'But he's moving on. He's not just making us look at our values.'

'Maybe he is still making us look at our values. Just that the values have got different.' Marsans finished his coffee. 'Or one could turn it on its head perhaps. Something you said earlier.

About the fact of one of the legends being modern being the point this person is trying to make. Perhaps it's the legends themselves we should be looking at. The victims are merely the product. Who they are is not that important.'

'I'm pretty certain of that already. But I think there's more. At least there is now. I think the actual victims ceased to be important to this man quite early on. What began with hate figures has evolved into something else. It's now the fact of using the legends that has become important, rather than the legends in themselves. I was hoping your field of research would help me see exactly what that was.'

'My field of research?'

'Iconography.'

'Symbology, to be more precise.'

'Is there a difference?'

Marsans gave her a look like he would a star student who's suddenly disappointed him. 'I look at the use of symbols to create a collective identity. And to preserve that identity.'

Elisenda stared at the coffee in her cup. Her mind rocketed through everything she and Marsans had been saying, everything that had been happening in the city. The victims and the legends. The sequence and the timing. The event and the aftermath.

'Identity,' she said, looking up. 'He's telling us we're losing our identity. Simply by embracing change and diversity, he thinks we're dissipating our own identity as a city, as a people. This is no longer about the victims. Or the legends. It's about us. All of us.'

Marsans looked doubtful. 'Which means?

'Which means that I know how to stop him.'

Chapter Seventy Four

Outside the café, Elisenda watched Marsans head off in the direction of Plaça de l'Oli on his way to the university and checked her watch. She was heading for the other side of the river.

Her date was waiting for her when she got to the shaded side of Avinguda Ramon Folch, opposite the law courts and forensic service. He was hopping from one foot to the other, trying to be inconspicuous behind a plane tree.

'Why are you limping?' she demanded.

Siset looked back at her and shrugged.

'Like the nose, by the way,' she added. 'Suits you.'

'You should see the other guy.'

'Completely unscathed, I imagine.'

Elisenda told Siset what she wanted him to do and he whined for a minute or two until she asked him if what she was hearing about Joaquim Masó was true. 'I'll pull him in if you like. You can identify him as the other guy.'

But Siset just gulped and shut up and did as he was told.

'And I'll have Mossos watching you,' she added, 'so no getting lost.'

'Why have I got to do it?'

'Because he's unlikely to notice you. He'd recognise one of my team.'

He sniffed loudly and she sent him on his way, watching him hop-skip across the road on his painful leg. No Mossos were going to be following him, but she figured he wouldn't know that. She then watched him wait until her quarry came out of the building and made sure that Siset did as he was told and scuttle after him. It was up to him now, all she could do was wait for his call and trust to his spirit of self-preservation. She knew that the person Siset was following would be coming out of the building at about that time. What she didn't know was where he was going. And she had no illusions that Jutgessa Roca would give even Àlex and his fluttering testosterone a warrant to interview this guy.

Siset's phone call came about quarter of an hour later, telling her where the man he was following had gone.

'Are you sure? Doesn't sound like his sort of place.'

'He is, I swear,' Siset pleaded. 'Can I go now?'

Elisenda ended the call and took a taxi from outside the post office to the bar Siset had named. It took ages to get through the afternoon traffic to the Eixample, but it was too far to walk given that she didn't know how long her man was going to be there. She drummed her fingers impatiently on the seat next to her and silently accompanied the taxi driver in his steady stream of invective against everyone else on the road. He had a nice line in sarcasm, she thought.

Inside the bar on Carrer Migdia, Elisenda walked slowly between the bright young things beavering away on laptops at the dark wood counter to her left and the floor-to-ceiling bookshelves to her right, scanning the room. She still half thought she wouldn't find who she wanted in Studio Store's urban-class chic. It really didn't go with his image.

But then she saw him, tucked away at a table at the rear of the room. He had his back to her.

'Gerard,' she said on walking round in front of him. 'Fancy seeing you here. Mind if I join you?'

She sat down opposite Bellsolà before the lawyer could object.

'I really didn't expect to find you in here,' she spoke truthfully.

He looked desperately uncomfortable, turning in his seat to look for the door, but the seclusion of his table now conspired against him. He was completely unsighted. Elisenda ordered a *café amb llet* and carried on speaking.

'Oddly enough, there was something I wanted to ask you.'

She opened her bag and pulled out a sheet of printed paper.

'Do you have a warrant, Sotsinspectora Domènech?' Bellsolà asked.

'Do I need one, Gerard? We're just chatting, surely.'

'This is most irregular.'

The lawyer turned in his seat and made to get up, but Elisenda put a firm hand on his to restrain him. 'I will get a warrant if I need one, Senyor Bellsolà. I'm just keeping it informal for your sake. For the time being.'

He sat down again, surprised at the coldness in her voice.

Elisenda placed the piece of paper on the table. 'An article you wrote earlier this year. Interesting. Apparently we're forgetting our past.'

'And?'

'It came out a week before the first attack. The one on Daniel Masó.'

The lawyer looked as though he'd been stung. 'No, Sotsinspectora Domènech. You are barking up the wrong tree. That is a perfectly innocent article.'

Elisenda picked up the top sheet and read aloud: "As the spirit of King Pau I lies dying amid the ashes of our faltering nation, and as the spirit of Rafael Casanova rails at the ineptitude of our failed institutions, the people of Catalonia are witnessing an influx of outside population and a dilution of our heritage that is far more insidious than anything General Franco ever dared dream of, and I say enough. The time has come for Catalans to say enough is enough and to stand defiant in defence of the values we have fought for so long to achieve and to invoke the spirit of our heroic past to fight for a better future."

She put the page down and looked at Bellsolà. 'Bit too florid for my liking, but you really do get your point across. Although some might find it just a little racist.'

'That is perfectly innocent. Since when has patriotism become a crime?'

'Patriotism? This is incitement.'

'I warn you, Sotsinspectora Domènech, do not enter into the fineries of the law with me.'

'Or is it a statement of intent?' Elisenda ignored the lawyer's splutter and took a second piece of paper out of her bag. 'But what interests me more is this.'

She placed the single sheet on the table in front of him. It was a printout from the website of a legal journal. An article with his name in the heading that made reference to the spate of attacks in Girona. Elisenda pointed to a sentence that Pau had highlighted in yellow marker pen.

'How did you know that the attacker left figures on the Verge de la Bona Mort to announce the attacks? None of that had been made public.'

Bellsolà looked up at her and down at the paper again. 'I'm a lawyer. It's my job to know.'

'Try again.'

'I will not, Sotsinspectora Domènech. But I will have your job, I promise you that.'

'And what do you know about the tiles?'

Before Bellsolà could reply, a figure rushed around the end of the bar and approached their table. 'I'm sorry I'm late, Gerard,' he said, pausing when he saw who was seated opposite the lawyer.

Elisenda looked up.

'Sotsinspector Micaló.' She looked back at Bellsolà. 'So that's how you knew.'

–

Elisenda paid at the bar for her coffee and glanced at the two men. They were studiously avoiding returning her look.

Micaló and Bellsolà. That explained a lot.

309

Outside, she was surprised to find cars with their lights on, breathing heavily in the glow of the traffic lights. The clocks had only just gone back the previous weekend, over the Sant Narcís festivities, and she was still getting used to the change of light in the early evening. She walked along Carrer Migdia back towards the city and turned right to head for Vista Alegre. Darkness was already beginning to fall over the river. A light switch had been thrown, ending summer, starting autumn.

Her phone rang.

She looked at the screen and was surprised to see Riera's name on it.

'*I have some more details for you, Elisenda.*' He spoke as though the altercation of the previous day hadn't happened. '*From what I can ascertain, Corominas died of a blow to the back of the skull.*'

'Thank you, Albert. Do you know what with?'

'*There are small fragments of stone in the wound. They're being examined now, but my feeling is that they're from a building in the old town. The colour and the composition seem to indicate that.*'

'Could it have been an accident?'

'*I couldn't say. It would appear that he either fell or was pushed against a wall or a step.*'

Elisenda thanked him and hung up. Walking back to Vista Alegre, she turned her thoughts to everything people were telling her. A lot of them had their own agendas. The question was which ones were just the small confusion of life and which ones actually meant anything. She was also reminded of something Albert Riera had said to her. About how our victims come before our personalities.

At the station, Àlex was waiting for her. 'Elisenda...' he began.

'I know how to catch this person,' she told him.

He was stopped in his tracks by her statement.

'You know who it is?'

'No. But I know how to catch them.'

He simply looked back at her. 'Elisenda, I couldn't get hold of you. Another tile's been found.' Her head dropped but Àlex continued before she could say anything. 'He's written your name on the back of it.'

'My name? Where was the tile?'

'On Carrer Figuerola, by the overhead railway lines. It's on the modern Rosa Serra statue.'

Elisenda's head snapped up. 'The one of the pregnant woman?' She caught her breath, able only to say one word.

'Catalina.'

Chapter Seventy Five

Elisenda's personal mobile rang.

She checked the caller ID. Her parents.

Her father told her that they'd rung around everyone but none of them had heard from Catalina. She could hear the quiver in his voice. She tried to make her own stronger not to upset him.

'Thanks, Papa. If you think of anyone else, try them. I'll call you the minute I know anything.'

She hung up and shook her head at Sergi, who turned back to his own mobile and stared at it blankly. Elisenda spoke to Montse and left them in the flat in Parc del Migdia. Outside in the park, she spoke to two members of Pijaume's team, who were watching the small artificial lakes and the pathways. Pijaume himself was in an unmarked car, roaming the city, the rest of his team assisting Elisenda's. Micaló hadn't offered to help search for Elisenda's sister.

The problem was Catalina hadn't been seen anywhere all day. She hadn't called anyone. They had no steps to trace back. Her car had gone from its parking space in the basement of the building where she lived, and there was no sign of where she'd gone.

Elisenda left the park in another unmarked car, a Seguretat Ciutadana sergent driving. She checked her mobile. She'd set off an expanding chain of phone calls. Friends, relatives and colleagues ringing on through the web, trying to track Catalina down, trying to trace her movements. But nothing was coming up. Just a couple of friends saying she'd seemed depressed. Right now, Elisenda would have taken that. It was better than the alternative. But then the guilt set in that she hadn't picked up on the depression. She knew her sister wasn't entirely happy. But depressed? And she felt guiltier still that Catalina hadn't confided in her.

Elisenda closed her eyes, knowing she had to change focus. Why Catalina? Why a pregnant woman? She couldn't see what it was that Catalina represented. The statue was merely a statue, not a depiction of a tale or legend relevant to the city.

Unless it was her. Elisenda. The attacker's real victim was Elisenda. Through her sister. She opened her eyes.

She thought of her own Girona. So different from her sister's. Catalina was married mothers in the newest part of town, the entrepreneur's wife, the woman who'd forgone her studies to marry. The woman who'd chosen that way to rebel against her upbringing. Elisenda was vocation. Her own choice of career. Liberated and single in her guilt. Another form of rebellion. Elisenda was old town.

She dialled her mobile. To tell the patrols to switch to La Terra, to the streets of the old town, to the sites of the now-disappeared bars for the bohemian and trendy she'd known in her youth.

To Elisenda's city.

Both new and what was left of the old.

–

'That's that fucking lawyer.'

'Shut the fuck up.'

'It is. It's that fucking lawyer. That Bell–something. The one who got us off that last time.'

'Bellsolà? No way. Where?' Manuel PM tentatively stuck his head up from behind the thick bush under the slender plane trees vanishing up into the night.

'Over there, by the trees.'

'We're in a fucking park. Which fucking trees?'

Cristobal HP unbent his knees and stood up straight, peering over the green wall. 'There. Where that path stops.'

They both ducked back down again and looked at each other, as much as they could see in the dark, and started to snigger uncontrollably.

'Bellsolà,' Manuel PM said, gasping for breath. 'A bender.'

That started them off again, the joint they'd shared and the beers they'd been drinking all evening playing their part in the hilarity.

'I told you,' Cristobal HP said between wheezing. 'Queers. They're loaded with money. And they're all too fucking ashamed at being filthy bastards to go to the police.'

They were in the Devesa, watching the single men drift silently into the bushes, listening to the muted noises coming from the undergrowth, clocking the burning tips of cigarette ends beckoning the initiates.

'So, do we do him? Bell-thing?' Cristobal HP asked.

'Are you fucking stupid? He's our lawyer.'

'Might recognise us?'

'Fuck that. We'll need him to get us off again some time.'

The two young men sank down further, racked by more induced laughter.

–

Àlex ended the call from Elisenda telling him to switch to the old town, unable to stop herself from asking if he had any news.

He had nothing to tell her. He looked over from his place in the shadows to where Josep was parked, watching the approach roads to the little traffic island in the dark where the statue of the pregnant woman stood, but no one had come near. He didn't expect them to. The attacker had not yet carried out his punishments anywhere near where he'd left his calling card, so there was nothing to suggest he'd do so tonight. The problem was they had no other specific site that had occurred to them.

He knew the frustration that Elisenda felt at that. She'd thought she could see into the attacker's mind.

Àlex left the spot where he was standing and went back to his car. He was roving through the city, ghosting through the few places they'd thought of trying, checking up with the Seguretat Ciutadana cars patrolling the streets, letting the members of his unit know he was there. He drove off, heading for the Pont de Pedret and the area around Sant Feliu. Elisenda's town. He knew it was pointless.

At the traffic lights, his phone screen lit up, a text coming in. He read the pre-set message, sent with just one touch, and swore.

He'd forgotten all about that.

—

'What we got?'

'Gimme a fucking minute.' Huddled up against the window in the back of the taxi to catch the street lights, Cristobal HP opened up the first of the two wallets they'd taken. 'Credit cards. All fucking credit cards. No fucker uses money any more. We should've taken them to a cashpoint. I said we should.'

In the middle of the back seat, Manuel GM was leaning forward between the front seats holding a thin-bladed knife to the driver's neck as he drove away from the Devesa. 'You find a fucking cashpoint round here, we'll take them to it.'

'Thirty fucking euros, a couple of watches and a necklace. And a joint.' He sounded happier at his last find.

Manuel GM faced forward again. 'You keep your eyes on the fucking road, granddad,' he growled at the driver. He caught the driver's reflection in the mirror. 'Hey, we've done you before.'

Cristobal HP peered forward to take a look and they both started laughing.

'Fucking moron, man,' Manuel GM went on. 'You never fucking learn, do you. We've done you before and you never fucking learn.'

Manuel GM told the driver to go to the same piece of wasteland to the north of the city where they'd made him go the last time they mugged him. He carried on laughing, the beer and the joint still working their magic.

'You never fucking learn.'

–

Pau stared at his mobile screen, trying to work out its meaning. He suddenly tapped the dashboard and made a phone call. Then he made a second one, this time to Elisenda.

'He's in the Devesa,' he told her. 'It's just come to me. Get as many people there as quickly as you can.'

Not giving her time to reply, he hung up and gunned the car engine, tearing through the quiet city streets to the darkened park. No other Mossos cars were there when he got out. Taking a torch, he entered the towering plane trees, heading for the undergrowth near the river. Shadows vanished in front of him, the men cruising the park quickly melting away from the light.

Except one.

An illusory figure emerged from the gloom and put a finger to his lips.

He beckoned Pau over.

–

Àlex continued to curse as he drove up the road winding past the archaeology museum. He had his duty to Elisenda, but he also had another duty. One he'd forgotten with the search for Elisenda's sister. One he couldn't ignore.

Up ahead, as the asphalt ended and the road gave way to track, he saw the lights from inside the car, its headlights still on, casting an eerie reflected glow back at it from the low scrub.

He'd switched his own headlights off before turning the last bend in the road, guided now by the small beacon of a taxi's courtesy light. He hoped he wasn't too late.

He brought his car to a halt next to the taxi, slewing sideways, kicking up a spray of small stones that rattled against the windows and rattled the two occupants of the back seat, giving the driver the chance to get out of the front seat and slam the door shut behind him before they could react.

'Are you all right, Senyor Pere?' Àlex asked, getting quickly out of his own car and taking a look at the taxi driver in the light thrown back at him. He was shaken but unhurt. Frightened but slowly exhilarant.

Àlex pulled out the police-issue Walther P99 pistol from his shoulder holster and got into the front of the car, kneeling on the passenger seat and pointing it through the gap in the headrests at the two muggers behind.

'Hello boys. You probably should have thought of taking your victim somewhere different this time.'

Manuel GM was the first to react. 'You can't arrest us for this. This is a trap.'

Àlex looked into his eyes, swapping the gun from right hand to left, and crushed the mugger's nose with a short, skilful jab of his fist. He immediately slapped the same fist sideways into Cristobal HP's slack, drooping jaw, breaking the bone.

'Who said anything about arresting you?'

–

Two other cars were at the borders of the Devesa when Elisenda got there, their headlights shining into the park. Another turned up as she got out, and she could hear more coming, their urgent sirens splitting the night. Steadily, more and more Mossos spread through the trees on foot, hurriedly searching. Many were anticipated by rustles in the bushes as the park's more zealous occupants finally drifted away. Shouts, becoming louder, reverberated through the slender trunks, an echo of the vanished funfair waltzers, now gone for the year.

Another more ghostly murmur brushed the leaves on the low undergrowth, its direction constantly changing, evaporating here and reforming there. The light cast from Elisenda's torch caught a glimpse of controlled flight, a spirit floating away from her, always out of reach.

More calls came from behind her, more shocked, more anguished. Elisenda shone her torch back to the quivering bushes in front of her as they slowly came to rest. Seeing nothing, she forced herself to turn back to the shouts. The torches were converging on a cluster of bushes towards the river. Walking out of darkness into a semicircle of hushed light shining on a tree, Elisenda stopped, the breath catching in her throat.

'Please, no.'

Montse came over to her and held her.

Another voice rose. Àlex, arriving through the trees. Anger and despair in his voice.

The wall of torchlight shone on a tree.

Held against its slender trunk, supported only by the thick rope that had garrotted him, was Pau, his head bent forward, his limbs loose, his chest unmoving.

Elisenda's phone rang out in the night.

Chapter Seventy Six

The members of her unit sat in silence in their office in Vista Alegre. They were all there. Denial, anger, shock, disbelief.

As morning broke, Àlex had gone with Pau once the judge had finally allowed the body to be removed. Elisenda hadn't wanted him to be taken to the mortuary alone. Neither had Àlex. He would stay with Pau as long as he felt was necessary. She was of more use back at the police station, with the members of her team who still needed her. Who wanted more than ever to find who had done this.

Puigventós came into the room while she, Montse and Josep sat in numbed horror. He was there to give them his condolences. 'And you have my support,' he concluded before leaving. 'All of you.'

'I should have seen the other angle,' Elisenda said once he'd gone.

'It's not your fault, Elisenda,' Josep spoke up. The first words he had uttered since coming in. And the first time he had ever called her Elisenda. 'You're not to blame. There's only one person responsible for all this. Not any of us.'

Montse nodded in agreement. Elisenda wished she felt she could entirely agree with them.

The other angle.

Before Pau's body had been removed, she'd asked Àlex to go with her to the statue of the pregnant woman. They'd driven the short distance to the little roundabout and pulled up on to the pavement by the overhead railway lines. She'd looked up at the unsightly concrete track, a relic of less demanding days, her mind oddly distracted by the thought that for the first time she appreciated the construction work carving up the south side of the city so that the new lines would come in underground.

'I got so obsessed with worrying that the attacker was singling me out, singling my family out, that I didn't think of all the angles.' She led him to the front view of the statue, their backs to the short road leading to Gran Via. 'Quite literally, all the angles. Look at this.'

He looked at the squat, white statue. It was a modern depiction of a headless, armless pregnant woman, standing in the middle of a flowerbed, the flowers now all gone with the summer.

'A pregnant woman,' he said. 'Understandable. It's what I would have thought.'

'Now look at this.'

She led him to the side, directly under the railway, to a point some ninety degrees from where they had been standing a moment ago. Àlex looked at the statue and his shoulders sank.

'I just didn't think,' she said.

Àlex looked up again. The view they both got from this side was the trick the statue played. From the front, a pregnant woman, from the side the figure that was represented was a phallus.

'The victim was never going to be a woman,' Elisenda went on. 'It was never going to be Catalina. He just used the statue to goad us.'

Àlex looked at her. 'You couldn't have known.' He gestured at the statue. 'That's exactly what he's playing on. Everyone's fears. We saw what he wanted us to see.'

'I got distracted.'

Elisenda shook the memory from her head and began to think straight, attributing tasks to Montse and Josep, listening to their voices, using the structure of investigation to overcome the grief and anger. To focus.

She left them silently and determinedly sifting through all the evidence they had and went into her office. On the way, she picked up Pau's folders of notes and then accessed his files from her computer once she'd sat down. She skimmed through some of the collated facts and suppositions on screen and was instantly struck by the thought that she was going to miss Pau's analytical mind. That hit her like a punch in the stomach. It was the man she would miss. She rubbed her eyes for a moment and went back to trawling through his handwritten and onscreen notes.

She began with his lists of people who had written articles and contributed to forums, but they threw up nothing she didn't already know. His handwritten notes were more off the wall. Otherwise improbable suppositions that he then worked back through to see if they held water, links anyone else might find unrelated, what the relationship between the clues left before the attacks might have with the attacks themselves. Most of them were connections that Elisenda had seen, but there were others that she hadn't thought of. One in particular that she found interesting. But the one question that kept coming back to her was why Pau and why the Devesa.

Her phone rang. The same caller ID as the one she'd got last night in the Devesa. She'd rejected the call then, but the caller had left a message: '*Eli, it's Catalina. What's going on?*'

With a sigh, she answered the call now. 'Catalina, where are you?'

'*I'm in Platja d'Aro. I've found your messages on my mobile. I had it switched off. What is it you wanted?*'

'Where have you been, Catalina? What are you doing in Platja d'Aro?'

'*I wanted to wake up and see the sea.*'

Elisenda closed her eyes. 'You wanted to see the sea. You have a house in La Fosca. Why didn't you go there? We could have found you there.'

'*I just wanted to get away. On my own. So I checked into a hotel on the beach.*'

'You could have told me, Catalina.'

'*I didn't want to tell anyone. I wanted to be on my own and not have to explain anything and sit and watch the sea. I just want to be on my own for a bit. I'm tired and I'm sick of having this huge bulge going everywhere I go. I feel it's defining me.*'

'I'm sorry, Catalina, I didn't see.'

'*Eli, for someone with as intuitive a mind as yours, you don't always see what's right in front of you. Why was it you wanted to speak to me?*'

Elisenda told her sister about the tile and about Pau.

'*Eli, I'm so sorry.*'

'I have to go, Catalina.'

Elisenda hung up and stared at her phone. What was it Pau had said when he called her? Something that had come to him? It seemed an odd way to phrase it. She called Montse in and told her to check Pau's mobile records. 'See if he sent or received any texts or calls from any numbers we can't account for.'

Montse was back half an hour later. 'I've applied for his phone records, but that'll take a couple of days, so I went to see a friend of mine in the Científica. We were at Sabadell together. They've got Pau's mobile, so she let me look through his calls made and received last night. He received a text message with just a photo. It was of the statue of the woman.'

Elisenda sat up suddenly. 'He was targeted.'

'I checked the number it came from, Elisenda. It was Pere Corominas' phone.'

Elisenda simply stared at her, too shocked to speak.

'Straight after he got it,' Montse went on, 'he rang a number that was none of ours. So I've just rung it. Antoni Sunyer answered. Pere Corominas' flatmate.'

'What did he have to say.'

'He said that Pau had rung him. He'd asked him if the statue of the woman had any significance. Sunyer told him that some gay men send the image to each other by mobile to say they're going to be in the Devesa. He told me something else. He said that someone from Sotsinspector Micaló's unit had interviewed him about it and that he'd told them about how the statue was used to send messages.'

'Micaló.' Elisenda tapped her fingertips on the desk and jumped up.

She walked out of the room and along the corridors into the Regional Investigation Unit offices. She pushed Micaló's door open and closed it behind her.

'Sotsinspectora Domènech,' Micaló said. 'It's usual to knock.'

Elisenda reached across his desk and pulled him towards her by the expensive lapels of his expensive suit. Her face was almost touching his.

'You knew. You knew the significance of the statue of the woman.'

Micaló remained calm. He tried to remove Elisenda's hands but her grip was too strong. 'You were too interested in your own interpretation.'

'You knew. You could have said something.'

'If you don't let me go...'

'What? You've threatened me in the past, Micaló.'

'I will have your career, you stupid fucking woman.'

'And I will make sure that everyone in the station knows that you withheld information that could have saved a fellow Mosso's life.'

'I suggest you let me go.'

'Certainly.'

She thrust him backwards with such force that he tilted over the back of his chair and was dumped on the floor under the wall bearing the framed certificates of his courses and commendations.

Back in her office, Àlex was waiting for her. He had news from the pathologist. Elisenda wasn't ready to hear it yet, so she sat down heavily behind her desk and told him of Micaló. She knew she was talking too much, holding the moment off.

'Pau received a blow to the head,' Àlex finally told her. 'But he died of strangulation. There were wounds to his hands and throat that show he'd struggled. He was conscious when he died.'

Elisenda knew that Científica had found a piece of wood inserted through the rope on the other side of the tree and used as the lever to strangle Pau. No forensics on anything.

'Garrotted,' she said. Corominas' stated preferred form of retribution. Only now Corominas was a victim too.

They stared at each other, no room for words.

Àlex spoke first. 'There was something you said yesterday, Elisenda. That you didn't yet know who this person was. But that you knew how to catch them.'

Elisenda looked directly at him.

'That's right, I do.'

Chapter Seventy Seven

Àlex's mobile rang as he was getting up from his chair to leave the room. Laura Puigmal. He listened in silence, glancing at Elisenda, then hung up.

'What is it?'

'It seems that two of the muggers who beat up Senyor Casademont were attacked last night. They're in intensive care. Someone attacked them, then left a message telling the ambulance where to find them. Anonymously.'

'I can't really get upset about that right now.'

Àlex nodded his head and left the room, closing the door behind him.

Elisenda watched him thoughtfully as he went back into the outer office to give support to Montse and Josep. She knew she needed someone like him as her sergent, someone who was able to bridge the gap between her and the unit and to pull the tricks she now had to be careful with, but there were times he frightened her.

She looked back to Pau's notes, also realising that she'd needed someone like Pau, who saw what others missed and who was able to plot and dissect them in his ordered mind. She read a paragraph towards the end of his handwritten notes and finally felt a tear come to each eye.

He'd written just three days ago that he felt the attacker was entering the end game, that his next victim would be his last. After that, he might disappear forever and they'd never find him. Another legend for Girona.

She dried her eyes and knew she had to get out. Montse had gone back to her friend in Científica to see if they'd turned up anything more at the scene. Josep was at a desk collating the information, instinctively taking on the job that Pau used to do. The seat Pau normally sat in was empty. Roaming the room, Àlex was straining at the leash, wanting to find and punish someone. Elisenda knew she had to get out.

She also knew exactly what it was she had to do.

–

Outside, it was coat and sunglasses weather.

Normally, she loved this season. The short parenthesis between the withering heat and sudden thunderstorms of summer and the torrential rain and fingering damp of autumn. When the city was warmed with blue skies and bright sun and cooled by a chill wind blowing in from the mountains. She thought of autumn Saturday mornings on the Rambla, bundled up on a café terrace with a small glass of beer, and mourned Pau and felt guilt in almost equal measures.

She held her face up to the sun for a brief moment and set off, heading away from the direction of the river, climbing through the steep streets towards the city walls and the university.

Professor Marsans was out.

'I really couldn't tell you where he is,' Aurora Torrent told her. 'Doubtless telling everyone how busy he is preparing for his trip to Columbia.'

'Will everyone who's studied history here have attended Professor Marsans' classes?'

'Of course. And mine, and those of most of the faculty staff. But not all of them become his chosen elite. Octavi takes more of a sniper than a scattergun approach to the furtherance of his career.'

'Do any of Professor Marsans' former students share his specialisation?'

Torrent turned away from her screen again and studied her. 'My dear, there's one thing you don't understand about Octavi. He makes sure his coterie of acolytes is in a position to help him whenever he needs it, but he would quite simply not countenance any of them challenging his own position. Now, if you don't mind, I am very busy covering for what I loosely term my colleagues.'

'Thank you for your time, Professora Torrent,' Elisenda said, leaving the academic jabbing sharply at her computer.

The slope leading down from the arts faculty led her to Plaça Sant Domènec, where she'd watched the demons jump in and out of the fire as she searched for the attacker's next victim. Her path took her past the top of the steps descending to the city centre. Past where the four muggers had stood and stared at her and Àlex as they walked by one morning an age ago. She knew that ever after, every part of the city would remind her of this year and, ultimately, of Pau's death.

'I'm sorry for your loss,' she heard a voice say behind her. She turned and was taken aback to see Joaquim Masó.

'Not a sentiment I'd associate with you,' she told him.

He stared back at her, his face impassive. 'He was always a nice kid.'

She held his gaze, past the cold eyes, unsure of what she saw. 'He was a nice man, too. I will find who did it.'

'I mean it.'

'So do I.'

She turned and walked away, not trusting herself to say any more, and carried on across the square and down Carrer Bellmirall to the small square in front of the main cathedral door. Locking Masó away in a corner of her mind, she stopped for a moment and took in the view, first down over the old town, then the new city beyond, and finally to the mountains in the distance. She could still be left breathless by the beauty of her own city. She just hoped she'd be able to enjoy it again one day. Walking down the steps, she was unable to resist glancing over her left shoulder to where the mugger had been left hanging. She knew it was impossible, but she fancied she saw his blood angel wings still in the ancient stone. At the bottom of the steps, she turned right and walked through the gateway under the statue of the Verge de la Bona Mort looking calmly down from her niche. Elisenda wondered how much had been excused in her name over the centuries.

Down by the river, she called Àlex but there were no developments. He'd call her if there were any. He asked how she was getting on.

'Coming together,' she told him.

Across the Onyar, she cut past the La Planeta theatre and went into the modern building housing the law courts and the Institut de Medicina Legal. She sometimes felt her life was walking endless corridors.

'Are you here to see me?' Albert Riera asked her. He was in a charcoal-grey suit today, not the forensic whites Elisenda was used to seeing him wear. She thought of her sister and how she claimed she was defined by one outward display, not her essence. We all were, Elisenda realised, almost failing to recognise the dapper silver-haired man before her as the forensic doctor.

'I wanted to set the record straight,' she told him. 'I overreacted the other day, and I wanted to apologise.'

Riera led her over to a window where the sun shone in. 'You and I both work at sorting out the vile things humans do to each other. We see what no one should see.' He paused as a young man in a sparkling lab coat walked past. 'Please don't think any more of it, Elisenda. I know I can sometimes be a little blunt and I apologise for that. We're the product of what we are forced to do.' He turned to walk away. 'And if you ever tell anyone what I just said, I will deny it strongly.'

Elisenda smiled and watched him continue along the corridor in the opposite direction. 'Never ever swear at me again, then,' she told his back view.

'We both know that won't happen.'

Outside again, she checked her watch. She had two more visits to make before she could get back to Vista Alegre. A ten-minute walk later, she was in the lobby of the newspaper offices, waiting for the receptionist to ring through to David Costa.

'He's in a meeting,' the receptionist told her.

Elisenda showed the young woman her badge and took the phone from her.

'I think you'll find you're not in a meeting,' she said into the mouthpiece before handing the phone back to the receptionist.

'I'll wait here,' Elisenda told her.

Chapter Seventy Eight

The newspapers finally got hold of the story of the tiles.

It was in the next morning's edition.

A tile had been found at the Jewish museum, in the upstairs interior courtyard, lying in the centre of the huge marble Star of David picked out on the floor. One of the last visitors of the previous day had found it and handed it in to the reception desk, thinking another visitor had dropped it. Fortunately, one of the members of staff who was leaving as they were wondering what to do with it was Meir Perlman, the visiting researcher. He saw the image of the Verge de la Bona Mort on the tile and recalled the figure of the bat he'd found on the statue a month or so earlier.

'We should give it to the Mossos d'Esquadra,' he told the people at reception.

They'd been sceptical at first, but he told them of the bat, so one of them dropped the tile off at the Mossos station in the old Hospital de Santa Caterina on their way home. The Mossos there knew enough to pass it on to Elisenda's team. No one knew who had told the newspapers about it. It could have been anyone from the museum.

Elisenda sat at the kitchen table in her flat and read through the article, her face impassive. She'd been down to the news kiosk on Plaça Independència to buy a newspaper before breakfast rather than spend any longer turning over and over in a restless bedroom. Finishing her breakfast, she went to the bathroom to brush her teeth and get ready for work.

When she went back into the kitchen, a young girl was at the table, staring at the breakfast dishes in front of her. Elisenda walked slowly into the room and stood by the window, looking at the girl. She was about six years old.

'You have to say something to me, Lina.'

She turned away, supporting herself on the window frame, staring at the river below. By the time she turned back, her daughter had gone.

–

'It's everywhere,' Josep told them all in the unit's office, putting the paper down on his desk.

He showed Elisenda and Àlex the website that Pau had been monitoring, which had seen a downturn in activity until first a Mosso had been found murdered and then the story of the tile had broken. The conjecture in the paper was outstripped only by the level of theories batted back and forth on the website forum. The one thing everyone knew was that it had to do with the attacks.

'At least they're not voting for each other to be next,' Elisenda commented.

She was right. All talk was about what the tile meant, and as the morning wore on, more and more of the forum was given over to trying to find a catchy name for the killer.

'But that doesn't mean to say they've improved any,' was Elisenda's coda to her previous comment.

Judging by the bags under their eyes and slow movements, Elisenda saw that everyone in the unit had had a fitful night's sleep, coming into work earlier than necessary. She and Àlex had gone through everything they had on Pau's attack, and Montse and Josep had fallen on his effects, released to them later in the morning, each one focusing on a particular aspect.

Midway through the morning, Àlex left the station to go to the forensic medicine institute, where Pau's post mortem was scheduled for eleven.

'I think one of us should be with him,' he told Elisenda.

'I agree. You go. Call me when you know anything.'

Throughout the rest of the morning, Elisenda gauged the interest on the website and looked at her watch.

Shortly before lunchtime, Professor Marsans called her mobile.

'I'm so terribly sorry,' he told her. 'I've just heard. Such a loss. He was a remarkably intelligent young man.'

'Yes, he was. I'll miss him.'

'We really must meet up and talk.'

'Yes, we must.'

An hour later, she looked at her watch one more time and told Josep and Montse she had to go out for a while. She looked at them both, their heads down, each intent on looking for the one thing they'd missed.

Elisenda hoped it would be pointless.

It was another beautiful autumn day to match the previous one. She retraced much of the route she'd taken the day before, turning right after crossing Plaça Sant Domènec and climbing Carrer Alemanys as far as the Jardins dels Alemanys instead of left to head for the cathedral. She stopped for a moment in the gardens at the foot of the city walls, the remains of the barracks where German mercenaries had been billeted in the seventeenth century in one of the many fights against the French, and took in the scented calm.

Taking a deep breath, she crossed the gardens and carried on through the Portal de la Reina, the old gateway leading out to the world beyond the city walls. She immediately came across huge boulders of ancient rubble, the remains of the Torre Gironella, destroyed by the French in the 1809 siege. Luscious grass filled the uneven ground between the slighted walls, some of it claiming back the manmade.

A man was seated on a small pile of stones, his back resting against a taller section of wall, his face in the sun.

He looked at Elisenda and spoke.

'I wondered how long I'd have to wait.'
Elisenda looked back at him.
'I really didn't want it to be you.'

Chapter Seventy Nine

The last blackbird sang in an autumn palm.

Apart from that, silence.

There were no city-break tourists, no office workers, no retired travellers nosing among the stones. No schoolchildren following a teacher's earnest games or elderly men sitting out time. The noise of the city and its traffic and commerce didn't permeate beyond the city walls into the world without.

There was just a woman and a man watching each other across a divide.

It was the man who spoke first.

'I take it you put the tile on the Star of David.' He sounded quite pleased with her, quite matter-of-fact. 'And you told the newspapers about it?'

'Yes.'

'You knew I'd know its meaning.'

Elisenda stared at him. 'You have no idea how much I wish I hadn't known.'

He looked around and patted the stones next to him. 'The Torre Gironella. Never rebuilt after being destroyed by the French. But that's not our story of it, is it? Correct me if I get any of my facts wrong, but it was 1391, wasn't it? A hundred and one years before the expulsion of the Jews and over four hundred years before the French turned it into this ruin. A mob ran wild through the city and the Jews were locked up in this old tower for their protection. You knew I'd see the connection between the Jewish museum and this place.'

'Yes, I knew.'

'The Jewish museum. In my day it was called Isaac el Cec. It was a bar and then it was a restaurant. And local people went there. And now they've turned it into a museum and no local people go there. Only tourists, who walk around it and come out again and still have no concept of this city. Our culture's no longer ours. It's a plastic image of itself for plastic people.'

'I also knew you'd only see half the history.' She gestured to where he was seated. 'The Jews in the Torre Gironella. They were locked up for their own protection, but many of them weren't allowed out until they rejected their faith and adopted Catholicism. And they were persecuted if they didn't. It wasn't some splendid storybook past to be proud of. It was real, with all its faults and foibles. All our history's like that. Every country's is. Previous generations were taught that Girona was three times immortal. That it held out against the French sieges. Then times change and the history changes and it turns out that French troops occupied the city and we'd all been fed a lie that suited whoever wrote the history that day.'

'That's not true.'

'It is true. You claim we don't know our history and that our culture's disappearing, but that's not true. History doesn't end. It's happening now. Our history evolves. Culture, society, people, we all move on. You can't take an idealised snapshot of a moment of your choosing and insist we all stay there. Culture, our culture, our identity, everything that makes us what we are includes our past, but it also includes our present. And our future. And you can't stop that.'

He cocked his head to one side. 'That doesn't interest me. It's not what I wanted to say. I was speaking out for our identity.'

'No, you weren't. You were speaking out for your own warped view of our identity. An identity that's changing, that's always changed. And that is something you can't accept. You've been inconsistent throughout. You evidently despise all that's new or doesn't fit in with your view of the old order, but you've used new legends to prove your point and old versions of history that have been discredited. You're as pragmatic as the rest of the modern world. You just excuse your own pragmatism in a way you won't excuse anyone else's.'

He looked surprised. 'You've come to confront me?'

'Of course I've come to confront you. With every gram of my being I've come to confront you.'

They stared at each other, both slowing down, both knowing they had to remain calm.

Elisenda broke the silence, her voice quiet again. 'Why have you come?'

'Because I've finished what I had to do.' He paused to consider for a moment. 'I've nearly finished what I had to do.'

'Why did you kill Pau?'

'You said so yourself. It was never about the victims.'

'Of course it's about the victims. It's never about anything other than the victims.'

He regarded her for a moment. 'Because I'd said everything I had to say. It was time to end it. People had stopped listening. They were more intent on petty squabbles than on where we were going wrong. No one could see it, which sickened me, and by the time you finally did see it, you'd all cheapened it and distorted it for your own purposes.'

'And killing Pau changes that?'

'Perhaps it wasn't necessary. I knew if I let him live that he'd eventually come to me. That's why I had to choose him. He had an even more analytical mind than yours. But once I'd killed him, I knew it was the end. That I didn't need to carry on any longer. You have no idea of the relief that brings me.'

'Relief? The relief it brings you?'

'Did you get the significance of the statue.' He looked at Elisenda in the sunlight. 'I see you didn't. It's because the statue is neither one thing nor the other. Neither a woman nor a man. By trying to be both, it becomes neither. And that was Pau. He was neither wholly Catalan, nor was he wholly Spanish. A hybrid of corrupted identity. The way we all are now. He and the statue are a symbol of the modern that is ugly, that doesn't add anything, that has no history, that has no place here.'

She shook her head. 'No. You are wrong. On every human level what you have done is wrong. I can understand about Masó, Chema GM, even Viladrau. But not the others.'

'Can you? And what do you think that says about you? Do you think you're better, then, than someone who sees the immigrant as an understandable victim, but not the priest? Worse than someone who doesn't accept the critic or the comedian as a deserving victim? Better than me because I say they're all as deserving of what happened to them? I heard you say they ceased to be hate figures. No, they didn't. Not for me. They never ceased to be hate figures to me because they were all part of what we're losing. From first to last they stood for everything we are losing. From first to last, I hated them.'

The blackbird stopped its song, the underlying silence more noticeable by its absence.

'So what happens now?' he asked her.

She gestured to his hands. 'You tell me.'

In one hand, he held a syringe, filled with a cloudy fluid. His arms were bare. In the other, he held a Walther P99 pistol. It was pointed at Elisenda. It had been all the time they'd been talking.

'The syringe is full of the stolen drugs, I take it,' she said. 'Who's it for?'

'I haven't entirely decided yet. Me probably.'

'And the gun?'

'That depends on you.'

He gestured with the gun for her to step towards him. Doing so, she caught a movement to her right. Turning to look, she gasped. Hanging by a noose from a tree, his hands tied behind his back, his mouth covered with brown tape, was Àlex. He was barely moving, his right foot clinging to a rock, supporting his weight, his eyes angry and imploring, looking at Elisenda. She made to move towards him, but the man fired the gun at the rock, almost causing Àlex to lose his footing.

337

'Please don't try to get to him,' the man said.

Elisenda looked down for a moment at the vivid green grass between her feet and then back up at the man seated on a ruined tower.

'Why, Narcís? Why did you do it?'

Pijaume looked back at Elisenda.

'My wife was ill.'

He sat in the breeze and stared bleakly at her.

'Terminal,' he continued after a brief moment. 'I couldn't keep up financially and the bank wouldn't help, so I had to turn to Daniel Masó. But then that got out of hand, too. My wife was dying and I had to worry about money. That is wrong, Elisenda. On every human level, that is what is wrong.'

'I'm sorry, Narcís. I'm sorry for your wife. I'm sorry for what you've had to cope with, but it excuses nothing.'

He carried on, not registering her words. 'I had to meet him in the building where you found him. He was thinking of buying it. With my money. With all his victims' money. And he was rubbing it in. I refused to pay and he pulled a knife on me. I don't know how it happened but I took it off him and he got stabbed. His nose too. I could see he'd bleed to death so I just let him. He was no loss to anyone. I'd been looking at the En Banyeta face just before I'd got there, and it struck me how fitting it was. Another moneylender dying, his nose rubbed away by someone desperate enough to do that.

'And then I saw those muggers, and I wanted them to know what it felt like to be a victim. I wanted people like them to know the city didn't want them, so I used the legends. And I used the Verge de la Bona Mort to show that I condemned them. That we condemned them. I saw it as our heritage fighting back. I even used Masó's van to take them. I thought it would be appropriate, one blight paying for the punishment of another. After that, it just ran away with me. I kept seeing people who deserved it. The priest, with his hypocrisy. The immigrant who came to this country and then complained about how he was treated. The comedian who sold out his heritage and bastardised his culture.'.

Elisenda pointed to Àlex, struggling to keep a toehold on survival. 'Why Àlex?'

'Because he sees himself as executioner too. As above the law.'

Pijaume fired the gun at the rock and Àlex lost his footing, his legs swinging out into space, the breath in his throat stuttering. Elisenda moved towards him but Pijaume shot into the ground in front of her feet. 'I am not afraid to kill you, Elisenda.'

She stepped back and watched as Àlex used the pendulum swing of his body to grasp for the rock again and catch onto it. The rope was still tight around his neck but she could see that he could breathe once again.

Elisenda looked back at Pijaume. 'And what makes you different from your victims, Narcís? From Chema GM?'

'I am not like him.'

'No? One or two of your scapegoats might differ slightly, but you're no better. He was responsible for an elderly man dying in fear and despair, you've got even more on your conscience. Daniel Masó thrived on fear, so did you, Viladrau is corrupt and so are you. Ultimately, you are corrupted.'

'Do not liken me to them.'

They stared at each other, separated by a common bond.

'So what did you achieve?' she asked him.

'Achieve?'

'With your victims? What did you achieve? Masó's business has been taken over by his uncle, people still owe him money. You still owe him money, that was where you got the swollen ear and the headaches from, isn't it? He got heavy with you. And the other muggers are out of prison already. The woman Viladrau abused and her son have been abandoned to fend for themselves. There was a better way to bring them to justice for their crimes. You're a policeman, you could have worked within the system and they would have been punished.'

'And Mònica Ferrer? How does the law punish her? It can't. What do we all do? Stop reading her bile? We can't. Everyone in the city loathed what she said, but we all kept her there because we all continued to read what she said. I did what I could. I used what I could.'

'But you achieved nothing. You made Mònica Ferrer suffer far more than any crime she ever committed, and now someone else has taken over from her with even more savagery. More immigrants and local people have suffered because of you. And the stand-up comedian. An entertainer, Narcís, that's all he was, not a threat to our culture. What do you think will change in the world because you brutalised a young man and left him to die in terror in a small city in Catalonia? You did nothing, you said nothing, you achieved nothing.'

She stopped for a moment to calm her voice before carrying on. She glanced over at Àlex. He was still safe. She spoke much more slowly.

'And I will never forgive you for what you've done to Girona. You've turned us against each other, neighbour against neighbour, colleague against colleague. You've brought out the most petty and vindictive in us and invited us all to see the worst in everyone else and demand that they be punished for it.'

'I can't bring out what's not there.'

'That's not a victory, Narcís. But in the end, you'll lose. You're not a legend, you're just a weak and fallible individual. We will forget you and we will get our culture back. Our real culture, not this artificial one of spite that you've created. We are strong enough to outlive you and move on.'

Pijaume looked across the gap between him and Elisenda and pointed the gun first at her and then at Àlex. He seemed to take a decision.

'We appear to have reached an impasse,' he told her. 'So now you have to decide. You have to take the decision who to save. And whether to let me die or not. Whether I deserve to die.'

He fired one more time at the rock, dislodging Àlex, already weakened, who swung heavily over the lush grass, struggling to regain his toehold, kicking with his feet, tightening the noose around his neck. Elisenda moved but Pijaume fired, this time at Àlex, narrowly missing him, making her freeze, caught between the two men.

He then put the syringe to his own arm and pressed. The cloudy fluid slowly drained from the plastic tube and he let out a sigh. Elisenda and Pijaume stared at each other as the gun drooped in his hand. Elisenda began to move, but he lifted the gun again. She waited a moment longer, Àlex's struggles becoming weaker, his legs in spasm.

Pijaume's eyes closed and Elisenda made the dash over to where he was leaning against the wall in the bright sunlight and knocked the gun out of his hand, kicking it away. She ran straight to Àlex and lifted his legs, trying to take the weight off the noose. Reaching up, she edged her fingers into his waistband, looking for the penknife he carried there, but she dislodged it and it fell down his trouser leg. She had to shake him, trying not to worsen the grip around his throat, until the knife finally fell through and onto the ground. She had to let go of Àlex for a moment to reach down and snatch the knife, hurriedly opening the blade and running to the tree to which the rope was tied and sawing desperately through the dense fibres. It gave way and Àlex fell heavily to the ground. Running to where he lay, she loosened the noose but couldn't feel a pulse, so she began pumping his chest and breathing into his mouth, punching his sternum to revive him. With a choke, he opened his eyes wide in panic and sucked air into his lungs, twisting against the rope around his neck and the pain of his hands tied underneath his body.

Elisenda made sure he was comfortable and then hurried back to Pijaume, kneeling down next to him. His eyes were struggling to stay open. She took out her mobile and called for an ambulance.

'I refuse to be made to decide,' she told him.

'I only meant good.'

She sighed. 'It was the wrong good, Narcís.'

His eyes flickered, the sight going from them, the whites clouding over.

'I didn't kill that young man,' he told her. 'Corominas.'

'I know you didn't, Narcís.'

He nodded and his eyelids began to close. He spoke in short breaths.

'My wife died. Last week.' He fought for breath. 'We might commit evil acts, but we can never be as evil as these illnesses that take innocent people and destroy them from the inside. Burrowing their way through everything that you love. That I loved. Her name was Anna. In the end, the past was all she knew. She was all I knew.'

Elisenda held him and watched the old world die, with all its good and evil, and she shed a tear for the second time in two days.

Chapter Eighty

One side of the church spoke Catalan. The other, Spanish with a southern accent.

Close family to one side at the front, his extended family behind, having made the sorry journey from Andalusia, filling the weeping pews in the parish church in Vista Alegre. The parish to where Pau's family had moved from Andalusia a generation ago and where Pau had worked in the Mossos d'Esquadra a lifetime of change later. Colleagues and friends on the other side, in black and dress uniform from the seats at the front to the standing rows at the back. The coffin carried in on the shoulders of six Mossos, Àlex and Josep at the front, the service in both languages, the police station empty of everyone but the reluctant minimum shift.

Outside, Elisenda let out a long pent-up sigh and spoke what words of comfort she could to Pau's parents. His mother told her that Pau had been proud to work for Elisenda. She watched them leave, going home for a private remembrance with the family.

The Mossos were walking in the other direction, returning in mute sorrow to the police station. Her own unit stood on the pavement together, their sorrow greater and more mute than anyone's. She caught Àlex's eye and they looked at each other for a moment.

He had come into her office the day before to ask what she would be doing after Pau's funeral, his throat heavily bandaged, his weakened voice barely audible through the dry-rasping pain.

She told him she'd be going and he asked her if she thought that was the right thing to do.

'I have to,' she told him.

He turned to go.

'Àlex.' She paused in what she was about to say. His hand was on the door handle. 'I was going to ask you about the two muggers who were attacked. I've spoken to them, but they claim they didn't see their attacker. I was going to ask you if you had anything to tell me, but I don't think I want to know.'

He started to open the door and she called him back.

'It's just that there are times, Àlex, when you're no better.'

Outside the church in the Vista Alegre parish, Àlex looked at her and nodded once before returning to the station.

'Are you ready, Elisenda?' a voice behind her asked.

She turned around. Inspector Puigventós was waiting for her, holding a car door open.

'I'm ready.'

They both got in and were driven along Carrer Emili Grahit and past the work on the new railway tunnel to the old garden suburb of Sant Narcís and its parish church.

The church was empty. Pijaume's wife's family had refused to come to the service and he only had one brother, who had evidently stayed away too, so his brief service was given in front of just Elisenda and Puigventós and two elderly women seated at the back of the church, who faded away at the end. Elisenda left the church, her shoes echoing on the polished floor. It was the loneliest sound she had ever heard.

'I don't know about you, Elisenda,' Puigventós said once they got outside, 'but I need a coffee.'

They went into an old neighbourhood café and sat at the pockmarked wooden counter with their own thoughts for a few moments. A slot machine in the corner of the bar played a tinny version of the birdie song on an endless loop over the low rumble of the TV news at the rear of the bar. Elisenda found it hypnotically comforting after the darkened hush of the two churches.

'So that's that,' Puigventós finally stated.

Elisenda watched the owner serve their coffee. 'Almost.'

The inspector waited until the owner had added the hot milk to their cups from the metal jug and moved away before speaking again.

'Did you know it was Pijaume?'

Elisenda took a small sip of her coffee and considered her answer.

'No. I didn't. But I realised that that wasn't the point. Just as I felt that the attacks were about the vehicle, not the victims, so I saw that the only way we were going to stop them was to see the attacker in the same way. I'd spent too much time focusing on who he might be that I was going around in circles. So I focused on the vehicle instead. On the symbol.'

She took another sip of the coffee. It was piping hot, so she put the spoon in to conduct some of the heat away and nestled the cup between the fingertips of both hands. Puigventós said nothing, but simply stared at her reflection in the mirror on the wall behind the counter, waiting for her to carry on.

'The attacker had used the city and its legends to turn them against us, and I realised that the only way I was ever going to stop him was by using his own weapon against him. The city and its history. Albert Riera said that what mattered was our victims, not our personalities. In this case, he was wrong. It wasn't the victims that mattered, not when it came to catching the person who had made them his victims. It was the personality of the attacker and the personality of the city. That's what put an end to all this.'

She took the spoon out of her cup and took another sip.

'Narcís told me before he died that he felt that Pau was closing in on him, but I don't think that was the case. I found nothing in Pau's notes to suggest it.'

Puigventós let out a deep sigh. 'Which makes it even more senseless.'

The car waiting for them outside took them back to the hill overlooking the city centre and a hotel where an informal lunch had been planned. Elisenda still wasn't sure how she felt about it. Pau deserved to be recognised, but she didn't know if any of them was ready for this.

Puigventós looked out of the car window at various people climbing out of cars and taxis and making their way into the hotel. 'And so we create a legend.'

Elisenda stared at the Mossos, the politicians and the great and the good of the city. 'We've got enough legends. He was just a man. That should be enough.'

Inside, Elisenda found the members of her team and stood with them, facing out at the rest of the buffet diners like a circle of wagons in the old Western movies that always played on Sunday afternoon TV when she was a kid.

'Is everyone all right?' she asked them.

They all nodded and moved closer.

'Good,' she said.

She leaned into Montse and whispered something in her ear. Montse stared back at her, a look of surprise on her face, and nodded.

Other Mossos came over to speak to her and her unit, and their little defensive circle fragmented as it became less necessary. Mosso Paredes offered his condolences formally to Elisenda and then went off, relieved after his duty, to talk to Montse and Josep. Elisenda watched them. Other younger Mossos went up and spoke to them, each evidently offering their support. The more senior officers did the same to Elisenda and Àlex, except for Micaló, who stayed close to the politicians and the money. He was studiously avoiding her, which suited her fine today of all days.

'Catch you later,' she muttered in his direction as he jostled for position between Puigventós and a senior councillor.

She turned to Àlex and chose her words. 'I'm sorry, Àlex, but I need to be able to trust you. You have to decide if you're going to carry on working with me. With my unit.' She looked away. 'I have to decide.'

346

He looked at her profile and nodded, his face expressionless, his voice unhealed.

Montse came to stand next to them. She looked exhausted.

'I wish we could go now,' the caporal whispered to her. 'Half these people didn't even know Pau.'

Josep joined them. 'And the half that did were baying for our blood.'

Elisenda spied a little vignette across the room. 'Talking of which.'

They looked over to where two figures were huddled in earnest conversation, David Costa, the newspaper editor, and Gerard Bellsolà, the third-generation lawyer. Each spoke to the other as though they were a slightly disreputable but necessary confederate. Elisenda had an instant image of the chain of information being quietly passed on. Micaló to Bellsolà to Costa.

They watched in silence for a moment before Elisenda spoke again. 'We go out for a drink tonight. To celebrate Pau our way.'

'El Cercle,' Montse agreed. 'That was his favourite bar.'

'El Cercle,' Josep echoed. 'No one but us.'

Elisenda signalled to Montse and they moved away from the group. El Cercle, she thought. The circle. The bar she'd told Mosso Paredes to go to for a brandy on that first morning, the day Daniel Masó was found hanging from a disused apartment balcony on Carrer Pla i Cargol.

And now the circle was about to close.

'You never met Pau Yáñez, did you, David?' she asked Costa. She'd backed him into a corner of the room after he'd finished his conversation with Bellsolà.

He stared back at her in surprise. 'No, I didn't. I'm here representing my paper.'

'Oh, I'm not questioning why you're here. I just wanted to talk to you about Pau. He was our colleague and we're here to celebrate him, so you should perhaps know a little bit about him.'

Costa looked increasingly wary, but Elisenda was effectively boxing him in between the tables laid out with a depleted array of food and drink.

'He had a remarkable mind,' Elisenda went on. 'He saw connections anyone else would miss. And he had a tenacity. He'd keep going until things would slot into place.'

'What are you trying to say? I thought we'd said all we had to say the other day.'

'No, I don't think so. I was asking you for help the other day. Perhaps I should have told you the tile in the museum was a fabrication but I don't suppose that really matters. No, David, I'm here to give you some help. I was telling you about Pau. I was going through some notes he'd made and I came across some interesting things. Take this website, for instance, the one that's turned this city on itself. Pau went through it, categorising postings and then cross-referencing them with articles in the local paper. Your paper, David. He also turned up a link between three computer hackers we were investigating and an article Carles Font wrote. Your journalist.'

He looked calmly at her. 'You won't be able to prove anything.'

'I won't have to. I'm telling you I know you're involved in the website and I'm telling you that it will shut down.' They stared at each other in silence for a moment. 'I won't tell you a second time.'

A hushing noise came from the end of the room, telling everyone that the top table was about to make its speeches.

'Catch you later,' Elisenda whispered to Costa and walked away to listen.

She listened and forgot. There was a definite inverse proportion between the length and sentiment of the various eulogies and the contact the person giving them had ever had with Pau. She caught Àlex's eye at one point and looked away in sadness and anger.

When they were finally over and everyone went back to their interrupted conversations, Elisenda sat down at a table and stared impassively at the people around her.

'So how are you, Elisenda?' a man's voice asked her.

She looked up to see Marsans pulling a chair nearer to her.

'This is a sour victory,' she told him.

'Sour?'

'I would willingly have let Narcís Pijaume pass into Girona myth if it meant Pau were still alive. And even Pijaume. And the reputation of the Mossos had remained intact.'

She let out a huge sigh and looked at the professor.

'I know,' she told him.

'You know what, Elisenda?'

'I know you killed Pere Corominas.'

Marsans simply looked back at her. Elisenda could see Montse and Josep watching them from a few paces behind the lecturer's seat.

'No,' Marsans said, shaking his head slowly. 'No, Elisenda.'

'I read the abstract of your paper in Columbia, Professor Marsans. And Professora Torrent's. They were remarkably similar. As was the summary of your new book to the new research she was getting into. Whereas your last book was a rehash of your previous three. You needed something new.'

'It was my research,' Marsans insisted.

'No, it wasn't. Professora Torrent spoke of your acolytes around the city. That's what Corominas was. One of your favoured few, now working for the city archives. I think you inveigled him into stealing Professora Torrent's work for you. And I think he did and I think he regretted it. And I think he threatened to tell her about it. But I know you killed him. And do you know what? If you hadn't tried to cover up your crime by linking it to the other attacks, you'd probably have got away with it.'

Marsans pinched the bridge of his nose and took a drink from the dregs of someone else's glass left on the table. 'My publisher was going to drop me. Unless I came up with something new. And then I saw what Aurora was doing.' He let out a dry laugh. 'Who would have thought that dear old Aurora would have come up with something so exciting.'

Elisenda signalled to Montse and Josep to come closer.

Marsans carried on speaking. 'Pere was one of the best pupils I've ever had. He would have been a fine lecturer himself. But he wanted to come clean about what he'd done. About what I'd done.' He looked at Elisenda. 'I couldn't allow that.'

Elisenda leaned forward and stopped him as the two caporals approached.

'Do you know what, Professor Marsans? I really don't care.'

Chapter Eighty One

Andrés Soriano pulled the zip on his fleece up tighter around his face and shivered. It wasn't so much the cold as the damp. Autumn was here with its dark mornings and thick air that got through to the bones and he was tired and angry.

He'd bought the fleece just a week ago and it was good quality and kept the wet chill out. But that was when he'd had a bit of money to his name. Before Daniel Masó's uncle had taken over from his nephew and started claiming the money he reckoned was owed to him. And with those two brothers from Barcelona that went everywhere with him, Andrés Soriano was not going to argue. He was going to shut up and tighten his belt like he'd done before.

'*Hijo de puta,*' he muttered at the thought.

He threw his broom into the little cart after he'd finished sweeping the cobbles at the foot of the cathedral steps and looked up.

And instantly staggered back.

'*Hijo de puta,*' he muttered again.

He looked again at the Verge de la Bona Mort in the gloom of the morning and saw it was nothing. He thought he'd seen something hanging from the foot of the statue with the impassive smiling face, but there was nothing there. Just a shadow in a niche.

Crossing himself, he climbed into his little motorised cart and accelerated through the medieval gateway as the sun slowly rose to scatter the damp of a Girona autumn.

Acknowledgements

I'm very happy to have to say thank you to a lot of people, who made researching and writing this book a huge pleasure and who all gave me their help, time and consideration with tremendous good grace and patience. All factual accuracies are thanks to them, the inaccuracies are entirely my own doing.

I was fortunate enough to spend time in Girona thanks to a Writer's Bursary from Literature Wales, which was invaluable as it gave me the opportunity to reacquaint myself with the city archives and wander the streets checking out locations and talking to people, and simply soaking up the atmosphere.

The Àrea de Comunicació of the Mossos d'Esquadra were very patient and helpful, answering all of my questions, no matter how trivial or grisly, or how many times I came back for more.

For the legends, I owe a big debt of gratitude to Pere Romans of the Girona Art Museum for going through sources with me and for hunting out numerous articles. I owe a similar debt to Elena Boix, conservator with the Art Museum, and Isabel Joan, curator of the Pharmacy Museum, for showing me around the seventeenth-century pharmacy in the Hospital de Santa Caterina and answering all my questions. I'd also like to thank the staff at both the City Archives and the Provincial Archives in Girona, who cheerfully found every single obscure article or book I asked them for. I would also simply like to thank the people of Girona for possessing such a beautiful and captivating city and for welcoming me back time and time again with such warmth.

Phil Rickman, author of the Merrily Watkins crime series, was gracious enough to interview me on his radio book programme for BBC Radio Wales about the Elisenda Domènech series, which gave me the encouragement to keep writing.

If you're going to get published, you can't go far wrong with my publishers Canelo and their extraordinary and uplifting blend of cutting-edge technology, talent and an old-fashioned desire for storytelling. They're also incredibly nice people, so I feel very lucky to work with Michael Bhaskar, Iain Millar and Nick Barreto, and with excellent copy-editor Helen Francis.

And before that, you have to have a really good agent. I've got the best in Ella Kahn, whose belief in me and perseverance and ability to see the essence of what I'm trying to say simply bowl me over.

And finally, I thank my wife Liz with everything I have for all her support, love and patience, and for knowing when wine was called for.